FINDING A WAY BACK HOME

NOMADIC RHODES
BOOK 3

SYDNE BARNETT

Copyright © 2024 Flame And Fiction LLC

All rights reserved.

ISBN:

Discreet Paperback: 979-8-9903198-1-3

E-Book: 979-8-9903198-0-6

Cover Art: Shanoff Designs

No part of this book may be reproduced in any form or by any electronic or mechanical means, including information storage and retrieval systems, without written permission from the author, except for the use of brief quotations in a book review.

This is a work of fiction. Therefore, the stories and characters in the novel are fictitious. All names, characters, companies, places, events and occurrences are fictitious. Any similarity to real persons, living or dead, or actual places or events is purely coincidental. Public bodies, institutions, or historical figures mentioned in the story serve as a backdrop for the characters and their actions, but these are wholly imaginary.

This book contains mature themes and is only suitable for readers 18+

For the 'too much' women, your Broderick will cheer the loudest. Go big, baby.

AUTHOR'S NOTE

Well, helloooo there, dahhling!

Thank you so much for joining Elora and Broderick for their story. I'm not even sure what I can say about these two. They were my sweetest, most stubborn couple to date, with a whole lot of rogue opinions about how their story would go. From the moment El showed up in the first book, they were jumping off the page, just waiting for their turn. This book is nothing like I thought it would be when I sat down to outline, and it's so much more 'them' because of it. If you're looking for a high stakes adventure, please check out my fantasy series, but if you're in the mood for a hug in a book, you've come to the right place. I think they deliver all the cozy, warm and fuzzy feels.

Finding A Way Back Home can be read as a stand alone, or after the first book, *South of The Skyway*, and second book, *Brewing Temptation*.

As always, your mental health matters!

Here are the content disclosures for *Finding A Way Back Home*:

Cheating (not between two main characters), explicit language, and explicit on page sexual content.

RHODES FAMILY APPENDIX

RHODES FAMILY APPENDIX

The Rhodes family is made up of twelve rowdy siblings, many many cousins and a handful of 'pseudo-siblings'.

*For simplicity's sake, I've **only** listed those mentioned in **this** book.*

MILO RHODES
Dad, captain of the *Rhodes Away*

JUNIPER RHODES
Mom, keeper of the chaos, deliverer of epic hugs and warm food.

I. JEANNE
Eldest sister, world-traveling surgeon, divorced, location unknown. Spontaneously appears on family text thread, usually around the holidays.

II. Rhyett

Eldest brother, entrepreneur, current location St. Pete, Florida. Adorably—some would say obnoxiously—optimistic. He has a daughter—Quinn, or 'Quinny'—with his wife, Brexley.

III. Jameson

Captain of the family fishing boat, located in Mistyvale, AK. In a relationship with Noel McShane. Bestower of sardonic witticisms and tough love.

IV. Elora

Traveling life & business coach and public speaker, single, nomadic but currently based out of Seattle. Designated family know-it-all and planner of events.

V. Axel

Fisherman, single, currently in Mistyvale, AK but travels for the winter. Equal parts sunshine and sarcasm.

VI. Paxton

Pro quarterback for the Windy City Wolves in Chicago, single. Gazelle-like focus on his career, hates the cold.

VII. Hadlee

Travel blogger and influencer, single, location unknown. Aka, Hurricane Hadlee due to a propensity for chaos.

VIII. Alessandra

Aka. "Alice", assistant to the CEO of Hart Investments, currently in Emerald Bay, CA.

IX. Finnegan
Aka. "Finn", digital nomad, we think he's in New York? That could change tomorrow though. Quietest of the twelve.

X. Leighton
Twins with Kaia, student and waitress, currently staying with Alice in Emerald Bay.

XI. Kaia
Twins with Leighton, student and waitress, currently in Emerald Bay, CA. Lover of all things beautiful, family makeup artist.

XII. Maverick
Attending college in Washington. Bogarts the good tunes, sympathy crier.

"Pseudo-siblings"
Broderick Allen—Best friends with Rhyett and Jameson, Philosophy Professor, single, collector of nice things, Mistyvale, AK.

Max—Best friends with Elora, Hadlee and Alice, right hand to the CEO of Jorogumo defense. Travels as much as an authentic Rhodes, single, impeccable taste in both clothes and booze, currently in Mistyvale, AK.

Cousins
Charlie—Town Sheriff, widower, two kids, June (11) and Sterling (7).
Jake—Fisherman, single, Mistyvale, AK

ONE

ELORA

October

"So, what's your body count?"

A laugh bubbled up my throat, but when Todd's blue eyes didn't crinkle, and his mouth slowly closed, the sound halted. *Awkward.* I swirled my merlot, still kind of waiting for a punchline. When nothing came, I scoffed, "Excuse me?"

"You know. Your *body count,*" he repeated with a derisive amount of emphasis, as though I simply hadn't heard him the first time. My nails dug into my palm beneath the table. "Like, how many dudes—"

"Hmmm...I don't know, do the ones in the freezer count?" Tone dripping in disinterest, I set my wine down to refrain from pouring it over his blond waves. If for no other reason than just because it was an exquisite year, and I didn't particularly want to waste it. Giving him a little wink, I added, "Or just the ones I've disposed of?" I shot a pleading glance at our server, who blanched but nodded. It was a shame, really, as this restaurant boasted the best chef in the city. But Todd was, unfortunately, only one in a *long line* of shitty blind dates, and my asshole tolerance was entirely used up.

The world's most perfect autumn afternoon came to a bumbling halt as he grappled for a response. Hell, just this morning, I'd sat in the booth recording an episode for my podcast, *TrailblazeHer*, with one of the most inspiring women I'd ever had the pleasure of befriending, celebrating her seven-figure year, only for her to shock the hell out of me and turn the celebration around with gushed affirmations over my book deal. When the show wrapped, we'd enjoyed a leisurely lunch sipping wine and eating mezé while Mara caught me up on her adorable four and six-year-old children, her husband's new affinity for fishing, and the book club recommendations she'd gained in the last year.

The two of us had been talking for ages about starting a foundation together, resonating with *TrailblazeHer*'s mission to empower women everywhere to reach their professional potential, and her daily mantra to raise the damn bar in all categories of life.

Evidently, Todd's 'bar' had somehow become ensconced in Hell itself, as he had the audacity to scoff in my direction. "What? I don't think it's too personal of a question to ask someone. You're beautiful, I'm, well—" he gestured vaguely at his entirely average-leaning-on-lanky body, "and we're old enough not to beat around the bush. If we're doing anything, have you been *tested*? A man's gotta evaluate the risks of dating a woman over thirty. If you're this easily offended, it must be terrible," he laughed as he swiped up his martini. *Some people's children, so help me.* Who in their right mind could ever think this was an appropriate conversation starter? What in the hell happened to *'Hello. How are you? What's your zodiac sign? Are you looking for a good time or something serious?'*

A dull ache brewed behind my eyes, gaze settling on his fingers where they twirled the olive toothpick as he shrugged and added, "I'm probably around forty."

Of course, you are. I didn't have to engage in this conversation to guess if I responded with a number anywhere near that–which it *wasn't*–he'd tell me it was too many. After all, only men are intended to enjoy their bodies. For fuck's sake. Deadpanning, I lolled my head sideways, blinking pointedly as our server made her way over. I held up my card with pleading eyes.

"God bless you. *Please* ring me up." To *Todd*, I demanded, "And what, pray tell, is your goal in asking?" Though placid, even I could hear the blade of temper threatening my composed tone.

"Just not big on sloppy seconds. I mean, you're what, almost forty?" *Thirty-two and about to go spend a stupid amount of money on a new eye cream.* "So, I know you've been around."

With a suffocated glare, I threw back my drink, wincing as too much liquid funneled down too tight a space and stood. Forcing an expression more grimace than smile onto my face, I turned my attention to the tool across the table, our server scurrying away. "Alright, that's enough for me. Todd, have the day you deserve."

His protest fell on deaf ears as I gathered my phone and purse, and followed the waitress' path to the bar, my heels clicking over the slick concrete floor. Music bombarded my senses with some modern calamity of heavy bass, the mouthwatering scent of steak worth selling a kidney for assaulting me. *Dammit, Todd. That smells amazing.*

My ride-share pulled up by the time I made it out the

front door, and I slunk onto the back seat with a huff, face falling into my hands as I rubbed my temples. Focusing on your career in your twenties was supposed to be the smart thing to do—the path to a happy life, or at least that's what every academic advisor said in my high school and college careers.

For the most part, it had been. Hell, I'd seen half the damn planet, visited countries we'd never even learned the names of in school to speak to leaders from CEOs to ambitious politicians. My golden touch came with me.

Prior to the dry spell of the century, I'd slept with whomever I wanted—which, admittedly, wasn't even half as many people as Todd's self-righteous body count. In my world, the need for company didn't overrule keeping my standards high—going wherever I wanted, chasing the clients I wanted... and I loved every. Damn. Minute of it.

My company had evolved from life coaching to holistic business coaching, and until this year, I'd regularly made it home to Mistyvale to see my family. Which was necessary with eleven brothers and sisters. My life was perfect. At least, it was until I opened my phone to the family text thread, where everyone was sharing holiday season photos. My oldest brother, Rhyett, shot over the cutest picture with his wife and daughter—with her perfect button nose painted black, whiskers painted on her sun-kissed Florida skin, those squishable cherub's cheeks sandwiched in a red lion's mane on for early trunk-or-treating. Tears pricked at my eyes, and the lump in my throat made me decide to book early tickets to Florida this Christmas to soak up snuggles before I had to compete with ten other siblings. I needed to lock down my spot as favorite auntie before the rest of the yahoos made their attempts to secure her affection.

. . .

ELORA
Brex, you make a very cute mama lion.

BREXLEY
Thanks! Papa lion with our lil cub is my favorite though.

THE IMAGE BOUNCED right into my inbox. Rhyett throwing baby Quinn up in the sky as her eyes vanished with the size of her open-mouthed, buck-toothed giggle. Noel, Jameson's girlfriend, followed it up with a picture of the two of them ice skating back in Mistyvale, bundled faces rosy-red with cold. By the time my younger brother, Axel, sent his selfie with his new girlfriend on a beach halfway around the world, my chest constricted, and I slid my cell back into my purse with a heavy sigh.

If careers were the most important part of our twenties —figuring ourselves out, establishing financial security— why did my heart ache so severely? And what was it about hitting my thirties that made it all feel so...*urgent*? I didn't want to find a man and jump right into child rearing. I wanted the whole fairytale. The love story. A romantic engagement. Planning a dream wedding with my sisters and friends. Time to travel and soak each other up before we were in the trenches of midnight feedings and spit up on my blazers. But, shy of sticking my eggs in a freaking freezer, it seemed like that fantasy was slipping right through my fingers.

Which led me here, in the back of a rideshare after yet another shitty blind date with the sticky heat of an Emerald

Bay fall fastening my thighs to the leather as my soft-spoken driver told me his *entire* life story.

My eyes glazed over, watching the traffic pass us by in a blur of gradually illuminating red light, the sun sinking over the horizon. Okay, so maybe living nomadically had its drawbacks. Drawbacks like no network of trustworthy referrals to men who were actually worth an hour getting ready and a subsequent thirty minutes in the back of some dude's Kia. Hell, I would rather turn on a good sitcom or curl up with a romcom and some tea than go out with a dud. I wasn't fucking desperate. At least this time, I wasn't alone in a random city. I was visiting my sister, just outside of San Diego, which was a personal paradise of mine.

The blue light of dusk filled the air when my driver pulled up to the curb in front of Alice's apartment complex, and I scraped my thighs off the leather and scooted out with a cordial 'thank you,' before heading for the gate. Past the coded entrance, I seriously eyeballed the pool, half a mind to just collapse in sideways like a tree, yelling 'timber' as I free fell, just to wash off the sensation of hungry-but-misogynistic blue eyes on my skin. There had to be more than this...*right?*

That was the question still circulating in my mind when I finally made it to the front door and found not only Alice, but our best friend, Max, planted comfortably on the sofa in front of the glow of the television. Two heaping bowls of popcorn—peanut butter for Alice and cheddar for Max—were surrounded by Milk Duds, Red Vines, and Hershey's Kisses, all neatly poured into cute teal bowls on the coffee table. We'd found Max some time in elementary school and decided to keep him forever. His neatly coiffed black hair was slicked back and complimented his coordinating cashmere sweater and slacks. The man had always possessed impeccable taste, right down to the shoes neatly lined by the door. He reached over to snatch up the remote, wincing as he took in my face and simultaneously paused the movie. My sister was draped across the couch with her feet in his lap, her long, dark hair flowing over the pillow propping her neck up, as she slowly ceased sipping on the chocolate milkshake I was certain she'd hogged. She lifted her phone and grimaced.

"Eight o'clock?" she said, followed by a sympathetic sigh.

"The dry spell of the century strikes again," Max lamented heavily, scooting over to free up a sliver of space for me between him and the armrest. We'd both been on a long run of crappy romantic luck, leaving me no option but to blow out a heavy breath as I accepted the gesture. Head on his shoulder, I sighed.

"Small talk aside, he opened the date asking about my fucking body count."

"What the fuck?" Alice scoffed, shaking her head as she returned to her dessert.

Max smirked, adding, "I would have told him I don't count bodies, just orgasms, and of those, there've been *plenty*."

An aggrieved sound, more sigh than laugh, bubbled between my lips before I admitted, "I asked him if the ones in the freezer counted."

Max's evil cackle was one of my favorite sounds on the planet. He took way too much satisfaction out of any kind of savagery, and I loved him all the more for it. "That's my girl," he said, leaning his cheek on the top of my head. "What about that guy from last week? The *foxy* one." I might not have been able to see him, but the Max that lived inside my brain absolutely waggled his brows. Sitting up, I turned to face them, greedily accepting the rope of licorice he offered.

"Carrick. He was nice."

"But...?" Alice hedged, not bothering to unwrap her lips from the straw.

"Bad kisser?" Watching as I snapped off a bite of my candy, Max canted his head with narrowed eyes.

"No, he was fairly decent in that department."

"No career path?"

"Shitty credit score?"

"Socks with sandals?"

"Bad tipper?" The two of them rattled off potential reasons for my rejection of Carrick, the semi-adequate kisser, like it had become a game to guess why none of the men I'd matched with were ever good enough. I couldn't help but laugh as Max amended, "Oh! *No* tipper?"

"Super religious, so you couldn't test the chemistry?" Alice said, a strangled shred of hope in her tone, like that objection might be redeemable. Hell, maybe it could be. My prospects were as abundant as the Sahara Desert is in trees. But they were proportionate with the amount of effort I'd given dating as of late.

The pathetic reality was that I was the absolute best at giving advice...so long as it pertained to anything aside from my love life. Try as I might, I'd been hung up on one asshole since I was fifteen. Every time I saw the same guy more than a few times and things got serious, my walls went up, because no matter how fabulously attractive or wildly successful they were, they weren't—him. The worst part? Broderick Allen was *anything* but an asshole.

We'd grown up as rivals in school—which wasn't really fair, as I had the advantage of being a few years behind him and made it my personal mission to break every record he ever set. *Petty?* Absolutely. But when he chose his friendship with my older brothers over our feelings for each other my senior year, I decided I no longer felt bad about our childish games. He picked them —honoring some stupid high school pact. Last summer was the first year we'd spent an excessive amount of time together since I'd left Mistyvale for college, and while I'd been endlessly subjected to everything about him I'd always loved—the gravel of his familiar laugh, the way the warm umber skin around those dark eyes wrinkled every time he smiled, his passion to advocate for literally *anyone* in need, even if they weren't his responsibility, and that gorgeous, clever mind—he never made a damn move.

It was high time to move the fuck on. So, I'd returned to life on the road, which was usually where I was happiest. These speaking engagements were what I lived for, even if my thirty-two-year-old body just didn't jump between time zones as easily as a twenty-something body did, and I was growing acutely aware of it.

Max's lips twisted to the side, Alice's gray-blue eyes growing concerned as they both stared me down, my silence evidently lingering far longer than appropriate. "It's just... he's not..."

It was Max who confirmed my spinster status and finished my thought. "Broderick."

His name made me groan, burying my face in my hands as I growled against them before jerking them away to stuff a handful of cheddar popcorn in my mouth. Aggressively chewing over the cheese-powdered deliciousness, I rolled my eyes. "The man has had over a decade since I was officially 'legal'—if he was going to do something, he would've by now—and I'm just being dragged along on a hook he doesn't even know exists and—*what is wrong with me?*"

"You know, they say we store our first love in the same part of the brain as a heroin addiction," Alice offered helpfully, as though I wasn't the one to tell her that after her first heartbreak.

"Great. So, I'm a junkie for a man that doesn't even want me."

The abrupt upheaval of the snack bowl punctuated Max's eye roll as he stood, setting the popcorn on the table. Grabby hands outreached for me as he demanded, "Get up, Elly. We're getting you laid."

"What?" I barked, laughing, but the man never relented and wasn't about to change now. Snatching my hands in his, he heaved me to my feet with an eager Alice on our heels as he led us through the living room.

"That's all you need. Hell, that's all anybody needs. One good fuck, you'll be right as rain, and you can focus on the important things again."

"The Summit's in a few weeks, right?" Alice redirected, flipping on her bedroom light as Max dragged me to the bed only to shove me onto the floral spread with a petulant bounce.

"Yeah, just before Thanksgiving," I said flatly, resigned to my fate. Once Max and Alice made a plan, there was no escaping it. Not alive, anyway. And while I would absolutely not be climbing a stranger like a tree tonight, drinks and nachos with these two yahoos sounded like the perfect distraction. *The Leaders in Thought Summit* was the event of my year—hell, my decade, if I had anything to say about it.

This year's conference was different. Having attended every fall since my first year in college, this was the year they had invited me back as a *speaker*. To say happy squeals had occurred the moment the phone was off would be an understatement. While my love life might've been barren, my ability to analyze a company and pull out their strength was what God put me on this earth for. In a few short weeks, I'd stand in front of colleagues and role models who'd inspired my love of the field and share what I'd learned with *them* for once.

"Good. That leaves us one week for fun, and two for prep," Max said, as if I didn't already have two completed drafts of my speech for that stage open on my laptop. "In the meantime, let's get the stick out of your ass, and let your hair down. Get out of that dress. It smells like desperation and blind date douche."

TWO

BRODERICK

November

"Eat an extra bear claw for me?" Rhyett's voice came through the Bluetooth headphones he'd sent me last Christmas.

"Obviously," I said, smirking as I stepped over a rain-filled gutter onto the sidewalk. Mistyvale existed in a perpetual state of hanging gray fog, especially through the winters. The harbor was full of bobbing vessels, their flags splotches of muted colors through the gloom. We held our annual winter carnival inside the new town mall to avoid this frigid mist. Even within those echoing walls and tile floors, we knew how to throw a party, and the predominant tradition was glorified fair food. I'd be indulging in every ridiculous small-town tradition tonight, alongside my friends. "How's Brex?"

"Fucking gorgeous," Rhyett answered without hesitating, making me grin like an idiot. "Motherhood looks so damn good on her, man."

If Apollo had a favorite mortal, it would have been

Rhyett. My best childhood friend was obnoxiously optimistic, and embodied sunshine, so it was fitting he'd settled in the state that shared the moniker. Even more so that he'd found his wife not a month after settling his feet on those white sand beaches. Just over a year and a half later, they had the cutest little cherub. Speaking of which…

"How's my niece? She's getting way too big." Their daughter, Quinn, was just about nine months old, which was incomprehensible. The older we got, the faster time slipped through my fingers.

"Dude, you're telling me. She's so chatty now—no idea what the fuck she's saying unless it's one of the signs Brex taught her, but she sure says it—and is officially a roll risk anywhere we set her. The other day, I walked to the bedroom for all of forty damn seconds to find my phone, and she'd somehow wedged herself under the couch." Chuckling, I jumped in front of a couple of gals, huddled in their winter jackets, and yanked the coffee shop door open, motioning for them to go inside. Nodding their thanks, they skirted past me before shuddering with relief at the warmth. "Did I just hear the bell to *Grizzly Grind*?"

"Are you a *bat* or something?" I demanded, following in the women's wakes.

"I miss home, man. This time of year, especially. Make sure Kara made the iced pumpkin cookies. Those are the town favorites." Rhyett started the *Grizzly Grind* coffee shop a few years before he left for Florida and had made sure we knew them for their fresh daily pastries as much as the java the girls were pouring. The hiss of milk steaming, and chatter of patrons greeted me as I dropped my hood back, leering around the line to the case, where the hand painted pumpkin-shaped cookies had dwindled to two.

"Got a few left, man, but the shelf is nearly empty."

"Good—that's good. That's what we like to hear."

"Place is hopping, McGraths are in the corner, Kara's behind the bar, only got...*two* open tables." I noted each detail as I peered around the bustling space, soaking up the chipper chatter and sugary scent of fresh sweets.

"Excellent. Now get off the phone, take out those ear buds and actually say 'hi' to your neighbors."

"Piss off," I groused, smiling to myself as I shook my head. "Not everybody feels the need to socialize every moment of their waking hours."

Rhyett's laugh warmed my chest. "Would do you some good now and then."

"That's what I have you for."

"Haven't been back since last summer. Worried you're getting lonely up there."

"That's yet to occur, but I'll keep you apprised of any changes."

"Yeah, yeah. Alright, say 'hi' to the girls for me."

"Will do, man. Say 'hi' to *your* girls for *me*."

The smile in his voice carved my own onto my cheeks. "Will do. Love you."

"You too."

The subtle click of the line dying punctuated the end of our conversation, and I begrudgingly pulled one ear bud out, tucking it into its case before returning the thing to my pocket. The eclectic shop was full of the subtle notes of Christmas music, never mind that we still had Thanksgiving to look forward to.

"Broderick!" My gaze snapped to the side where a familiar freckled face beamed back at me. Noel emerged with a sleeve of new to-go cups, waving over her armful of merchandise.

"What the hell are you doing here?" I barked back,

smirking at her bright smile. Rhyett had set Noel up with a spot here at *Grizzly Grind* last spring, while his manager was out on maternity leave and Noel was rebuilding her life. But she'd walked away when that was over, pouring her inspirational level of enthusiasm into starting a nonprofit for survivors of domestic violence, like her. The woman had a smile to melt icebergs if there's ever been one.

"Brinn's out with a sick toddler. Least I could do was lend a hand this time of year."

Grinning, I shook my head. "Do you ever sleep?"

"Not if I can help it." The line shuffled forward, the last group stepping to Kara's side of the counter to order, leaving me to lean forward and kiss Noel's cheek, her chaotic red curls making my nose itch. "What can I get you, handsome?"

"A red eye would be great," I said, leaning back and stripping the leather gloves from my hands and stuffing them in my coat pocket. Her skeptical brows winged up, and I shrugged, supplying, "I've got two more lectures and papers to grade before the festival tonight."

"*Mmmkay,*" she said, punching the order into the POS. "You still coming to dinner?"

"Wouldn't miss it," I assured her as I handed over my credit card. My best friend—Rhyett's younger brother, Jameson—had wasted no time winning over Noel, and the two of them played host to most of our gatherings. "Captain get off the water last night?"

"Yeah, he's probably still huddled up by the fire while knocking out this week's accounting."

"Good deal."

The bell rang behind me, and she jerked her head toward the end of the bar. Taking my cue, I scooted my way down to the drink drop-off as two giggling female forms scooted forward, dropping their hoods to reveal a couple of my sophomores. Big city professors likely had the luxury of avoiding their students far more than I ever could. They eyed me at the end of the counter before their giggles escalated, and I shifted nervously, their gazes on me while they exchanged muted whispers.

"Hi, Professor Allen," the first said, nerves betraying her smile and putting a squeak in her voice. I tugged at my collar, giving a stiff wave back as the second echoed the greeting, smiling coyly as she tucked black hair behind her ear. *Oh boy.*

"Tara, Ciara," I nodded curtly, rubbing a hand over the back of my neck as heat rushed to my face before scowling at Noel, her knowing grin taking way too much pleasure in my discomfort. I snatched my coffee cup from her freckled hand, glaring as she snickered, and abandoned my plan for a cozy coffee in, instead backing toward the front door.

"Sarah coming tonight?" Noel asked, louder than necessary in a not-so-subtle sign of solidarity.

"Yeah, I'll pick her up after work."

"See you then!"

Noel, at least, had the decency to extend an olive branch, even if she didn't care for my plus one. The Rhodes siblings, however, all turned their noses up whenever Sarah was mentioned. My on again, off again girlfriend of the last decade had pretty much burned her bridge with them on breakup number three. Noel, mercifully, had missed that fiasco. With one last wave, I headed out into the cold.

WITH THE TANTALIZING promise of laughter to look forward to, I walked the three blocks home from the university in a rush after work, opening the front door with all the tact of a linebacker. Finding the living room empty, when my girlfriend should have been yanking those sexy little boots into place, I hollered, "Sarah, babe, we're gonna be late!"

Kicking off my shoes by the front mat, I shirked my jacket off in the next motion and set it over the back of the couch. The uncharacteristic warmth of the evening lingered on my grateful skin, even as I rounded the corner of our outdated little townhouse for the fridge. Dull seventies yellow and sinus-infection green had evidently been all the rage in Mistyvale during the nineties.

Noel was an amazing cook, naturally insisting on covering all the bases, except for wine, which she was wise enough to defer to me. I was opting for a steadfast red for the roast beef dinner and a chilled dessert wine to complement her cherry croissants. My feet halted halfway to the fridge when a sense of unease settled in my stomach.

"Sarah?" I called again, motions slowing to take in the furniture that was usually just-so, now sitting askew on the rug, and her sweater carelessly tossed on the floor. The first time Sarah and I dated, she'd been slightly chaotic, but when we got back together for another go of things, she'd gotten better about matching my love of all things orderly. It wasn't like her to leave things haphazardly strewn about. "*Babe?*" It was the muffled sound upstairs that sent my pulse running. Like a cry or *yelp*. Mind whirring, I bolted up the staircase, images strobing against my eyes, varying from an ax murderer...to what my gut already knew to be the reality I'd find behind our bedroom door.

Bursting through, not sure what I was hoping to see beyond the threshold, I came face-to-face with a naked Sarah. Her eyes flew wide as some skinny fuck plowed into her from behind, his hand wrapped in her blonde strands of mussed hair. Bile rose in my throat as I turned, cursing as she shrieked and the man barked, *"What the fuck!?"*

It was going to be a long goddamn night.

NOEL'S FAIR, freckled fingers hesitated as she went to set a croissant on my dinner plate later that night, her evaluative brown eyes surveying my frantic pacing, like a beast trapped in a cage. She bobbed her head before setting two croissants on her and Jameson's plates and placing the entire platter piled with them on mine like a peace offering. Quiet and scowling, Jameson's only sign of life was the rapid bounce of his leg, hand bracing his jaw, those signature Rhodes' blue-gray eyes glaring at the table between us as I finished my explanation.

"I can't fucking believe she'd do this. Fuck. Yes, I *can*. I knew—*knew* something was off these last weeks—but didn't want to rock the damn boat by asking her about it."

His gruff sigh was somewhere in the neighborhood of a bear chuffing. The man was my ride-or-die, but I monopolized our allotted number of vocalized thoughts, leaving Jameson with the scraps. "Sorry, man. Never cared for her." Dark brown hair shifted under his hand as he yanked fingers through his loose curls in frustration.

"I know. That's the shittiest part. You guys were right. You. *Rhyett*. Noel," I said, nodding her direction as she grimaced, those brown irises heavy with what I could only describe as sympathy.

"Rhyett's always right," Jameson begrudgingly admitted. How the same parents had produced the sun beam and the terse bastard across from me, I would never understand. But I fucking loved him all the more for it. "He's like El in that way."

El. Elora. "Oh God, please don't tell El," I muttered, rubbing my temples as a dull ache pressed against the back of my eyes. Speaking of annoyingly upbeat siblings, their little sister was terrifying to even the best of us, her accomplishments enough to make a neurosurgeon grimace and hug the sharp corners of their framed degree just for reassurance. She'd no doubt have a damn field day with this, having loathed Sarah from the first go around. Just one more confirmation: she'd dodged a bullet with me all those years ago. Obviously, I still hadn't figured out the whole *keeping a woman* part of the relationship description.

"You couldn't have known," Noel offered softly, snapping me back into the moment as she came back over with the pot of freshly brewed coffee in hand. None of us were rage drinkers, opting instead for figuring out a game plan together. She topped off both our mugs with a steaming dark roast before turning back for their kitchen counter, only for Jameson to snake an arm around her waist. His other hand liberated the coffee pot, setting it on a marble platter she'd had ready to receive the dinner spread prior to my raging arrival fucking up our entire plan. Falling into his lap with a little yelp, Noel quickly nuzzled into place, my eyes going foggy as he buried a kiss against the deep red curls that spilled down her shoulders, like he could get to her neck through the beautiful mess of a mane.

That.

I'd always wanted that, and never had a clue what it felt like or how on God's green earth to get there. Honestly, I'd be wise to write off the idea of dating altogether at this point. *Had I just become a confirmed bachelor?*

"Who's that obnoxious girl in *Friends*? The one that

won't leave Chandler alone?" Jameson asked nonchalantly, though it sounded as if his words had traveled down a very long tube to reach me. His girl burst out laughing, shaking her head as she snapped her hands over her mouth.

"Yes! *Janice*. Sarah is your Janice."

"For all our sake, please let this one go," James instructed dryly, though I'd known him long enough to spot the tension in his jaw, the sympathy in his eyes. The man knew this level of betrayal far too keenly.

"Oh, we're done," I growled, rubbing my hand over my jawline, tracing the five o'clock shadow that felt a bit more like ten o'clock than it should've. "In *my* damned room, no less."

"I'm so sorry," Noel said, the waver in her voice making me feel guilty for yammering on about my first world drama. She certainly took the cake in the competition of shitty exes of the three of us. I shook my head, not wanting her pity, and certainly not deserving her sympathy. It might've been morally reprehensible, but Noel's toxic ex brought her here to us, and her need for protection gave me a new friend I never would've admitted I needed. Mostly, she lit James up in a way nobody ever had, and that alone would have earned my stamp of approval. Forget the fact that she was a saint with a heart too damn big for her own good. "But I am. You don't deserve this. Not any of it."

Quiet for a long moment, I nodded. "Thanks, Noel."

"Eat up, champ. Nothing says *wallowing* like warm cherry croissants, a scoop of vanilla ice cream, fresh coffee, and a good movie."

"What about the festival?" I asked, although even my ears heard how hollow the words were. The last thing I needed was a crowd of locals asking me where Sarah was.

"We went last year," she said with a nonchalant shrug

before kissing Jameson's scruffy cheek. "Came. Saw. Conquered. Ate bear claws until they came back up. No need to revisit that particular experience."

A soft smile accompanied the warmth she planted in my chest, and with a sigh, I stood with her. Jameson followed behind us, his unspoken frustration like a storm cloud in our wake.

"That conference thing. When is that?" he asked softly.

I shrugged, more irritated than anything else. "Might not go this year. Kinda... feels pointless, if I'm honest."

"Bullshit," he scoffed. "Don't let this bitch get in your head, man. Go learn. Isn't this their big decennial thing—that grant you've been babbling about all damn year?"

Sighing, I admitted, "Yeah, the New Leaders' Grant."

"Then, you're fucking going. That bitch took your time, but she doesn't get your fucking future."

Reluctantly, I straightened my spine, meeting that intense glower I'd grown up interpreting for everyone around us. When I gave him a nod, Jameson returned it before leading the way to the couch. I just had to keep my head on straight long enough to get there.

THREE
ELORA

"You're a sadist," I snarled as my shaking arms finally succumbed, nearly collapsing on my face as I awkwardly lumbered onto my back.

"That may be, but my evil ways have given you a delectable ass, so you're welcome."

"Fffffs," the attempted curse came out like a hiss and Max snickered as he gracefully lowered to the mat beside me.

"Tell your assistant to stop giving me the stink eye."

"Christopher? What's he going on about?" Blinking over at his too-pretty face, I forced both eyes open to the cell phone he had pointed at me, my spectacularly styled and obnoxiously punctual assistant glaring back at me from the screen.

"*He's* going on about the fact that Max promised you'd be done by ten," Chris said dryly.

"*Yeah?*" I panted, blinking back at him.

"It's a quarter after."

I fought back the smile that threatened the corners of

my mouth. "Is there a meeting I'm forgetting about? I thought Jenna was on the calendar for noon."

"Yes," he snipped pointedly in that blunt New Yorker's accent. Chris and I met at a gala that my younger brother, Finn, invited me to a few years back. The event benefitted the art society in New York City, and I'd known that night I'd have to spirit him away on my own. When the pandemic shut down the life he'd loved in Manhattan, he'd chomped at the bit to join my predominantly-remote team until he proved so invaluable, I bribed him to follow me from gig to gig until—and unless— some beautiful blonde swept him away and demanded he put a ring on her finger. "But if you don't eat between now and then, there will be nothing in the way of productive conversation and everything in the way of a hangry velociraptor. Ten-*sixteen*," he added for emphasis. Raising my hands in reluctant surrender, I rose to stand before turning to hoist Max to his feet.

"Okay, okay, I'll hop in and out of the shower and be ready to go."

"If I promise to feed the tyrannosaurus, will you get your ugly mug off my screen?" Max griped. I wrinkled my brow. Chris was anything but ugly. Six foot one, sandy-brown hair, gentle green eyes framed by smile lines, a sexy plaid cashmere scarf wrapped around his lean neck—*how* the man was single was beyond me.

"Fine."

"*Fine*," Max bit back. My brows had likely merged with my hairline by the time his gaze landed on mine after ending the video chat and slipping his phone in his pocket. "That man bugs me."

"Jealous?" I teased.

"You were mine *first*," he lamented with a theatrical whine as we turned towards the locker rooms.

Looping our arms together with a grin, I assured, "And forever shall be."

"Don't you fucking forget it. Okay, shower, brunch, Jenna—what's next on our calendar?"

"Touring that building downtown to see if it's a good fit for the school."

"I still think it should be virtual."

"Of course you do," I said, rolling my eyes. Max practically ran a cyber security firm called *Jorogumo Defense*; his computer was more of an appendage than an autonomous tool. "Not all of us speak in code, Maxi."

"You could if you slowed down long enough to listen to me."

"That would require one fewer shot of espresso in my morning oat milk latte, and *that* just ain't gonna happen."

"At least you're a cute little energizer bunny." His words made me smirk, and I shook my head. "Aren't you lucky you have me?"

"Obviously," I said as we split ways to gather our things and slink into fleece lined coats to fight off the frigid air. Reunited, Max pushed open the front door of the gym and I winced as the brisk Chicago air bit at my skin, the promise of the season's first snow an abrasive greeting. The fact that Max dictated his schedule and loved sightseeing enough to meet me all over the country would never get old.

Sometimes, it was for weeks at a time, others were just for lunch, or a night on the town, but his arrival always brought a little piece of Mistyvale with him, and I clung to it like a buoy. This stop had been particularly fun, as we got to watch one of my younger brothers, Paxton, play football, facing off with his rival as he quarterbacked the way to victory for the *Windy City Wolves*.

Having a literal dozen of us scattered over the country

was brutal, but there was something fun about having someone to visit and cheer for everywhere I wandered.

Chicago promised me not one, but *three* speaking engagements this week, and now we'd be parting ways, which always put a lump in my throat. Max was heading home to Alaska, and I was bound for Vegas for the summit. Anticipatory nerves twisted in my belly as the clock ticked down inside my subconscious. It was almost go-time, and I was beyond prepared. But for today, I needed to soak up my limited hours with my best friend and little brother. We likely wouldn't cross paths again until after the holidays, and I loathed the perpetual distance.

"I still say it's too damn cold here. The *Windy City*," he scoffed, tightening his black jacket against the frigid air.

"As though that's any less appealing than *Mistyvale*," I countered. Our little Alaskan island lived up to its name, shrouded in a perpetual state of slate gray over the climb of spruce covered mountains. Nevertheless, none of us could help but wander back in a steady rotation. "Besides, Chicago needs a program like this. With poverty rates at an all-time high, the best thing I could do is empower women to close the income gap for themselves. They just need the right resources."

Wrinkling his nose, Max said, "Fine. But if you land here, I'm appointing you a bodyguard. Murder rates are ridiculous, Elly."

I laughed, but when he just glared at me, my mouth popped open. How much money did the man make at that tech firm, anyway? "You can't be serious."

"As a diabetic in a shaved ice parlor."

"You're worse than Jameson."

"I learned it somewhere," he snickered. I was close with all my siblings, but some had more helicopter tendencies than others. Jameson was certainly in that category. "Alright, food, conquer meetings, tour your bodyguard's future haunt. Got it."

"EL, you're looking at some major renovations here," Paxton noted that evening as we toured my potential school. Like me, that wasn't necessarily a deterrent so much as a statement of fact. We Rhodes were raised with a 'how can I' attitude, not a 'can I' handicap. "You're going to need at least a million just for the building."

"Which is why we're applying for more than one grant," Mara reminded him with just as much enthusiasm as I had through the phone screen as I rotated her angle to see the entire width of the room. "Oooh! Those windows!" she gushed.

Paxton had been the first of my siblings to pledge a chunk of cash towards our school under the condition that he was a silent investor, and we didn't publicize his involvement. The press was savage, and always looking to poke holes in the personal lives of anyone successful, star quarterbacks included. If a pissed off reporter didn't get the interview they wanted with Chicago's heartthrob, it wouldn't take them long to turn their irritation on the project in a petty attempt at revenge. I didn't like it, but if Pax felt like that would protect our mission, so be it.

"We're gonna need a few more," he grumbled, snapping a piece of rotted trim off the doorframe with his bare thumb. I winced.

"Okay, and maybe we're still hunting for a better location," I agreed. "I don't want the entire grant going to structural stability. I'd like a portion left over for salaries and equipment."

"A different location, like somewhere *sunny?*" Max asked hopefully as he used the rubber eraser on his pencil to poke at water damaged drywall.

"I can't say I'd be mad about another reason to visit Florida," Pax noted, careful to keep his tone neutral and shifting back to look at me as he slowly sipped his black coffee. He'd already been down to visit our big brother, Rhyett, and his wife in Tampa at least half a dozen times since our niece was born.

Most of my brothers looked very much alike—the same easily tanned skin, those trademark gray eyes, and varying shades of loose brunette curls—save for Rhyett and Axel, who somehow ended up blond. Paxton had always been one of the more agreeable of my brothers, with a high willingness to take part in shenanigans and a higher tolerance for being doled out roles that came with pain. His years playing in the NFL had wracked his tall frame with muscle that I would very much be needing if we were going to accomplish this restoration during his off season. He had one more year on his contract with the *Wolves*, and then nobody knew where he'd end up. I couldn't picture him giving up his career at thirty, but it seemed to be the norm for the industry—bow out before his body forced the decision. Running a broad palm over his neatly styled short hair, he tongued over a canine, eyes scouring the room I was already envisioning as a lecture hall with its gorgeous, high stretching metal framed windows, and exposed brick wall dividing it from the neighboring space.

So what if there was a little water damage, and a whole lotta drywall damage? That's literally what renovations were for. The natural light would keep it cheery year around, even through the dreary months of back-to-back blizzards. The acoustics were perfect, and if the crew could restore the hardwood floors, it would be magical.

"I'm not saying no," Pax said gently, "but I am saying we should keep our options open. I don't see this place flying off the market in this condition. Get through the summit, secure the funding, then we look at all our options, whether they're here in Chicago, or somewhere…warmer."

"*Thank you*, QB," Max said smugly, rising from where he'd been examining some sort of moisture buildup behind the trim with a sneer so disapproving his lip was about to curl.

"Okay, okay," I said, glancing down at Mara on my phone screen, whose expression was equal parts amused and exasperated. "We keep hunting?"

"Aye-aye, Captain."

I laughed before exchanging quick goodbyes and pocketing my phone, following the guys down the stairs and out of the massive gothic building, where we all eyed the enormous exterior. "I just love the—"

"*History* of the place," Pax finished.

"Yeah," I agreed before Max's hands landed on my shoulders, yanking me toward him.

"I say this with love, Elly. But don't sink this ship for aesthetics. You've got too much potential, and too much time wrapped into it to not be pragmatic with this."

"I know."

"Okay. As your best friend, it's my job to make sure that head of yours stays at least distantly connected to the earth."

Laughing, I wrapped an arm around each of their waists, and turned to walk to our lunch date, somewhere we hoped Pax could enjoy his double chicken breast on salad without being recognized behind a thick beanie and aviators. "Thanks for coming with me, guys."

"Anytime," my not-so-little brother said, giving me a squeeze as we marched in sync down the sidewalk. "You have fun in Vegas—but not too much fun. I don't want to wire you bail money—and don't make your competitors cry too hard, okay?" Mostly, I was just hung up on the fact that he probably *would* wire me bail money if I needed it. Fighting back my smile, I led us to our last Chicago dinner of the year. This was going to work. Tomorrow would be a day of a few dozen emails and one decent layover before I was in a much warmer climate. And then my fun would begin.

Broderick

"YOU ALL PACKED UP, TEACH?" Jake asked at guys' night the day before my flight out for the summit. I had, in fact, purged my house in the three weeks since I kicked Sarah out, starting with the damn mattress she'd defiled with who knows how many men. The long-overdue renovation had officially begun, starting in the outdated kitchen. Poker nights were a biweekly ritual for all of us these days, although they'd felt like a goddamned life preserver this month. The guys helped me keep my head on straight, sights set on winning this grant as I dealt with the fallout of the official end of our relationship. I wasn't a social guy, by any means, but when you grew up with the Rhodes family, just their bloodline ensured a decent obligatory social circle. Jake was one of their innumerable cousins, and coincidentally, one of the easiest guys to get along with. His brother, Charlie, was the same, despite being our town sheriff.

"Yeah," I sighed, keeping my poker face as I stared him down, waiting to see what he would do. Jameson tapped his cards against the table impatiently, while his younger brother, Axel, laced his fingers behind his head.

"I'm sure he was color coded a week ago," Jameson said dryly, smirking in my direction. Yeah, I liked organization, so what? If I didn't properly pre-plan, I'd inevitably forget something crucial.

"If you bothered to wear anything but black, you could try it some time," I snipped back as Jake tossed his chips into the pot, raising the bet. To Jake, I added, "Flight out is at seven am."

"Nice. You'll be warm by sundown."

"Thank God for that." A thirty-degree difference would feel insanely awesome.

"Need to run through your presentation again?" Charlie offered helpfully, always a willing encourager.

"I think he could sign it, mime it and Morse code it," Axel countered with a chuckle. He'd endured more than a dozen renditions alongside Jameson and Noel as they all helped me prepare for the trip.

"Good," Charlie grunted, raising his beer. "Cheers to new beginnings."

"I can cheers to that," I said, lifting my beer as the guys all did the same. The clink of glass was accompanied by a chorus of, "To new beginnings," and, "To Broderick," and my chest tightened. It would disappoint more than just me if I failed this quest, so I had to ensure I didn't.

FINGERS LACED like a net behind my head, I floated in the hot tub, staring up at illuminated palm trees twenty-four hours later. The last glimpse of blue light faded away when I finally peeled myself out of the resort hot tub, toweling off before I stepped into flip-flops. After a shockingly uneventful travel day, I'd settled in, ordered an early dinner, ran my thoughts like a hamster on a wheel in a fierce internal debate over re-writing my entire presentation, though I ultimately left it as is.

Instead, I stripped down, stepped into swim trunks and swam my laps in the heated pool before forcing myself to sit still long enough for a thirty-minute soak in the saltwater sauna. I was ready to hunker down with a good book before getting into bed at a time that would make my grandfather proud. Tomorrow was registration day, and that would inevitably entail a tremendous amount of social interaction I certainly couldn't care less to indulge. Tolerating *that* required extra sleep.

That anxiety churning in my stomach was only exacerbated when I stepped back into the hell-scape that was the casino floor. The entire resort was a labyrinth of intricately designed pathways that led to more debauched chaos. "Excuse me, sir, where are the elevators?" I asked a man dressed in a gold, lame piped uniform.

"Follow the patterned carpeting to the flashing lights," he said without bothering to even look at me as he power-walked through the sea of slot machines.

Left with the least helpful set of directions in the history of all humankind, I chose the least offensive pattern and followed it. As luck would have it, I chose the wrong pattern and found myself wandering past innumerable shops, restaurants, card tables, and slot machines, all hoping to milk a man for every last penny to his name before spitting him out into the cruel desert heat. To paraphrase the Eagles, you can checkout anytime you like, but your *money* can never leave.

A new sense of apprehension slowed my steps as the chatter of the bustling lobby swallowed the soft slap of my flip-flops on white marble. Countless voices bounced off the intricately carved walls and mural-painted ceiling. But my attention zeroed in on a lean female form poured into a classy black dress and red heels. Brunette hair cascaded down to her shoulder blades, frizzy from an inevitable day of airport insanity, judging by the two carry-on sized bags at her feet. Shoulders tense, she set her long, manicured hands on the desk pleadingly, and goosebumps walked down my spine as a knowing set in. Cautiously edging in closer than necessary to pass them on the way to the elevator, I confirmed what I already knew when she turned, yanking her hand through waves I knew from experience were like silk to the touch.

Holy hell.

More beautiful than my memory ever did justice, Elora Rhodes looked exhausted and uncharacteristically discouraged as she knelt to retrieve her discarded luggage. Her hair had grown out since I'd seen her last, and she'd dyed it darker, making those gray-blues impossibly brighter. More definition had built into her biceps, like she'd been honing her strength towards impossible perfection.

If she wasn't Rhyett and Jameson's little sister, I probably would have asked her out fresh out of high school. The moment she was legal, I would've done the whole roses and a boombox outside her window deal—or something equally pathetic in an effort to woo her. As it was, a teenage pact amongst the guys barred any of us from crossing that boundary. James got his heart stomped on by El and

Hadlee's friend, and when she became impossible for him to avoid–plaguing the house and after event parties until Rhyett caved and told the girls what she'd done to their brother–we'd all vowed to stay away from our best friend's sisters or sisters' best friends. In a town as small as Mistyvale, it only made sense, and we'd all honored it like law ever since. There was a section in there about moms and aunts too, but I didn't think that had presented an issue for any of us. The worst part? I'd pushed him into that relationship in the first place, and the weight of his bruised heart had been my burden ever since.

Even now, a neon warning sign flashed in my mind screaming *off limits*. As I watched her nervously lick her lips, I'd never regretted that agreement more in my life. With a huff, El straightened, and when those blue eyes landed on me, her red lips popped open in surprise.

Well, shit.

FOUR

ELORA

"*El?*" Broderick's evident shock gave way to one word: just my name as he blinked and staggered forward. I couldn't say the same. Exhausted, flustered, and more than a little pissed off, it took all my faculties to remember how the hell to close my mouth. *Fuck. Me.* Nearly all six feet of warm umber skin and lean muscle were on display and glistening wet from an apparent dip in the pool. I followed the line of his gorgeous abs down to those navy-blue swim trunks before my brain caught up and yanked my gaze to those perplexed brown eyes. He was already closing the gap, broad hands gripping the towel haphazardly wrapped around his broad shoulders.

"H-hi," I finally managed to stammer. What the hell was that pathetic broken syllable? I'd delivered keynote speeches to thousands of people, live streamed lessons to three times that, argued with CEOs of billion-dollar companies about the long-term impacts of their economic choices, but my hormone-induced high school heart throb reduced me to utter stupidity with his audacity to possess abs and say my name. Just like that, I was sixteen years old again, pouring my heart out at my junior prom, only for him to walk away, leaving me staring after him into the mist blanket over the parking lot.

An entire lifetime took place between then and now, so many fresh memories of his laugh, his quick wit, his ability to analyze a situation in a circle until everyone in the room was questioning their sensibilities. He'd been there for me—for us—through hell and high water, through losing Pops, and nobody had hesitated to volunteer him when we needed an extra hand. Rhyett and Jameson called him one of our 'bonus brothers' alongside Max. But he'd never been that for me. He'd always been...*Broderick*. Somehow, the fifteen years of new memories didn't erase the ache in my chest as I watched him close the distance.

"You okay? You look stressed."

"Oh," I sighed, eyes sliding shut as I forced myself to swallow my pathetic unrequited feelings and gather my composure. Travel had been exhausting in the most literal sense, only to arrive at this clusterfuck. "Evidently, speaking at an event doesn't guarantee your room these days. They double booked."

Brows winging up, his gorgeous brown eyes rounded. "You're... you're speaking this week?"

"If I can find somewhere to crash in this damn city, yeah. Principles for Women in Leadership on Wednesday morning. But everything's booked. We're vying for space with an NFL game, and Taylor Swift, and apparently not even Vegas was prepared for all three of us at once." Tears pricked at my eyes as the explanation poured through my lips. Kicking myself, my brain tried to muddle through if I was close to my cycle, just overstimulated from the long day, or if an unexpected Broderick sighting had triggered memories of home.

Aaand, now I'm homesick, for the love of God. Annoyed with myself, I sucked down a steadying breath and huffed, "It's fine, honestly, I'm just tired. I'll figure it out. I'm sure there's something on the outskirts of the suburbs or a town or two over."

His brow furrowed, and I studied the familiar amber flecks in his eyes as they darted past me, his hand vaguely damp where it settled on my shoulder. "Hi, ma'am, there must be a mistake. Ms. Rhodes and I are associates, and I can assure you, she leaves nothing to chance. Surely, you and I can both agree that if she's speaking at the event, she needs a room on site, and it would be insane for the resort to not prioritize making this right."

In that one blink, he swapped from my Broderick to Dr. Broderick Allen, and my damn knees went weak. Pathetic. *Honestly, Elora, we are above this,* I hissed to myself internally. Brain Elora and body Elora needed to get on the same damn page.

"As I told your friend, Mr—"

"Allen," he supplied with a smile that could make any female buckle. I watched the front desk girl's skin go muddy as she attempted to keep her composure with the deity now leaning on her marble counter.

"*Dr.* Allen," I chirped dumbly, as if that elevation in title would somehow help our case.

"Yes," the little blonde smiled sympathetically, a trace of pink coloring her pretty cheeks when she met Broderick's gaze. *Same babes, same.* "Well, Dr. Allen, as I told your friend, unfortunately, we had a huge system error. We are deeply sorry for the inconvenience, but there is nothing I can do. The computer booked nearly twice as many guests as rooms, and we didn't catch the error until the convention began checking in. We're offering an incentive to attendees to allow speakers to stay in exchange for credit, but so far, there've been no takers."

"Well, surely you have rooms in a sister hotel?"

"I'm sorry, sir, but we're completely booked."

"I understand you're just doing your job, and this isn't your fault," he cocked his head to catch her name plate, his voice patient and level as ever. God, why was that hot? I ground my teeth. Everything about Broderick had been hot from the summer when he showed up with puberty-induced veins in his forearms. "*Hallie*, but I'm sure you agree this is unacceptable. Who can we speak with to resolve this for Ms. Rhodes?"

"Broderick, it's fine," I interjected. "She's exhausted her resources; I'll just go call around—"

"Worst case, you crash with me," he supplied matter-of-factly, as if nothing about that would be in the least bit uncomfortable. The sudden catapult of my heart begged to differ.

I blinked, tucking my now-haggard curls behind an ear. My gaze traced over that immaculate, lean frame, a lone water droplet making a race down the length of his torso. Absolutely not. In no universe could I survive a week in five-hundred square feet with *that*, without humiliating myself like I did all those years ago. Broderick's loyalty had always been, and would always be, to my brothers. There wasn't even a discussion to be had, *of that* he had been *abundantly* clear. "Don't be silly. I could never impose."

"Like I didn't practically live on your couch growing up." He squeezed my shoulder. "I know Hallie can help us out. If you grab yourself a cup of tea, I'll meet you by the fireplace when we have some solutions. In the meantime, call around as much as you'd like. We'll all figure this out."

My eyes narrowed, ego bristling. "Like I just said, we've

already exhausted her resources."

"So, I'll exhaust someone else's," he countered cheerfully with a little smile that spelled a hellish mental loop for whoever they doomed to respond to the escalation call. I almost felt bad. *Almost.* If it weren't for the ache in my fingers, still clinging to my luggage, I might have sincerely dragged him away before he latched onto his next target. The manager appeared at that moment, and with a sigh, I turned to find out what I could.

AS LUCK WOULD HAVE IT, nobody within a ninety-minute radius seemed to have vacancies. Well, unless I was brave enough to march down to the seedy-looking hotel available by the hour, but I needed to shower just from talking to the front desk guy on the phone. The Summit's social media forum was full of attendees, all reporting back as we found new information, and they'd begun a roommate file. Beds were filled as quickly as people posted them, and I'd just hocked my phone into my bag to massage my throbbing temples when Broderick sidled up beside me on the front curb of the resort, with a prime view of the illuminated valet booth. He tossed a gold foiled envelope in my lap and sat shoulder-to-shoulder with a sigh before placing a keycard in my palm.

"They had something?" I chirped, hopes instantly dashed when I saw the stiff smile as he feigned nonchalance. I knew him too well to believe it.

"They had an extra *keycard* for my room," he said, shrugging. "And you've got over a grand on that gift card to use at any of their locations. You and Hads are the only people I know who might actually get their money out of that." My younger sister, Hadlee—or Hads, for short—was a travel blogger, and bounced around just as often, if not more than I did.

"Well, thanks. I'm sorry for interrupting your swim, or whatever you were off to."

"Nah, I was done, anyway. I'm sorry they fucked up your trip."

"Well, thanks anyway."

"Anytime, El. You know that."

"Yeah," I said, forcing a smile. He'd always had my back...just not in the way I wanted.

"So... I'll show you to the room?" He clapped his hands to his thighs before standing, swiping a suitcase in one hand and offering me the other. I stared at it for a beat before accepting the help to my feet.

"Broderick, I'm not so sure I should—"

"This is what pullout sofas are for."

I bit my lip and didn't miss the way he tracked it before gluing his eyes to mine. That was why he was so infuriating. Everything about our private interactions screamed I wasn't alone in my infatuation—at the very least, attraction—but in the more than decade since I'd been of age, he'd never made a damn move.

Move on dot org. That needed to be my new life motto. It was high time I just trucked right along and forgot about him. But as that bright smile flashed wider, my stomach flopped, and I resolved to be single forever.

"Stop thinking so hard and come invade my space."

"You swear it's not a bother?"

"I swear. You won't even notice me. I'll sleep on the spare bed and be gone before you wake in the morning."

BRODERICK

WE BOTH STARED, slack jawed, at what I could only describe as a crime scene on the hideaway mattress. Gouged holes leaked stuffing from the already-thin cushion. A dark rust-colored stain spread out in a great circle with small splatters across the corner. My livid call to the front desk resulted in as much progress as my passionate petition of Hallie and her manager. A credit to the restaurant—dinner, on the house—as an apology for the inconvenience. The hotel was as hyper-extended as a leaf spring with too large a load.

My eyes were still closed, thumb and forefinger pinching my temples as El paced from one side of the room to the other.

"What the hell do I do now?"

Sighing, resigned to the seventh level of hell I was damning myself to, I motioned to the bed.

Her eyes flew wide. "Absolutely not."

"Got an alternate?" I countered.

"I'm working on it." She lifted her phone and demanded, "Anything?" Her scowl said whoever filled the line didn't have answers, either. "Come on, work your tech magic. There's gotta be something."

Smiling wryly, I said, "Hey, Maxipad."

She shot me a glare, but amusement tugged on those glossed lips. "Broderick says hi...yes, that Broderick... He's *attending*, what do you *think* he's doing here? ... He's got me in his room at the moment, but there's gotta be another option... No, of course not." Her gaze flicked back to mine before she whirled towards the city, lowering her voice to a hiss I couldn't decipher as she inevitably retaliated Max's snark back in his direction.

This was fine. This would be fine. We were both adults. Professionals. *Off fucking limits*. It's not like we hadn't been camping together dozens of times. This time was just...*alone*. With a murder scene in the corner. On one queen sized mattress with—

Nope. Nope, I was fucked. And there was no unfucking once properly fucked.

Needing to do something with my hands and not stare at the disturbing stains any longer, I walked over and folded the hideaway back into place inside its disarming exterior—which did nothing to ease my need to wash my hands. Maybe I'd hop on the forums and find a room full of dudes, and just crash in there. I sure as hell wasn't leaving El to find a place in filthy Sin City alone.

No room for one of their speakers, for fuck's sake. Who got fired today?

"Yeah, okay," El said with a forlorn sigh. "Keep me posted, please? Yes, I'll eat... No, I won't be a bitch... Okay... Yes please... Love you, Max."

The call disconnected, and she rocked on her heels before saying, "Welp," popping her lips on the 'p' like Jameson so often did. I swallowed hard. Oh, fuck. Max knew. Which meant Alice would know. Which meant Paxton and Finn would hear and Jameson would inevitably pick up the trail at some point. And then I was well and truly fucked. How does a man explain his way out of this? What grown man would believe the tale?

El grimaced with a little shrug. "How do you feel about Mexican food, roomie?"

HOW I MET *Your Mother* played softly on the television as background noise—a nervous tic El developed in high school, usually reserved for when she wasn't feeling well.

One thing that always impressed me about this woman was how much food she could put down. I knew NFL players that couldn't eat what she could in one sitting. Maybe it was growing up gorging during our football games, and maybe it was competing with eleven other mouths for food at the table. Eat it or lose it. Whatever the reason, her ability to inhale an entire combo platter and follow it up with dessert had always been entertaining.

Sometime during her nervous pacing, after she'd ordered takeout but before she flipped on the television, I'd remembered to go shower and clothe myself. She'd been marginally less frantic when I returned, the too-small bed covered in a towel and aluminum tins full of our favorites. We ate in silence, watching someone else's shit show for a few minutes before returning to our own. She was playing it cool, like I was, but I could see those cogs turning.

"We should get some shuteye," I stated, hours after I'd intended to pass the fuck out. She nodded, but her eyes were far away, and I waited, even as her long fingers nervously fluttered together.

"Ground rules," she declared abruptly.

"Pardon?"

"We should set some, right?"

I raised a lone brow, equally amused and apprehensive about what was about to come out of her smart mouth. Nobody in Mistyvale could push my buttons quite like El. "I've known you for thirty-one years, but sure, yeah, *ground rules.*"

"No sleeping naked," she blurted out as color stained her tan cheeks.

I barked a laugh, blinking pointedly. "You really feel like that needed to be stated?"

"Well, *I don't know*," she said, nibbling on her lower lip

and motioning vaguely at me. "I don't know if you sleep clothed. I *do* know that was plenty of exposure for my eyeballs for one week this afternoon. Which reminds me, if you bring someone back to the room, put a sock on the damn door."

"Now, *come on.*"

"*What?*" she questioned innocently. The woman had one hell of a poker face—predictably learned from her brothers—and I couldn't for the life of me figure out if she was being sarcastic or not. "My eyes would never recover."

"You seriously think I'm voluntarily rooming with my best friends' little sister and I'm going to bring back a hookup? Shit, El, at least pretend to have an ounce of faith."

"Okay, my bad. I just...this is weird, right? This is weird," she repeated, as if seeking my confirmation.

"Only because you're making it weird," I pointed out, shoulders tight as I fought the need to defend myself. Her brothers and I might have done the whole free-love thing in college, but it had been years since I'd been a casual hookup kind of guy.

"See! It is. It's weird."

"You afraid I can't keep my hands to myself or something?"

"I didn't say it was you I'm worried about."

Something I couldn't read flashed in her expression. That was odd. I could usually read everyone, especially El. "Are you insinuating I need to worry about wandering hands?"

"I'm notoriously...a cuddler," she said. If she weren't so clearly uncomfortable, it would have been fun to see the illustrious Elora Rhodes fumbling for purchase.

"Well, *I'm* notoriously a space heater, so that should

mitigate that concern. Plus, I doubt you'll be up for canoodling once I state my proposed bylaws."

"Bylaws?" she yipped, a broad smile cracking through her discomfort.

"You get roommate rules, but I don't?" I countered, smirking.

"I'm not saying that. Hit me, Professor."

Shaking my head, I supplied, "Funny you should say that. I get one philosophical musing per day, and you have to deal." She groaned dramatically and suddenly I was seventeen, standing back in the Rhodes' basement, bickering about Hypatia and the value of philosophical freedom. Chuckling, I said, "That's the price, El. I get to pick your brain on a concept a day."

"Fine," she said, rolling her eyes as she finally reached to unclip her sleek high heels. "But I'm not a teenager anymore. I need my beauty sleep. No midnight musings."

"Breakfast, mid-toothbrush, all fair game."

"Speaking of mid-toothbrush. You're not like my brothers, are you? No clumps of toothpaste in the sink." She wrinkled her cute little nose as I shook my head. "It's disgusting."

"I'll give you that one." Running a palm over my jaw, I suggested, "We trade shower days. Even dates for me, and you take odds."

"*What?* That's ridiculous. Besides, I shower daily."

Immediate regret filled my bones, because now I was picturing her in the shower. *Dumbass move.* Filling my mind with random regurgitations from my dissertation, I looked anywhere but at El, running a hand over the back of my neck.

"Listen, we can trade, but be prepared for negotiations."

Smirking, she jabbed, "Like there's ever been any other option for us."

"Gotta keep you on your toes, Rhodes."

"I think you have that backwards," she teased, tossing her shoes toward the murder sofa. She had me there. It had always been Elora pushing me to do better, stealing my records a few years behind us, always in the back of my mind when I was tempted to settle for my version of mediocrity. Honestly, I'd been shocked she didn't make herself go out for the football team just to see if she'd be a better running back.

"Yeah," I agreed, a tense silence falling between us. When she rolled that lower lip between her teeth again, I smirked. "El. It's fine. You're not in the way. I'm not letting you march out into Sin City to find a room all alone. I have contained the evidence inside the couch, and we have to be downstairs in—" I glanced at my wrist but realized I'd taken off my watch and fumbled for my phone instead. "Seven hours."

"You're right. It's...just like old times," she said with false bravado, flashing that smile she used for YouTube and stage appearances. It was the Elora the rest of the world got, not the one I grew up with, and I immediately remembered how much I loathed it. I was about to agree with her anyway when my phone rang, and I looked down to see my mother on the screen.

"I should take this."

"Say hi for me?"

"Will do," I said, rising to step past her, and absolutely not inhaling the subtle lilac perfume lingering on her skin. The snick of the patio door clicking shut returned the air to my lungs a beat before I slid the answer button and said, "*Hey*, Mom."

FIVE
BRODERICK

"You always make us proud, baby. Don't be so hard on yourself," Mom said about a half an hour later.

"I know, Ma. Competition's going to be tough."

"That's a given—it's in the name."

"Yeah," I agreed, thinking of Elora, wrestling with whether to give her more details about the turn of events today and opting to avoid any additional opinions. I loved my mom, and she'd always been supportive. Not easy to please, but quick to support. She didn't care if my marks fell, so long as she knew without a doubt that I'd given it my all. Dad was the same. Happy and healthy, with a good sense of integrity was their greatest concern. It was *me* having panic attacks if that percentage mark dropped toward a B. But Marley Allen made us dad's favorite gumbo whether my team won or lost, whether I'd taken first place or last.

"Brod?" Her tone told me I'd lingered longer than appropriate, concern laced into that one syllable, making it feel longer. "Everything okay?"

"Yeah, just tired," I allotted. It wasn't a lie, but I glanced over my shoulder to the closed patio door automatically. "Bumped into Elora Rhodes in the lobby today."

"Elly!?" she chirped, her adoration obvious. El and Mom were birds of a feather, both so driven it would put most men on edge. "What on earth are the odds? Oh, how is she?"

The door seemed to grow in front of me as I gave her crumbs when a feast of information sat at the tip of my tongue. "Looks great—she's speaking on women in leadership—told me to say hello when I talked to you next."

"Please say hi back! Always did love that girl."

"I know," I said, smiling. *She wasn't the only one.* "Look, Ma, it's getting pretty late here—"

"Oh! Honey!" she said, blatantly frustrated with herself. "I'm sorry, I've kept you on too long. Just missing you already."

"You're fine, Mom," I chuckled. "But I'm gonna hit the hay."

"Okay. You get your sleep and kick some ass this week."

Grinning at her enthusiasm, I said, "Alright, Ma. Talk soon."

"Talk soon. Love you, baby."

"Love you too. Tell Dad I love him, please."

"I will, the moment I pry him away from that old rust bucket."

Laughing, I shook my head. At some point, my white-collar father decided to restore a '52 Chevy pickup. For the most part, he just painted the garage in various fluids and shavings of metal, but he was bound and determined to do it himself. "Sounds about right. Night, Mom."

"Night, Brod."

Shoulders dropping, I blew out a breath that had wedged in my ribcage, and slowly eased into the room, eyes immediately scanning for El. Never in my thirty-five years had I been so grateful for hoodies and sweatpants instead of some frilly girly silk thing. Elora was either passed the hell out or a fantastic actress, her chest rising and falling steadily in an oversized green *Grizzly Grind* sweatshirt—paying homage to Rhyett's coffee shop back home—when I finally returned from my call. She'd always been precious, but especially so in sleep. My Pixie girl—tiny, but capable of unleashing absolute chaos on any who provoked it. When we were kids, her petite stature had earned the nickname, the attitude growing to match over the years. I could never have left her in this shit show alone. Regardless, her brothers would fucking kill me. This was a terrible idea. I should sleep in my rental car.

Stomach in knots, I peeled back the comforter and had to fight the need to burst out laughing. She'd lined two pillows down the center of the bed like a down-filled barrier between her side and mine. Marginally less apprehensive, I slunk under the stiff, starched sheet, momentarily distracted, wondering who actually liked their sheets chemically straightened.

Laying back on a thick pillow, I laced my fingers behind my head and surveyed the textured beige ceiling, listening to the soft exhales of the woman to my right. I was eighteen the last time we'd fallen asleep together. We'd been on the trampoline Mom gave me for my birthday, my last summer break before college. It was one of those unheard of balmy Alaskan August evenings, the sun finally tucking behind the horizon around midnight, and the two of us fell asleep shoulder to shoulder beneath the stars.

Something about her proximity brought me back to that night. They had suspended Jameson for fighting—which was *bullshit*, because he didn't start the fucking thing—and

El had been beside herself because of our inability to help him. Somehow, my idea of comfort for the too-fucking-cute *fifteen-year-old* had been telling her all the folklore I knew about the stars. We'd drifted off in the middle of an indigenous fable, and all those years later, I fell asleep to the same soft sound of her breathing beside me.

THE HOTEL ROOM was silent when I woke to the early light of morning. Startling upright, I looked around, blinking into the dawn as I looked for any sign of El or her things. The room was freakishly tidy, right down to the hastily straightened sheets on her side of the pillow blockade. Like most American hotels, our room was the proud host of hideous carpet and chunky blackout blinds that doubled as a home to an inordinate amount of dust. No doubt that was what I could thank for the fact that my face was aching, sinuses stuffy, forehead throbbing. What was it about whoever designed these corporate monstrosities? They all felt the same, like one ongoing nightmare showing of *The Shining*. It was the green light of the miniature coffee pot that finally caught my attention.

Once I had a full cup in hand, I wandered to the bathroom, about to call her name, when I saw the door was cracked open, revealing chaos beyond. *There it is.* A cloud of hairspray lingered in the air, and I glanced over the open packs of makeup and still-steaming hair styling tools. Her pajamas were tossed over a towel rack, the vague moisture in the air telling me she'd showered. Had the sound of her leaving woken me up in the first place? How in the hell had I slept through all of this?

By the time I dressed and made it downstairs to register

for the event, the banquet room was filling with eager attendees. Name tag hanging from my new lanyard, I surveyed the chaos, my eyes immediately finding El as she worked the room like a pro. Her little frame looked long as she buzzed from one group to another, beaming and shaking hands as though they were all old friends. She tossed her silky hair over her shoulder.

"Professor Allen?" When I found green narrow-set eyes blinking up at me, I realized I must've missed her first attempt to get my attention. Clearing my throat, I smiled down at the little redhead in a deep green dress, her round face trained on mine. Young enough to be one of my students, she stood tall and bold.

"Hi—yes, that's me," I muttered, offering her a cordial smile and stretching my hand out. She accepted instantly but shook with more vigor than I was frankly expecting, nearly pulling me forward.

"My name is Clara. I'm a junior at UC Davis, and I'm absolutely obsessed with your dissertation. I just needed to introduce myself."

"Oh!" I blinked at her as she rolled her lip between her teeth. So...*young*. So obviously shoving herself out on the line that I almost felt bad for shuffling back a step. How on earth would she know about my dissertation? It was *ancient*. Grasping for the proper response, I pulled at my collar. "I'm flattered, thank you. Are you a philosophy major?"

Elora

"FANTASTIC MEETING YOU, Miss Rhodes. Will we see you at the bar for drinks after the presentations today?"

"If I ever slow down long enough to stop dancing, absolutely."

His laugh warmed my chest as the man—that just introduced himself as Pierce—released my hand and I returned it to the strap of my event-branded tote bag they'd distributed at registration. He was handsome, if you were into that whole blond *J. Crew* vibe.

Hand stuffed in his slack pockets; Pierce flashed a dimpled smile I'm sure won him all number of dates. "Excellent. Well, I'll know where to find you."

"Sure thing," I chirped, relieved when none other than Mara Correa came skidding around the corner, her short, silky black hair secured away from her face in a tiny bun as her eyes landed on me. "If you'll excuse me—"

My sentence was cut off by the elated screech of a woman hellbent on a mission, Mara's beeline headed directly for us. Pierce didn't have a shot in hell at responding, because she collided with me with a yelp. The air rushed from me in a laugh as I threw my arms out to steady us, tote crinkling a beat before it fell from my arm to the floor, and I wrapped her up with just as much enthusiasm.

"As I live and breathe!" she squeaked, crushing me.

Shoulders shaking with laughter, I squeezed her right back. "Nice to see you, too."

"I'm so glad you're here! I got a little nervous yesterday."

"Flying out of Chicago in November was not my brightest idea." My delayed flight had eliminated any possibility of catching the connector, crafting one big clusterfuck of a day before the room debacle last night. I rolled my eyes in exasperation.

"It's not normally that bad," she allotted with a one

shoulder shrug. "But you're here now!! Come, come! Who have you already introduced yourself to?"

"Gosh, it feels like half the room."

"Can't exactly say I'm even a little bit surprised. Here, Johanna King is in the corner, and she just freed up," she trilled excitedly, snatching my hand in hers and dragging me away with enough force that I barely retrieved my bag from the floor. Johanna was another podcaster—though her following was double mine—and one of my most anticipated speakers for the week. Beyond that, she'd be sitting on the panel for our grant, which meant if anyone had the inside scoop on what the judges were looking for, it was her.

I stood a little taller, lifting my chin and running my free hand through my hair before we cleared the distance. It was that final swipe of my tongue over my teeth as I checked for stray bits of bell pepper or hash brown that came to a halt as abrupt as my footsteps. Broderick appeared to be deep in conversation with a curvy little redhead a good decade younger than me, braced with his shoulder against the wall with one ankle crossed over the other. Sickly green oil swirled in my gut for the heartbeat before Mara's face appeared in my line of sight, a deep groove between her brows as she locked eyes with me.

"Babes, you have a stroke or something?"

Clearing my throat, I shook my head, even as my insides knotted. Ew. What was this revolting somersaulting rage—*fuck me, I'm jealous*. This should not have been a new sensation. I'd been a victim of the acidic waves of envy since high school. It hadn't rattled me then and it absolutely wouldn't rattle me now. Schooling my features and yanking my shoulders back, I said, "Nope, just thought I saw someone, that's all. Where's Johanna?"

Just then, the lights dimmed, and the music increased in volume, a steady base suddenly rippling through the floor as everyone looked up and toward the stage placed along the long wall. "Tonight. We'll track her down *tonight*," Mara promised, although she looked just as eager to go find seats as she'd been to meet a legend in the industry. Fingers clutched—more tightly this time—in Mara's, I followed her straight to the front of the room, where she promptly yanked me down into an uncomfortably padded metal chair with blue brocade upholstery that would match the drapes in our room.

Still fighting the unsteady sensation in my center, I leaned an elbow on the table, bracing myself as I inched towards Mara's ear. "Pssst. Are you here alone?"

"Are you hitting on me? Because while I'm flattered, I'm otherwise engaged," she teased with a wink, tossing her short, dark strands. "I'm bougie, but not that bougie. Kent and the kids are with me."

"Ahh."

"Why?"

"No reason," I said with a smile, jerking my chin back at the stage as a sophisticated-looking man in a navy suit took his place at the podium. I wondered if Mara and Kent's hideaway bed looked like it also pissed off the mob.

THE CONFERENCE OPENERS were all freaking fantastic, as were the four cups of complimentary coffee now coursing through my veins and sending shudders down my frame. Anticipating the close of the segment, I gathered my pens and notebook and slipped them back in the tote bag. The downside to compulsive coffee consumption was the accompanying bladder requirements, and I was dying to get the hell out of here and back to my bathroom before lunch opened up.

My ambitions were halted by none other than the mile long, blonde and beautiful Johanna King as she stepped on stage to raucous applause. Mara and I exchanged grins as we joined the room in their enthusiastic welcome, hands stinging from clapping and face a little numb from smiling so much.

"How is everybody today?" A chorus of whoops went up, and she smiled impossibly brighter. "Let's give our opening speakers another round of applause!"

"God, her dress is impeccable, isn't it?" I whispered to Mara as the room broke out into cheers. She nodded enthusiastically. The rush of the day poured right through the moment as Johanna's mic gave a little pop of feedback a beat before she continued.

"Now, I will not delude myself into thinking you're all eagerly awaiting my every word on the edge of your seats. By now, you're likely salivating over that roast turkey and mashed potatoes they've been wafting through the air vents for the last hour and a half." Polite laughter filled the room as she surveyed the space. *Magnetizing*. She wasn't doing anything spectacular beyond simply existing, and I found her magnetizing. "But we have an announcement, and I wanted you all to have time to process and strategize before we reconvene this afternoon to break into small groups." I didn't know what she was going on about but was suddenly fairly certain I wouldn't like it. "*The New Leaders Grant* received an outpouring of interest that was exponentially higher than we could have ever anticipated." A round of claps cut through the space, but my stomach was sinking with each breath, and Mara's hand jutting out to grab mine did nothing to ease the nerves. "In order to expedite the application process and keep the rest of this week on track, we took the liberty of reviewing your applications and narrowing them down to the final five—"

It was at that point in her explanation that my mind went...*blank*. Completely. Utterly. Deer in headlights. Blank.

What would we do if we didn't even get a shot to plead our case, to pitch the endless hours of research? *Five!?* Five contestants out of the two hundred sitting rapt in this room?

I wasn't sure I heard another word out of Johanna's mouth, but I was entirely sure that Mara was suddenly yanking me to my feet and colliding with me like a Prada-clad football player as she hopped from one foot to the other and the chaos of the room came roaring back. I snapped my eyes back to the stage to see one duo making their way up the stairs and an obliviously cheerful Johanna beaming down at us as Mara shoved me forward and we made our way across the floor and up the steps.

The first women reached out their hands beneath nervous smiles, and I shook them both as we took our spot and Johanna called out names and the purpose of their applications.

Pierce and Cheyenne were siblings from Wyoming, building orphanages with 3D printers in third world countries.

Alexandria was funding scholarships for minority families to attend universities.

A weighted pause settled over the room as I realized the beaming faces in line were suddenly...our competitors. I didn't want to compete with any of them, as they shifted on their feet nervously, suddenly at center stage. All their ideas were worthy of receiving the money. For the first time, as my heart pounded in my chest, I realized how hard this would be.

"Our fifth and final candidate is applying for the funds to start up a center that would provide after school care, meals, tutoring and extracurriculars for teens whose parents cannot be as involved in their lives as they'd like." So, a youth center. Oh, for fuck's sake, I'd be robbing bunnies to feed raccoons in this fiasco. But her next words snapped my attention to the back of her perfect golden hair. "From a rainy little community in The Last Frontier. A small fishing town called *Mistyvale*, Alaska." *No. No way.* My breath stalled as I scanned clear across the room, finding him against the back wall, as though my mind had never lost track of him in the first place. My stomach sank as his eyes found mine through the gold frames of his reading glasses. No freaking way. "Professor Broderick Allen."

SIX
BRODERICK

The level of dread mirrored back at me in those Rhodes blue-gray eyes from across the room was an accurate depiction of the panic in my chest. *Of course.* Of course, they'd reduce the competition for efficiency's sake. That or the fates had been sorely lacking in entertainment and decided to shake things up a bit. And, *of course*, it would be me facing off with Elora. It was always me and Pix.

I was the swim team captain my sophomore year, before Dad made me pick between that and football. That was two years before she swept the board, claiming every damn category and setting the state record for metals collected. My shoes as Student Body President were filled by none other than Elora Rhodes, with ten more votes than I'd acquired. I was awarded Valedictorian with a four-point-oh, so she took AP classes and took the title with a four-point-five.

A four. Point. Five.

What kind of psychopath could get a GPA like that? My best friends' baby sister. That's who.

As her eyes slipped closed, she looked less than thrilled

at the current matchup, and with good reason. Our competitors all had fantastic, heart-smashing causes. And if she was anything like me, she'd been preparing for weeks and knew that more likely than not, it would be the two of us standing as finalists by the end of the week.

It always had been.

Cursing, I made my way on stage to shake hands with Miss King, and my new competition, hesitating awkwardly in front of Elora. Did I shake the hand of the woman I'd known practically my entire life? Go in for a hug and make the entire conference awkwardly aware of our friendship? What were the odds a tiny Alaskan fishing town would produce *two* of their finalists? We had a four-figure population. So...None. Absolutely incomprehensible.

Swallowing audibly, my shoulders relaxed when she extended her hand and gave a practiced smile. As I accepted, she practically crushed my palm, and I canted my head as one of her sculpted brows arched incrementally in challenge. The warning was implicit, as they all had been back home.

This means war.

A war I wasn't entirely convinced I wanted to wage. But as she released me, I slipped my hand in my pocket, clutching my lucky silver dollar like a grown man's support blanket before we all leaned together to pose for a photographer who'd scurried up on the stage.

Eyes working to get rid of the flash's retina abuse, I thought about the absolute chaos we caused as teenagers. And while that was inevitable in a small town—hell, especially a fishing town where we grew up earning grown men's wages to burn on fun—there were so many kids with parents on the water, or in the cannery, and nowhere to go without getting into trouble. Mistyvale needed this. Hell, after Sarah, *I* needed a win. You know what? El had always pushed me to do better—*be* better—and this wouldn't be any different.

Game on, Rhodes. Game. On.

MY BRAVADO ENDED AS ABRUPTLY as it started the moment she caught up with me in the hallway in my naïve attempt to flee. A woman on a mission, you'd have thought she was attempting to ignite me with the glower she shot my direction.

"A youth center, huh? Couldn't have made this easy on my conscience and opted for some football program expansion?"

There wasn't a point in fighting my smile as I glanced down to where she fought to keep up by my shoulder, heels clicking against the slick tile. Slowing to accommodate her little legs, I sighed. "Didn't know I'd be pitted against you in the first place, Pix."

Those delicate lips twisted sideways at the moniker, but she didn't acknowledge it. Instead, she said, "You should withdraw. Save us both the effort."

"*I* should withdraw?" I quirked a brow, shaking my head as we reached the elevators, and I pushed the tacky plastic button. I made a mental note to sanitize my hands when we reached the room. That was one too many handshakes and one too many very public, vaguely dirty-feeling surfaces for my liking. "Absolutely not. Women are eligible for all kinds of scholarships in male-dominated fields. We don't have anything like this on the island."

"We had even fewer amenities when we were kids and we all turned out just fine."

"Half our peers had criminal records by the time we hit nineteen," I pointed out. Mind you, it was predominantly petty theft and equally harmless small-town indiscretions, but a handful were hit with assault charges due to the inevitable bonfire brawls that broke out when kids had nothing to do and nobody at home waiting for them. "Not everybody had loving homes to retreat to, El."

She looked down to her feet, scowling as she stepped into the now open elevator, and I quickly followed her in. My parents were both phenomenal, high achievers, but with that gift came long hours and missed games. If it hadn't been for Rhyett and Jameson dragging me into their mother's sights, my childhood would've been so much emptier. Loved. But quiet.

"I've been preparing for this for months," she added, only my familiarity with her giving away to the irritation hidden in her matter-of-fact tone.

"Same."

"Mara and I need the funding for the school. Contrary to your insinuation, there isn't another program like ours in the country. We'd be the first of our kind."

"Listen, El. The idea is great. But you have three other competitors to worry about with causes far more compelling than mine."

"Like fate would ever be so kind," she muttered dryly, rolling her eyes before they fell to her feet. "It's always fucking been you."

The words hit my chest infinitely harder than they should've, my throat suddenly thick as I turned to face her, the scent of her overpowering my senses. Fuck, she'd always smelled so damn good. She blinked up at me, her determined mask cracking to reveal something heavy as she held my gaze. Had she meant that to feel as weighted as it did? In the sixteen years after that prom, we'd never really...*talked* about what happened between us. Never thought it needed to be said. I'd been out of line, and it wouldn't happen again. But a part of me always wanted to know if she'd seen it that way. If...if anything was different now that we'd grown up.

Tone quiet, curious, and laced in reproach, I managed to squeeze her name out in a pathetic little, "*El.*"

The lift *dinged*, light illuminating a beat before the doors whooshed open, sending us both flying back a step to opposing rails as a group of people rushed in, reeking of Nevada heat and cafeteria food. Their obnoxious chatter did nothing to cut the tension that had just settled into the space, especially not when Elora's eyes locked on mine a beat before the doors opened again—*not* on our floor—and she snuck past the bustling crowd, leaving me cornered in the back of an elevator that smelled of BO and cheap suits.

I'D PRACTICALLY PACED a hole in the tacky carpet of our room by the time I caved. This sitcom-level disaster needed a sounding board. Swiping my phone off the crisp bed covers where I'd hastily discarded it, I hesitated. Scowling, I slowly lowered onto the edge of the bed with a stone in my throat. My thumb hovered awkwardly over Rhyett's name, and then Jameson's before tossing it back onto the bed. Hell, my entire friend group was comprised of Rhodes. Hadn't been an issue until I needed an unbiased opinion. I scrolled down the contact list before staring at Max's name. He already knew. He could tell me what the hell to do, right? But Max's loyalty was firmly planted in Camp Elora, which meant he'd probably give me the finger and curt instructions to bow the hell out of her way.

I should, really. It would be the ethical thing to do. The gentlemanly thing to do. It's what my father would do. I shouldn't compromise her drive to do this, and knowing Elora, my presence on that lineup would. Besides, even if I won the damn thing, every penny in that account would stink of betrayal. It would feel like stealing from her. But Mistyvale kids were on the fast path to throwing their lives away and being trapped on fishing boats whether they wanted that life or not. They needed this.

I needed this. To prove it wasn't all for nothing. To prove I was more than just some small-town community college professor. That I could make an impact and put our town first, like my parents. It was their legacy that led me to rush across the room and yank open the dresser drawer to retrieve my gym clothes with enough force to throw it off its track.

Maybe a good run would clear my head.

Elora

"*THAT'S* 'PROFESSOR HANDSOME'?" Mara demanded, although I couldn't tell if the pinch in her brows was denial or challenge. As we'd gotten close and she'd noticed my...less than encouraging track record in the romance department, of course she'd heard all about Broderick. I just didn't ever think our two worlds would collide so abruptly.

"In the glorious flesh," I said, sinking into the stiff brocade armchair in the corner. Fuck me, he was gorgeous, and so damn captivating. Of course, he made the top five.

Of course, fucking Johanna King had noticed Broderick Allen. "We're hosed."

"Now, now. Slow down," she said with a laugh as she lowered into the chair beside me in her hotel room, bending to pop her heels off. Her adorable little family was down at the resort water park, soaking up the sunshine and entertainment while mama was kicking ass and taking names. "Didn't you always best him?"

"When I could study his game plan, identify weaknesses and improve it? Yeah. But we were never neck and neck. I was always just taking one extra step beyond his precedent. *He* set the bar."

Shaking her head, a coy smile crept up her face. "Ornery little thing, aren't you?"

"I thought it would get his attention," I admitted with a huff, pursing my lips and wishing I could go back for a very firm conversation with teenage Elora about pride and priorities.

"Likely did more than that," she snickered. "So, how do we beat him?" Something uneasy churned in my stomach, but it must have shown on my face because before I could vocalize it, Mara was cutting me off. "Absolutely not. *No. Nada. Ni.* We didn't come this damn far to only come *this* far. You're not backing out because of a pretty face and a mind with a penchant for spouting off Proust."

"It feels shitty."

"To be pitted against your childhood flame? No shit. But we're not quitting."

I wrinkled my nose. But any trace of humor vanished as quickly as the guilt settled in my chest.

"Fuck, I know that face. Stop it right now."

"What?" I mumbled weakly, not even convincing myself that I didn't know exactly what she was saying.

"Why does this bother you so much?"

"Broderick."

"*Jesus*—yes, I got that," she said with a pointed eye roll. "I mean, *why* does the idea of beating him bother you *this* time?"

"Broderick...plays everything close to the vest."

"Okay...?"

"He sticks to Mistyvale, aside from the occasional work trip."

"Still missing the point," she said, irritation slipping into her tone as she motioned to move it along.

"He never—and I mean *never*—does anything for himself. He tried out for football because Rhyett and Jameson were going to play, and he wanted to spend the summer with them. When he became the best running back on the team, he kept playing because the coaches begged him to. Now he's buddy coaching the high school football team with Jameson, because with the summer salmon season, James would miss too many practices." With a huff, I shrugged. "He volunteers in town because his mother was the mayor for half our childhood, and proofs contracts for the local legal aid program on his off time because it's his dad's pet project."

"So, we're robbing a saint, is what you're insinuating."

I huffed a laugh, my cheeks aching. "I've never seen him go for something he wanted because *he* wanted it. As unfortunate as this is, I'm kind of...super proud of him for being here. For taking the shot, you know?"

"He's not aiming to buy an Aston Martin; he's trying to help a bunch of punk teenagers with too much time on their hands."

"Punk teenagers just like *we* were. Mistyvale kids have always been too bored for their own good."

With a pinch between her brows, she immediately countered, "You guys turned out just fine."

"We were lucky," I pointed out with a laugh at the irony, like he had just forty minutes earlier.

"And our aspirations are no less admirable just because his are also noble." Leaning back, Mara crossed her arms, lips twisting to the side as she focused on me.

I shook my head. They weren't. Women still faced such a radical disadvantage in the workplace, in pay gaps, in a country bound and determined to kill off new moms through medical negligence, if not actual malicious intent. God forbid you take the time to heal and bond to your newborn, or get your breasts back to a non-painful, cantaloupe-sized state before being thrown back into the workforce. Don't get me started on the lack of paternity leave—as though fathers shouldn't bond with their babies and look after healing baby mamas. Such an *anomaly* that the suicide rates are astronomical.

We needed this. A school that didn't just equip but empowered. A network of like-minded, badass business babes that would rally and support each other as we figured our shit out. First as students, then as associates, both near and far. Mentors in their industries. Professionals in marketing, advertising, and finance to lean on even after graduation. This mission was about cultivating long term success after equipping them to envision and engineer their reality in the first place. Entrepreneurship was the one way we could guarantee our own benefits in the long run.

A school like ours didn't exist, and it was about damn time somebody made it happen.

"No," I begrudgingly agreed. "The dream hasn't lost value, just...the ease with which I intended to bring it to fruition. I didn't know the competitors. It was easier that way."

"Hey, we don't even know if we'll both survive the first round of elimination. The judges could make this easy on us." I inclined my head, aiming for a disapproving glare, but the involuntary tilt to my mouth obviously ruined the effect, as she burst out laughing. "Yeah, okay that sounded too easy, even to me."

"This is going to suck."

"*Or or or*" she exclaimed as she leaned forward conspiratorially. "It doesn't have to suck. It could be fun."

"Fun?" I drawled dryly.

"Look, he's not actually Mother Teresa. The man broke your heart in high school and rejected you when you fileted yourself open again as a grown ass adult. Perfectly capable of consenting. Perfectly capable of making your own choices, away from the prying eyes of your meddlesome-as-fuck family."

"Ahh, yes, I just love reliving romantic trauma. Please, *continue*."

Ignoring my dripping sarcasm, Mara forged ahead uninhibited. "He's not some innocent little doe, El. Maybe, you use this opportunity to show him what he's missing out on. *Maybe* one last shoot out is exactly what you need to get him out of your system." She flashed a cheeky little wink, adding, "Or...what he needs to get *into* it."

SEVEN

ELORA

Mara's husband, Tony, returned with their littles, and I stepped out to give them privacy as baby Nate started to cry, prompting Mara to whip out a breast like that was the answer to any infant ailment. Surprised—but also slightly relieved—to return to an empty room, I snuck over to my suitcase to change into my gym gear, then whisked my hair into a top knot. There was nothing like a hard run and a heavy lift to clear my head, and if Mara and I were going to walk away with this endorsement, it needed to be positively crystalline.

Eyes on the prize, I laced my shoes and headed out of the room and down the hallway, popping in my earbuds as the elevator lit up, and belched out a swarm of tipsy resort-goers. Did everyone in Vegas just perpetually reek of alcohol, tobacco, and something vaguely smog-like? When the last straggler was gone, I stepped inside, stretching my neck, arms and legs on the way down. I could do this. I'd always been one to conquer a challenge. And Broderick would be happy for my success because he'd see the impact, just like I'd support his if he took home the check. The man would bless so many kids if he poured these kinds of resources into our tiny town.

Stronger by The Score came on by the time I hit the first floor, and I found myself matching the beat with my footfalls as my body stretched just a little taller. A good sweat was all I needed. At least, that's what I was convincing myself of right up until I stepped into the gym and was rooted to the spot.

The glorious, long pace, the shredded biceps glistening in sweat, the splotchy tank clinging to pecs any straight woman would want to lick. God help me. Broderick had always run like it was effortless—a glide, rather than stride. Blue headphones rested over his tight curls, his jaw was set, shoulders back and defined legs gobbling up the track. I watched for a heartbeat as those arms pumped—did I mention the man was mouthwateringly vascular, because *dear baby Jesus in a manger*—as some distant part of my brain came online and demanded I gather enough dignity to get the hell out of there.

A throat cleared and I startled, blinking and ducking my head as I stepped aside to allow an irritated looking blonde into the room. She made a beeline for the Stairmaster, and I glanced back just as Broderick's footwork stumbled in an uncharacteristic falter. He jerked his hands up to the controller, rapidly tapping the down arrow to slow his admirable pace to a hurried walk, slipping the headset down around his neck as his eyes tracked me in the mirror.

"Pix, you alright?"

"Y-yeah," I said awkwardly, clearing my throat to excuse the stammer as I begged the floor to swallow me whole. Smiling stiffly, I skipped onto the treadmill beside him and cursed whoever decided the hotel only needed two. "Just clearing my head. You know, getting in the zone."

"Yeah."

"Yeah." Awesome. Twenty-four hours in and losing intelligence at an alarming rate. "Sorry, didn't mean to throw you off your game."

"You didn't," he argued, shaking his head as he pursed his lips. The blonde eyed us skeptically and I nearly burst out laughing when Broderick's forced smile mirrored mine nearly identically. Had anyone ever been more awkward in the history of the word 'awkward?' I didn't think so.

Irritated with myself, I said, "Oh, good. Please commence running."

"Alright," he said, slowly shifting his headphones back into place.

Of course, he was fucking down here. It was one of the things I loved about the man—we shared a long list of compulsively healthy coping mechanisms. Exercise for stress being one of them. But leaving now would be more ridiculous than just doing what I came here to do, so I activated my machine and then tapped my watch as it slowly crept to life, the smell of rubber thick in the air.

I started the workout tracker and then tried to focus on the metrics on my screen, but deep brown eyes locked on mine in the mirror, a gentle curl to his lips as he watched me pick up the pace. When I scowled at him, he chuckled, shook his head, and focused on his virtual screen—a mountain path, naturally.

The slowly increasing cadence of his feet on the belt beat through the music in my buds, and I huffed, forcing myself to complete the warmup before increasing my pace until I knew I'd be scrambling to keep up.

This. This is what I loved about running. The freedom —or illusion of it, in the case of an indoor gym—the roar of my blood through veins begging for an escape, the burn of muscles. Running silenced the outside world and ceaseless chatter of my mind, forcing me to focus on just putting one foot in front of the other, one step at a time. A hell of an accomplishment for a mind so often stretched over multiple topics and goals at once.

Out of my periphery, I saw Broderick increase his speed, sweat glimmering across the glorious tendons in his forearms. Increasing my own pace, I gauged how hard my body was working, glancing at my heart rate, relieved to see that despite the aching in my chest, it was still solidly below that eighty percent mark.

We ran like that for at least the length of a song before I decided to slow down and catch my breath in preparation for another interval. But he pushed himself faster, and before I processed what I was doing, I ramped up my speed too.

Dammit the man made me stupid. Feet soaring, lungs screaming, muscles protesting, I lengthened my stride, feeling the stretch of my calves as they fought to push me farther with each step. A mature, self-respecting business coach with a six-figure book deal should be beyond petty competition. Alas. Broderick Allen reduced me to teenage levels of stupidity. Which is why, against all better judgment, I matched his next increase, taking my much shorter legs to a full god damn sprint.

I was going to die on a treadmill. Like a frantic, oversized hamster launched off the back of the track, dying in a head-on collision with the free weight rack. Oh god, what a humiliating way to go. Max would never stop laughing. I would trip on a shoelace, and die of concussion by fallen free weight, but they'd inevitably label it faulty footwear, and Max would follow me out, victim of cardiac arrest via aggressive laughter.

To the utter relief of my wailing lungs, we both passed the mile mark and eased to a walk before stepping off the machines. He gathered his water as I walked in a slow, tight circle, bringing my heart rate down before turning for the free weights I was still grateful not to die beneath, and grabbing the twenty-fives before claiming a mat.

Broderick

WHY WAS SHE WEARING THAT? Why. In God's name. Was she wearing *that*? Yeah, the leggings were high-waisted, but skintight, leaving nothing to the imagination, and the strappy sports bra was so fitted it lifted her perfect tits until they kissed in the middle. No. I hadn't meant to notice. But *fuck*, she was gorgeous, and no straight, red-blooded male could see that much skin on a woman that drove him mad, and not want to reach out and touch it. Jameson would promptly beat me to a pulp if he knew half the images running through my head.

She was doing a drill we called the 'slow death' in the gym back home—essentially kneeling to the ground before rotating the opposite hip to step back up, with the weights cradled at her shoulders. The tight lines of her abs flexed, lean little muscles taut with effort, her brow set in concentration. El was the kind of fierce most men only read about but never have the terrifying pleasure of encountering.

Her brow winged up, eyes locked on mine in the mirror, but before I could look away, she mouthed something that had me dropping my headphones back around my neck and panting, "What?"

She breathed a laugh before quipping, "You catching flies over there?"

Brows pinched; my brain grappled before realizing she was telling me to close my mouth. *Like I'd been gaping.* My skin buzzed in response. Scoffing, I countered, "Is there a reason *you're* watching every muscle in my body, or did you trade life coaching for anatomy without my knowing?"

"Something wrong with enjoying the view?" she asked, tone taunting. Slowly, El bent over, using perfect deadlift form—ass out, core tight—to set those weights back on the ground in front of her mat. Every ripple of muscle was accentuated in those damned leggings, the perfect globes of her ass on display like a pert invitation for me to sink my teeth into one. *Sue me, James.* It wasn't my fault this girl had somehow grown up to be a smoke-show not even a priest could avoid appreciating. Even the crease under her ass was sexy.

And I was going to hell for noticing.

"Nope," I said, shrugging like she wasn't driving me up a wall. "Besides, I'm just making sure you're not going to tear a muscle. I'd hate to see you have to bow out of the competition with so much on the line."

"Seriously?" she drawled sarcastically, straightening and popping a hip in one sexy little motion. The crease at her waist just begged me to close the distance and wrap my hands around her middle. Little Broderick, unfortunately, was taking notice. *Off. Fucking. Limits. Asshole.* "You're gonna 'gym bro' me? Save the lectures for your classroom, Professor. Chris and Max hooked me up with a personal trainer ages ago."

I felt my jaw flex under the pressure that phrase elicited. Last thing I wanted to think about was some douche stretching her out after a sweaty session. "Suuure."

One word, but the tone in it had her brows winging up as she motioned to her weights. "By all means, if you think you're more qualified, come give a demonstration."

"No need to make you feel inadequate," I said with a wink. When she grinned back, I added, "I know how competitive you get. Don't want you pulling a hammy."

"Psh, *chicken*," she scoffed back, that maniacal smirk hooking wide to one side as mischief sparked behind those familiar gray-blues. God, I missed that ceaseless mouth. I did not, however, miss wishing I could put it to better use. "I'm not daft enough to think I'll outlift Mistyvale's favorite running back."

"Been a long time since anybody called me that."

Something warm slid behind her smirk, a fond nostalgia hidden behind her sass. Likely of pre-game carb-a-thons and the tinny smell of high school bleachers. El always came to all our games. I knew because she had a whistle so loud it crossed the chaos of the crowd—a straight shot to my chest, like a power up—when I was on a good run. It was always her I found in those stands, hands boldly raised, when I scored.

"Maybe because these days you just start arguments you can't seem to finish. You going to show me up over here, or what?" She threw her hands up, jerking her chin towards the barbell rack in challenge.

Shaking my head, I held her stare, the heat in my chest a flashing red light screaming a warning to back off, to put some space between us. But I held my ground for once. "Over *there*? Nah. On that stage this week?" I gave her a nod, a promise. "You're going down."

I knew the moment her eyes flared, her cocky smirk twisting into the coy smile of the she-devil hidden inside that compact little package, that I'd said the wrong thing.

There was nowhere to back pedal before Elora's eyes tracked down to where I knew my shorts had grown tighter than comfortable. "Would you like that?"

Dead. I was so dead. I glanced over to the blonde still climbing flights of stairs, her headphones mercifully on, and was about to open my mouth—to say *what*, exactly, was still to be determined—when my eyes snapped sideways because the door opened, and in strode Pierce and Cheyenne. Her attention shifted just as abruptly, that pretty little column of her throat bobbing as she faced them and I rolled my eyes, returning my headphones, and squatting down to lift my weights.

Fucking *Pierce*. Man had eyes for El the moment he fell into her orbit. Couldn't exactly blame him, but with that polished wardrobe and thick head of blond hair it was like competing with *Thor* in Lululemon. Which was a dumbass thought in the first place because she wasn't mine to compete for. But as he flashed that too-white smile, and Cheyenne skipped into the gym and wrapped a giggling El in a hug like they were the oldest of friends instead of competitors that met *this morning*, my stomach bottomed out.

Irritated, I increased the volume on my noise canceling headphones, and tried to focus on getting in my reps, and not the fact that she had my cock at half-mast. But every time I set down my weights, I caught sight of the three of them—El's headphones now hanging around the slender column of her neck—laughing together in the mirror. She was evidently unaffected by our little verbal sparring match.

I thought it was annoying when Rhyett made friends in a blink, but nothing irked me quite like seeing her smile... *for him.*

She never smiled for me like that. Smiles with me were always more reserved—guarded and laced with some old echo of the day I ruined everything. Huffing and panting, I dropped my gaze, squatting down and snatching my weights again. It was the moment I saw the exchange of phones between the *Marvel* superhero incarnate and my smart mouthed little Pixie that I decided I didn't need to lift nearly as badly as I needed to get out of this room.

Blowing out a harsh breath, I scooped up my phone from where I'd set it on the bench and, with a cordial nod to the saints building orphanages, rushed from the room. I couldn't hate the man any more than I could blame him for liking El. Watching her jump from date to date had been agonizing back home, but I'd survived it then, and one week in a resort wasn't going to undermine years of discipline.

With a huff of irritation, I jammed the button to summon the elevator. The echo of laughter down the hall had me aggressively pushing it on a loop when my name bounced off the walls.

EIGHT

ELORA

Max was going to be *thrilled* with me. Six-foot-two, blond, well dressed and beautifully articulate, Pierce was exactly Max's type, and—lo and behold—recently single after his last boyfriend moved to London a few months back. *Months*—which meant it was a perfectly acceptable amount of time later to move the hell on. A pop in my step, I practically skipped down the hallway, grinning as I shot off a rapid-fire text with his handle and phone number, because that's what best friends do when they meet a Greek god brought to life.

Glancing up as I tucked my phone away, I spotted none other than my temporary emergency room mate stepping into the elevator. My stomach tightened, but after a brief internal debate, I called out, "Broderick!"

When he slowly turned back my way, begrudgingly holding out an arm to keep the doors open, my brows dipped in a scowl. What had his boxers in a bunch?

"You okay?" I asked, a bit out of breath after the gym and quick jaunt down the hallway.

"Dandy," he said in an unconvincing monotone.

Okaaaay. Shrugging off his irritation, I said, "Pierce and Cheyenne seem great, don't they?"

"Sure," he muttered, pulling the headphones off his neck and powering them down without meeting my eyes.

"I mean it," I pressed. "Their foundation is freaking incredible." When his eyes widened irritably, and he tongued a molar, I demanded, "What's your problem?"

"Just, not a fan of bonding to the competition."

"*Competition*," I scoffed. "We were just brainstorming other ways to generate startup capital. If you'd bothered to say hello, you might've picked up a backup idea or two."

This time, those dark browns landed on me, an intensity burning within as he said, "Never wanted a backup." I hesitated at the weight of the words, brain trying to muddle through them for the meaning he seemed to weave between words.

"Doesn't hurt to have one." Elbowing him playfully in the ribs, I said, "Come on! We're going out for drinks. Come with, get those juices flowing."

"You can't be serious," he muttered, barely audible as he rolled his eyes skyward.

"Who pissed in your Cheerios this morning?"

"Nobody."

"Then what the hell is wrong with Pierce and Cheyenne?"

"Nothing, I just think it's a waste of time to connect with someone whose dream you intend to crush in the next three days."

"Jesus, Broderick. Did you ever think about the fact that networking with these people could move your foundation forward faster than the grant even could?"

"I promise you; Pierce has nothing to offer you that I don't."

Scowling, I shifted my weight away from him, irritated with the judgmental tone, and a bit taken aback by his closed mindedness. The universe had more than enough resources to go around. All our causes were worthy of funding, and if I could make connections that would be mutually beneficial, all the better for it. "Jaded much?"

"I'm not jaded, just irritated by your naïveté."

"*Naïveté?*" I barked, scowling at him as my temper bristled.

"You can't think he actually wants to help you. He's our opposition, not our friend." Palming the back of his neck with an irritated huff, his eyes fell to the floor, and he shook his head. "Misdirection is a classic tactic to outmaneuver an opponent."

"And what are you implying—that they're going to try to distract me with their *friendship?*"

"That's exactly what I'm implying. Throw you off your game. Play on your emotions. It makes sense."

"No, it doesn't. You're thinking so small mindedly." I crossed my arms. This moody, broody bullshit was the part of Broderick I didn't usually fall subject to. This was what Rhyett and Jameson had to coax him away from, and frankly, I wanted no part of it.

"Well, you do whatever you want, but I'll be keeping my distance to avoid any bullshit distractions I can't afford. Not all of us can just phone up our brothers and start a nonprofit."

My jaw dropped so violently it popped audibly, images of cartoons flashing in my vision as I fought back the pissed off desire to slap him. "*Excuse me?*" I barked.

"Why did you even put your name in the hat in the first place? You don't need the money."

"As flattered as I am that you believe that, I can't actually fund this myself."

His scoff brought to mind how satisfying it would be to knee him in the balls. Just to top off the insult sundae with a cherry from planet dick head, he added, "No, but between you, Rhy, James and Pax, I think you're plenty covered."

"My success will not be dictated by the achievements of *my brothers*," I snapped. Chest heaving, head beginning to throb dully. Okay, yes, Pax was an investor, but that was different. He was partnering with us—not giving us a handout.

"No, *you'd* prefer it was dictated by the influence of men that just want to lure you to bed. I thought your brothers taught you better than that."

"What in the hell is wrong with you?" I demanded, whirling to face him as the whirr of the elevator began to slow incrementally. "It's not like that."

I was about to tell him to go eat a Snickers and bring back *Dr. Jekyll* when he said, "What are you thinking, hanging out with a guy like that? Don't kid yourself into thinking it's just drinks or a *friendship* he's after."

The vision of my fist cracking against his face and blood spurting down his nose sent my teeth grinding together. Hell, I could even hear Rhyett scolding me for breaking Broderick's stupidly pretty face as Jameson chuckled in resignation, assuming he'd earned as much. In reality, my stupid mouth popped open in shock, eyes narrowing as I latched on to the undeniable blade of jealousy in his tone before snapping it closed. Was he serious, right now? *Fuck. Right. Off.*

"So, *what*?" I looked up to the flashing red number on the wall counting the floors as we rose, needing nothing as violently as I needed the hell out of this tiny box. "Even if that was the case, Pierce is a perfectly adequate prospect. Smart, successful, cute—"

"He's just not the guy for you," Broderick barked before I could add the crucial caveat to the end of the lineup.

Duh. But he might be the guy for Max. Instead of saying that, I yanked my eyes off the ticker and trained them on his face, nearly staggering under the seething weight of his gaze on me. If Broderick wanted to have an opinion on who I was or wasn't dating, or to act like some jealous neanderthal, he should have made a move in the last *fourteen* fucking years I'd been an adult. Hell, he should make a move *now*. Fucking own up to this thing we both knew had always been lying dormant between us.

Giving him one last chance to grow a pair, I lifted my chin defiantly, tone cold as steel, and demanded, "Then *who is?*"

He held my glare, the pinch in his brows not easing as his eyes roamed my face. Jaw ticking, he just stared back.

Disappointment crashed through me, any last shred of fool's hope dissolving into resentment as the doors finally whooshed open. "*Exactly*. If a successful, beautiful man actually has the balls to pursue love and risk the vulnerability that entails, he might stand a *chance* at being happy."

As I rushed past him for the freedom of the hallway, my teeth ground together and I decided I no longer gave a shit what Broderick Allen wanted.

NINE

BRODERICK

Foot meet mouth. Seriously. Could that have gone *any* worse? Rubbing a hand over the back of my neck, I sucked down air and wondered what in the hell had climbed up my ass, because in no universe did anything that happened in the last ten minutes make any sense. Never once had Elora ever leaned on her older siblings for her success, and insinuating as much was like lighting a match in a pool of gasoline and not expecting to turn into a human torch.

I knew that Sarah got in my head, but holy fucking shit, El was as far to the opposite side of the spectrum as a woman could get. It was a damn cheap shot, and her grabbing her backpack and slamming the door on the way out of our room just hammered that final nail in my coffin.

It was irrational. Hell, even as I said it, some part of my brain knew I was being an idiot, but I couldn't stop this slimy constricting sensation in my chest, the ugly head of jealousy suddenly alive, well, and rearing. Pacing the length of the room, I scowled at my phone where it lay discarded on the bed. This was the stuff I would normally talk to Rhyett about. But El and the girls had always been, and would always be, firmly off limits. I'd made a damn promise. And as ancient as it might have been, I was a man of my word. Always had been. It's how Dad raised me.

The value of a man is rooted in his fortitude and integrity.

That's what he told me as a kid. Some boys get bedtime stories, others grow up on superheroes. Robert Allen raised me on life lessons and parables—no doubt planting the seeds of my obsession with morality. But our word was as good as law—a hill worth living and dying on.

Phone as heavy as a dumbbell, I stared at my favorites screen, both of her brothers looking back at me from their tiny icons. But it was the names beneath them that my eye traced one too many times. *Noel McShane. Brexley Rhodes.*

Treasonous. This idea. Hell, I'd probably be better off calling Max or my father. But that knowledge didn't stop my thumb from tapping the selfie of my three favorite blondes—Brex, Rhyett and Quinn, all boasting broad, cheesy grins.

Oh, fuck me, this is a horrible idea. I was just dropping the phone from my ear, my stomach in absolute knots, when the line clicked to life and a familiar—albeit breathless—voice broke the silence.

"Broderick?"

"Hey, Brex, how's it going?"

A little giggle was audible in the background, a smile breaking through my anxiety. "Good! Just chasing Quinny around. She's quite the scooter these days, but she pulls herself up on *anything* and *everything,* so it's a twenty-four-seven game of catch the baby over here these days."

That explained her lack of oxygen. "Ahh," I grunted lamely. "Where's Rhy?"

"At the bar, he got an order this afternoon."

"Makes sense," I said, nodding as my throat thickened. "And you? How you doing, pretty mama? Rhy said you've got a book on a deadline?"

"Yes," she exhaled in a whoosh, as if she collapsed into the nearest chair. "The sequel to my fantasy is due next Wednesday. I'm just about there—I *think*. I mean, it could be absolute trash. It probably *is* trash. Actually, now that I'm thinking about it—"

Laughing, I cut her off, "It is *not* trash, Brex. It's going to be great. I loved the pages you sent me."

"You're just saying that."

"I'm *not*," I insisted, chuckling. "I think the sequel will be even stronger than the first book."

"You really think so?" she asked, a strangled note of hope underlying her anxiety. I loved Brex, and honestly, she was one of few people in my life who could relate to the suffocating uncertainty of a mind that ran in circles until the body collapsed in a sweaty pool of panic.

"I really think so," I echoed back. A relieved exhale was punctuated by another baby giggle that her mama immediately echoed.

When my throat tightened and the silence lingered for a beat too long, Brex softly asked, "You okay, Allen?"

Smiling at the endearment she put in my last name, I blew out a breath. "Can I, uh...talk to you about something?"

"Obviously, anything. What's going on? Are you okay?"

"Something just between us?"

"Broderick, are you in some kind of trouble? You know James and Rhyett would flip their lid if you needed help and—"

"No, nothing like that." I said, chuckling at the panic creeping into her tone. Slowly, I eased my pacing in favor of leaning against the wall beside the front window, staring down at the chaos of the strip. "I promise I'll talk to them at some point, if it proves prudent. But for now, can this conversation stay between us?"

"I have a nine-month-old."

Blinking, an ache planted in my brow as it furrowed in confusion. "Yes, I'm aware. But I don't see how Quinn—"

"I am covered in a combination of homemade baby bottle food, spit up, a fluid I can't confidently identify, and can count the cumulative hours I've slept this week on my fingers. I'll be lucky to remember this conversation in twenty-four hours, let alone have the energy to relay it to someone else."

My laugh slowly dissipated into something more in the ballpark of a sigh. "Alright. Point taken. This is like, skull and dagger, sworn to secrecy level of—"

"*Christ*, Broderick—spit it out."

Chuckling nervously, I pushed off the wall and collapsed into the armchair, leaning forward to brace myself on my elbows. "Look," I admitted on a loaded exhale. "The guys would kill me for even saying this, but I kinda have always had a thing for El."

"Yeah."

There wasn't a hint of surprise. Not a trace of it in her tone or blunt delivery. Confused, I clarified, "Elora. *Elora Rhodes*."

"Yeah."

"Their younger sister."

"Oooooooh," she said dramatically, tone dripping in sarcasm that made my mouth pop open. "*That Elora!* I was confusing her with *another* Elora Rhodes. Continue, but please get to the point before Quinn sprouts another tooth."

Stunned, I managed to stammer, "You knew I was into El?"

"Honey, anybody with eyes knows you're into El."

"The guys—"

"Oh, well *no*, not the guys. As much as I love them both, they're not the most perceptive when it comes to emotional intelligence. Sometimes I think that Rhy suspects, but he hasn't said anything."

"Jesus," I mumbled, mouth hanging open as my mind whirred through the implications of that assumption.

"You didn't honestly think we were all oblivious, did you?"

"Kinda," I admitted gruffly, frowning at the tacky hotel carpet as I palmed my jaw. Her laugh was light, like this was the best entertainment she'd had in a decent stretch of time.

"Honestly, Sarah felt like a self-destructive bandage of procrastination."

"Your writer brain is showing," I muttered, squeezing my temples between my fingers, but breathing a little deeper when she giggled.

"Okay, so you've come to terms with the fact that you're into their sister. Why are you calling me?"

"I don't really...have anybody else I can talk to about this shit."

"What shit?"

"So, El and I are both at a conference, competing for a... life-changing amount of money via a leadership grant."

"No way," she cut in enthusiastically. "Rhy told me you were going to that, but I didn't realize she was too!"

"Well. We're here. And she couldn't get a room—they double booked, it's a long story. So, she's crashing in my—"

"You're sharing a room?!" she squeaked. "Shut up, please tell me there's only one bed?"

Scowling, I turned to glare at the singular mattress I was adamantly avoiding, and then at the murder sofa in the corner. "How did you know that?"

A trill of laughter carried through the line. "*Classic*," she muttered, tone way too satisfied for my liking.

"I'm beginning to think this was a mistake."

"No!" she yipped, and it sounded like the speaker brushed against skin. "This is textbook *fate*, Allen. People write this shit all the time, I sell it every day. Do not—I repeat, *do not*—fuck this up."

Wincing, I begrudgingly admitted, "I might've already. But this isn't a thing. This isn't—"

"It is totally a 'thing' that you don't want to screw up. Also, what on earth did you do? *No!*" The abrupt barked demand startled me so severely, I yanked the phone away from my ear, glaring back at the screen before tentatively returning it.

"What?"

But she was still reprimanding quite vocally, and it took me a second to make sense of what the hell she was saying. "We do *not* chew on cords. That is a *no*, Quinny. Sorry," she muttered, now back towards the phone as a happy little coo sounded near enough I knew she must've picked up the baby. "How did you screw it up?"

"Look, I just wanted to get through this week with some pride intact. But...the idea of competing against her was bugging me, and there's this guy that's just all over her, and it was grinding my gears, and I said some stupid shit."

"Broderick Allen, *jealous*. Never thought I'd see the day."

"I am not jealous," I stated matter-of-factly. "You

should see these guys, Brex. It's ridiculous. We've been here twenty-four hours and they're surrounding her like scavengers."

"Sure. Such a very disinterested, not jealous observation. Go on."

"I am *not* jealous."

"Mm—hmm. So. What did your *not* jealous mouth say?"

"That she should drop out of the competition." The line went entirely silent save for the quiet baby babbles in the background. "And that if she asked, the guys would back her foundation.

Brex's dramatic groan did absolutely nothing to ease the tightening in my belly. Nor did the irritated exhale that followed.

"What?" I demanded.

"Seriously?"

"Yes, seriously."

"Dude. What the fuck?"

"It's bad. Isn't it?" Honestly, it wasn't really a question. I was fucked.

"The only way this could be worse is if you told her she'd somehow ridden someone's coat tails to success."

Grimacing, I rubbed my thumb and forefinger against the bridge of my nose.

"Your silence doesn't bode well," she noted flatly.

"I...may have told her that networking with the men here was looking to win based on who wanted to lure her to bed."

"Jesus Christ. I'm a writer, not a miracle worker. What is wrong with you boys? I swear to God, Rhyett got all the sense of the three of you."

"Don't I know it," I mumbled. After a long moment, I said, "So? What the hell do I do?"

"You mean besides grovel?"

"Yes," I sighed.

"Start with the groveling. *Profuse* groveling. And then we have to move into offense mode."

"Offense mode?"

"You called me to win the girl, right?"

"I, uh..."

"*Oh please.* If you can't be honest with yourself, just don't lie to me. It's insulting. You want her."

"The guys would never forgive me—"

"For robbing you both of a happiness you deserve and have waited far too long to claim? Yes. I agree. So, what we need is a strategy."

"Strategy," I repeated stupidly.

"Yes, you big, loveable asshole."

"*Hey,*" I complained, but Brex was already moving into boss mode. What was with all of these world conquering women in my life?

"Don't 'hey' me. You admitted it yourself. That was a total prick move, and we gotta compensate. Phase one? Grovel. Apologize. Phase two? Remind her of what you two *do* like about each other. Phase three? Win the girl."

"You sound way too excited about this."

"My only company has a one-word vocabulary, so I've been feeling a little isolated. This is the most excitement I've had in ages."

Shaking my head as I ran my palm over my hair, I said, "Alright. So, I need to tell her I'm sorry. I'm shit for verbal communication, so do I write a letter?"

"*Shit for verbal?!* Broderick, you literally lecture

America's youth for a living. What do you mean 'shit for verbal communication'."

"That's different," I argued, commencing my pacing.

"How so?" she demanded, and I could just picture Rhyett's five foot six powerhouse popping a hip expectantly.

"It's not emotional, it's *logical*. It's information I have time to research and prepare for before I'm opening my mouth."

"Research?" she scoffed. "Hell, Allen, how much research do you need? You've got thirty-one years of research, from where I'm standing." Her words brought me up short, pausing as I thought that through.

"Yeah, uh...I guess I do."

"Duh, you do! You get to bypass all that awkward favorite color, what's your sign bullshit and skip right to the good stuff."

Yeah. Right. If she'd even have me. If I could avoid choking on the betrayal. Nodding to myself, I turned on my heel to pace a new groove in the carpet. "Yeah. Okay, so where do I start?"

"What about a peace offering? Not a letter—grow a pair and *talk* to the woman. Something that she'll love. That will make her feel seen."

"Well...food is her love language?"

"Good! That's good. What's her favorite?"

"Um...Mexican is a safe bet."

"Anything that you do just the two of you? That's a bit generic. Unless you once shared a romantic flan on a mountaintop or something."

Chuckling and grateful she was willing to crack my tension with humor, I weighed my options, thinking about our life on that windy fishing island. "We always got sushi together. We both like the same rolls."

"Good! Yes, okay, we can work with that. Do you know what she likes with it? She a soy sauce girl? When it comes to women, details matter, Allen."

Christ, didn't I know it. On a huffed laugh, I added, "With enough wasabi to make your eyes bleed."

That earned a cackle. "Excellent! Okay. Next up—favorite color?"

"Didn't realize I'd get a pop quiz on this phone call."

"Oh, yes, you did. It's why you called me and not Noel." She had a point. "So. Answer me, Allen."

"She'd say red, but it's actually purple." Growing up sandwiched in brothers, El tended to lean into her masculine unless she was around her sisters, or it was just us. I got to see those pieces of her that James and Rhyett didn't.

"Not even gonna ask. Flowers? Shells? What's she like?"

"Uh, roses, and those great big balls."

"Great. Big. Balls?"

"Oh, fuck off."

The cackle crackling over the speaker was absolutely maniacal. "Come on, you gotta give me that one."

"Did you and Noel share an egg at one point?" Seriously, no wonder these two were best friends. Double trouble.

Her laughter was renewed, breath a little shallow as she said, "I wish. Honestly, we're probably closer this way. Come on though, stay focused. You gotta have something beyond *balls*."

Smirking, I added, "The big, soft, fluffy ones." Brex's ensuing laugh seemed to earn one from Quinn, the happy little coos making me smile. Questioning myself, I guessed, "Peonies, I think?"

"Ooooh, we don't have those here. They die too fast to ship. But they're awfully pretty."

"I think they're out of season?"

"So stick with roses. Can't go wrong if she likes red. Now, what's something you can do together?"

"Umm..."

"Come on Allen, you're in *Sin fucking City*. Your options are unlimited."

"I uh...I think I have an idea."

"Well hurry up. Out with it."

TEN

ELORA

"This means war," Alice chirped from where I'd propped her sweet face on the table.

"Yeah!" Max said with gusto. "What the fuck Broaddick?" The rest of his words were drowned out by our collective laughter.

"I don't think that image is helping our girl," Mara noted, smirking from the corner chair where she was nursing baby Nate.

"Fine, poor pun—but I'm not wrong. He's being a real prick."

"I think he's jealous," Mara stated flatly.

"Of *Pierce*," I pointed out with an eye roll.

"The man is *fine*," Max said, shrugging. "Thanks for that, by the way."

"Anytime."

"That hair!" He swooned, with a dramatic eye roll.

Smirking, I countered, "Those eyes."

"Rescues orphans, for pity's sake."

"With his sister."

Brows arched theatrically, Max conspiratorially asked, "How's the backside?"

"Guys," Alice whined. "Focus."

"Right," Max said, grimacing. "We need a plan."

"We have a plan," Mara objected. "Goodie goodie over here didn't want to execute the plan for fear of bruising the dickhead's poor wil' ego."

"Not anymore," I said with a huff, throwing my hands up as I returned to pacing in front of the propped-up phone. Max and Alice tracked the movements through the screen. *"Have my brother's fund it.* For Christ's sake. We're talking millions of dollars here, not some thirty-thousand-dollar startup. Even if the guys had that kind of cash—okay, so Pax might have that kind of cash—but that's irrelevant. Even if it was an option, it is *not* an option."

"No way," Max said, purely in solidarity.

"You are a strong, independent woman," Alice added for good measure. "You don't need no man. Not even our brothers."

"Except for...well...you know, Pax's pre-existing investment," Mara pointed out.

"Hey," Max and I barked simultaneously.

"Whose side are you on?" I demanded.

Shrugging, she adjusted baby Nate in her arms before saying, "Just pointing out the facts here." She bobbed her head, short, silky hair shifting as both faces on the screen looked in her direction with skeptical arched brows. "Fact one," she held up a free hand and raised her index finger, "he's being a jerk. But I think it's because—*fact two*—he's in love with you and thought Mr. tall, blonde and beautiful was making a move."

"Objection denied," I quipped, crossing my arms. "The prosecution holds that if he has feelings, he's had fourteen years of me being a legal prospect to make a move and hasn't. Regardless. Belittling my accomplishments is horse shit, and now he's going down."

"In his dreams," Max mumbled, stifling a laugh when I shot a glare in his direction. He ran a broad palm over dark black hair, pushing it away from his eyes. "Look, Elly, you two have done this dance for over a decade. I'm sure he's at least dreamed—"

"Max!" I yelped, collapsing onto the mattress in exasperation.

"What?" He raised his palms in surrender.

"I mean, Max is right. He's wanted you since you both were in high school," Alice agreed. "And he's not that much older than you. The whole 'you're not eighteen' thing was chicken shit."

"*Guys*," I whined, dropping my face into my sweaty palms. "I gave up on Broderick ever wanting this last summer. Remember when we stayed with Noel when her psycho ex was literally stalking her in Mistyvale?" They all nodded solemnly. "He had weeks of time with just us hanging out in Jameson's house, keeping eyes on Noel, and he never said or did anything. When I went to broach the subject, he *answered the fucking phone*." I crossed my arms in frustration.

All three of them winced, but it was Max whose expression turned into a grimace. "Right. But wasn't that the morning after Jameson beat the daylights out of said psycho?"

Rolling my eyes, I stared skyward as I puffed air into my cheeks. "Yes," I begrudgingly admitted.

"And wasn't James convinced that the psycho would retaliate—which *he did*."

"Yes," I griped.

"So...Broderick wasn't supposed to answer a call from his best friend who was likely going to prison for beating a senator's kid half to death for assaulting his girl." Irritated, I swiped my coffee off the table and chugged down a scalding mouthful. Taking that as answer enough, Max said, "So, maybe cut the guy a little slack, because as much as I love you, *your timing* was shit."

"And then you left a few days later," Alice pointed out. "Broderick has always been a processor. He has to have all the data first so that he can analyze it before he makes any kind of conjecture. And then needs time to sit with the conjecture before moving on to implement it because he won't act unless he's certain."

"Are you guys seriously ganging up on me right now?"

"We're not ganging up on you, Elly," Max said with another shrug. "We're just...presenting all the factors."

"I can't let myself even entertain this notion right now. The point stands. Fourteen years. It wasn't just last summer. He's had over a decade to say something. I can't let myself even think he might finally do something because then I won't focus on the grant, and that needs to be my priority."

"Oh, yes," Max said, thrumming his fingers together like a cartoon villain. "Now *that*, we can tackle. Two birds, one stone."

"What?" I said, the word more of a laugh.

"Bird one. Make Broderick lose his mind. Drive him crazy. Taunt, tease, tempt until he caves and bends you over the—"

"*Max!!*" I shrieked.

"Right. Sorry. It's been a very dry year, okay? Bird one, make Broderick admit his feelings. Bird two, win the grant."

"I'm supposed to woo him whilst robbing him of his dream?" I blinked pointedly at that absurd combination.

"You're supposed to lure him in with your feminine wiles while *reminding him* you are Elora motherfucking Rhodes, and you don't need anyone's help knocking your goals out of the park."

ELEVEN

BRODERICK

BREXLEY
Tom Petty?

BRODERICK
Check.

BREXLEY
Peace offering?

BRODERICK
Philly rolls with extra wasabi.

BREXLEY
I'll allow it.

Any idea when she'll be back?

BRODERICK
Not a clue. But we reconvene at eight am, so I don't imagine she'll be out very late.

BREXLEY
Alright. I expect an update in the morning.

BRODERICK
*Saluting emoji.

. . .

I blew out a breath as *Wildflowers* started playing over my Bluetooth speaker. Petty had been a favorite growing up, but this song in particular always made me smile, because it made me think of Elora. Elora, who needed nothing as severely as she needed to feel free. She soaked up sun like a hibiscus and needed the wind on her skin and sand beneath her feet or she'd wilt within a month. She blended in with the city girls as well as the next woman, but her heart had always—and would always—call to the wilds of Alaska. She could toss a net or tie off the boat as well as any Mistyvale-born man and look adorable doing it.

Okay, the Philly rolls might have been slightly self-motivated, but it was one of the many things we'd always enjoyed together. Might remind her that under the ego, we were friends...usually. Sushi was one of the consistent delicacies on the island. Our little town was host to very few luxuries, all of which the mainlanders took for granted. But we were never short in the fish department—a fact that was entirely attributed to families like the Rhodes that kept our economy flowing.

Staring at the sushi tray, I popped the lid off only to clip it back into place. I waited...and *waited*. All the while, nerves burrowed into my gut. Gradually, I became Professor Pit-stain, which resulted in my stripping, showering, and applying an absurd amount of antiperspirant before returning to pacing the length of the room. Deciding I needed to tuck the peace offering safely away in the mini fridge where I couldn't eat them all myself, I climbed into bed, reinforcing El's pillow moat before flipping the music off and TV on. Normally, I'd pull up a favorite true crime series, but with reconciliation on my mind, I flipped it to *How I Met Your Mother*.

Peace offering number two.

This was fine. It would be fine. El and I always drove each other entirely crazy, but we were just as quick to hash it out and move on. *Usually*. Prom had made things weird. Last summer made them weirder.

Sushi was probably not even going to touch the level of discomfort I'd just created between us. Guilt and anxiety gut checked me like a linebacker, and I shifted uneasily, glancing to the door and wondering where she was. If she was okay. Anxiety wasn't new to me—I think I was born with it. This compulsive need to check and recheck, to guess and second guess every minute detail of my life. Maybe it was a byproduct of two abnormally productive parents, but maybe it was just...me. Which meant that awful hollow burrowing sensation in my stomach was undeniably the beginning of a spiral. I should never have made her second guess herself. Should never have suggested that of the two of us, she should be the one to bow out.

It was those thoughts that were interrupted by the late-night electronic chirp of the lock followed by the heavy creek of the metal door. I was prepared for her to come in looking as uncomfortable as I felt, or even to burst into the room ready for round two. Instead, she didn't even bother to glance my way, her hair mussed, headphones in her ears as she balanced a restaurant serving tray on her hand, a drink in the other as she gracefully spun into the room, bopping to music I couldn't hear.

The nod she gave me seemed no more significant than a frat bro *sup* and, bewildered, I sat up to assess the firecracker now wordlessly settling into the little corner table where they'd stacked generic postcards and notebooks with hotel branded pens that no one had ever used even once in hotel guest history.

Looking content with herself, Pix scooted everything aside so that she could spread out her food. My eyes shot to the mini fridge, mouth making to form the words but falling short. *El. Hey. How are you? I grabbed you a snack, although it appears you came prepared. I'm sorry for being a colossal shit sandwich.* Something. *Anything.* Instead, a thick silence settled between us, awkwardly filling the space. Or...it was awkward to me, because El looked entirely at ease as she neatly lined out her dinner, headphones still playing some sort of symphony worth subtly swaying to.

Watching her slowly unclip the tacky plastic lid from a hot sauce container, I thought back to all the times we'd retreat from the chaos of the Rhodes house, just the two of us, hiding in the other's silence. El could chatter just as much as the rest of them, but she had this inherent sense for when the insanity overwhelmed me, and I needed quiet. Something Jameson understood, but Rhyett had never comprehended. To him, the more the merrier. A dozen siblings, and he was always the first to invite extras in.

It had been her companionable silence in which I found my home. She scowled, the abrupt change in her expression pulling me from my reverie as she set her sauce ramekin down in favor of a brown napkin, which she promptly dabbed in water and took to her shirt, where red sauce had splattered. With a huff, she scooted back on the wheelie armchair, and slowly reached for the hem of her sweater, slipping slender fingers beneath the fabric before scraping it up and over her torso, revealing bare, tan skin and a form-fitting short camisole cropped above a belly button ring I sure as hell hadn't ever seen before.

My swallow ached right along with my jaw as I clenched it, sending my gaze skyward. *Taxation is theft. The government is corrupt. Morality is a matter of perspective. Polar bears are starving. Jameson would beat me to death if he knew I just got hard watching his baby sister take her sweater off to prevent a stain.*

Seriously—what the hell was wrong with me?

Replaying Brexley's words in my mind, I blew out what I hoped was a calming breath, sliding free from bed and wandering over to the fridge, attempting to channel an inner nonchalance that hadn't existed since the siren in front of me hit puberty.

She paused her stain dabbing to glance my way as I knelt and retrieved the sushi container. I set it on the table beside her plethora of options, nudging it toward her as she held my gaze. Those Rhodes blues narrowed slightly as she gingerly plucked an ear bud out.

"That a peace offering?" she questioned dryly, surveying the little carton. I smirked at her wording, knowing full well that's exactly what this was. She seemed to finally notice what was playing on the television as well, her eyes flying to the side of the room as she removed the second headphone.

"That depends... Is it working?"

One dark brow arched as her gaze flicked back down to the sushi. The presentation wasn't Michelin-star by any means, but it wasn't exactly convenience store quality either. Drizzled in some kind of house-special aioli, they hadn't held back and delivered it with an abundance of soy sauce, pickled ginger, and wasabi. Good. At least one thing in my favor.

Eyes narrowed in accusation, she gingerly pressed her own box closed, grabbing the chop sticks, and snapping them apart in one only semi-aggressive motion. She twirled them between her fingers before plucking up a piece and popping it between her lips in one bite, chewing slowly as she eyed me. Holding her gaze should have won me an award. Seriously, Medusa could take notes. But I saw the flicker of satisfaction as the flavors finally hit her tongue. Saw the memories spark in her eyes, like I knew they would, because some invisible wall seemed to dissolve within them.

"Maybe," she begrudgingly admitted around her mouthful of rice and smoked salmon. "Depends on what follows up the cream cheese and seaweed."

"I'm sorry," I blurted out gruffly, irritated with myself all over again. "I didn't mean it. Not the way it came out. That was a dick move, and we both know it."

"Continue," she prompted, pinching another piece with her chopsticks before poking them toward me.

"I'm not an imbecile, El. I've seen how hard you've worked. So have your older siblings—none of them would ever insinuate your success was anything other than earned." I dipped my head to capture her gaze. "That was super shitty. And...I'm sorry."

Her eyes widened incrementally before she jerked them to her food, throat working around a swallow. "Good sushi," she said softly, scooting her prior meal aside in favor of the carton. That had to be a good sign, right—a kind of acceptance? Was that hoping for too much, too quickly? Smiling, I took the chair beside her and snatched up the second pair of chopsticks, cracking them apart and swooping in for a piece, smirking when she slid the box away from me, eyes wide beneath arched brows as the corners of her lips twitched. The expression spelled out her sentiment exactly—*excuse me?*

Fighting a smile, I reached forward again, only for her to slide it farther away, her eyes narrowing to slits, a hand poised to slap mine away as she said, "Thin ice, Professor. *Thin.* Ice."

Chuckling darkly, I gingerly placed the chopsticks on a napkin between us before raising my hands in surrender. She smiled as she returned the tray to the center of the table, and I put a safe amount of space between me and the evidently off-limits peace offering.

"So," she said around the next mouthful. "What's your strategy for presentations tomorrow?"

"Really think we should hash out battle strategy together?" I countered, my chair creaking as I slowly rocked in it to dispel some of the extra energy seeping from my body.

"Like I would bother to adjust mine the night before. I've had this thing planned down to the second for weeks."

Holding her stare, I thought long and hard before saying, "Mine is highly statistic motivated. For our population size, we have an unacceptable number of young people with criminal records. That's my angle."

Nodding, chopsticks pointed my direction as though demanding an answer, she said, "Kind of like a *Big Brothers, Big Sisters* idea?"

"Kind of," I allowed, leaning down to fish a sparkling water out of the mini fridge. Cracking the lid off the glass bottle, I said, "I want to make sure we have the funding to bring on tutors and keep a good ratio between kids and counselors. Nutrient-dense food, so the kids who don't go home to hot meals have somewhere they can drop in and fill their bellies with more than vending machine food."

A furrow implanted between her brows, and she ran her tongue over her front teeth as she created a wasabi-soy sauce mix in the tray. Stirring the concoction with her chopsticks, she admitted, "It's a noble cause, Brod."

"So is the school," I pointed out quietly. Those steel blues lanced me to my chair as she twirled her next bite in her wasabi sauce concoction that made my sinuses burn just looking at it. I could do with a little bit here and there, but she really soaked it on there. Evaluation evidently over, she nodded. "Where there's a will, there's a way, right?"

"Absolutely." A delicate, one shoulder shrug.

"There will be other opportunities for funding for whoever doesn't get it."

"What is meant for us, will find us," she recited like a reflex. I smirked, the words an old familiar echo of so many days past. Pix was nothing, if not consistent.

"You've said that for years," I pointed out.

"I still believe it," she shot back without bothering to shift her focus off the next bite. I watched as she popped the piece into her pretty little mouth, tracking a drop of sauce that fell from the corner. Thumbing it away, my fingers hesitated for one beat longer than appropriate before I realized I was still touching her.

Clearing my throat, I pulled my hand away from her now sauce-less lips. Before I could stand—which, honest to God, was my intention—she scooted the tray my way with the last Philadelphia roll still intact. She set her chopsticks down pointedly.

"Apology accepted," she whispered, quickly snatching her Mexican food off the table and tucking it into the fridge below our desk. "Thanks for dinner. I'm going to jump in the shower."

We both rose so abruptly that we nearly collided. Her

face was an inch away from my chest, mouth popping open and eyes rounding as they slowly tracked up to mine.

"Sorry, I'll just, uh—" Her words trailed off as she stepped to one side just as I did. Wincing, I made to move back, but we were like a couple of magnets, synchronized in our abysmal attempt to disengage. "Sorry, I can—" Again, her thought cut off, but this time we bumped into each other. Chuckling awkwardly, I clamped my hands down on her shoulders, holding her steady while I untangled my legs from the spokes of our chairs, stepping aside to grant her space to vacate as well. My heart was hammering faster than a nail gun on a new construction Coast Guard house Friday night at a quarter to five.

Her nervous, breathy exhale hit my chest, warming the skin through the fabric of my shirt a beat before she dropped her gaze to our feet, then nodded and turned for the bed, where her suitcase lay open. She hurriedly gathered clothes, but I was too busy staring skyward and blowing out a slow, pained breath to inventory what she escaped to the bathroom with.

Cursing internally, I slid my phone from my pocket as it buzzed.

> BREXLEY
> The suspense is killing me, Allen. Update?

> BRODERICK
> Could've gone better.

> BREXLEY
> Could've gone worse?

> BRODERICK
> I guess?

> **BREXLEY**
> Continue as planned. One step at a time.

> **BRODERICK**
> *Saluting emoji*

TOSSING the phone onto the murder sofa as a frantic rodent burrowed in my gut, I reluctantly retreated to the bed, hoping I'd fall asleep before El made it out of the shower.

Elora

I AM ELORA MOTHERFUCKING RHODES. So, what if he apologized so sincerely, equipped with a perfectly thoughtful little peace offering? Max, Alice, Mara, and I had a plan. And, at thirty-two, I was years past being easily manipulated by that stupidly perfect mug of his, or the equally stupidly gorgeous smile he wore when he was nervous. Deep brown sad puppy dog eyes or not. No man had a right to look so sexy while also pitifully apologetic. It wasn't legal.

Blowing out air like a leaky balloon, I looked over my reflection one last time, giving my hair another scrunch and missing how easily the curls came out to play when it was shorter. The romper was blush and silky, the black lace hitting the top of my thighs. Bright and airy, it was perfect for Nevada heat—when I wasn't crashing with my older brothers' best friend. This was...conservative, really. I usually preferred much less clothing, for fear of waking up with the sensation of strangulation. Or that's what I was convincing myself as I straightened the spaghetti straps at the edge of my shoulder. A deep V-neck traced against the tan skin of my chest, which now shimmered lightly after applying the tinted lotion. I cocked my head, lifting my boobs and wishing they were twenty-one-year-old perky instead of early thirties *meh*, but they'd have to do. A bra would defeat the purpose of the silk.

Geez, Max was diabolical. I kinda loved that about him. Smiling over the mouthful of nerves threatening to choke me before I even made it out of the glamorously tacky en-suite, I snatched up my discarded clothes, tucking them beneath an elbow before grabbing the towel. I whirled for the bedroom. Casually scrunching the towel in the ends of my hair, mostly for something to do with my hands, I made a beeline for my suitcase at the foot of the bed. Tucking them into the dirty bag, I prayed I looked casual as the metallic teeth of the zipper purred, and I moved it to the desk where we'd just been.

I could feel him watching me, like a heat across the back of my neck. Some fucked up kind of satisfaction wound through me then, curiosity begging the question; 'is Max right'?

When I turned back for the bed, his full lips were parted, eyes half-hooded as they unabashedly trailed up my very bare legs. *Sweet baby Jesus in a manger*. Was it hot in here? 120-degree-Arizona sunshine-hot? My heart hammered, a nervous sweat pricking at my low back and suddenly tingling palms. Quirking a brow, I closed the distance as he snapped his gaze to my face before clearing his throat and muttering the tightest goodnight mankind had ever heard.

Broderick turned into the cutest six-foot blanket burrito in history, his back to the pillow moat—and me—as I slid beneath the covers. With one last fortifying breath, I grabbed the pillows from the center of the bed, tucking one between my legs and the other against my chest, strangled by anxious arms as I turned my back to his, and unsuccessfully attempted to find sleep.

TWELVE

ELORA

The persistent ring of my alarm forced my eyes to creep open but proved leaden with sleep. Disoriented and abnormally, *pleasantly* warm, mouth dry, I blinked into the gloom of a resort room blacked out to the morning light and hummed appreciatively at the hard embrace of long arms and a firm body cocooned around mine. The sensation was exquisitely similar to coming home until my groggy mind made sense of the *very* firm—

My eyes flew open, body fighting the desire to bolt upright as I realized *Broderick's* impressively hard dick was pressed against the curve of my ass. His gorgeous, dark, vascular forearms locked around my waist, breath hot against the back of my neck as he nuzzled into me, emitting a deliciously rough, growl from somewhere deep in his chest. The amount of mortifying teenage dreams replaying through my mind sent my willpower skittering for cover as I launched myself away from him. But my feet were trapped in a web of twisted, tangled sheets, leaving me nothing to land on save for the palms of my hands as I attempted to yank my ankles and calves free from the boa constrictor of determined bed linens.

"What the fuck?" we both said in simultaneous confusion. Mine more of a mortified, muttered curse as the unrelenting white sheets landed me face first on the scratchy hotel floor, rolling away in my misguided attempt to flee. Broderick's in an adorably groggy bout of early morning bewilderment.

"El?" he rasped, as I ab-curled up to tear the sheet from my limbs, only to yank it off his body, which was now boldly on display. The glorious top-half anyway—at some point he'd stripped his hoodie, and evidently kicked all the blankets off and onto my feet. He wasn't kidding about the human space heater thing. A thin sheen of sweat covered my skin, and the dry, itchy spot on my chin convinced me I'd drooled the equivalent of a small pillow lake in the Broderick-induced comatose that had implanted this impenetrable fog of insanity in my brain. As for the second? Well...that enticing bulge he'd just had pressed against my all too eager ass was now pitching an impressive tent in the dark gray sweatpants draped low across his damn hips. Like Broderick junior was determined to salute the day. Or. Me.

My mouth popped open as I traced up that line of dark hair, fingers wondering how soft or coarse it would be beneath them, before shaking the sleep and lust from my muddled mind. Broderick was gorgeous in the way ancient statues were gorgeous. He wasn't bulky, but long and lean, like a swimmer, or runner. Which made sense, since he first became a hometown hero in high school for his ability to fly down the field like a bird on the wind. A skill which came in handy when he beat the rest of us down the bank and fished that kid out of that frozen lake senior year. That was the day everyone forgot he'd ever been a football star.

But *knowing* he was an athlete and admiring the evidence usually hidden beneath tweed blazers or fancy vests were two very different things.

"I uh, *sorry*, just—um—woke with a start. Late. *We're late*. Presentation day! It's morning. I have to—"

My incoherent babbling seemed immensely entertaining, as a slow, mischievous smile spread over his cheeks, stoking the inferno taking up residence in mine. His stupidly gorgeous, defined cheeks. Something glinted in his eye as I clumsily flew to my feet, running my fingers through disheveled hair and cursing as I bowed my forehead into my hand.

"I'm gonna get ready—shower, I need to shower—for my presentation. Your presentation. You finish first. I mean—" I shook my head, wondering when the hell I'd ever been this flustered, if ever. But God, he felt even more delicious than he looked. Of course, he had to be even better than my fantasies. "Your presentation is on the schedule first, so if you need to shower before me, that's fine. I can wait. I showered last night, actually, so I'm fine. I can just. Um. I'll be going now." To my untimely grave, *please God*, just swallow me whole.

A low, breathy chuckle emanated from the side of the room I would absolutely not be glancing toward as I retrieved my clothing from the table. Jiminy Cricket on a camel. Could that have been any more humiliating? Good thing I'd gotten my fill of Mistyvale hikes because under no circumstances would I be returning to an enclosed, captive proximity to this man again in my life. Presidents of billion-dollar companies—no problem? Hell, I'd met Alice's sexy-suit-daddy asshole of a boss, and immediately confronted the company's carbon footprint. But sharing a bed with my brothers' best friend, and I was a babbling, bumbling imbecile.

BRODERICK

DAD
How's it going?

BRODERICK
So far, so good.

DAD
When will we know results?

BRODERICK
Finalists will be announced tonight.

DAD
I have no doubts you're one of them.

BRODERICK
My competitors are all more than qualified for their causes, so I'm not getting my hopes up.

DAD
Your competitors might be qualified, but my son is too humble.

How's Elora?

I blew out a heavy breath, wishing I could hear the tone of the question. Dad was the only person I'd ever confided in about my feelings for the guys' little sister. How was Elora? *Breathtaking*. That's what I wanted to say. Instead, I slid the device into my pocket as I tracked her through the space. Elora, in a sleek black jumpsuit with a diamond cut out of the back, whisking around the room, making introductions, and helping the first-time attendees was an insane turn on. She was gorgeous. But the polished version of my Pix held nothing to the sleep-disheveled, babbling beauty that tore me from bed this morning in a flailing, sheet-stealing fiasco. I'd never seen her so...frazzled. Some purely primal, male part of my brain took a fucked-up kind of satisfaction at her sudden onset inability to articulate. And even more fucked-up satisfaction as her eyes locked on my body, that mouth popping open. Like she didn't hate what she saw. A woman like Elora noticing you was the highest kind of compliment, but for her to gape like that...my mind concocted very different uses for that mouth before I reigned in my rogue imagination.

Off limits.

Despite my brain repeating the mantra, the image of that skimpy lingerie clinging to her curves flashed in my vision. So did the pert peak of hard nipples. And I in no way meant to catalog the way the silk clung to her perfect ass, but here I was, fighting a hard on at a conference for the nation's most brilliant young minds. What in the hell happened to that blessed hoody? Was she trying to drive me into madness?

But herein lay the problem: I wanted her. Had always wanted her. Had never had the guts to admit to her brothers how deeply I needed this woman in my life. But Elora had. Not to her brothers, of course. They'd never let her live it down. But to me. I'd royally fucked up in how I responded...*twice*. But at least at some point, the bombshell holding an entire posse of businesswomen rapt with her words had cared for me. Shared in my pathetic attraction to the one person that wasn't an option.

Over the last year, I'd convinced myself she'd somehow turned it off. But based on El's reaction this morning... Brexley Rhodes might very well be onto something.

Maybe, just maybe, I hadn't completely fucked myself out of a chance with her... if I was willing to risk the only friendships I had back home.

A gentle throat clearing pulled my attention to the chair beside me. I'd settled at a table in the back of the room, the white cloth draping it now covered in half-heartedly discarded cups of coffee, cell phones, even a few bags belonging to women who evidently deemed me trustworthy enough to keep watch of their belongings.

The blue slipcovers over the chairs coordinated with the tacky hotel carpet, and now perched on the one beside me, was none other than Johanna King, hostess of the event.

"Afternoon, Professor Allen," she said with a smile, too practiced to be real. Johanna was the kind of polished that belonged in magazines. Her sleek golden hair came down just past her collar bones, curled enough to look impeccably effortless without becoming disheveled. She had too much neck, not enough warmth in those calculating hazel-green eyes and moved a lot like she rehearsed each intentional shift of her limbs or weight. A dancer on a stage rather than a woman sitting at a table. It made my stomach uneasy. Instincts screaming that all was not as it seemed, despite her pleasant demeanor and hospitality.

"Afternoon, Miss King," I said, giving her a cordial nod. My gut instincts might be rearing, but that didn't negate her success in her field, or the impact she would have here on this congregation of ambitious minds. Professional formality was more than owed. "What can I do for you today?"

"Just wanted to drop by and make sure you're enjoying your time at the event or remedy it if you're not."

My mind immediately flipped to the groggy memory of Elora cradled against my body, and how long-awaited the sensation had been. Smiling, I said, "Time of my life. Thanks for orchestrating such a unique opportunity." Not that she could take credit for the booking glitch, though I certainly wasn't complaining.

She laughed, and when she leaned forward in apparent recovery, her delicate hand came down on my forearm, where I'd rolled my button up sleeves to the elbow. My eyes dropped to where she gave me a squeeze, her skin on mine. That was... not my favorite. If it hadn't been for the Rhodes being just as touchy-feely as my parents, I likely would never allow a stranger within a five-foot radius. But they'd beaten physical affection into me over the years, and it was that and that alone that kept me from disentangling from her too-friendly clutches.

"My pleasure. This batch is especially promising, don't you think?"

"A little bias, I'm afraid," I said, leaning back in relief when she removed her hand from my arm, tucking a long strand of honey hair behind an ear baring precisely one gold hoop.

"Oh, don't be so modest. You've earned your place on that stage."

Smiling, my eyes drifted back to Pix. It certainly wasn't my cause on my mind as I crossed my arms to move them out of range. She'd been brilliant today. Engaging the audience, not afraid to answer questions on the spot or crack a witty joke. It had been magnetizing to watch. Even

Mara was on fire during her portion of the talk. "My competitors are all fantastic. You don't happen to have secondary grants hidden up your sleeve?"

She laughed lightly, straightening the arm of her blazer. But she ended the laugh by laying her hand on my shoulder, shaking her head. "So humble, Mr. Allen. And unfortunately, not this time around. Although, in the future, we'll have to account for this caliber of talent."

"That might be in your best interest," I agreed. What organizer wouldn't want their name on these causes? Elora's was fantastic, but I could begrudgingly admit the others were also just as worthy.

"Although, between you and me, I think you'll be quite pleased with the score tallies this afternoon." Her voice climbed up, a brow subtly arching as though she expected a much larger reaction to that line of bait than I gave her. Unbothered, she continued, "You and your fellow Alaskan are solidly in the lead. What are the odds of two of you coming from the same tiny town, huh?"

"Statistically? Nonexistent," I breathed, gut crashing as Pierce made his way over toward Pix.

"Must be one hell of an island."

"The best," I grunted noncommittally, eyes flicking between that eager, press-worthy smile and Elora, as she embraced *Thor* the *Abercrombie* model, before trading for his sister, to my immense relief. "Though it certainly poses its own unique challenges."

"Challenges that have inspired you both to engineer admirable remedies."

"A good silver lining."

"Are you an opportunist, Mr. Allen?" Something in the shift of her tone brought my focus back to the woman sitting well within my personal bubble. She slowly eased forward with conspiracy written across those pretty, strategic features.

"A realist, I'm afraid," I said matter-of-factly. Her chime of a laugh did nothing to disarm my unease around her.

"You impressed some powerful people in your presentation today. People that could make or break this grab for the grant. I don't think you need to worry about moving on to the next round of finalists."

Oddly enough, I was uncharacteristically at ease after my pitch. I was prepared, confident, well-organized, and it showed. Whether I made it to the next round of qualifications was out of my control, and for once in my life, I wasn't obsessing over the outcome. No, I was obsessing over something worse. Something I shouldn't want and couldn't have and yet was rapidly deciding to pursue, anyway. Because nothing and no one had ever fit in my life quite like El in my arms this morning. And nobody had ever gotten my blood pumping like her adorable rambling.

My mind left the conference the moment she landed in my hotel room.

"Thanks for that—I did my best," I said, aware the delay in my response was likely more than noticeable.

"Well, it showed. You know, a few of the panelists are going out for drinks tonight. If you want to come along, I'd be happy to introduce you."

"That sounds uncomfortably like cheating," I said, glancing back her way just in time for her brows to furrow.

"Nonsense, silly. Networking is half the reason we're all here this week, isn't it?"

"Perhaps," I allotted, thinking back to Elora's words. Would she go if Johanna extended the opportunity to her? Probably.

"It's not *cheating*. Shaking hands doesn't garter any

favors." But even as she said it, it felt as though it naturally would. Maybe she was right, and this was a classic case of overthinking. But if I was going to meet the panelists, I'd be doing it beside Elora. Elora, who was heading out of the ballroom beside Lief Erikson, reincarnated.

Now or never, Broderick.

"If you don't mind, I actually owe my fellow Alaskan a drink. Made a little wager. She kicked my ass. She's a hell of a presenter, isn't she?"

"Very impressive," Johanna agreed amicably, though the change in subject deepened that subtle pinch in what had to be Botox enhanced brows. "But don't count yourself out just yet," she added, canting her head as she brushed invisible debris off my shoulder, trailing her fingers down my arm until she squeezed my elbow. I stood, nodding as I disentangled. *Christ, she was forward.*

"Thanks for stopping by, Miss King. I'll see you around."

"It's Johanna," she corrected cheerfully, beaming and giving a little wave as she added, "See you around, Alaska."

Shaking off the feeling of her fingers on my skin, I made to intercept Elora. I pulled my phone from my pocket and fired off a text. Just one question. The answer immediately popped into my inbox.

BRODERICK
You sure this is a good idea?

BREXLEY
You said she loves her music.

BRODERICK
Since high school.

> **BREXLEY**
>
> So, what are you texting me for?
>
> Go get her. Quinny and I will accept nothing shy of victory, Allen.

Point taken, I sighed, tucking the device away and resigning myself to the inevitable, irreversible free fall off this bridge I was crossing.

Spotting Mr. Tall, blond, and perfect was easy in the sea of much shorter frames, but it was the bombshell in black my eyes trained on next.

"El!" I lengthened my stride, coming up beside them a little faster than frankly acceptable if I was going for casual. When she turned, her broad smile faltered for only a second before giving way to something...tentative? An adorable hesitation warring with the spark in her eyes.

"Broderick! Hey!" she chirped excitedly, like she meant it, and was obviously back in control of her ability to orate. "You were amazing today. You remember Pierce and Cheyenne? Guys, you remember Broderick Allen?"

"Of course," Pierce said, too authentically cheerful for my liking. Couldn't even hate the bastard properly. "Nice to see you again. Thoroughly enjoyed your presentation today."

"Same, same," I said, smiling. "Very inspired by the neighborhoods you planted in Bolivia."

The man's grin went sheepish, as if he was modest under that jock-ish exterior. "Didn't feel like we could even make a dent in things."

My chest constricted. Of course, he actually cared. *Dammit.* "To those mothers, it meant the world," I reassured.

"Yeah," he said wistfully, nodding. "One at a time. At least, that's what I'm telling myself."

"That's all any of us can do," Elora added with a genuine grin that warmed my heart. Her sincerity was contagious. Like a hug in human form. "One woman, one kid, one house at a time."

"True enough," life-size *Ken* said thoughtfully before turning his attention to me again. "So, Broderick, you coming out for lunch? We had eyes on the enchilada stand down the street."

Smirking, I glanced at El. *One guess whose idea that was.* "I, uh, would love to, but might have to take a rain check. El, can I have a minute?"

Blinking, she quirked her head, a hint of a blush creeping up her cheeks and warming my own. "Um, yeah. Pierce, I'll catch up later!"

"Sounds good. Broderick," he extended a hand, his shake sincere as I accepted. *Prick.* "Good to see you again."

"Likewise," I said, nodding to his sister. When our companions were out of earshot, El turned on me, holding her posture, but the subtle shift on her heels told me she was either as nervous as I was or picking up on my own anxiety, which seemed to grow as Pierce's back shrunk on the horizon.

"Hey, what's up?"

Now or never. Holding her stare, I smiled before asking, "What are you doing tonight after the finalists are announced? I talked my uncle into getting me tickets to Taylor Swift tonight, and I'm in the mood to celebrate. With you."

THIRTEEN
ELORA

I needed a drink. Strong. Whiskey. Neat. Never in my life had my stomach been flopping on such a relentless cycle unless I voluntarily strapped myself into a death mobile on a rollercoaster. And those butterflies were electively endured, not set loose by my teenage fantasy deigning to acknowledge me. My phone buzzed incessantly as my emotional support humans freaked out nearly as much as I was. Broderick got us seats for the concert *tonight*, and even scoped out an authentic Italian restaurant near the event center. First Mexican, then sushi, now my weak spot for authentic marinara and favorite musician from high school?

> **ALICE**
> You have got to be kidding me.
>
> **MAX**
> So help me god, if you don't climb this man like a tree, I will fly down there to kick your ass.

MARA

Climbing the competition is generally frowned upon.

MAX

Frowned upon but not specifically prohibited. Fine by me.

ALICE

I can't believe he's doing this. HOW is he doing this?

MAX

One does not ask questions when handed sold out tickets to Taylor Swift.

ALICE

Isn't she sold out all week? Aren't seats like a grand a pop? How'd he even get them?!? If he didn't know you were coming, he couldn't have planned this ahead of time, which means he got his hands on these this week.

MARA

The conference has been three consecutive ten plus hour days. I would also like to know how Professor Handsome pulled this off.

ALICE

Did Mr. Allen defend somebody in the mob? Win some kind of favor Broderick cashed in?

MAX

A gambling ring, maybe?

In all my searches, I found nothing but squeaky clean, obnoxiously bright sunshine and rainbows regarding the Allens. Believe me. I do my research.

ALICE

Sissy, you're going, right?

MAX

Of course she's going.

Right, El?

Elora Rhodes, so help me. You answer this phone right now.

Dammit, Elly. You don't pass up the opportunity to see the Queen beside tall, dark, and freakishly compassionate.

ALICE

Sissy?

WHEN I FINALLY REMEMBERED HOW TO lift my jaw off the marble floor, I'd stammered a measly, *"What?"*

"I distinctly remember one too many Rhodes sisters' renditions of *Teardrops on my Guitar*, and rants about her empowerment of women, ongoing charitable contributions, *Guinness World Records* set, and some nonsense about her funding music schools—"

"Music departments in colleges," I cut in before my mouth fell open again, fingers lamely coming to settle against my lips as nerves rode bulls inside my stomach.

Broderick didn't miss a beat, even as the corner of his lips quirked, he continued, "Along with some briefly fixated and then forgotten goal to get her on your show. Or has your infatuation changed, and I'm totally off base?"

Jaw cracking shut, I shook my head, unable to suppress my smile. "You're serious."

"As a heart attack." Did the man have a single clue

what that slow, sexy smile did to me? The rare show of confidence? I was equal parts transfixed and terrified because even the suggestion was making me feel the things I wasn't prepared to be feeling for the same guy that rejected me...*twice*.

Dammit, this was dangerous territory.

Was this a *friend* thing? A bonus little sister thing? Or... as significant a gesture as it felt? If I accepted, I was setting myself up to get my heart smashed again when we went our separate ways—him back to my big brother in Mistyvale, and me onto my next adventure—and not even my comfort music would peel me off the bathroom floor this time, because even her new albums would remind me of him.

Cautiously, I clarified, *"Tonight?"*

"Seven pm," he confirmed with a sheepish little smile and nod, bringing a palm to tug on the back of his neck.

"On the strip." He'd chuckled as I echoed back the pieces of information he'd hurled at me with the stumbling finesse of a semi-truck descending stairs. My fingers were suddenly ice cold where they settled on my lips, which were still sticky with stain. I watched that little spark in his eyes, body remembering what he felt like against mine in that tiny bed this morning. When he lifted his gaze and slipped that hand into his front pocket, rocking on his heels, I saw something in him that hadn't been there before. He leaned in and for the briefest inhalation, I thought he was going to kiss me, right there in the hallway as attendees rushed by us in a river of chatter. But he gently tucked my hair behind my ear, stealing my breath as he grinned down at me.

"Go make your pro-con list. I'll be by the room at six. Be ready if we're going, or I'll be making some strangers on the strip very happy with these," he waved his cell phone, where the digital tickets were still proudly displayed on the screen.

With that, the man melded into the flow of passersby, and I was left standing, gaping like an idiot as I attempted to process what the hell just happened, and all of the—if there were *any*—implications.

Hair curled and sprayed, makeup set, I took one last fragrance-tainted breath, and grabbed my phone from its incessant buzz on the counter.

ELORA

What does this mean? To him, I mean. Am I making something out of nothing?

MAX

It means that your sexy nighties were hotter than intended?

ALICE

eye roll emoji Jesus, Max.

MAX

Am I wrong?

ALICE

It means that Broderick is the most thoughtful man we know, and maybe he's capitalizing on time, spent with just the two of you to see if there's anything there.

MARA

If he can't see what's there, he might be pretty, but he's also blind, and dumb as rocks.

MAX

Agreed.

> **ALICE**
> The man is loyal to a fault. Cut him a break.

> **ELORA**
> So…I'm doing this?

> **MAX**
> Send us a selfie first.

I OBLIGED, snapping a close up of my makeup, and then reversing the camera to show off the form-fitted black cocktail dress that cut off mid-thigh. It dipped low in the back, showing off the delicate tattoos on my spine. Rolling my eyes, I watched the replies bounce right back into the inbox.

> **ALICE**
> Damn. Good luck, Broderick.
>
> **MARA**
> *bowing emoji* YASS goddess.
>
> **MAX**
> Elora-2 Broderick-0.

> **ELORA**
> You're sure I shouldn't go with the red one?

> **ALICE**
> You are literal perfection.
>
> **MAX**
> Don't you dare fuck up your hair with an outfit change.

> **MARA**
> You'll have to tell me where you get blowjob-red lipstick.
>
> **MAX**
> Stand tall. Get it, babe.

SMILING, I shook my head and headed for the suitcase, where I fished out a matching clutch and tucked my phone away before transferring my ID and cards.

And I *would* stand tall tonight.

Out.

With my long-time crush, in a strange city, where nobody knew us, so no ridiculous ancient pacts of small-town brotherhood could be broken.

What happens in Vegas, stays in Vegas. Right?

That's the mantra I gave myself when there was a subtle, rhythmic knock on the door. Before opening it, I stood tall, closed my eyes, blew the last trace of nerves out, and turned the handle.

What I didn't expect was for Broderick to be extending one long stem rose in front of that ear-to-ear knockout smile.

"A congratulatory token for making the top three," he said gallantly. *Prince Charming* had nothing on Broderick Allen. And God, were those *nerves* adding gravel to that gorgeous baritone?

It wasn't until he'd closed the distance, his thumb brushing over my lower lip, that I realized I'd clamped my teeth into it. Tentatively, eyes narrowed suspiciously on his face, I accepted the smooth stem, and brought it to my nose to inhale that intoxicating scent.

"Broderick Allen, are you *wooing* me?" I said over a smirk that barely contained the grin begging to be set free.

"Just practicing my graceful loser routine, like they do before the Oscars."

"I wouldn't count yourself out so quickly."

"I would be an idiot to underestimate my competition," he countered, smiling with something like pride in those deep browns. It was of no shock to Mara and I that the three finalists moving on to the next round were us, Pierce and Cheyenne, and Broderick—fate clearly had a sense of humor. Taken aback, I studied the sincerity there, my breaths coming in faster, shallower little pumps of air when he didn't yield. Nothing about this felt like a bonus little sister outing.

"Thanks," I mumbled, throat constricting in some invisible turtleneck as I turned back, wishing for some way to put my rose in water. Broderick sidled into the room and leaned casually against the entertainment center, hands in his front pocket, watching as I gingerly set it across my pillow. He was always so damn classy, and today was no different. Sleek charcoal slacks complimented a pale blue button-up shirt—the sleeves rolled up to expose those gorgeous forearms he'd used to cage me against him—beneath a navy vest. It was the moment he slid those bronze glasses on as he studied me that I was well and truly done for. My heart had grown *wings*. Wings that fluttered like the happiest little hummingbird as I turned back to face him. God, that smile might just kill me yet.

BRODERICK

BE READY AT SIX. That was the indication I'd asked for in order to feel her out. To see if this was okay with her. And damn, Elora didn't hold back.

I was still getting used to her longer locks of hair down and free flowing, since she almost always had it pulled back. That silky dark brown framed her face tonight, curled in a sexy, messy way, just begging me to wrap it around my fist. Her lips were a gorgeous shade of red that snagged my attention the moment she all but threw the door open, but her eyes were still beautifully, perfectly, Elora.

It was the dress that did me in. Tight in all the right places, a midnight black fabric hugged the supple lines I'd ardently attempted not to focus on for my entire damn adult life. I needed to taste her. To know what her soft curves would feel like beneath my palms. It was that primal urge that kept me anchored to the table with my hands safely tucked inside my pockets. El loved nothing if not a woman who refused to make herself small. This concert was an ode to that. I didn't know a single song, but when Brex asked me what I could do for some grand gesture, I put in a call to my uncle, who had a buddy from college on the inside of the event scene here in the city.

Judging by the way the invitation had robbed away her coherent words, I thought I hit it outta the park.

This was insane.

I knew it as I watched her set the rose on her pillow. Knew it as she nervously ran those pearly teeth over that tempting, painted bottom lip. Some part of me clung to the fact that her brothers would kill me for the amount of time I allowed my eyes to linger on those strong bare legs or the swell of her ass. As for the rest of me...

Well, ultimately, for tonight, I was just going to do what

made her happy. If that took us down a new road, fine. If not...at least she was smiling at me.

At least I would always have this picture of her tonight, flustered and beautiful...*for me*.

When she reached my side, I stretched out my hand in offering, preening like a damn bird when she took it. "Got your ID?" I asked, needing to say something to break the silence, to make sure nothing would stand between us and a night she'd remember.

I HAD TO ADMIT, the pop princess put on one hell of a show, and judging by the permanent smile on Elora's face as she rattled off every single fact she could think of about the music empire, she was thrilled with it. I'd been hoping for the opportunity to dance with her, but it wasn't really that kind of show. Too much screaming and giddy, uncoordinated flailing about with drinks held upright by women much younger than us. I now knew a disturbing amount of information about the thirty-something icon.

Dinner had been just as disconcertingly smooth, and watching our chipper, round little waitress entirely enamored by Elora putting down *another* basket of breadsticks might have been the highlight of my evening.

We'd opted to walk back down the strip, rather than trying to compete for a ride share in this chaos. The flash and glow of the omnipresent neon colored her skin as she prattled on beneath the roar of car horns, tires grinding across asphalt and the constant chatter of voices. Props to Taylor for creating such a feral fandom. But it was that *smile* I watched.

"You still want to meet her someday?" I finally asked as

a limo passed us with feather-boa-baring women woo-hooing through the sunroof, saluting the city with raised middle fingers. Grinning at the surrounding insanity, El slowly glanced my way.

"I mean, obviously," she said, like the question was ludicrous. "Who wouldn't?"

Well. Me, for starters. But that didn't need vocalizing.

"Can you imagine how much I could learn in thirty minutes with her on the show?"

"I love that you're always learning." I did. It was one of the sexiest things about her.

"Grow or die, baby. Grow or die."

Chuckling, I shook my head, simply smiling at *her* smiling.

"What about you? If you could have dinner with anyone, who would it be?"

I slid her palm back into mine, pleased when she curled her fingers around me. "Present company aside?"

That tiny hitch in her breath as her eyes darted to me before returning to the bustling sidewalk was sexier than it had any right to be. Mischief sparked a beat before she used her free hand to toss her hair over her shoulder with a quippy eye roll. "Obviously."

"Living or dead?" I pressed as I guided her behind me while a group of boisterous young men took up more than their share of the walkway. She gave a thoughtful little hum, barely audible against the onslaught of the city.

"Living."

"Mmm. Keanu Reeves."

"What!?" An elated little yip burst out of her lips as I guided her back to my side, trading her hand for my arm over her shoulders, tucking her against me. She reached up the opposite hand to lace through my fingers, my heart hammering harder. "Like *The Matrix* guy?" Her eyes narrowed as she studied me for some kind of tell. Knowing El, she'd find it if it was there to find.

"Why so surprised?"

"I just...expected a scientist, or philanthropist, or maybe one of the less corrupt politicians," she said thoughtfully, still studying me.

"Too predictable," I supplied.

"Is it the tragic backstory or the charitable contributions?"

"Dude just seems...inordinately *good*. All of that pain, and he still goes out of his way to help people. Of all the celebrities flashing their wealth around, I think an hour with Keanu would be...wholesome. Insightful. I bet he knows things the rest of us don't."

"*I know Kung-Fu*," she said in a hilariously accurate imitation, those years in theater class resurfacing.

"Ahhh, I should've known I'd regret this."

She cackled skyward, and I gave her hand a little squeeze, not willing to head back to the hotel yet. Not willing to let this little bubble of...stolen time burst.

"Nah, you're right," she said, hip bumping me and giggling as our path bent in that direction for a beat before getting back on course. "I bet he'd be pretty chill. Insightful, but chill."

The ostentatious drive and classy illuminated sign for our resort became visible ahead, right as another rowdy limo zoomed past us. Too soon. I wasn't done with her. With us. Doing something fun for once. Glancing around, I thanked every member on the event board for selecting this insane city for our meeting point, because down half a block and across the street was a glowing sign for a gelato shop, with a line of people out the entrance after ten pm.

Long live Las Vegas. I jerked my chin in that direction, watching as she tracked the movement.

"Still a cookies and cream girl?"

Her eyes widened as a slow smile hooked her lips to one side a beat before she shrugged off my arm, catching my hand as it fell away so that she could yank me toward the light that just went red, the crosswalk filling with pedestrians. Demanding little thing.

Flashing a grin over her shrugging shoulder, she quipped, "Always."

FOURTEEN

ELORA

Fingers still a little sticky from the gelato, I wiped them against my dress before swiping the photo booth strip from the machine and waving it at Broderick. Much to my satisfaction, he rolled his eyes before I glanced down to the evidence of our evening on the town. The man actually stuck his tongue out in the last one with me.

"Awe, it's cute," I chirped, grinning down at our goofy ass faces. Even clowning around with me, the man was fucking adorable.

...Especially clowning around with me.

There was something so liberating about being away from home—maybe that's why we loved to travel so much. To go somewhere we could shed our skins covered in labels bestowed by neighbors who still remembered us in diapers and exchange them for suits all our own. Whether they were silly, free and lighthearted, or quiet and reserved after a lifetime of serving, travel brought out...the authentic layers in people they rarely revealed otherwise.

Vegas brought out the version of Broderick few ever saw. And as I watched him march off ahead of me like the photo booth wasn't his idea in the first place, I canted my head, admiring how that perfect bubble butt filled out his dark slacks. Because nobody here cared. Not a soul was watching the childhood friends gallivanting through the streets, at the mercy of our whims, wondering if it was something more. There weren't any Mistyvale alumni to make a jab or tell my brothers that Broderick spent the evening with my hand in his, or his arm looped around my shoulder. There was an entire city, entirely barren of fucks to give. And I loved it.

This is why people love Vegas. Not just the gambling or hookers or shows—the freedom of it. The nameless face among the tens of thousands on this condensed strip of endless sin and entertainment.

"Oh, come on!" I teased, feeling like a Chihuahua chasing a Doberman as my stubby legs attempted to keep up with his long stride. "You can't tell me we're not cute," I added as I caught up, lunging forward to wrap around his swinging arm and force him to slow to my pace. At least mild amusement laced his features when he turned my way, begrudgingly accepting the photo strip. I swore I watched him stifle his smile.

"*You're* cute," he said, quirking a brow. Heat rushed my face, and I broke away from his gaze in favor of our feet over the dirty concrete, careful to avoid a suspicious pile of something viscous.

We were quiet until we turned down the over-the-top drive of the resort, great arching palms to either side with twinkling lights everywhere. For the most part, Vegas felt like what would be vomited out if one could eat neon lights and an ashtray. It took getting to the outskirts, the suburbs against that gorgeous expanse of desert, to see the appeal in the enormous metro. But the resort, while over the top for my taste, at least attempted to class up the tacky surroundings of tricks and illusions.

After a beat too long, I said, "Thanks for tonight, Broderick. I had a blast."

"Good," he said simply as the splatter of the fountain misted our direction, and we rounded the corner to the grand, domed sunshade. As we entered, smiling at the bellmen to either side of the automatic glass doors, he added a quiet, "I'm glad."

With his hand at the low of my back, sending jitters through my insides, we made our way through the bustling lobby and down to the elevator bay without speaking again. The longer we stewed in our silence, the thicker the air seemed to get, crackling with some kind of turbulence I didn't want to acknowledge as the heat of his palm against my dress pulled all of my focus from the cacophony of voices and echos of omnipresent machines around us.

In and up, we moved in contemplative static energy, my heart gradually picking up tempo in anticipation of something—*anything*—happening. A switch to flip. The way his eyes tracked my movements made the hand on my back seem like a kind of ownership my entire body thrummed to accept. By the time we reached our door, my heart was fluttering in my throat, and my nearly nonexistent oxygen supply halted entirely when he caged me against the busy wallpaper with his exquisite body, chest heaving, determination in his eyes.

Like a dumb fish, my mouth opened and closed twice, but words failed me. Broderick's shallow breaths were hot on my face, his exhales dancing with my short inhales, the taste of him on the air coasting through my parted lips. God, over the years, I'd fantasized countless times about what it would feel like to finally kiss him again. To taste him and feel those hands on my skin without that measly three-year gap between us damning it all.

His gentle finger tucked my hair behind an ear before his warm, smooth palm slid down to cradle the side of my neck, his focus entirely trained on my mouth. Desperate to touch and feel and taste, a stuttered little breath stalled in my ribs when the flat tip of his straight nose bumped the end of mine. My desperate hands scraped up his arms, settling on his biceps as he nuzzled our cheeks together, burying his face in my hair and inhaling audibly. Like he needed to commit my scent to memory as badly as I needed to anchor myself in his spiced musk.

When his forehead settled against mine, I wet my lips, but as I shifted my chin to meet him in the middle, his gaze snapped to my eyes like I'd shocked him, something like panic flaring in those deep browns. A little pinch formed between his brows a beat before he closed his eyes in something like painful resignation, a tiny shake of his head and flex of his jaw the only warning I got before he turned away. The door beeped as he slid his card free, returning the air to my lungs in a whoosh of disappointment as he rushed inside, running a palm over his short hair before wordlessly vanishing into the ensuite.

My mouth popped open, confusion battling the devastation suddenly making my heart plummet for an entirely different reason as I stood there, dumbfounded and wondering what the hell had just happened.

Was it all in my head? I quietly shut the door, locking the bolt and the top latch before slowly leaning into it, craving the icy metal support to stay upright as my brain whirred through the last several hours. Had I read it wrong? Or had he been weighing our options just as heavily and yet again decided I wasn't worth it? There was no way I'd just imagined the want dripping off that man. I wasn't alone in this, so what the fuck was holding him back?

Broderick came back into the room in a rush, frustration tensing his brow as he tongued a molar. His mouth just opened when my cell phone rang. Without glancing to the screen, I declined it. As I made to break the horrendous silence with some pathetic deflection and announcement of bedtime, it rang again. My eyes slid shut, and I chewed my bottom lip.

"You should answer," he breathed. Swallowing, I pulled my phone up, scowling when Alice's photo flashed across the screen.

Bringing it to my ear, I answered the call, my eyes back on conflicted deep browns. "Sissy? You okay?"

"I'm gonna fucking kill him."

"Oh boy," I sighed, pinching the bridge of my nose as I wandered toward the patio. "Greyson?"

"No. Santa Claus. Of course, Greyson. It's always Greyson. I fucking. Hate. Him." The last two words seemed to come through gritted teeth, and I winced. With one last glance over my shoulder, I found Broderick staring at his feet, his hand at the back of his neck. "I finally had a date planned this weekend, but nooooo, the dragon needs me to accompany him out of town to a luncheon where he can't be bothered to remember a god-damned name, so he needs me there to remind him who's who. This is fucking insane."

With a sigh, I pushed open the door and stepped outside into the cool city air. It might've been smoggy, but at least it was brisk, and didn't emanate with that insane energy occupying the space between me and my *roommate*.

"So quit," I suggested for the millionth time, already well aware of what her answer would be. It had been the same since the first day he told her a little country bumpkin would never make it in the city, let alone in *his* company. Little did he know, the fastest way to make a Rhodes double down was to tell us we couldn't do it. Alice even more than most. She might have been one of the quietest in the bunch, but she was resolute, and only an idiot could mistake her silence for stupidity. The woman missed nothing. Which is why Greyson Hart had been eating his words for the last year and a half as she became his begrudging right-hand woman. Purely out of spite to prove him wrong, of course.

"And let him win?" we both said in unison. Mind you, mine was dripping sarcasm, and hers was more of a pissed off pterodactyl. She choked on something like a laugh, but I let her be the one to finish.

"*Never.*"

Broderick

STUPID. Selfish. Reckless.

I almost kissed my best friends' baby sister. It didn't seem to matter how hard I ran sprints in the gym, or how heavy I lifted, the guilt of that didn't dissipate. Not even the endless string of pull-ups seemed to help. Hell, any time the two of them wanted to scare off some low life showing a little too much interest in their sisters, they called me in for backup. I was supposed to look out for them, not memorize the outline of her curves in that dress. What the hell had I been thinking? Taking her out. Indulging that idea for any period of time when I'd sworn she was off limits—safe with me—to the only two people that had always had my back.

It wouldn't have stopped at a kiss. I knew it. Hell, the portrait on the wall across from us in that hallway knew it.

If I tasted those soft, red lips and let my hands roam up her athletic little frame, that would be the end for me. If she didn't stop it, I certainly wouldn't have what it takes to peel myself off her until I'd laid claim to every inch of Elora Rhodes. Fulfilled every forbidden fantasy that had accumulated over the last eighteen painful, albeit entertaining, years.

But some distant part of my brain—probably the one responsible for survival—thought of Jameson's face, if he knew I had Elora up against a wall, about to claim that pretty little parted pout before shoving her inside my hotel room. A room where she had no escape plan if she felt like I crossed a line. With no spare rooms in the city, we had to survive two more days of this event—preferably without her knowing I was sporting a perpetual chubby and fierce case of blue balls. She had to be focused enough to give a presentation the day after tomorrow, and after all our years together, I owed her at least that much.

Best-case scenario, if she didn't think I was a creep taking advantage of a shit situation, and still returned the sentiment, I knew her heart enough to know getting involved would be an enormous distraction and compromise her conviction in the competition.

By the time I made it back to the room and showered, El was asleep on her side of the mattress. I hesitated, watching her turn in her sleep, thinking of how sweet her little body felt, safe in my arms. I bowed my head and released the breath holding my lungs captive. Resigned to old vows and guilt-tangled fantasies, I grabbed the spare blanket from the dresser and curled up on the murder sofa.

AVOIDING Elora was about as easy as circumnavigating viruses in a kindergarten classroom. If my self-preservation instincts were better, I would've bailed on the lessons today, except for the fact that two of my favorite speakers in the lineup were scheduled two hours apart from each other. But...she was everywhere. And when I concealed myself in a corner of her absence, attendees were still discussing her talk yesterday. Like a song on the wind, her name seemed to carry, keeping me on edge everywhere I went. Because every time it surfaced, I winced at the image of a pissed off Jameson, who would inevitably react in one of two ways. Option one—and this was the most favorable of the two—is he'd knock my ass out with one right hook. I was tough, but not grew-up-on-the-Bearing-Sea tough. Defending myself wouldn't have been an option under the circumstances. Option two—and realistically, the more likely of the two—was that he'd go inside that thick skull of his, and let that betrayal deepen until he couldn't look at me without the fires of hell in his eyes, and that would be the end of our thirty years of friendship. As for Rhyett...I wasn't sure what to expect of Rhy. But disappointing Rhyett Rhodes was in the same ballpark as murdering a six-year-old girl's pet rabbit. It likely didn't help that my neck was kinked from cramming myself onto the loveseat in the corner and failing to sleep for the majority of the night.

Immanuel Kant would tell me that my loyalty to them needed to supersede this gnawing, aching desire in my gut. To slink into the shower for a date with my fist, burn off this tension on my own, and send her on her way on Saturday. On the opposite hand, the fathers of Utilitarianism would argue that if I made Elora happy, her joy would make Max, Mara, and her sisters happy. Maybe—*maybe* Pax and Finn would side with us? Lord knew my mother would be beside herself, finally having the hope of a daughter-in-law on the horizon. That meant more joy could be derived from me succumbing to my own weaknesses than disappointment. Right?

But the moral reprehensibility of breaking that promise...

My stomach flipped uneasily every time I reached this point of my inane internal debate.

Forty-eight hours. I just needed to endure this for forty-eight hours, and we could go back to our lives. Mine, alone, renovating my townhouse back in Mistyvale, teaching at the college, and hating most of the world. And El could return to... Well... blessing anyone lucky enough to rub shoulders with her on her widespread adventures. Nobody would be any the wiser. It's not like Taylor Swift and some gelato crossed a line we couldn't come back from.

But fuck, *I wanted to.* That was the problem.

Pursuing Elora would likely end my two closest friendships. But avoiding her after leading her on would be the final nail in the coffin of our relationship. Which was a much more agonizing thought than it had a right to be.

I SPENT Thursday tucked away in men's bathrooms, and fleeing the lectures before they wrapped up so that I could exit the building and hide somewhere off campus to eat during the breaks. But I'd successfully avoided a direct confrontation with the world's most glaring distraction. I went out with a few professors from mainland universities, and nursed a beer late into the night, hoping to return after she'd fallen asleep. It was the subtle vibration of my cell that had me pulling the cursed thing from a back pocket and swiping it open.

> JAMESON
>
> Good luck tomorrow, man. How you feeling?

FUCK, *wouldn't you like to know?* No, actually, you probably wouldn't like to know that the prospect of winning the grant now soured my stomach, because those funds could go to Elora. Could go to her school. Could back up a mission she'd put her whole heart into. And you really wouldn't like to know that if the only thing I accomplished in life was making your little sister smile, it would be enough.

> BRODERICK
>
> Prepared. Competition is tough. Did you know El was entering? She's in the top three with me.

THREE DOTS APPEARED and vanished twice before my screen lit up with a picture of Jameson and Noel with beanies tugged tight over their heads, and noses red with cold. Cursing, I swigged the last of my beer before swiping to answer. There was no hello. Not that I expected one with James. Just a curt demand for more information.

"Hold up. My El?" *No, fucker. My El. I just don't have the balls to tell you that.* "She's at the conference?"

"She gave an entire speech yesterday about women in leadership. Do you *ever* check the family text thread?"

An irritable scoff came through the speaker. "Don't know if you've noticed, but there are twelve of us, plus Skittles and Brex. By the time I get back into cell service, they've rattled off hundreds of updates about lunch plans and who's going to visit who. I'm not about to sit and scroll for hours to catch up. Kinda figure if it's important, I'll hear about it."

"Well, you didn't hear about *this*."

"Apparently not. That's sick. I mean, she speaks all over the country these days, so I guess I'm not surprised. What the hell is she competing for?"

"Her and Mara Correa are working to secure funding for their women's business school."

There was the subtle scratch of a rough palm over unmanaged stubble. "I thought Pax bought into that."

"He's a silent investor, but he's not bootstrapping the whole thing. El says they need a few million just for the building. She's got a five-year plan for moving the project into the green, but she needs the five years funded first."

"Tracks. Damn." His dark chuckle made me bristle, irritation staying my hand where I rocked my beer glass on its rim.

"What?" I bit out before adding, "If you say it feels like old times, so help me…"

His chuckle turned into a full laugh before he pointed out, "You said it. Not me."

"This shit sucks."

"Oh please, you two seemed to love wiping the floor with each other as kids."

"This is different."

"Why?" he asked flatly.

Because I've been pining for her since I was sixteen, asshole. Killing time with poison like Sarah when everyone knew she was trouble the moment she came into my life. Instead, I said, "I never would've entered if I knew she was vying for it. She'd *wipe the floor* with anybody else on the lineup. Frankly, it feels like I'm the only other contender. At least according to Johanna King."

"Johanna who?"

"Never mind. Not important. I just...wish I'd known, you know?"

"I guess. Look, man, I love my sister. But if I can tell you anything, it's once she decides to do something she'll make it happen. I know you. Which means you're digging yourself into a hole over there, overthinking the morality of winning when she wants it. And that's bullshit. If El loses, she'll find her money some other way. Just..."

"Just what?" I bit out when his words drifted off into the air.

He released a low, prolonged sigh. "You deserve this, man. Don't wig yourself out before tomorrow."

"If you were a half-decent brother, you'd tell me to bow out."

"If I were a half-decent brother, I'd tell you to swing harder because it will push her to win," he challenged. "As it is, I'm betting on El crossing the finish line with or without this one endorsement."

Something like pride battled the anxiety in my chest a beat before irritation swallowed them both. "That a backhanded compliment, Cap?"

"Nothing backhanded about it."

"Are you saying she'll find a way, but I won't?"

"I'm saying…El has made it her business to do whatever it takes to make her dreams a reality. It's like…a game for her. And I'm just…proud of you, I guess, for taking a chance, getting off island. Don't wig yourself out worrying over her. She'll figure it out. She always does."

I sat for a moment, studying the warm glass in my hand before catching the bartender's eye and holding it up. Talking to him about the genuine source of anxiety would be the adult thing to do. Just. Broach the subject. Be honest with him. That's what a proper friend would do, right? According to Brex, the guys probably didn't even remember that old pact, and would want me to be happy.

But right as I opened my mouth to ask if we could talk about something, he muttered, "Damn."

"What?" I asked softly, nodding as the bartender set down a fresh glass and swiped my old one. I ran a thumb over the rapidly gathering condensation on the chilled edges.

"Skittles just served dinner." His nickname for Noel had originated from her explosion of color in a climate made entirely of shades of gray. But there was an underlying insinuation in his tone that made me shake my head.

"Why does that sound like a euphemism?" I sighed.

"Didn't say what she was wearing."

"TMI, man. That woman is like a sister to me."

"Good, cause that means I don't have to kill you."

I laughed, glancing up to the television as the bartender flicked between channels, landing on recaps of the games this weekend, and predictions for the following. Hoping a change in subject could absolve the guilt unsettling my dinner, I said, "Looks like Pax is favored by two touchdowns on Sunday."

"Can't underestimate the underdog."

"Good point. He won't."

"Never does."

"Alright, I'll let you go. Say hi to Noel for me."

"Will do. And Broderick?"

"Yeah?"

"I mean it, man. Don't hold back. You finally found what lights your soul on fire. You told me only idiots don't chase that." Of course, logically, I knew he loved my enthusiasm for the youth center, but all I could picture was Elora's face, arms painfully aware of the memory of her frame against mine. I'd told him that when he wasn't letting himself pursue Noel for his own concocted excuses for hesitating, and couldn't help but shift in my seat as the irony set in. "Set your sights and no matter what happens, don't let go."

Like a coward, I just said, "Thanks, buddy. Talk soon."

"Call me after the awards tomorrow."

"Yeah, alright."

"Noel says she loves you."

That earned a little smile as I said, "Love her, too. Kinda even love you, but you're a pain in my ass."

His laugh made me smile for a beat before he said, "Love ya, fucker. Have a good night."

The call disconnected a beat after Noel's laughter filled the line, and slowly, feeling like a coward, I set the phone on the bar and wiped a window clear on the glass, watching beads of water slide down its slick surface. My heart felt heavy, and I kicked myself for not saying something while I had his attention.

To my relief, El was asleep when I finally slipped into the hotel room. But the solace halted when I took in the tempting silky pajamas draped heavily over her strong frame. Pix might've earned the pet name because she was petite, but these days she looked more gymnast than starving ballerina figurine. Strong. Disciplined. You had to be to build that definition. My palms buzzed with the need to trace her edges, cementing the subtle feel of them in my mind.

As I watched her sleep like some psychopath, I thought about what it felt like to have her smile for me...*because of* me, and anxiety ate me from the inside out like a five-course meal. Because if I took the Utilitarian path, and risked it all —my friendships, my *bonus parents* and home away from home, not to mention my at least moderately attractive face as I knew it—I couldn't very well look her in the eye while professing my feelings if this grant money lined my pockets when it could have been in hers. Beneath the war in my mind, a little voice spoke up, and I knew exactly what I had to do. And it started with paying a visit to Johanna King.

FIFTEEN

ELORA

The Besties Chat:

MAX
Chin up, babe. You've got this.

ALICE
Call us and report back tonight!

ELORA
Love you guys.

RHODES FAMILY CHAT:

ALICE
El goes on for her grant presentation in twenty!

RHYETT
Break a leg, beautiful!

JAMESON

Jesus, harsh man. Didn't know you wanted B to win that badly.

RHYETT

Fuck off, J. You know what I mean.

LEIGHTON

You've got this, big sister!!

KAIA

You're my hero, Elly! Knock them dead!

MAVERICK

So violent. Jesus.

ELORA

You guys are ridiculous. I fucking love you.

PAXTON

Money's on you, El. Literally. Go lock it down, Sparkplug. Either way, I'm so fucking proud of you.

TEARS IN MY EYES, throat thick, I stared at the messages, giggling at my chaotic brothers and eternally sweet sisters. I missed them all so damn much, a wave of homesickness competing with the pre-stage jitters for who would sabotage one of the most crucial sixty minutes of my career. But it was the moment our oldest sister's name popped up on my screen that my eyes flew wide. We almost never heard from Jeanne outside of holidays, and even then, service in third world countries wasn't exactly dependable.

JEANNE

Just landed. What are you doing, sissy?

RHYETT

Holy fucking shit, where are you?

JAMESON

Christ, good to know you're still breathing. *eye roll emoji*

AXEL

Jeanne! Holy hell, girl. It's good to see your name.

HADLEE

Where you at Jeanie?

El!! I'm so fucking proud of you. Go rock it.

MAVERICK

'IT'S ALIVE' gif

ELORA

Damn sissy. Good to see your name. I'm pitching for a grant for Mara, Pax, and my school.

JEANNE

HELL YES. Go and grow, baby! I believe in you.

FINN

Jeanne, see you soon!

El, you've got this. Go kick ass. We're all rooting for you.

MAVERICK

What does one wear to an award ceremony these days?

JAMESON

Just don't arrive naked.

AXEL

Well, that shoots my plan in the foot.

> ELORA
>
> No one is arriving anywhere, and certainly not in your birthday suits. Gotta roll. Jeanne, let's chat later?

> JEANNE
>
> Tomorrow? I'm wiped. Gotta clean up.

> ELORA
>
> I fly out for Seattle at noon. After?

> JEANNE
>
> Perfect.

> JAMESON
>
> Wait. Wtf did Finn say 'see you soon'? You better not be in NYC without telling the rest of us.

FOR THE FIRST time in years, anxiety had tightened my belly as I prepared for my last pitch...right until the yahoo crew sent me snickering as I slid my phone into the tight, silky pocket of my favorite cobalt blazer. Partially, the nerves reared their heads because I'd be speaking in front of the attendees and panelists again today, but mostly because Broderick hadn't been back since the night of the concert. Some kind of body snatcher had swapped him for his body double all over again, and I'd been reeling since.

I thought the night had been a freaking dream right until he went all *Star Trek Vulcan* on me and then vanished into the ether. Even Evel Knievel would have whiplash hanging around this man.

I'd known he was around, because Johanna told me how 'very much' she enjoyed chatting with my 'foxy professor friend', and I decided maybe she wasn't quite as fabulous as I'd originally thought. As a matter of fact, I actually didn't care much for her at all.

And then he was there, opening the day bright and early, and owning every inch of that stage like the professor he was. He was so introverted, so introspective—always stuck in his head—that sometimes it was easy to forget that he literally spoke to a few hundred students for a living. I watched with rapt attention right until that bright smile cracked his face at the sound of boisterous applause from hundreds of members of the audience who'd engaged with him before their coffee even went cold on the last morning of the event. Hell, I'd been impressed at how many attendees were in their seats, sans toothpicks to hold their eyelids apart.

As for Broderick...he was magnificent. And also, a total fucking sneak, because I rushed out of the room the moment he wrapped up, weaving through the now standing bodies as fast as I could manage, and still didn't catch him before he vanished. I checked the room during intermissions, to no avail. The shithead was *avoiding* me.

Pierce closed out the morning segment of the day, leaving me with the task of opening after lunch.

When I arrived down in the conference room, I canted my head, studying the stage, which was now missing a podium. In its place was a solitary armchair. Curiosity quirked my brow just before the unmistakable clearing of his throat had me turning to find Broderick smiling softly, holding up an impressive cup of coffee in offering.

"That's a rather manly serving there," I said, narrowing my eyes before accepting and asking, "What's this for?"

"You always like to present like you're sitting across a table from your audience," he said, nodding to the chair on the stage. My mouth popped open. When I turned back to him, he was backing away into the hallway like that was all the explanation I'd get.

"You watch me speak?" I asked, a not-so-subtle heat creeping up my neck at the idea, spreading to my chest when he grinned conspiratorially.

"Didn't think your hometown forgot about our golden girl, did you? Hell, I play your lives for my students."

I tracked his movement, taking slow steps toward him as he backed up. Simultaneous amusement and overwhelm tugged my heart along on the invisible leash in his hand. At a loss for words, I wrestled out, "Broderick, thank—"

"No biggie, Pix," he shrugged. "You deserve this. Break a leg out there," he said, turning to vanish into the steadily flowing sea of post-lunch attendees finding their way inside, their gradually growing chatter bouncing off the walls.

What the hell was he doing, playing ghost for two days straight just to drop in for the kindest gesture I'd ever seen, only to vanish again without an explanation? Confusion burrowed into my belly. He was the most infuriating man I ever had the displeasure of infatuating over. I was just about to chase after him and demand some straight fucking answers when a beaming Mara appeared in my sight, clapping me enthusiastically on both shoulders.

"Good morning! Looking beautiful," her eyes widened at the enormous coffee clutched between my fingers. "Looking *caffeinated*. Ready to go kick some ass?"

Blinking, I said, "Yeah, I guess."

"That's the spirit!" she chirped sardonically, turning me around and smacking my back to encourage our movement toward the curtained off prep area. Still a little dazed—and a lot confused—I followed my friend to the side of the stage, where the happy but flushed faces of a bustling IT team greeted us and began wiring me to the mic.

Johanna came in, beaming that stage worthy smile, and I couldn't help but return the hug she offered before pulling back and dusting invisible lint off my shoulders.

"You're on in ninety seconds, Elora. You ready?" she said cheerfully as she adjusted her own mic on that perfectly pressed ivory blazer. I sucked down a deep breath before straightening my spine and beaming back at her.

"Born that way."

I closed my eyes when Johanna nodded and turned for the stage. Hanging onto the rail at the bottom of the three quick steps, I envisioned walking up and across the stage, saying hello, working the audience, and then inviting them to refill their coffees from the table carafes, and settle in like old friends. I envisioned what it would feel like to hold their attention, earn their laughter, and make them ask the hard questions because they felt comfortable enough to. I shook out my shoulders and pulled on memories of the jitter of applause from my chest to my toes and held that right until Johanna called my name. My heels clicked up the stairs, the walk out music blaring through the enormous speakers.

Chest up. Head tall, I took the stage with a smile, a strut, and a cheery wave.

PIERCE AND CHEYENNE were the first smiles I recognized in the crowd's chaos as they mobbed around me to ask questions in the hallway after my talk. God, it was a rush unlike any other. Better than performing, knowing that not only had I planted the idea of this school in the universe, but also equipped the crowd with lessons and skills they could all use to grow their own businesses and charities. The latter hurled her arms around me with so much enthusiasm, I would've eaten carpet if not for Pierce steadying us both with a laugh.

When she pulled back, her beaming face was echoed by Mara, who finally forced her way through two rather eager looking young men who had flocked to my coat tails on Monday and just kept finding their way back.

"You were incredible," Cheyenne squealed.

"Legendary," Mara agreed with zealous nods.

"A shoo-in, and I can't even be bitter about it," Pierce said, playfully nudging my shoulder, his pearly teeth on display in a dazzling smile. *Oh, yeah. Max owed me.* "Who's your mother? Who the hell raised you?"

Laughing, I shook my head, hands up in defense. "You guys did amazing, too. I don't think the judges have an easy task awaiting them." The gorgeous siblings both started showering more flattery, but my eyes locked on dark browns across the heads of new attendees tentatively working their way forward to ask their questions. Broderick's smile was subtle, but so fucking reassuring with that glow of pride that my heart seemed to slow just holding his attention. A tentative grin crept up my cheeks before I bit my lower lip, and he gave me a nod.

"Gonna answer that?" Pierce's chipper baritone brought me back into my body and I blinked, swallowing hard as I realized the device in my palm was singing a merry little tune. Yanking myself from my stupor, I glanced down to see *Christopher Calling* written over the screen.

He knew where I was. Hell, he was supposed to be tuned into the lives. Perplexed, I hesitantly answered with a simple, "You okay?"

"Fuck yeah, I am. So are you, by the way. Are you sitting down?"

"No?"

"You should be."

"Chris, what's up? You're freaking me out." I glanced up to find Broderick's column now vacant, disappointment slumping my shoulders as I waved to my friends and extricated myself from the chaos, Mara tight on my heels.

"On second thought, maybe don't sit. Maybe walk, but not on steps or near water."

"Chris."

"Is Mara there?"

"Yes."

"Thank God, because I don't know if I can contain this any longer and I needed you both. Get somewhere you can stick me on speaker."

Some bizarre anxiety-anticipation combo settled in my throat like I'd forgotten how to swallow. As a matter of fact, my mouth was suddenly parched, body gearing up to fight some invisible threat as my assistant continued to babble in the background, like he was talking to someone else.

When we rounded a corner, I shoved inside a conference room where—at least judging by the enormous, oblong marble table and abundance of chairs down the center—big-wigs had their meetings. *The Godfather* would approve of the four-inch slab and looming presence of the armchairs. I scooted one out as Mara locked the double doors before joining me.

"Jesus fucking Christ, are you two ready yet?"

Laughing, I said, "Yes, and out with it. You're killing me here."

"Just got off the phone with Lionel."

"My agent?"

"No, dummy, *Richie*. *Yes*, your fucking agent, I swear to God, El, sometimes."

"*Chris!*" I snapped, growing more than a little impatient and a lot nervous.

"Right." He sucked down a long breath, like he was steadying himself, and my eyes flicked up to Mara's, but she just shrugged, brows winging up to mirror my confusion. "So, we may have been conspiring the last few weeks, and taken the liberty of pitching the school to some pretty major producers in some very major networks." My heart...stopped. Apparently, so did Mara's, judging by the pit-bull-jaws-of-death level grip she had on my arm. He wouldn't have gotten us alone and built up all this anticipation if that effort had been fruitless. "There were a handful of little fish that took the bait...and a couple of very, *very* big fish sniffing around too." I heard the chatter of a keyboard being typed in rapid succession as he sucked down another long breath, either unaware or not caring that I was holding mine. "Two made bids, Lionel worked his magic, and they just delivered their highest and best offers. Which is why I'm calling. They watched our lives this week, El, and they *both* want you. But I just sent you the offer from the one we're most excited about. You could pick between Chicago, New York, or Los Angeles, and I know you wanted to be in charge of location, but just wait until you get a look at these numbers."

I was already two steps ahead of him, swiping over to my email. The world seemed to shift on its axis. This...this changed everything. Buildings already owned by the network. Plans and funds for not only equipment but the staff, as well as a small scholarship account. My throat constricted as Mara and I both pressed our hands to our lips in tandem.

Sucking down a breath, I reminded myself not to get

excited until it was a done deal, but holy mother fucking shit.

"Do I keep the hiring process?"

Without missing a beat, Chris said, "Yes. I weeded out anyone who wouldn't budge on that. It's a school first. Mind you, they get a say because we can't have a Debby Downer or Bertha the Curmudgeon tanking ratings, but you get an ultimate sign off."

"Who determines scholarships?"

"Joint venture. But you get to field the first round and let them pick from the finalists based on camera tests and interviews. They want to pull some characters in, keep people engaged."

"What happens if the show gets canceled? Do we lose all of it?"

"This is why you're the CEO. First, there's no way you'd get canceled. I can already see the way you'd spin spotlights for female-owned businesses and then past students. The first few years, the funds are minimal as the school gets going—they'll document any necessary renovations, and setup, and then they ramp up once you have students prepping for graduation. That's when filming would start. The alternative would be poaching business students from major universities and dropping them into their senior years. But I told them you wouldn't like the first subjects being students who were primed by other educators. You'd want to highlight women who got the complete experience. Should something happen to the show, yes, we'd lose the allotted annual funding, but the building, the gear, that all stays."

Nodding, I blew out a heavy breath. This is what we'd been praying for. I just...never expected it to come in this form. It was that initial startup that was killing us. That was the thing about manifesting. It rarely arrived like you imagined it would. All I could do was send my intention into the universe and trust it would deliver what was meant for me.

This...this was so much more than I dared to ask for.

"Why aren't you more excited? Did you get down to the funding part of the proposal? The five-year plan?"

"What? No, not yet. Did you run this by Max?"

"Or risk getting his eyes plucked out? Of course he did," Max's voice was suddenly on the line. Throwing a hand up as if to say *what the fuck is this*, I glanced to Mara, finding a mirror of my bewilderment.

"Wait, are you two together?"

"No, Elly, my sweet summer child. He just patched me in. I went through the fine print last night."

"You know I have an agent for that, right?"

"And yet, you asked for me," he pointed out with no small bit of satisfaction.

"You did," Mara agreed, smirking. "Literally, just now."

"Okay, and you approve?" I pressed, somehow earning laughs from both men on this impromptu conference call.

"In spades, baby. This is it, El. This is that big break we've been waiting for. Hurry up and read through it, so we can all be on the same page."

I shook my head, puffing air into my cheeks before admitting, "I'm still trying to wrap my brain around this whole thing."

"Well, don't think too long," Chris cut in. "This is fucking brilliant, El. Not the thing you hem and haw about, you know? They're going to want an answer—"

I scrolled until I saw the numbers at the bottom, my heart a full throttle race horse as I blew out a long *phew*. Twice. Twice what I'd applied for—not just here, but total.

Which meant...we didn't need the grant if we took this. I could tell Johanna I withdrew, and at least based on the responses today, and our scores prior, that would leave Broderick in the lead. I adored Pierce and Cheyenne, but I loved Broderick more. My heart galloped harder. If Broderick could take this home to help the island's kids, *and* Mara and I got our funding...

Holy shit. My eyes locked on Mara's as she gave a decisive nod and mouthed 'fuck yeah.'

"Sure that's not a misprint, Chris? That is a lot of zeroes behind that nine."

SIXTEEN

BRODERICK

Too eager to sit still, I slowly paced the full circuit of the back of the ballroom, swishing the ice in my drink against the glass and watching the crowd as they all mingled. I'd never been much for *mingling*. But knowing there was no way Pierce's presentation earned him enough points to bypass El had me buzzing with anticipation as Johanna stepped on the stage. Dramatic music and a rapid dimming of lights silencing the crowd in a heartbeat.

She'd pushed back when I'd finally wrangled her into a meeting today, immensely displeased with my decision—swore I was miraculously in the lead—and was not shy about vocalizing it. But I watched with bated breath now, my focus rotating from where El was mingling with a group of people, to the woman holding the future in her hands.

I recognized Pierce, Cheyenne, and Mara, even in the dim lighting, but some twisted sense of hope bloomed in my chest when I realized El's head was still on a swivel. Was she...was she looking for me? It was stupid, but I hoped she was. Because I sure as shit kept my eyes on her.

"Well," Johanna said, clapping her hands to command

our attention, as if everyone wasn't waiting for this conclusion of our week together. "What an incredible event. Thank you to every single one of you for making it so special." Applause went up everywhere and I rolled my eyes. Applauding yourself for attending seemed asinine when there was an announcement actually worth making, but alright. "Thank you to our speakers." More clapping, more irritable, anxious pacing. "To all the contestants, and especially our top five. Thank you to the wizards behind the curtain. This event wouldn't be worth attending without our incredible IT team."

"For fuck's sake," I muttered to myself, earning a surprised side eye from one of the older attendees I'd chatted with at length. Gray, springy curls, dark skin, boring outfit and an equally bored expression. She stared at me for a moment before catching herself. But not before I grimaced and gave her an apologetic nod and wave.

Really, I was just trying to slow my breathing. It had to go to El. It's the only thing that would make it worth it. I should've cared about the sound crew and camera guys, the PA's and producers, the donors and ten million, six hundred thousand and forty-eight other fucking names she rattled off in her seemingly endless closing speech, but there was only one person—*one woman*—in this entire building that I gave a shit about and she was standing with her arm slung around Pierce fucking Christensen like they'd both be happy either way. Good for them. I wouldn't be happy unless this went one way. The right way. The way that gave my Pix the money she needed to chase this big, beautiful dream of hers. She was always built for greatness, and it was time the world saw it on a much larger scale.

"Without further ado—" *Fucking finally.* I froze midstride, my fist propping my head up, elbow braced on the arm beneath it. My oxygen supply amputated abruptly, eyes locked on Johanna, praying she really had proper brain cells in that pretty head of hers and hadn't gotten where she was based on a sex tape or some other scandalous method of acquiring fame I'd been too trusting to look into. "The winner of this decade's Leaders' in Thought Grant is..." Of course, they'd do a drum roll. *Jesus*. "Pierce and Cheyenne Christensen!"

Fuck. Me.

My eyes snapped to where I'd seen them last, though there was a dull roar of applause somewhere past the cotton in my ears. I spotted them. Right as El stopped patting his back in exchange for a tight hug with Cheyenne, that practiced, internet-approved smile on her beautiful face.

No. *No*. I didn't understand. She was light years ahead of them. This didn't make sense. This was *bullshit*. I wanted to demand a recount, but then they were making their way up onto the stage, and Elora was wheeling around on her heels. For a moment I thought it was toward the exit, but when her eyes found mine across the room, she froze, shoulders slumping as she offered an apologetic smile, like she was disappointed for *me*, instead of herself.

Of course she was.

I was in love with a saint, and she didn't even know it.

"HONESTLY, I don't know what his end goal was, but there we were, stuck bobbing in the south Pacific..."

Johanna King liked to talk. *A lot*. And was, evidently, immune to social cues because nothing about my grunts in response, or placid expression, seemed to tell her to *please fuck off* quite like I hoped they would. A handful of us had reconvened downstairs in one of the many hotel restaurants with a built-in bar, including dancing. Go figure. I wasn't sure what was making my mood worse, the woman to my right who was incapable of catching a hint, or the woman on the dance floor letting the store-brand Chris Hemsworth run his paws all over her waist as they laughed and spun the night away celebrating his asinine victory. Seriously. Who the hell did he fuck to beat Elora?

"Have you ever been?" Johanna chirped. Blinking, I just shook my head, rotating my glass on its rim. In all honesty, I lost track of where the hell she'd been in the most recent story of grand adventures somewhere after Hawai'i. Regardless, I hadn't really traveled much anywhere aside from Alaska, Washington, and Florida, so it was a safe wager to go with no. "Oh, you just *have to* make the time! It's enchanting!" she gushed as I knocked back the last of the whiskey. A dull throb formed behind my eyes, and I wondered if one could die of defeat. Spontaneous combustion would be ideal.

All of that strategizing and running in circles for nothing. I glanced up to where Pierce and El were dancing, and she winked at me from across the room before returning to their celebrations, as if all were well with the outcome of the day.

"And the food! My God, Broderick, you wouldn't believe it."

"Sounds amazing," I said simply. I was about to motion for the bartender, hoping to snag my tab and get the hell out of here, but a ball of infectious energy slunk onto the stool beside me, and I didn't have to turn to know El had just arrived.

"Miss Rhodes," Johanna chirped cordially, "looking

good out there!"

"Ahh! I'm so sweaty," El said as she fanned herself, grinning as our eyes locked. "Pierce is relentless."

Fucking Pierce.

"Wore her out, I'm afraid."

I closed my eyes at the sound of his voice, working to summon enough energy to be professional with the guy feeling up *my* Pix all night. Attempting to mimic a neutral expression, I turned to face him.

"Broderick, my man!" he exclaimed, reaching out to grasp my hand. I hated that he felt sincere. Like he gave a flying fuck about me when I'd just been envisioning tearing him off her. Maybe breaking his face. Jameson would've.

"Hey, congrats," I breathed.

"Thanks, buddy. Just gonna dance the night away, soak it up, do the whole Vegas thing before we gotta ship out to reality tomorrow morning."

"Nice," I said, bobbing my head and bringing my gaze back to my drink. I could feel El watching me intently, surprise pulling my attention sidelong again when he turned to our hostess.

"Miss King, I believe I owe you a dance!"

"I couldn't leave Broderick moping alone over here," she said, smiling in a way that made me feel wholly uncomfortable.

"I insist," Pierce said so kindly only a psychopath would turn him down.

"I'm not moping. Go have fun," I encouraged. "I was about to head out, anyway."

"*Boo*, party pooper," Johanna teased before smiling up at the victor himself, much to my relief. "Alright, I'll take you up on that offer."

And just like that, they skipped off to join the crowd of

strobe light infused, gyrating bodies. Knowingly, I turned on El, who was grinning victoriously. "Did you just ride to my rescue, Pix?"

She scooted in closer, bumping my elbow before she waved down the bartender. "You looked a bit cornered."

I glanced over my shoulder to make sure they were safely out of ear shot before admitting, "I *was*, holy hell, she can talk."

Elora laughed, shaking her head. "Some things don't change, huh?"

Fuck, how true that was. I studied her features for a minute, the sleek, petite lines of her face, and once-precise curls weighed down by one too many spins and a healthy sheen of sweat.

"Yeah. Some things," I agreed. Like how much I fucking wanted her. Even now, all these years later. Suddenly the condensation on my glass became immensely interesting, my thumb rubbing little windows clean on the cool surface.

"For example, there's still nobody I'd rather lick my wounds with," she added lightly, my gaze snapping over to that sweet smile. The same one she wore when we got in trouble as kids, like she knew it was wrong, but had deemed it worth it. Because we'd managed the mischief together. All I could think was I'd like to lick *something* but I managed to bite down on my need to say it, nodding instead.

"So," I said softly, "where's the magnanimous Elora Rhodes off to next?"

WE SPENT the next hour nursing our drinks as she ran me through her next few months of travel plans, and then asked me every imaginable question about this semester's workload, who my favorite students were, who was causing trouble, and who I expected to see the most out of. We talked about our families, although my two loving parents' hectic lives took a fraction of the time that recounting all eleven Rhodes siblings did. As if the sheer number of them didn't make it hard to keep track, the fact that at least half of them traveled for a living certainly did.

No matter how many tales we told, I still couldn't shake the lingering irritation that I'd bowed out of her way, only for Pierce to walk away with the money anyway. I'd been avoiding the subject, not wanting to add insult to injury, but the infuriating reality was niggling at my gut. "Look, El, I'm sorry about the results tonight. I—"

With an adorably wrinkled nose, she shook her head as she cut me off. "Enough talk of competition. It is what it is." She waved away the conversation, but I didn't miss the pinch in her brows. *Right. Don't rub salt in the wound, you idiot.* Elegantly, El swirled the last of her red wine before setting the glass down with a quiet thud that left no room for debate, then spun it by the stem. "You wanna get outta here?"

Still leaning back in my bar stool, I crossed one arm over my chest, the other braced against my jaw as I listened to her. I feigned thought for a moment. I didn't need to process that answer, but smiled and asked, "Where to, Rhodes?"

She shrugged, her cheeks flushing a bit, which did nothing to tamp down my need to touch her. "Maybe Pierce has the right idea."

"Sweaty, *untied tie* Pierce?" I said skeptically, amused, grinning as we both glanced at *Thor* himself, still dominating the dance floor. She giggled, staring at her empty glass before meeting my eyes with a spark in her own.

"I mean, neither of us are gonna drink away a loss alone. What are the chances the two of us will ever be in this city together again? Why not...*do Vegas?*"

My imagined version of 'doing Vegas' had more to do with one too many drinks and a humiliating Elvis-ordained wedding than slots and blackjack, but I never could say no to this woman.

"Alright," I agreed.

"Really?!" she squeaked, rising to her feet in an instant.

"Don't ruin it," I muttered, knocking back the last of my drink. I'd passed *pleasantly buzzed* about twenty minutes ago, now teetering precariously on *tipsy*. She mimed zipping her lips, and I chuckled as I slid my wallet from a back pocket to pay the tab. "What all does that entail, Pix?"

"Let's see, drinks—*check*. Maybe loitering behind old women and then stealing their slot machines?"

"You watch *Friends* too much."

"Come on, let me blow your dice."

I choked on my laugh, flicking a skeptical gaze her way. The bartender wordlessly took my credit card from me, vanishing to close out my tab. I wet my lips before saying, "That's what you're thinking about? Blowing on my *dice?*"

She grinned. But the part of me I was desperate to kill could have sworn there was a playful insinuation in her tone when she said, "It's a start."

With a theatrical sigh, I stood, grabbing my jacket off the back as she wiggled in her seat before doing the same. I motioned towards the front entrance and said, "Lead the way."

El threw her arms up in victory, a smile making her face glow. "To the Craps tables!"

SEVENTEEN
ELORA

"That's it. You're my lucky charm. I'm never letting you go, Pix."

I desperately tried to keep my walls up in the hours of drinks and laughter, of clasping his big hands in mine to blow into his cupped palms, hoping to bless his dice with luck. The blur of lights, bells, endless shouting speakers and cheers or groans of sloshed patrons surrounding tables all mixed into a chaotic concoction with the occasional moments of clarity. Moments like his hand sliding to the small of my back as we crossed the casino. Moments like his lips brushing my cheek after we won an impressive pile of chips. Moments like Broderick pulling me into one of the tacky gift shops and nudging me toward the tower of postcards.

I'd laughed and said, "Oh my gosh, *you remember!*" Because for several long, pathetic years, every new place my travels took me, I never forgot to send one home to him with a recount of the trip's highlights and a 'wish you were here'. He never wrote back. Just thanked me via text and we'd chat for a moment before he'd vanish again.

"I remember *everything*, Pix." Those were the words that cracked through my walls as I sheepishly stared up at him under my mascaraed lashes. Scrambling to stay in control, to stay lighthearted, to not waste this one opportunity to build memories with him, I scanned the assortment and snatched up the Bellagio with its beautifully illuminated fountains, waving it in the air in victory.

I remember everything, Pix. The words played on a loop right until we were standing in the cashier's cage, the sounds from all directions bombarding my senses, while his praise sailed full speed into my chest, and my pathetic defenses crumbled like castles made from Play-Doh after someone left the lid off the container. *I'm never letting you go, Pix.*

Broderick's eyes were no longer glossy with one too many fingers of scotch, and it was the clarity in his vision as he said it that threatened to destroy me. Just a stupid little girl, with my stupid childhood crush in a city full of lights and glamor, wishing he meant them like I wanted him to. Instead of saying any of that, I swallowed and smiled, ignoring that it felt watery even to me.

Clearing my throat, hoping the emotion would go with it, I asked, "How'd we do?"

"Made out like bandits. I mean, after the slots."

Laughing, I agreed, "Yeah, that sucked. Blackjack and Roulette too."

His brow pinched in the most adorable display of confusion as he tucked his wallet—our winnings, along with it—into his jacket pocket. I couldn't remember the last time I'd seen the man even remotely intoxicated. He was cute as hell. "I forgot we did that."

"Poker was decent."

"But not like Craps—should've just stayed there in the first place." His eyes narrowed in contemplative curiosity, and I canted my head, watching as he stretched his arm to pull his sleeve up. Eyes on his watch, he muttered, "Perfect."

"What?" I asked, confused but still grinning, and willing away the want in my chest in favor of a mask of entertainment.

"Come on."

"Come *where*?" I demanded petulantly, but when he stretched his hand out, I took it. At least if he iced me out this time, it would be from many, many miles away and I'd be none the wiser.

"Just humor me. Come on." Rolling my eyes, I followed Broderick's lead as he dragged my ass through and out of the casino on legs that still felt more like rubber than actual limbs. After a few crackling moments of silence, he asked, "Do you remember that year we were all camped out by the lake and got to see the Northern Lights?"

"Yeah?"

"Just...thinking about the two of us keeping each other warm under that blanket."

I snorted, shaking my head at the fondness in his voice. "You mean the night James almost decked you for 'fondling me'?"

"I *did not*," he insisted irritably, earning a laugh.

"Oh, I know. I was there, remember?" He'd actually been an infuriatingly perfect gentleman, hand firmly planted on *my arm*, as he tucked me against his side and we chattered into the chilly air together, refusing to call it a night and move into the tents away from the fire. For me, that had everything to do with the fact that I'd be sleeping with my sisters, and not the gorgeous twenty-one-year-old overwhelming my senses with his warm hug and cinnamon-laced scent. Not that Jameson saw it that way, the overprotective teddy bear he was. "Not gonna lie. I actually loved that Old Spice shit you wore."

"God, *that* was a phase."

"One of my favorites. That was the year I left Mistyvale." What I didn't say was *in no small part to get away from you.*

When Broderick opened the side door of the resort onto the bustling street, he glanced back to me, his eyes far away and pinched in the center, a heaviness to his tone when he spoke. "Believe me, I know."

Stepping out into the brisk evening, grateful we were in Nevada and not anywhere farther north where the air would bite this time of year, I squeezed his hand. Fairly certain he'd been avoiding me with the same level of dedication the last forty-eight hours, I softly asked, "Where you been, Professor? The last few days?"

"Thinking, Pix. A lot of thinking."

"Care to share with the class?" I pressed.

He shook his head, cheek curving with the tiniest of smirks. Somehow, my never-ending references to his career path had yet to get old. "Just you."

Two words. Two words weighed down with so much unspoken implication that my feet felt heavy with them. There was no way I imagined that. It was only his hand in mine, leading me down the strip, that kept me moving.

Voice gruff, he asked, "You remember the day you broke your arm?"

Surprised by his question, I nodded. I'd been fifteen and fell while bouldering with the guys. The look of resolute horror on his face as they made a makeshift bind for my agonized arm was permanently etched in my mind.

It was a different fear than my brothers showed. I'd known it then, just like I knew it now with the weight of those deep browns on my face, and tears pricked in my eyes. Fully incapable of holding that intense gaze, I looked to the concrete, even as he squeezed my fingers. I breathed a nervous laugh.

"You held my good hand all the way down the mountain. Held me in the back of Rhyett's truck. Wouldn't leave my side until they took me back for x-rays."

"That was the scariest day of my life. The idea of something hurting you—even back then—absolutely eviscerated me." My stupid, smitten brain got held up on the emphasis of the past tense. Like, somehow, he cared more now than then. But he was talking again, dragging my muddled brain and hammering heart right along with him. "The year you had braces, I didn't smile in a single group photo, so that you wouldn't be the only one hiding your teeth."

My cheeks flushed, eyes wide as I watched his profile, his gaze fixed ahead of us. Hell, I thought I'd imagined that. "I remember," I breathed, suddenly incapable of having enough oxygen to power proper words. *Where in the hell was he going with this?*

"When that blond douche, Brian Moretti, stood you up on prom night, I wanted to physically tear him limb from limb. Feed him to the sharks."

"You shoved him off the dock," I recalled, smiling softly and pushing my legs to keep up with his determined stride. I'd never seen Broderick move with this sense of urgency, unless he had a football in his hands. He powered each step with an unspoken purpose that I didn't understand.

A dark chuckle rumbled in his chest as he nodded. "I have countless screw ups in my life, El. I'm far from perfect

—kind of a fuck up, really." When my mouth popped open to protest, he whirled to face me, setting his warm fingers against my lips and instantly rendering me silent. "But the worst of them all has been hurting you."

"Brod—"

"I'm sorry," he cut me off, closing the distance as he brought those big hands to my arms, pulling me into him, soothing the length of them. We froze within the stream of the city, forcing the scattered pedestrians to split around us like an island in the flow of a river. "I never got a chance to tell you that. Never knew how to say it. But there it is— *I'm sorry*. I'm sorry for hurting you. First, during your junior prom."

Heat flushed my cheeks, the memory of his mouth on mine and hands on my body flooding the corners of my mind. God, I'd never been so thrilled with myself as I was in that moment. He was my *nirvana*...until he wasn't. He'd pulled away, muttering apologies for stepping out of line, and when I attempted to reassure him, he told me he should never have kissed a minor. A *minor*. Like I hadn't been in love with him since I knew what love was. Like we hadn't served as the other's safe harbor for years. That old ache echoed back at me as he studied my face, my mouth, finally locking on my eyes.

"Again, last summer, the day James got arrested. And every damn year in between." He stroked the gentlest caress down the length of my cheek, goosebumps rippling in his wake. Undeniable hunger filled those crisp brown eyes, shadowed by sadness. "*Sarah*. The gym this week. Taylor Swift." He shook his head, chin dipping. "So many screw ups."

Heart falling out my ass, I made to pull back, but panic flared across his face as it snapped to mine, and he wrapped an arm around my waist, pulling me to him, caging me against his hips as frantic eyes flicked between mine. His other hand suddenly forked through my hair, coming to cradle the back of my head and sending the air rushing between my parted lips. My startled hands settled against his chest.

"Broderick? What are you saying?" That was the thing about internal injuries. The physical ones would clot and bruise and web together over time. But the unseen ones? Those are forever. Those old scars smarted just the same as they had when he'd left them, and I stifled the hint of hope his words planted. I wasn't *allowed* to hope. Especially when he held me just like this days ago, only to vanish on me altogether. Not even as he held me, like he cradled the world in those broad palms.

Sheepish eyes dropped between us before coming back to trace my face, lingering on my mouth. "That I've been a coward, Pix. That I've been terrified for years."

"Terrified of *what*?" I wanted the words to come out like a demand, but the fear, the sincerity in his eyes robbed me of my strength, leaving in its stead a confused, desperate kind of want... A want reflected back to me in dark eyes, his pupils blown wide, and dropping to my lips.

"That I'm too late," he said as my hands slid over his where they cradled my face. A gentle thumb traced over my cheekbone. "That a better man would scoop you up and I'd never get to apologize or admit the truth of it. To tell you how fucking brave I think you are." Another stroke of my cheek that fueled my rapid-fire heart. "I'm scared I'll never get to tell you that your brothers have nearly killed me with this pact of theirs. That *every day* I see you and can't touch you is a slow kind of death." One warm palm eased down my neck as if he could coax me back into breathing where

I'd solidified to stone beneath his touch. Beneath the lunacy of the words hovering in the air between us. "I've been terrified of what would happen if I screwed everything up and let myself have you."

The world stopped. Tilted. Like we'd been submerged in water, the chaos of the street vanished and my entire body ignited under the intent in his gaze, the heat of our skin where it met. Because his forehead was resting on mine, his inhales robbing the air from my chest.

"Terrified to ask you to forgive me." His warm hands slid up and tilted my chin, our mouths nearly brushing before he leaned back, just an inch as if to search my eyes for an answer. He must have seen *something*, because he leaned back in, breath hot on my face as he said, "To ask you if there were no other factors, would you still want me?"

I gave a tiny, breathless nod...and then the world detonated. I hadn't even realized where he'd taken me until an enthusiastic symphony of saxophones blared to life on speakers *everywhere* as the enormous *Bellagio* fountains burst into synchronized dances to my left...and Broderick Allen ripped away every ounce of sense as his lips claimed mine.

Broderick

I KIND OF EXPECTED ONE of two things to happen when I kissed Elora Rhodes. One—she'd hesitantly kiss me back, more of a 'letting it happen' before letting me down easy. Easier than I'd let her down, at least. Two—she'd rear back, cock that arm like we taught her to, and ring my bell. Maybe tell me I was an idiot and missed my chance. Either reality seemed liable to happen, and I'd deemed the gamble worth taking.

What I didn't expect was for the world as I knew it to implode in her tiny fists where they gathered my shirt like she hung on for dear life. Frank Sinatra's *Luck Be a Lady* blared through the center of the strip as she raised on her toes, the full weight of her leaning into me like she was about to collapse. I pinned her against me. Wanting more. *Needing* more. I cupped the back of her head, fingers threading through her hair, urging her tighter against me. In the same heartbeat, she scraped her manicured nails beneath the hem of my shirt, and along the skin beneath. A shiver wracked my spine, and I nipped her bottom lip, swallowing her breathy moan that followed before running my tongue over it to soothe away any sting. El's nails dug into my oblique, her other hand cradling the back of my head as I tightened my fingers in her hair. El pressed her hips against mine, and I knew she could feel exactly how badly I needed her. Spine tugging, I barely groaned her name.

It was the abrupt crescendo of saxophones, the ensuing cutoff of the music from the speakers, finale of splashes, and round of applause for the show that peeled us apart. The same wild need burning me alive was shining in her steel-blues as a stunned kind of silence settled between us, and slowly, the growl of the city buzzed back into my consciousness.

She'd stolen away every sense when she returned my kiss like her life depended on it. Chest heaving, unable to stifle my smile, I breathed, "Hey, baby."

Her response was an uncharacteristically tentative smile back, and breathy, "Need you," and then she snatched my hand and was pulling me back toward our hotel. For the first time in our life, I felt no guilt watching the sway of her hips and pert, perfect ass.

It wasn't until we were trapped in an elevator with a middle-aged Japanese man in a slick suit who kept nervously looking between us like the tension was palpable that I finally got my heart rate—and hard on—under control. I cleared my throat, giving him a curt smile and nod. All the while, I was fully aware the pull between us felt like electricity popping off in the air. Poor guy skirted out the doors the instant they opened, and El impatiently jabbed at the button to close them until they finally banged shut. Which, admittedly, felt pretty damn good, knowing she was just as desperate to get back to me as I was to her.

Even better when she turned, still looking stunned… and absolutely edible. In the next beat, she closed the distance, leaving the last few inches for me, like she was giving me space to change my mind.

Instead, I bent to grab her ass—and *fuck me*. She was perfect. Strong and round and just small enough for me to hoist into the air. El immediately complied, wrapping me in those shapely thighs and descending on my mouth with the same fervor from the fountain. I backed her into the mirrored wall as the elevator climbed, yellow fluorescents flickering softly as they buzzed. I was too busy to care. Tasting, teasing, tugging at those soft lips until her tongue slid into my mouth. She held me tight between her legs, like if she released me, I might vanish. I echoed the sentiment, palm in a desperate rush over every inch I could reach. The feel and flavor of her engraved themselves into my memory eternally. Along with her desperate, breathless voice.

"*Broderick.*"

I pulled back to study her, checking in and finding her just as taken as I was. Her flushed cheeks, swollen, parted pink lips, wide eyes, and dark, fluttering lashes all shot the last drops of blood from my body to my cock. Fucker was already painfully hard as I claimed her mouth again, one hand roaming while the other arm held her up. Her hands were everywhere, but as the elevator slowed, they came to my shirt, fumbling with the collar, and then the first button. Second. *Third*. All without breaking the kiss.

When the doors whooshed open, she made to disentangle. But I shook my head.

"Someone could see us," she panted, and I grinned against her mouth as I carried her down the hallway.

"Don't care," I breathed back, earning a nervous laugh that I swallowed a beat later. Somehow, we managed our way down the hallway and into our room without setting her down. She had at least half my buttons out of the way when the door clicked behind us, the lock buzzing closed by the time we hit the bed.

With her splayed out beneath me, chest heaving, eyes tracing my partially exposed torso, I shook my head, smiling in disbelief. Reverently sliding my palms down her sides, I trailed the length of her gorgeous, muscled legs, and hooked her shoes free, dropping them to the floor as her sharp eyes tracked the movements.

Praying she didn't change her mind, I demanded, "Tell me you want this."

She nodded, and for a breath, I thought she wouldn't speak, but she managed a quiet, "I need you. *This*. I need this." Her feet hooked behind my back again, pulling me onto her.

"Too many clothes," I complained, slipping my hands beneath the hem of her loose pants, sliding them down as she laughed.

"I agree," she breathed back, fingers snatching the edge

of my shirt. But instead of continuing to free the buttons, she slid her hands flat, roaming up my chest as her eyes followed, and then yanked me sideways with her legs. Laughing, I rolled with her, certainly not complaining about the goddess looking down at me with lust-hooded eyes and a curtain of hair draped over a shoulder.

She smirked in a way that could *only* spell trouble, and before I could reach her wrists, or utter a warning, popped my button-up apart in one demanding yank, sending buttons flying and skittering across some hard surface.

"*You—*" my complaint was silenced when she lunged to kiss me, the words lost on her lips.

"Faster," she said against my mouth. I rolled us back, pinning her beneath me this time. It didn't stop her from tearing the shirt off my arms as I ripped the flimsy fabric from her top, revealing what I assumed was a very expensive bra to match her black thong. And a body I'd never dared to let myself admire. Long. Athletic. A purple gem glinting on her belly button ring.

"You're so damn beautiful." I palmed her narrow waist, thumb tracing the line of her abs before making my way to her soaked center. My head fell back at the slick feel of her pussy against my fingers.

Thumbing aside the thin scrap of lace fabric, I said, "Look at you, so wet and needy *for me*."

"It was *always* you," she panted back, no small trace of desperation in her voice. Every inch of my body froze, gaze slowly tracking away from that perfect pink pussy, up the defined lines of her body to her face, where her eyes mirrored every ounce of weight she'd placed in those words. Refusing to let go of her, I kept a palm against her clit, the other braced on the bed as I dove for her mouth. El's hands wrapped around either side of my neck, taking my demanding kiss and pulling me tighter, a near bruising pressure.

It wasn't enough. Could never be enough. I nudged her jaw aside to lick and nip and suck down the line of her neck. Needing to taste all of her.

"*Please*, Broderick," she said on a trembling breath. That was all it took for me to thrust one finger into her wet heat. Her head rolled, back arching and exposing more of her neck for me to lick and kiss and claim.

"Fuck, Pix, you're so tight." Her moan was all I got in response as I added a second finger, curling them as I kissed down her collar, her chest. Memorizing her lines. I shoved away the bra and sucked one perfect nipple into my mouth. Her answering gasp shot straight to my cock.

Five minutes in, and Elora had my dick weeping like some college kid finally getting his first lay. I needed this to last. Needed to impress her. Prove we were worth the wait. But fuck, she was *perfect*. Coming undone beneath my hands, those little whimpers and moans destroying my resolve.

One hand curling two fingers inside her while the other worked her needy, swollen clit in gentle little circles.

"More...clit," she panted desperately.

Smirking, I arched one brow, but complied, shaking my head. "Fucking hell, you're *still bossy* when I fuck you?"

"*Especially* then," she huffed through a giggle.

"Mmm," I hummed thoughtfully, adjusting until her body arched, eyes rolling back as I increased the intensity. Fuck, she looked good coming undone beneath me. "Funny, I don't mind it so much at the moment," I noted. She smiled until her breath hitched in three quick pants. When her legs fought me, thighs shaking, I eased just enough to keep her writhing without taking her too far. "Tell me what you like, baby. Slow and sweet?" She shook her head, unable to open her eyes even as my smile grew. "Needy little thing. Faster?" Another head shake. "Harder?" I guessed again without shifting the pressure. She gave me another 'no', and I canted my head as lust-leaden eyes found mine.

"You're perfect...I need your cock."

It twitched in response, aching and heavy for her. I knew she'd find my head slick with pre-cum when I finally freed it. "Not yet." Her pout came to an immediate halt when I leaned down and roughly sucked that nipple into my mouth. "I've waited over a decade to have you, baby. I wanna take my time with you. I want you dripping down your thighs for me—want to make you come so hard that you don't think you can give me another. *That's* when I get to fuck you, baby. And I want you to finish while screaming my name, so this whole damn hotel knows who makes you feel this good."

And with that last promise, she did just that. Head thrown back, body clamping down around my fingers, Elora gave a breathless cry. *Just my name.*

"Broderick!"

EIGHTEEN
ELORA

"Holy...hell," I panted as Broderick lowered his body onto mine, the weight so delicious my eyes closed as I soaked up every inch of skin contact. Had I ever come that hard? I didn't know a woman *could* come that hard. Like I physically shattered around his hand before he put me back together with gentle caresses and gentler kisses. It was his promise-laced words, as much as the physical pleasure that unraveled me entirely. Like a cheap damn rug, and he ran off with the frayed edges and left me in tatters.

Only...he *didn't* leave... Instead, when I peeled my heavy lids open, the deepest brown eyes were looking down at me with a kind of admiration I'd only ever dreamed of. Like I'd just rocked his world instead of the other way around. His warm, broad hands took turns brushing the hair from my sweat-slicked face in adoration before cradling it between them, gaze roving over me like he couldn't get enough. Couldn't bear to look away. Like I was every ounce as precious–as *wanted*–to him as he had always been to me.

Dazed and panting, I raised a hand to cradle his face,

stilling when he turned to bite into my palm before kissing it. Tears burned in my eyes as I stared up at the man who had owned my mind and body since before I had a right to love him. When he turned his attention to my face, the sentiment was reflected back, his eyes closing as he pressed more languid kisses into my palm.

"Hey baby," he said as a low chuckle rumbled in his chest, a rare cocky smirk hooking his lips. "I could get used to watching you shatter for me like that."

"You're cute when you're smug," I teased, instantly rewarded with the full wattage smile that few ever saw. Fuck, he was gorgeous. Having evidently granted me enough time to catch my breath, Broderick captured my lips, my hands flying to wrap around his back, and feeling the muscles bunch as he ground against my hips. Goosebumps pricked across my skin when he ran his nose over the length of my cheek, his warm breath a caress of its own. I traced down the long, lean lines of his body until I hit the damn belt between us, fingering along the edge of leather until I slipped between our bodies to unfasten the thing. He rocked us together again, my body coiling as if he hadn't *just* released all that pressure.

For all his big talk about wringing me dry, when I whimpered, "Please?" his cheek just twitched, and he popped his hips up into plank to make it easier for me to shimmy his pants below that tight curve of his toned ass. When his cock sprang free, my eyes dropped between us because fuck, he was big. *Long*, thick and veiny. I salivated just looking at him. Breath coming a little faster, I looked up, locking on his gaze as I wrapped that steely, tantalizing length in my fingers. It was the moment my thumb ran over the slick head, spreading that bead of pre-cum, that a shudder ran through his body, eyes sliding shut.

I peacocked internally as a sigh rumbled through him. "Dammit, El. Your touch is incredible." He reared back, glancing around and patting at the pocket of his half-discarded pants before his eyes slid shut in frustration and he muttered something inaudible that sounded a lot like a curse. I laughed morbidly as realization dawned.

"You don't have condoms?"

"I certainly had no interest in bringing someone else into this room, and thought it was good insurance to not break the pact."

"Fuck the pact."

He winced, but joked, "*What happens in Vegas*, right?"

"Fuck me, Broderick. Just us."

His eyes rounded in surprise. "What?"

"I'm protected and all clear, and I trust you."

For the first time, he seemed hesitant, lips popping open as he said, "El, there's a lot we can do together and I'm not asking you to give me that."

"*You're* not asking. I am. *Fuck me*, Broderick. Please. I've wanted to feel you since I was seventeen, and like hell am I waiting to find a fucking condom if you say you want me back."

His full lips fell open as his eyes searched mine, and then he was moving, nipping down my body line before the flat of his tongue licked straight up my soaked center, sending shudders of pleasure up my spine.

"You taste so damn good. I don't know what I want first."

"I can relate." That was all she wrote. If for no other reason than Broderick Allen was fucking me with his mouth, a blunt finger sliding home again.

"Soaked for me," he muttered, almost reverently, before sucking my clit between his lips, sending my back arching.

He slipped another finger into me, licking, sucking, pulling, eviscerating my ability to articulate as pleasure wracked tremors through my limbs. I grasped at his muscled shoulders, the sheets, my own desperate body. "Damnably perfect—I never stood a chance," he growled as my hands found my breasts, palming them over the fabric of my bra. "Sit up," he ordered, abruptly standing and stripping the pants and briefs from his legs, where I'd abandoned them. My thighs tightened at the demand in his tone, and I did what he asked, curious to see where this was going. "Bra–off."

Well. Fuck me sideways. The girls always said it was the quiet ones that blew the roof off. "Mmm, sexy, bossy Broderick does things to me."

"He's about to," he countered as I contorted to unclip my bra. When I slid the final strap aside, freeing my breasts with a little bob, his nostrils flared, gaze darkening as his eyes looked over me. And I finally let my eyes drop down the length of him. All six feet of glorious, warm umber skin stretched over muscles that demanded I memorize their lines with the tip of my tongue. Goosebumps pebbled my flesh, and it had nothing to do with the purr of the heater kicking on in a gust of chill wind.

"Of course, you're fucking perfect," I muttered as I traced the outline of those muscled thighs, a gorgeous adonis belt, and a dick so proud it looked almost painful. Some primal part of me preened at that. That *I* did that to him. I needed it in my mouth like I needed my next breath. Slowly, watching his eyes for any reaction, I sat up and poured myself onto the floor at his feet.

"Oh, fuck me," he muttered as I tossed my hair behind my shoulders and gripped his erection.

Chuckling darkly, I said, "That is the idea, Professor. Suck you off, let you fuck my throat."

"Jesus Christ," he snarled, dropping his head back to look skyward, hands settling against my cheeks like he couldn't *not* have his hands on me. I knew the feeling. "*That mouth.*"

I gave him a wicked smile a beat before I wrapped my lips around his cock and sucked him deep, savoring the salty bead of pre-cum and throaty growl I earned in one blunt motion. Wrapping his fist in my hair, Broderick acted as a guide, but it was my turn to growl when he *slowed me down*, a hand resting on the side of my face as I pulled him to the back of my throat.

"*Easy, Pix.* The first time I come, it'll be in your perfect pussy, not your mouth."

I nodded as much as possible around a mouthful of cock. And then slid down as fast and hard as I could until he hit the back of my throat, my eyes watering as I gagged. Fighting against the reflex, I pulled him in again, my cheeks hollowing out as I urged my jaw to relax, to fit all of him, as futile as the effort might be. That hand wrapped in my hair tightened as his thighs clenched, and I pressed my tongue into the base of him, nails digging into his perfect ass before sliding back off with a little *pop*.

"Stand up," he ordered, but his hands were already scooping beneath my arms, hoisting me to my feet so he could devour me wholly. "Need you. On the bed. Hands and knees."

Nodding, I stole one last decadent kiss, our lips swollen with lust and sex, skin glistening with sweat. I turned over, crawling up onto the bed, the stiff white sheets crinkling beneath my hands and knees.

"Ass up, baby." Broderick's decadent hands wrapped

around my waist, halting my movement, and pulling my ass against his hips, where he stood at the end of the bed. But then his entire body went rigid, a sharp intake of breath the only sound in the silence as one warm hand slid up my spine before veering left to my ribs, tracing the line the bra left on my skin.

"What's this?" he asked, that rich baritone raked over coals. I smiled softly, not needing to glance back to know which tattoo his fingers found on my trap, where it hid beneath the straps of bras and bikinis. Just for me.

"Wildflowers," he croaked, the gravel in his voice betraying the emotions that penetrated his lust as his fingers firmly traced the outline of the word, the spirals of vine and Alaskan wildflowers that sprang away from the lettering. Every drive out the road, late night beach bonfire, stolen hike, front porch sunrise, and cuddle under the northern lights played through my mind. Because we always played Tom Petty when it was the two of us. It was the sound of home.

"Baby," he breathed, and I knew better than to glance back as vulnerability washed over me. But I did, finding his full lips parted in awe. In the next heartbeat, he dove forward, his fingers wrapping around my jaw and pulling me over my shoulder to claim my mouth. His hand snaked between us, notching his cock with my entrance. In and out, he teased with just the head, sending shivers up my spine as his breath traced my neck.

"You were always supposed to be mine," he whispered, and then thrust forward in one smooth motion, sending every scrap of air out of my lungs. Leisurely, as if we had all the time in the world, Broderick slid back, before rocking his hips forward, halting when he met resistance, sending my body trembling.

"So damn full," I gasped, convinced he'd just stretched me to my max.

"Almost there, baby. You gotta relax."

"What?" I squeaked. "*Christ,* Brod."

"Never thought about the challenge of you being tiny until now," he muttered, and I laughed, my core clamping down and earning a satisfying pulse of his cock. A victorious smile split my cheeks when he growled, "*Don't* fucking do that. I'm not done with you."

Smirking, I stifled my laughter, trying to relax instead, but God, it wasn't easy. "Never," I said, smiling as his hands roamed down the length of me. At least, right until he impaled me on that miraculous weapon of a dick. Air was a foreign concept. *Everything* trembled. Delicious ache and pleasure danced in my core. There was well equipped, and then there was Broderick motherfucking Allen.

"Broderick!" I cried out, fighting to brace myself as he filled me entirely, every damn wall aware of each glorious inch of him.

"That's it, baby. That's *my* girl—finally taking all of me." A low groan rumbled from him, and then he was shifting, picking up a slow rhythm, like he was easing me into it. "Your pretty little pussy looks so good stretched around me. I wish you could see what I see."

"Enjoying the view?"

"Abso-fucking-lutely," he growled before clapping my ass, and then soothing the sting with a gentle caress. Then his fingers were digging into my hips, owning my body as he scraped them up my frame.

There were no words. Just a shaking nod. We spent our lives lost to the world, always wishing we could just get lost in each other, and miraculously, it was an even more magnificent sensation than I'd even imagined. *He* was more magnificent than I'd imagined.

"That's my girl," he said again, each syllable dripping with pride and lust and something that felt a lot like love. Nope. Wasn't going there. Too soon. "My clever, beautiful, sexy girl." The snap of his hips picked up tempo, and I threw my head back as he filled me to the brink. I arched into him, tilting my ass up in offering, somehow needing more, even as he bottomed out. Impossibly full. *Achingly* full. In all those fantasies, it was never like this. This *desperate*. This divine. My body sang as he ran his hands roughly over every inch, slowly sliding home like we'd been carved of the same stone. Urging my body to adjust around him.

"You won't break me," I promised, and his dark chuckle rumbled through me. Broderick wound his hand into my hair again, tugging my head back with a delicious sting. When he finally started thrusting, I breathed a desperate, "*Yes!*"

Just like that, he severed the outside world. All he left was bruising pleasure, the tickle of sweat on my body, and the slap of his skin against mine. The obscene, wet slide of our bodies mixing with my desperate moans and his pants and grunts. And I got lost in him. Lost to Broderick Allen. The man I always wanted but never believed I'd have. The man who held my soul in his beautiful, gentle hands. Gentle hands that were deliciously *not* gentle as they wreaked havoc on my nervous system, running over every inch of skin, tweaking my nipples, slapping my ass between demanding thrusts that stole my breath. Again and again, he relentlessly jackhammered into me like our lives depended on his performance. One hand in my hair, the other slid up to tweak my nipple, and I cried out as the combination of sensations overwhelmed me.

"You close? Fuuuck, I'm close," he panted, dropping that hand down to play with my clit, applying just the right amount of pressure. The other shoved me forward, the side of my face collapsing to the mattress as he hammered home. Expertly working my clit as though he'd memorized what my body liked in the first round, now masterfully driving me to madness.

"Yes!" I cried.

"Good. Come with me, baby."

"Yes!" I moaned again. And then he was swelling against my walls, the sensations impossibly intense. He picked up the pace against that throbbing bundle of nerves as release barreled forward. More. "I need—"

"I know. I've got you, Pix." His tone was guttural–a primal kind of growl as he obliterated me, pleasure overwhelming my senses, sending tingles through my body to the roof of my mouth. Fingers digging into my hips, he growled, *"Mine."*

"Yours," I sobbed back as that claim shattered me. And together, we hurtled over the edge into the abyss of euphoria below.

At some point, he eased me onto the mattress and wrapped my body in his, those strong, dark arms pinning me against him, his breath hot on my neck. My head was spinning, body limp and numb, soul singing an incandescent serenade only he had ever coaxed from it. Sex had never been like *that*. That was an...*out-of-body* kind of bliss.

The oxygen was finally finding its way into my lungs, our skin just beginning to dry when he breathed, "El?"

"Yeah?"

"What if I don't want this to stay in Vegas?"

BRODERICK

ELORA'S SKIN pebbled beneath my touch, although I wasn't sure if it was my fingers on her spine or the question I'd left hanging between us. I ran a thumb over the word *wildflowers* formed by fireweed, lupin, and the aggressive wooded vines our island was known for. She'd tattooed our song on her body. I'd been in love with this woman since we were teenagers, and she'd *inked* our favorite song on her skin. I'd known from the beginning if I let myself taste her, there would be no stopping.

I couldn't even blame the whiskey, or Vegas, or anything else that happened tonight. Sober as a preacher on Sunday morning, I took what wasn't supposed to be mine. There wasn't an ounce of guilt left, even as her bewildered eyes found me. Everything about her felt...right. Like we just fit. Like we'd always been.

Her lips were parted slightly, gaze still heavy with echoes of pleasure. I could eat her out for the rest of the night, and it wouldn't be enough. Nothing temporary would. I needed Elora Rhodes like I needed the air in my lungs, and one taste would never be enough.

El eased onto her back, her hand naturally coming to settle against my cheek. Her evaluation made me want to shrink into myself, but I held her gaze, my fingers trailing along her ribcage, memorizing the lines of her breasts. Slowly soothed the side of her ass where my handprint was still pink. She was so sinfully sexy, it shouldn't be legal.

"What do you want, Brod? We didn't really...talk much." Uncharacteristic vulnerability laced her tone, gutting me. Because there was fear in her voice. And with good reason. I'd given her *nothing* beyond admitting I wanted her.

"*You*, Pix." I answered simply, pausing that featherlight caress and allowing my palm to slide up and settle in the well between her breasts. "It's always been you."

"What would that even look like?" She breathed before her jaw tightened, like she was bracing for disappointment. I hated myself for planting that in her. Hated that I'd retreated inside my skull for years, that I hid behind my loyalty to her brothers for so long she was blatantly preparing for me to fuck this up. I deserved the trepidation in her eyes. Even if it shredded me. It might take a lifetime to make it up to her, but I decided right then that I would.

Fighting to swallow, I shrugged a shoulder, opting to answer truthfully. "I don't know, baby. But I know I'm sick and tired of trying to not want you. Sick and tired of not holding you, of not coming home to see your smile or hear your voice. Your laugh. Of lying to the people that matter the most to me about how much you mean to me."

Nodding, she rolled her lower lip between her teeth, and I raised a hand to her face, thumb freeing it before I leaned over to brush my lips over hers. We weren't feral this time. The touch gentle and...almost aching.

"What about my brothers?" she breathed shakily when I freed her mouth, leaning our foreheads together.

"Fuck it, baby. I can't keep this from them anymore. I just...I can't. Not *now*."

A relieved puff of air hit my lips, and then she tilted her chin, stealing sweet kisses. *Leisurely* kisses. Not the kiss you share with someone you love who's getting on a plane in twelve hours.

"You know," she finally breathed, "I've waited my

entire adult life to hear you say something like that." The way the end of her sentence went quiet had my gut nose diving.

"Why do I hear a 'but'?"

"But...what are we doing? What do you want from me—from us?" She lifted onto her elbows, and I ran my palm down her torso to her hip, turning her into me. Needing her closer. Needing to stay tangled up in her toned legs. "How would this even work? I travel full-time. Hell, I can't even remember the last time I stayed in my apartment for more than three consecutive nights. Getting home to Alaska happens less every year, especially since my parents retired in Florida. And you...you *are* Mistyvale." Her gentle stroke against my stubble did nothing to ease the ache of the truth in those words.

The bridge of my nose stung, so I took a minute to tighten my grip on her hip, to admire the blooming hickey I'd inflicted at some point on her neck, down to the faint pink tinge of stubble burn on her thigh, where she had it draped over my leg. I loved seeing her disheveled like this. Evidence of my touch everywhere.

That didn't stop the dread pooling in my stomach. I pulled my eyes back to her face, stroking a lazy line up her side. "What are you saying, Pix? This is just a one-night thing?"

"I don't know."

My chest went tight, so I cleared my throat. "What *do* you know?" I prompted gently, trailing my fingers down her bicep.

"That you don't enjoy rocking the boat. That telling my brothers about this—about us, *whatever* that means—would *seriously* rock the boat. And that I don't want you to risk losing them over whatever this is unless we know it's gonna stick." She shrugged like that suggestion wasn't just a new form of torture.

"You asking me to lie to them, Pix?"

"I'm just... you guys made that dumb rule so that you weren't alienated if things didn't go right. We're both mature adults—certainly too old to make drama. I'm never home to intrude on your space, anyway. So, let's make sure it's going right and *then* worry about telling them about our private lives."

"A lie of omission is still a lie, El."

"We've both been bullshitting them for years as it is. Why is this different?"

"Because that was out of loyalty," I dipped to press kisses to her sternum, and each side of her collar bones before leaning back and finishing the thought. "And this feels... like a betrayal."

"So, don't then." She shrugged. But in the next breath, she brought her fingers to trace my ribs as she added, "I just don't want to be why you three fall out if this isn't a forever thing."

"And if it *is* a forever thing?" I countered, not missing the tiny twitch at the corner of her lips. I rolled my body over hers, and she laid down, smiling when I cradled her face in my palms, pressing kisses to her forehead, the tip of her nose.

Breathily, she said, "Then we cross that bridge when we get to it. Tell them together. I just want to take our time figuring all the answers out as just us first. Does that make sense?"

It did. And *didn't*. My stomach did that uncomfortable flip flop that meant I was toeing the line of wrong and right. But when El tilted her chin to press her lips to mine, she silenced that unease. Silenced the world. Because the woman of my dreams wanted me back, and that had to be enough. "For now, just... let me worship you."

Her concerns seemed to vanish as I slid down her body, hands roaming, dropping kisses along the way until I could bury my face between her legs again.

NINETEEN
ELORA

Once we'd rung ourselves dry, Broderick used one deft finger to scoop his cum *back inside me* in some primal unspoken laying of claim. Perverse, filthy, and toe-curlingly delicious. I *loved* it. Loved knowing our bodies had melded entirely. Loved his sly smile as his insatiable eyes followed the lines of my body to my face. My bones went liquid. I was lying in a pool of my own sweat, acutely aware of the skin his fingers had just set alight before he eased off the bed to the bathroom. It was there that my spinning mind came to a very important conclusion: I'd never really lived until my lifelong flame had orgasmed fifteen years of pent-up angst and desire out of my body in one sitting. Like we were a bomb that needed to be defused before it detonated, and we'd watched that ticker count down to the last possible second. The most adoring praise always followed his filthy words. That approbation, combined with his skilled, oh-so-responsive fingers and a cock the gods would envy, reduced me to an incoherent puddle of languid limbs draped across sheets that smelled like *us*.

That smelled like *him*.

"Hey, baby," he whispered huskily as he lowered his body around me and I inhaled deeply, soaking up the scent of lust and home and unadulterated bliss. Two simple words wielded so confidently, and he had me swooning even in my unresponsive pool of vibrating euphoria.

"*Mmmm*," I practically purred as his warmth enveloped me. It was as close as I was getting to a word. Seriously, who attached anvils to my eyelids? Because they couldn't remember how to open. I knew I loved the man—knew every poor fucker that tried to date me had been unfairly held against his flame—but this was fucking ridiculous. Who knew concealed under the ties and tweed, the recited Proust and Kant, lay a delicious lover just waiting to devastate me? To ruin me for anyone else.

But as his warm arm wrapped around my waist, his face gently nuzzling into my neck, and my ass wriggling into his dick, I hummed contentedly. Because yeah, Broderick could fuck better than a porn star, but I'd never felt so... *cherished*. He'd gotten me off, then cleaned me up. I returned the favor, and we laid there, just reminiscing. Slowly, tenderly, he shifted his body over mine, cradling my face as he peppered it in kisses before we made love. The sweetest, most intimate kind of love. The deep-in-my-core, only-in-movies kind of sex I'd never known. We cuddled, ordered room service, ate, laughed, and talked about dreams... and then he came back for more, like he could never get enough.

Which was a relief because I knew I could never get enough. He was right. Whatever this was, it would not stay in Las Vegas. How could that thrill me just as much as it terrified me?

"You hungry?" he whispered groggily against my dewy skin.

"Mmmmm," I hummed. Maybe? I couldn't locate my stomach to check in. That quiet laugh raked over my overloaded senses.

"Is that a yes, Pix?"

"*Mmmph.*"

"I'll just go with yes to be safe." He kissed my cheek, my neck, my shoulder, then bit into the sensitive skin where the two met. Smart man. How was he still so damn coherent? He'd emptied me of lust and brain cells in one go. When he leaned away, some desperate part of me wanted to protest. But even as he shifted on mattress springs that squeaked subtly, my body melded further into the sheets, breath a little deeper as I settled into this contentment.

It seemed like no time had passed before he was nudging me out of my stupor. My nose was the first part of my body to come online.

"Is that...bacon and brie?" I questioned, perplexed, as I peeled back heavy eyelids.

"Fanciest grilled cheese of your life, with marmalade on sourdough. Complete with a tomato bisque that smells amazing, if I say so myself."

"Jesus," I muttered, blinking and rubbing at my sleepy eyes as he chuckled.

"I also grabbed a basket of hot wings and a steak fajita quesadilla just to be safe."

"I ever tell you that you're too good for me, Mr. Allen?"

His smirk infected every syllable as he said, "Just fighting to be good enough, Pix." The smorgasbord spread over the mussed sheets was enough for at least four people, and I'd never felt so much love for one person.

"Food is my love language," I admitted as I stretched out grabby hands for the fancy brie and bacon grilled cheese. Because why the fuck not?

Broderick chuckled a simple, "I know," and handed me the plate. The first bite sent me moaning, head lolling back against the headboard, my reaction making him laugh harder. "And here I thought I was the only one who could elicit that sound from your mouth."

"To be fair," I said, covering said mouth as I reached for a water bottle. "You *are* still responsible. It's just not your dick I'm swallowing this time."

"Jesus Christ," he muttered, but I saw the smile as he dropped his face and palmed the back of his neck. "*Your mouth*, Pix."

"Seemed like you were a pretty big fan of it about an hour ago."

"Woman, you will be the death of me." That sent me laughing, fighting not to choke on my mouthful of decadent sandwich, which only seemed to amuse him more. "Only Sin City delivers five-star room service in the middle of the night."

It was as he popped the clear lid off the Styrofoam quart, the scent of tomato and cheese wafting my way as he held it out to me that I breathed, "Viva Las Vegas."

ONCE WE FULLY SATISFIED OUR appetites, Broderick cleared the leftovers into the fridge. "This will make for the weirdest breakfast spread on record."

I snorted, shaking my head. "If you think this is the first time I'll eat hot wings for breakfast, you're sadly mistaken."

"Medical marvel," he grumbled, eyeing me up and down. It was the first time I saw his eyes on me without a trace of embarrassment...only...*appreciation* in his gaze. And damn, if that didn't feel exquisite.

"They're having me studied," I teased as he sat back down beside me. "For *science*, obviously."

"Obviously."

"Metabolic wonder woman."

"Sure it's not a psych ward for illusions of grandeur?"

"*You're* a psych ward," I retorted, scowling and sending him chuckling into his palm. "Honestly, though, some women work out to look good. I work out so I can *eat*," I groaned.

"You've always looked good to me."

I bit my lip, shaking my head as he eyed me up and down like I didn't just stuff my face like I was about to be put to death. "Ready to pass out?"

Broderick grinned but stood abruptly. "Hang on. One last bucket list item."

"Are we dying?"

"Slowly but surely," he said with a smirk before vanishing... into the bathroom? The crash of water confirmed my suspicion, but I still furrowed my brows skeptically as his head popped back around the corner. "Coming, Pix?"

"To take a bath?"

"Humor me," he called back. Shaking my head, I rounded the corner to a very-naked Broderick, thoroughly appreciating that perky backside as he stepped into the immense tub. When he caught me ogling, his brows winged up.

"Appreciating the view?" he asked, throwing my previous words back at me.

"Abso-fucking-lutely."

If I wasn't braced for it, his smile could have knocked me on my ass. "Come on, baby. Let me take care of you."

Well, how was a woman supposed to say no to that? Smiling to myself, I accepted his outstretched hand and gingerly stepped into the hot water. When we were both safely seated, I leaned back into his chest, his legs settling to either side of my hips as those broad hands wrapped around me, giving my breasts a little squeeze before dunking a washcloth and running it across my decolletage. Heaven. I'd survived the week of hell and ended it in heaven. Once he'd painstakingly washed me down, my hair included, Broderick relaxed into the bubbles, pulling me against him and weaving our fingers together. My light tan was in stark contrast to his rich, warm brown. He sighed blissfully, bringing our threaded fingers to my chest. Chills coasted over my skin when he leaned in to whisper in my ear.

"Pierce may have won the grant, but I promise you, I'm the one walking away with the greatest prize, baby. You're all I ever wanted, and never dared to ask for."

"SO... WE'LL TALK?"

"Yeah," I agreed cheerily the following morning, even though nothing in my body was remotely cheery. Our sex-a-thon gave way to the brutal reality that we were flying to two very different cities today. I was standing outside the gate for Seattle, staring at the man I always wanted, and only finally tasted, wishing his flight had room for me. It didn't. He'd checked first thing this morning and again when we checked in for our respective departures. Broderick had classes on Monday, and I had a meeting with the team tomorrow after Chris wrapped up church. So, there was no delaying the inevitable. He had his duffle thrown over his shoulder, fingers hooked in mine, his other hand cradling the back of my neck.

Seeing right through my facade, Broderick hooked his finger beneath my chin, lifting it and bringing his mouth to mine in a caress that felt way too much like goodbye for my liking.

Everything ached. And it wasn't just the fact that I was walking like an old west cowboy who'd ridden their steed for too long. I'd never understood why women talked about holding a cold soda can between their legs until Broderick eviscerated me wholeheartedly. Sounded like it might soothe at this point. It was this soul-deep fracture through my chest. Because I didn't want to let go of his wrists, where I'd wrapped my fingers around them, trapping his broad hands cradling my face.

Eyes stinging, I decided closing them was safest as I leaned into his hand, kissing his palm. "Maybe forcing ourselves to be out of arms' reach will be good on the communication front? Force us to talk," I suggested, working to keep my tone light when I just wanted to crumble. Because even if I couldn't define it, something had changed irrevocably last night.

"I still say we found better uses for our mouths."

I snickered despite myself, a flush creeping up in my cheeks. Judging by the smug little smile he gave me as he ran a thumb over one side, he saw it. Enjoyed the effect he was having on me. "Obviously," was my choked reply.

"Come on, Pix. You can't cry. You know I won't get on the plane if you cry."

"Is that a bad thing?"

"The university would say it's a terrible thing."

"Yeah," I grumbled, hanging my head forlornly.

"We'll talk," he repeated. "I'll come see you in Chicago

after Thanksgiving." When I just nodded, he added, "We can go see Pax play a game. Eat some deep-dish pepperoni pizza—the genuine stuff." I nodded again. But he lifted my chin for the second time, those dark eyes boring into mine. "Tell me we'll be okay, Pix. Tell me you're in this."

"I'm in this," I repeated, lifting my chin, feigning a strength I certainly didn't feel. "We'll talk."

"Okay," he said, sighing as the attendant made the final call for his flight. My chest physically ached as he kissed me one last time, and I palmed at my heart. 'I love you' sprinted down my mouth but got trapped on the tip of my tongue. Too soon. No use in being the crazy overbearing girlfriend, even if I'd always known it.

Letting him walk down that ramp was one of the hardest things I'd done in my life.

Broderick

THE WEEK LEADING up to Thanksgiving break was one of the longest of my life. Catching up on grading papers, teaching lectures, and my morning and evening calls with Elora were the highlights. But it wasn't enough. I wanted to wake up with her in my arms, kiss her breathless before she went out the door in the morning, pleasure her into that euphoric comatosed sleep at night.

Between those bright spots was mostly... a lot of gray and mist, and I hit the gym with James in the mornings and their cousin Charlie in the evenings just for something to keep my hands busy. I even put the finishing touches on my kitchen the Tuesday before Thanksgiving. Good thing, too, because the oven at the big Rhodes house 'took a colossal shit'—Jameson's words, not mine. One downside to island life was how long it took to freight appliances in, and the very limited selection on our oversized rock.

My parents were hitting Cabo this year for their anniversary, which left me celebrating with the Rhodes, in my new kitchen. I wasn't complaining. I always landed at their place after dinner, anyway. It was just... my favorite Rhodes was missing.

Couldn't exactly vocalize that as we all piled into my townhouse Wednesday night, and Noel put us all to work. There were few things the Rhodes loved as much as pie, which made the annual pie baking marathon as much of a tradition as the dead bird and mashed potatoes. Noel was hovering around the boys' shoulders, eyeballing their handiwork as I came into the room, eyes flicking between my companions and El's text thread.

> BRODERICK
>
> Miss you, beautiful. Sleep well.

ELORA

Miss you, handsome. Happy pie night. Say hi to everyone for me?

> BRODERICK
>
> A bit of a giveaway, don't you think?

ELORA

Maybe. *winking emoji*

To be fair, if they take one look at my face when I think about your magic dick, that will be the end of this charade.

> BRODERICK
>
> Thinking about me in your mouth again, baby?

> **ELORA**
>
> Every damn day.
>
> In particular, that growly thing you did when I licked up your balls and sucked one side into my mouth while I jerked you off.

I CHOKED ON A LAUGH, nearly inhaling my mouthful of whiskey. I'd buried my fingers in her pussy, peppering her body in kisses while she deep throated me. The memory of her coming down my hand as I painted her skin in cum had me getting hard in an instant. Hacking, I waved away a disapproving glance from light brown eyes in a freckled, scowling face. When she saw I was stifling laughter, Noel couldn't quite keep her frown in place, shaking her head instead as her mouth tipped up. I waved her off and watched her go back to micromanaging the pie making process before trying to subtly adjust myself.

> **BRODERICK**
>
> Christ, woman. Your mouth.

> **ELORA**
>
> Didn't seem to mind it so much between your legs.

> **BRODERICK**
>
> Certainly my highlight of the week.

> **ELORA**
>
> Don't you forget it.

BRODERICK

Never. But baby, you can't get me hard when I'm five feet away from your brothers.

ELORA

Just tell them you're watching porn.

BRODERICK

In the kitchen on pie night?

ELORA

I was replaying you coming all over me in my mind during my meeting this morning. Same thing, right?

BRODERICK

Um. Real memories trump porn.

ELORA

Damn straight. I intend to erase every image of another woman in that brilliant mind of yours.

BRODERICK

So, maybe the porn was a bad suggestion after all.

ELORA

I didn't say to *actually* watch it. I said that was a viable excuse for little Broderick standing at attention.

BRODERICK

Sure. I always fill my spank bank while my best friend and his girl bake in my kitchen. That's healthy.

ELORA

Spitting out water laughing gif

> **BRODERICK**
> And need I remind you there's nothing little about 'little Broderick'.

ELORA
Oh, I know. I just started walking normally.

Dammit, I can't talk to you when I'm going commando.

> **BRODERICK**
> Killing me here, Pix.

ELORA
Talk to you before bed?

> **BRODERICK**
> Yeah. I'll text first so I don't wake you up.

ELORA
By all means, wake me up. But be naked when you do it.

Alright, sexy, I gotta catch a ride. Make good pie.

> **BRODERICK**
> Take care of my girl. Counting down to Chicago. Booked a place not far from Pax. Easy to sneak off to.

ELORA
See you soon, handsome.

"NOT SO THIN, *NOT SO THIN*," Noel reprimanded, snaking her way under Jameson's bulky arm to grab the rolling pin. More than a little amused, I went to set my phone on the counter before thinking better of it and sliding it in my back pocket. Last thing I needed was her brothers seeing her name pop up with a list of the filthy things we did together. Fuck, I loved that woman. Who would've thought the illustrious Elora Rhodes would have such a dirty mouth.

"Don't crush it, *Hulk* hands. Sweet baby cheeses. Roll it *gently*." Noel rushed to set down her Hot Toddy and take over to salvage it. She'd just poured two mugs, which felt a little ambitious for seven pm on pie night.

I snickered as he scowled at the top of her red curls, not dumb enough to argue with her. "Where the hell is Max? He's always good at this shit," Jameson groused.

"He'll be here in a bit. Don't be such a baby."

Side-eyeing the thickness Noel expected for the crust, I did my best to mimic it before holding my hands out like a kid presenting their clay turtle to their teacher.

"Yes! Perfect, Brod, just transfer it over to the pie pan and stab the bottom a few times with a fork."

Running my tongue over a molar, I arched my brows as I glanced at a still-scowling James, feeling a bit smug.

"Oh, fuck off," he grumbled as Noel re-rolled his piece of dough.

"You're just jealous."

"I did *not* crush it."

"Totally did," Noel said lightly, shooting him a glance as a stray red curl fell in her face. I snickered, grabbing my whiskey and clinking it to his before raising my own in salute. James smirked and was still shaking his head when he picked his glass up and brought it to his lips. Much to my relief, my best friend had never been the one to chatter or gossip, and beyond learning I hadn't won, had asked no pressing questions about me or El. Which meant I'd yet to have to outright lie. Honestly, that was a tremendous relief. One I thanked the universe for as I set down my glass.

Axel raised on his tiptoes to peer over at my approved pie dough, mouth pinched as he studied. "About a quarter inch?"

"That measurement should be real familiar to you, little brother," James said, a wry, crude grin on his face. I shook my head.

"Fuck off," Axel said, rolling his eyes. The fifth of the dozen, Axel was essentially a younger, more mountainous version of Rhyett. His long blonde hair gave him an unhinged, baby Brad Pitt circa *Troy* vibe, a fact his siblings weren't shy about reminding him of. Stubborn fucker still wouldn't cut it. This was the quietest a Rhodes gathering had ever been. Their parents were happily roasting in their Florida retirement escape. Rhyett and Brex, Jeanne, El, Hadlee, and Finn were all in their respective homes. Pax had a home game on Thanksgiving Day, so he was stuck in Chicago. The twins were visiting Alice in Emerald Bay, and Maverick was deep in his first semester at school—although I suspected he'd crash at El's for Thanksgiving.

We'd have the cousins and their kids for the actual day, but tonight was...*small*. Freakishly intimate, having grown up around this enormous tribe of weirdos. Despite years of being overwhelmed by the noise and chaos, and barrage of physical affection, I kinda missed them all.

"That's twice in as many minutes, Wolverine," Noel chided, smirking over her hot toddy. "That might be a record, even for you."

"Not my fault Axel's worried about his quarter incher."

"Personally, I think thicker is better," Noel said, somehow keeping a straight face like Jameson wasn't insinuating his brother had a micro penis.

"Oh, *I know*," James said, failing to do the same as he

grabbed another dough ball from the bowl and dusted the counter.

"Gross, guys, *seriously*? Don't ruin pie for me."

My head snapped up when that familiar voice cut through the groans and laughter. Standing in the doorway, looking equally smug and anticipatory, was my girl. Elora's face was pink with cold, her nose red like a little upturned cherry. My fingers ached to brush away the windswept hair falling free from the messy bun piled on top of her head. I tightened my grip on my glass instead.

"*Heyyyyy*!!" Axel threw his arms up in victory, sending flour flying *everywhere*.

"What the fuck are you doing here?" James barked, sloshing the whiskey as he slammed his glass down and made an open-armed beeline for the front door. El laughed, tossing her purse onto my couch like she belonged here. Was at home here. Maybe it had been Sarah that made her so uncomfortable the whole damn time.

"*That's* how you greet your baby sister these days?!" she scolded, rolling her eyes, but she threw her arms open to wrap herself around his torso as he crushed her against his flannel-clad chest. Max came in my front door behind her, shaking off a black umbrella before doing the same thing to his hair. Like he was neatly planting all the loose droplets on my floor mat.

"Max, did you do this?" James barked, not hiding his grin. A twinge of guilt battled the elation in my chest as Max shook his head, hands raised in surrender. He could act as grouchy as he wanted to, but Jameson was the world's biggest teddy bear for his family. To his sisters, especially. *Not much longer*, I promised myself, grinding my teeth in restraint, keeping my distance. Axel was next to wrap her up in a bear hug, lifting her feet off the ground in a fit of giggles. He gave her a good spin, and I eyed the exposed skin between her deep red sweater dress and furry knee-high boots. *I can't talk to you when I'm going commando.* She'd been catching a ride *here* when she dismissed our conversation. And knew full well exactly what I'd be thinking of with those strong legs on display. The promise at their apex. The image of yanking her into my bedroom and bending her over my desk to see that pretty pink pussy had me clearing my throat and studying the last of my drink.

"Miss her, Allen?" Noel nudged my elbow, watching the reunion with a satisfied smile on her face, and *two* mugs in her hands. That little shit. I couldn't help but assess her, wondering if her best friend had relayed our conversations during my time at the conference.

"I miss them all when they're off island." Not a lie. I'd be thrilled to hug Alice or Pax or Finn. But not *this* thrilled. Not itching to close the distance. To slip my fingers under that too-short-for-Mistyvale dress and revel in her sweet heat beneath.

"Sure," she chirped, flicking her eyes up to me in a way that said, 'how dumb do you think I am?' and I wondered if Brex was right. Were we so terribly obvious that everyone noticed except for the two that needed to? "That why her eyes are locked on you like a homing beacon?"

I snapped my face toward the Rhodes siblings, wincing when Noel snickered.

"Gotcha!" she muttered. But she wasn't wrong. El had eyes only for me, and I wondered how Jameson was still oblivious to how intently she kept looking back at me, making eye contact with Max and her brothers as they talked, only long enough to avoid being rude. Noel nudged my elbow and said, "Happy Thanksgiving, Brod."

"Happy Thanksgiving," I muttered back a beat before Noel closed the distance, launching herself into El's arms right as they opened, drinks held out to either side like precarious little wings.

"Welcome home, Elly!"

Elora's laugh was better than the rare peek of winter sunlight. "Hey, Skittles!"

"*No*, none of that," Jameson growled firmly, shaking his head as the girls both burst out laughing. "You don't get to call her that. That's my thing. Exclusive. Not sharing. She's *my* Skittles. You get Noelie-Bear or Bean or whatever shit you two concocted," he said, pointing between El and Max and then pulling Noel back to him possessively. "Hey, man," he added to Max as an afterthought.

Max gave him a cheerful salute, but his eyes locked on me with way too much understanding on his face, and my stomach bottomed out as he made a beeline in my direction.

"Professor! Good to see you. You got any more of that?" Max nodded to the whiskey in my hand before slinging an arm around my shoulders and rotating us toward the kitchen. "Have a feeling we'll both need it."

TWENTY

ELORA

"I'm so proud of you, Noel. That's amazing!" I stirred the heaping skillet of apple pie filling, breathing in the sweet spices as Noel swirled her wine glass, leaning against the counter beside me. Noel and I had been working on her non-profit all year, and her calls and brainstorming sessions were some of my favorites.

"It's just exciting to finally get going," she said, but I didn't have to glance up to hear the smile in her voice. "All the boring paperwork and startup stuff is done, and now we can really build on that foundation."

"Absolutely," I agreed, setting the wood spoon down on the edge of the steel pan. "You're going to touch so many lives, babe."

"Yeah?" she asked, not able to hide the hope in her voice.

"Yeah," I assured, right as Jameson snaked his arms around her waist, stooping to kiss her neck. I grinned. Jameson had walls a mile high before she broke them down, and I loved seeing him so happy. Some petty part of me wondered if I was finally going to know what that felt like. Still grinning, I looked up to find Broderick, where he sat at the table, handing Max crust cut-outs of leaves and pumpkins so he could decorate our filled pies.

Jameson tugged Noel into his chest for a cute swaying hug dance to whatever Christmas music they had playing, and I flipped off the burner, grabbing my wine from the counter.

"Got room for one more?" I asked the crust decorating team of disgruntled men. There was a chorus of *mehs*, but Broderick's eyes slowly dragged up my body, his lips quirking before he wet them. His nod was succinct. "Love the updates, Brod," I noted as I pulled out a chair, raising my wine glass to motion to the surrounding room.

"Brightened it up a bit, I suppose," he said humbly.

"More than a bit," I countered. "It's beautiful. Love the new countertops and that island is worth its weight in gold."

"That might be an overestimate," he chuckled, setting the tin cookie cutter aside and sliding the leaves over to Max, whose brow was furrowed with concentration. I hadn't missed the two of them exchanging hushed words–like some clandestine pow wow–prior to Axel joining their lineup and made a note to interrogate one of them later.

"Hell no, did you see how many pies we could fit on there? That thing will pay for itself for years."

His eyes dragged over my body before flitting to the expansive marble counter and back. "I can certainly think of some uses."

My cheeks flamed, and I swirled my glass, if for nothing else than something to do. Lifting my chin and holding that smoldering gaze, I said, "I'd love a demonstration."

"I'm sure you would."

"Got anything specific in mind?" I asked innocently,

smirking when Max scanned between us before he wrinkled his nose and returned to placing leaves around the rim of the pumpkin custard. There'd never been a part of my life the man wasn't privy to, and as he'd had a conference play-by-play, he was my only chance for a sounding board this week. With mock scolding in my tone, I said, "When it comes to getting consistent results, details matter, Professor."

He let his gaze drop over my body like a physical caress, and I squeezed my thighs together as the spring in my core wound tighter. We'd been dirty talking over text and on the phone all week, and at this point, a feather and a pretty promise would probably knock me right over the edge.

"Don't insult me by insinuating I don't account for the details, Rhodes."

Incapable of suppressing my smile, I swirled my wine before taking a long pull. Axel, however, *growled* under his breath and scooted back from the table.

"Welp. My details suck," he said, clapping his hands on his thighs as he stood. "You're up, El. Grabbing a refill—anybody need one?"

"No thanks, I'm good," Brod said. Max and I both shook our heads as Axel glanced between us. He gave an oblivious shrug and turned for the kitchen as I watched Broderick's expression, wondering what kind of mischief was running through his head. With a smile, eyes trained on me, he added, "Got everything a man could want right here, anyway."

"Can you two just go bang this out somewhere else?" Max muttered under his breath. His quiet tone didn't keep us both from kicking him in the shins beneath the table. "Ouch," he complained before we all burst out laughing.

"Come on, let me lend you a hand," I said as I set my

glass down, waving both hands in a motion to pass me the bowl of dough.

One dark brow winged up. "You'd enjoy that, wouldn't you?"

"Down to the last drop—" I grabbed the bowl of pumpkin filling as my brothers and Noel wandered our way, "of filling," I added, smirking as he slid over a prepared pie pan and I poured the last portion into the shaped crust. Using the plastic spatula, I scraped the edges of the bowl clean, ensuring all the filling landed as intended. I ran a slow finger over the spatula before flicking my eyes to his and sliding my finger between my lips. He sucked on a canine as *I* sucked off the pumpkin, shaking his head before dropping his eyes below the table and snagging the glass of whiskey he'd been nursing since I got here.

"Save some for me," Axel complained, bumping into me as he dove for the bowl. I burst out laughing, turning my face into my hands, certain it was flaming red. But it was Broderick's foot, tapping mine beneath the table that had me grinning back up at everyone.

"FUCKING *FINALLY*," I muttered when Max headed out into the blustery evening, leaving us alone. Evidently, the sentiment was mutual, because before I'd clunked the deadbolt into place, Broderick was behind me, body enveloping mine. I stuttered in both step and breath, leaning my forehead against the door as his hands scraped up my sides, grazing over my breasts before making their way down to my waist, where he squeezed as he rocked into my ass.

A breathless little giggle escaped between me as he turned me around, pinning me to the front door with his hips. "You're a cock tease."

"Not my fault you can't keep your head out of the gutter. I was *just baking pie*."

"It was *absolutely* your fault, you little minx. *Commando*. Christ, woman."

Laughing, I dropped my head back to the wall as he dove for my throat, kissing, sucking, nipping at the skin between my neck and shoulder. I'd never felt like a man was starving for me, but there was no denying that he'd missed me like I missed him. After grappling with telling me about his feelings for so long, Broderick certainly wasn't shy about showing me. His hand dropped between my legs, hoisting a thigh up around his hips before he slipped beneath the hem of my dress, growling when he found me bare—and wet—for him.

"Are you trying to kill me, Pix?"

"Gotta keep you wanting, Professor. Can't have you wandering off."

"Never," he snarled, and then plunged a blunt finger inside me, knocking the air out in a sudden rush of sensation. "Glad it's not just me. You're dripping, baby."

"Since the moment we talked about your balls in my face and your cum painting my tits."

"*That wicked mouth*," he muttered, amused, before claiming it with his own. I giggled, loving that for all his filthy words, mine made him seem sheepish and uncertain, but it was swallowed by the overwhelm that was Broderick Allen as he slid his finger out, only to replace it with two. The sudden intrusion sent my back arching, pleasure overwhelming my synapses as he hit that perfect spot inside me. Leisurely strokes, as if he had no intention of rushing this, of satisfying that desperate, needy spring in my core.

The moment his lips were on mine, I needed him *everywhere.* As though the world fell out from below my feet, and I plunged down into the pool of him with no hope of surfacing for air as he pumped against my walls. I didn't *need* air here. Just his decadent touch as he curled his fingers, that spiced scent filling my lungs, and the taste of his tongue as it plundered my mouth.

"I've got the shower warming up for you," he breathed when he peeled away, slipping his fingers out of me to give my clit a little tap, every inch of my body protesting the absence of his mouth robbing me of oxygen.

"*Mean.*"

"I'll just let you pretend that wasn't your first thought when you landed."

"You saying I stink or something?"

He gave my ass a little clap and squeeze, brushing his nose over mine as he shook his head. "I'm saying you spent your day hopping airports, and I've never seen you last this long without 'washing away communal seats'."

I wrinkled my nose, glancing down at myself before shrugging, "Couldn't wait to see you."

His smile was akin to pouring hot wax directly down my spine, heat blooming to life like it would consume me entirely. "I couldn't be happier to have you home, baby."

"Yeah? Not ruining your bachelor's pad?"

"It's long-past time this place filled with your light, El." Smiling to myself, I leaned into his chest, breathing him in, memorizing the lines of his back with the pads of my fingers. "Now, if you want to wash the plane off of you, go do it before I snap and bend you over that island you were admiring earlier."

Smirking, I said, "That doesn't sound sanitary."

"Believe me, there's nothing sanitary about what I want to do with your ass in the air for me."

Cheeks flushed, I shook my head, rolling my bottom lip between my teeth. Glancing down to the clothes that had seen a ride share, two planes, and a handful of very public benches, I wrinkled my nose. "It's somehow sweet and irritating that you know me well enough to know that's bothering me."

"I've been studying you since you lost your cooties, Pix."

"Just love what you see?" I teased, yanking the tie from my hair and sending it pouring over my shoulders in frizzy, undone waves. His pensive face twisted incrementally in the sweetest hint of a smile.

"Yeah, baby. Now, *go*, before I change my mind," he said, clapping the side of my thigh and jerking his head back toward the hallway to his bedroom. The goosebumps on my neck told me he followed a beat before warm fingers brushed my hair off over one shoulder. By the time I got to the steam-filled bathroom, his hands were tracing my collar bones, warm lips pressing a line up the back of my neck. I leaned to the side, revealing more skin for him to work with as my heart ratcheted up in anticipation. Gentle fingers hooked my bra strap, pulling it down over my shoulder as he pressed kisses across the skin, breathing me in. His hands slunk down my body to the hem of the dress, slowly easing it up. When I raised my arms above my head so he could slip it up and over, he hummed contentedly.

"You're remarkably beautiful, baby," he said, words like honey over my skin as he trailed his fingers back down my arms, my ribs, my waist, fingers eliciting a flip in my low belly when he traced the crease between my thigh and hip.

"I'm dying to be buried in you again. Hurry, okay? I mean—take care of yourself but do it quickly."

Breathlessly, I nodded. "You're cute when you can't decide if you're sweet or horny."

"Can't I be both?" He nipped at my ear before stepping away. Head spinning, I watched as he pressed a button on a plastic contraption in the corner. A moment of study told me it was a towel warmer.

"*Boujee*," I teased, grinning as he chuckled. For as long as I could remember, the man always had exceptional taste in all things. He patted the doorframe twice before leaving me in the coastal-craftsman style bathroom. These old townhomes were a hodgepodge collection of decades' worth of cheap updates, but Broderick brought it into this century with sophisticated gray and white subway tile. The black and white hexagon tiles on the floor and chunky window trim seemed the only remnants of its original bones.

As eager as I was to get my hands on him, the man was right. I didn't realize how dirty and sore I felt until the hot water beat against my tense muscles. I dropped my head to my chest and let the onslaught massage my neck and shoulders. Bubbly suds spiraled and collected around my feet as I finally gave myself a moment to breathe. The week had been long, his glaring absence suddenly agonizing now that we'd poured ourselves out for each other.

Finished and feeling relaxed and squeaky clean, I headed out into his room. He was decently tidy for a bachelor. But the platform bed wasn't made, and a jacket was haphazardly tossed over the foot of it. A stray shirt lay crumpled in the corner beside a luxurious looking, but likely uncomfortable armchair—too shallow to actually cozy up in. But that was the extent of the *clutter* in the space. A rich espresso brown bookshelf sat beneath the window, organized with his collection of favorites. I noted an intricate balance between classic names, memoirs and more contemporary stories. He had an entire shelf dedicated to the Alutiiq on the island, and my fingers traced over the titles. Some I recognized from school, and our great aunt who kept the old traditions alive. Others were foreign, their names tripping up my tongue despite years of effort to acclimate. Knowing Broderick, he had them all memorized.

Straightening, I turned for his closet, pulling it open and smiling at the heaps of unwashed or unfolded clothes spilling from the hamper onto the floor, relieved to see he wasn't a total freak. At least he made it into the bins. My room usually looked like the lingering damage after a natural disaster. Running my fingers along the line of hangers, I found his gray Tom Petty t-shirt. I slipped it off the hanger and over my head before laying down across his bed. Every muscle in my body seemed to release a collective sigh, like they'd all held their tension until this moment, when we could finally melt into his mattress. Maybe it was the way his scent lingered on the sheets, or just subconsciously knowing we were back together.

I'd just drifted off into the strange place between sleep and awake when a floorboard croaked, bringing my eyes to a pensive, beautiful Broderick. *My* beautiful Broderick. He leaned against the door frame, a pinch in his brow as he looked down my body. I rolled to my side, dropping my knee to the bed, which pulled his shirt up to the edge of my ass.

"You okay, there? You look like you're in pain. Not backing out on me, are you, Brod?"

He wet his lips, shaking his head softly as he

confidently said, "Never, baby. Just... regretting all those wasted nights when I could've had you like this." He closed the distance, sitting down at the foot of the bed, where his hand quickly settled on my bare leg to give it a squeeze. "Wearing my old shirt, smelling like my body wash."

"The clove is quite refreshing."

He smirked softly before leaning down to press reverent kisses down my leg, pulling it with him as he straightened. Strong hands stroked down the length as I rotated onto my back, bracing on my elbows so I could watch him.

"You and Max seemed to have a long chat before Axel intruded? He promise to ruin your life if you hurt me?"

A snort of amusement escaped him before he said, "I'll give him points for creativity. Jameson would just threaten to break my face."

Something sour twisted in my belly, knowing I'd asked him to keep this from him. Still, I said, "Slow, thorough, torturous destruction is more Max's style."

"I'm not going anywhere, so I'm not worried."

"And if I ran off?"

"You won't."

"So confident in that? I haven't exactly done *serious*."

"That's because you were with the wrong guys."

"Willing to gamble your future against *Jorogumo Defense*?" Max's firm certainly tiptoed the line between legal and not.

"Worth the risk," he said, grabbing onto my calf possessively, which did strange things to my insides. The alien sensations intensified as he kissed and touched up my legs until he hit the apex, my cheeks flaming as he inhaled my sex before peppering my pussy with kisses. Raw, primal sex was one thing. It felt...physical. *Chemical*. But this near worship level of adoration? That was a kind of vulnerability I'd never known before. Something in his soft touches stirred a part of my soul that had laid dormant. It made me squirm, which, infuriatingly enough, made *him* chuckle.

The hot exhale of his humor against my clit was the last sensation before he sucked that bundle of nerves between his lips, making mine pop open as my ears went buzzing.

"It's not possible for you to feel this good," I breathed, struggling to stay composed as he lavished me in licks and kisses, hot palms pinning me in place for him. There was a satisfied spark in his dark eyes when they flicked to me.

"You watching me eat you out is an insane turn on."

"Yeah?" I asked, smirking as he nodded into my pussy, breathing me in before lapping straight up my center, silencing any remaining thoughts my mind might have had. His fingers sliding home would've done it if his tongue hadn't already rendered me silent. Torturous pleasure wracked through my body, collapsing me into the mattress as I arched into him.

Riding Broderick's face and fingers set my heart racing, that coil in my core winding tighter with each hungry pull and precise curl of his fingers. It was like he was calling my release forward with each movement, pleasure building pressure through my veins as my breath went ragged, hands grappling for purchase on his neck, shoulders, the sheets, anything within reach as he pushed me toward that edge. Right as a cry tore from my throat, he halted, sliding out and leaving me empty.

Disbelief popped my jaw open as I gaped down at him. "Hey!" I croaked. "Not fair."

"Trust me, baby, you've had me on edge for a decade. I think I owe you this."

"Oh, fuck off," I barked, *mostly* teasing, but not

bothering to hide the desperation in my voice as he chuckled, raising his brows expectantly.

"It'll be better this way anyway, or that's what I've heard."

"No—*nono*. Orgasms are better. *Orgasms* are *always* better."

"And you'll have one—"

"*Was about to*," I interjected petulantly.

"When I say so." Okay, so that was hot, but not nearly as hot as his warm palms clamping down on my thighs and tugging me beneath him in one solid yank, towering over me with expectation written over every inch of his face. "Do you know how long I've wanted you in my bed, El?"

Panting, desperate and a little pissed, I shook my head. God, he looked so victorious, so determined that my frustration ebbed away as he moved his fingers to his slacks to undo the buttons. I reached for him, but he froze, a mischievous smirk lifting his cheeks as he jerked his chin toward the headboard.

"Trust me, baby, I'll make it worth it. Keep your hands above your head."

"Excuse me?"

"Or I can just leave you laying there panting after me?" He shrugged, as though the outcome had no effect on him. The bulge straining against the zipper of his pants told a very different story.

"I never realized you were evil under that nice guy façade."

"Remind me how evil I am when I have you spilling all over our bed, okay?"

"Not gonna happen."

"We'll see about that."

I laughed, but pure, horny desperation saw his confidence and wanted to raise the bet. Eyes rolling, I stretched my arms over my head, grasping one wrist in the opposite hand as he stripped, and I watched, mesmerized by each revealed masculine line of muscle. Was it possible for him to be more breathtaking after a week apart? It shouldn't have been, but my mouth popped open, chest pulling in ragged gulps of air, just as expectant as the first time.

"Good girl, keep your hands up there or this stops again, understand?" The man must've robbed me of my brain cells when he robbed me of that orgasm, because suddenly, I was nonverbal, hands fisting in the supple fabric over my head as a very naked Broderick dove between my legs, kissing my swollen, pulsing clit before using his fingers to rub tight circles as the other slipped two fingers inside me, curling again, and sending me into a feral kind of frenzy.

"Oh shit," I breathed. "Fuck, baby. *Oh fuck.*" My muttering continued as my body writhed under the overload of pleasure. "Broderick!" I cried out as the first roll of an orgasm wrapped around my core.

He withdrew, a defiant squawk tearing from me as he leaned back, but before I could protest, he hooked my feet onto his shoulders, hands on my thighs, and lined up with my entrance. The spark in those eyes promised me we'd relish every moment of this night.

One inch at a time, he smoothly slid down into me, the sensation rippling through me, head falling back. "Oh, God," I panted.

"That's a generous upgrade from *Professor*."

My laugh only tightened the tension in my center before he started a steady rhythm of gentle thrusts.

"So damn beautiful, baby. Look how you stretch for me."

I did, my mouth hanging open as it took every ounce of willpower to keep my eyes from slamming shut. But that attempt was futile the moment he began a vicious thrust.

"Oh, shit—" I threw my head back, eyes sliding shut as he jackhammered into me. There was sex, and then there was a claiming. There was pleasure, and then there was euphoria. Shattering beneath Broderick was the latter in every sense.

"That's my girl. God, you look so good, El. So damn perfect. So responsive."

I think I nodded, but my soul was hovering somewhere outside my body, looking back, watching as he obliterated me entirely. My hands slammed down onto his shoulders, nails digging into his skin as he stuttered to a stop.

"What?" I breathed, the tone as close to begging as a woman with any sense of dignity could manage. *Everything* in my body had a pulse. "Broderick," I groaned as he slipped free.

"What'd I say, Pix?"

Blinking, I scrambled to catch my breath. Scowling up at him, I barked, "I can solve this myself, you know?"

The wry smile that painted his features would've had the best woman liquefying at his feet. "Sure. But you won't."

"Who's the tease *now*?"

"Who broke the rules?" he countered without missing a beat. That cheeky self-satisfied smirk would've irritated me if it wasn't so damn cute. Rules. *Hands*. Above my head.

"God dammit," I growled, throwing myself onto the mattress. "Move over. I have a vibrator in my purse."

His laugh wrapped around my chest, filling my heart

with some kind of molten oil. "Oh, but you'd miss out on watching me fuck you until you come so hard you see stars as you soak my cock."

Dammit. My eyes fell to said cock as one of his broad hands wrapped around his length and gave it one steady tug. Another. Eyes narrowed in accusation on his face, I hurled my hands above my head and relished how hard he seemed to fight his need to smile.

"That's my girl. I promise to earn your trust, baby. I'll always take care of you. You've just got to let me." Before I could make sense of up or down, he'd plunged his fingers back inside me, the tender touches from earlier gone, and in their place was a ferocious, expectant thrust, his demanding fingers finding my clit as his mouth descended on a breast. Lavishing it in demanding pulls, Broderick had me whimpering beneath the sensations. He was too good. I needed him *everywhere*.

"Broderick!" The keening cry sounded far away, my back arching as I flexed and balled my hands to keep them in the sheets above my head. Writhing and bucking beneath the onslaught of pleasure, my throat felt raw, eyes heavy as release barreled forward.

"You come all this way to see *me*, Pix?"

"Yes," I panted without hesitating. It was true. As much as I loved my family, this trip had nothing to do with pie day. Eyes closed under the weight of impending detonation, I could hear the joy in his next words.

"God, do you know what you do to me, baby?" His movements got impossibly more intense, sending me soaring toward that beautiful abyss. "You came so far to see me. I think I can give you more than one of these."

And like he'd flipped a kill switch, Broderick curled

those fingers, hitting that perfect spot. I imploded in a release so violent, I did, indeed, see stars.

But it just. Kept. Going.

Even as my legs shook, rolls of pleasure waved through me, and he stayed relentless. My thighs clamped down on his hands as the pleasure overwhelmed me. This time when my hands wrapped around his arms, he didn't relent, ripping wave after wave of pleasure from me as I came down his hand, soaking his wrist, warmth spilling from my body.

"There's my girl," his voice rumbled through me as he dragged the release out in slow steady strokes. My body shuddered as he slowed and stilled.

"H-holy sh-shit," I stammered, incapable of inhaling as the last shockwaves stuttered through me. The world spun like I had cartoon birds flying around my head. *"That's* why people edge."

"You're welcome," he chuckled. When Broderick pressed his fingers against my lips, I opened automatically, his warm chuckle heating my cheeks. "Suck, baby. God, you're so beautiful. You taste so damn good." He slipped his fingers into my mouth and my eyes fluttered open as my tart release hit my taste buds, landing on a satisfied smile. "That's my girl. Told you you'd spill all over our bed."

Our bed. I hummed at the realization that he made this place mine, too. On one hand, the feminist in me was freaking out because how could he *possibly* when we just got together? But... the rest of me? Being with him came as naturally as breathing. As though it always had been. And while the sex was new, the man was not—no, this was a *long* time coming. Perhaps we'd gone our separate ways to become who we needed to be, and now it was just about finding a way back home.

Home to me was Broderick. Even if I couldn't say that yet.

Needing to tread on safer territory, I breathlessly whispered, "I was promised I'd get to come on your cock."

"And you will," he stated simply. In the next breath, he swooped in for a kiss, snaked his hand between us to line himself up, thrust home, and made damn good on his promise.

TWENTY-ONE
BRODERICK

"Sheets are in the closet on the top shelf," I said when El started poking around in my dresser drawers.

"Ahh, perfect," she flashed a smile over her bare shoulder, and I debated pinching myself to make sure this wasn't some elaborate dream. Pix in my shirt was more delicious than she had any right to be. But Pix in nothing but the delicate gold chain around her neck, with a satisfied smile on her face, prancing around my room like her nicknamesake?

There weren't words. My face ached from smiling as I rounded the corner into the hallway to toss the sheets into the wash. Because I'm a man of my word, and did, in fact, make her come so hard she soaked the bed.

That moment would inevitably play on loop in my mind from now until the end of eternity.

I'd just pumped the detergent and was about to close the washer lid when a thought occurred, and my gut dropped like it did when I was about to be forced on stage as a kid. An unexpected vulnerability washed over me, and I swore under my breath as I rounded the corner.

"El! Baby, I'll get the sheets down," I called back to her right as I heard a crash and a *'whoops'*. Clenching my jaw, knowing exactly what the whoops had been, I rounded the corner. Elora—back in my Tom Petty shirt—was kneeling in my closet behind the sheets, which were now halfheartedly tossed onto the end of the bed. One hand pressed to her lips as the other held out a postcard. She flipped it over, her brows pinching as a slight tremor rattled the cardstock.

"Brod, what is this? *What are these?*"

I leaned into the door, just wearing the towel I'd tied around my waist after our post-sex shower that *also* featured some indulgent enjoyment of each other's bodies.

"What do they look like, baby?"

She scrambled to right the shoe box that had evidently come soaring out of the closet when she yanked the sheets down. I should've thought it through from the start, but honestly couldn't even bring myself to feel embarrassed. She knew what she meant to me now. This wasn't news anymore.

El's throat worked as she ran her fingers across the mess of postcards and she settled down on her bare ass, crossing her legs. Chuckling, I snatched up the blanket that lived at the foot of my bed and crossed the space. Kneeling beside her, I gingerly wrapped her up in it. She didn't say a thing, just pinched it in her fingers around her throat, the furrow in her brow not giving way as she scoured through one after the other, gently setting them back in the shoe box.

"You...you kept my letters."

"Yeah," I grunted, the word heavier than it ought to be in my mouth. Like a stone where water should be. The next one was fresh—unbent, the ink not yet faded—and I knew what she'd see when she turned it over in her fingers. The Bellagio looked back at her, and when she turned to me with parted lips, her eyes were more than a little glossy. "You kept all my postcards."

"Even our new one. Well, except for the Leaning Tower of Pizza, but that's because your brother spilled a beer on it, and I couldn't exactly salvage it at that point."

She giggled, shaking her head as she added, "I still say a stack of pizzas is way cooler than a crumbling ode to ancient architecture."

"I guess if I had to lose that one, I'm glad it was from Chicago."

"Dear Broderick," she cleared her throat, eyes flicking to me expectantly before continuing to read. "We're in Austin this week. It's hotter than Hades' seventh circle, but the street tacos are decent, and we're hitting the downtown music circuit, so that should be fun. Wish you were here." She arched a speculative brow. "Not exactly something to write home about. *Dear Broderick*, turns out Manhattan isn't really any better than any other overcrowded, overpriced, over-hyped city. But the plays are wonderful, and the food is spectacular. Met a musician that would put Miles Davis to shame, and I know you'd never admit that to me, so I won't ask you to, but go give him a listen. And your secret is safe with me. He's better, isn't he?" Smirking, she looked up to me like I owed her an answer.

I leaned back into the bed, studying her, studying me. "He was good, but no Miles."

"Bullshit."

"Nah. You oversold him. Or maybe it was the live performance."

"God, the food there was impeccable."

"Yeah?"

"Yeah. Even your snobby ass would be impressed."

"I thought you liked my ass."

"I didn't say it wasn't bite-able. Just a lil' pretentious."

"Come here, you have something on your face," I teased, lunging forward as I licked my thumb. She squealed and rolled backward, but I pursued, settling my body over hers and planting an obnoxious, over the top kiss on her cheek. Laughing as she dramatically wiped at her face, I kissed the tip of her nose. "Oh hey, I remember that one." I snagged one stray that had gone flying away from the pile. "Dear Broderick—"

She snatched it from my fingers, holding it up above her face, revealing an idyllic tropical beach with a lawn chair on the front. Frankly, good for her, because now I could return my attention to kissing down her jaw and neck.

"Dear Broderick, it finally happened. I found the man of my dreams—oh my gosh, I remember this. I was so sloshed that night—Never mind that he's seventy-three and happily married to his high school sweetheart, Ronald makes the best jerk chicken in the Caribbean and can recite the entire rugby team roster. His wife, Ester, is also very kind, but her jerk chicken just didn't kidnap my heart like Ronald's did. Wish you were here."

"That one made me laugh. You would pick a man based on culinary prowess."

"Yes, well, food *is* my love language." She shook her head, looking down at the stack of images and faded written notes. "I cannot believe you kept all these."

"Yes, you can," I countered flatly. "It was always gonna end up being me and you, El."

Those gray-blues looked like I'd just ignited them. Like a molten core churned beneath the steely surface as she studied me. "Why did it take you so long, then?"

"You know why," I choked out, throat thick. Guilt had consumed so much of my life. Guilt for wanting her when I shouldn't. For harboring that truth away from her brothers. Guilt for being entirely uninterested in all of my mother's blind dates, despite knowing Sarah wasn't a healthy alternative. Hell, even now, finally having what I always wanted, guilt was my companion for not immediately telling Rhy and James the truth of it.

"And why is this different?"

"Because some losses are survivable. Others are not. Watching you drift away was the slowest kind of death. But seeing you slip through my fingers in Vegas, when I had you right there... that was an accelerant."

Pensive, Elora studied me, and it took every ounce of my spine to hold her inquisitive gaze. "Are you saying I moved into the latter category?"

"Yes," I breathed back, even as that invisible elephant popped a squat on the center of my chest. Shaking my shoulders out, as if there was any hope of dispelling some of that energy, I finally said, "Tell me I'm not alone in this, Pix."

"It was never my feelings that were in question."

Fuck, that hurt. I hated myself for the echo of rejection in that molten gray fire. Hated that I put it there. "No, it wasn't," I agreed. I moved for the bed, pulling her with me as I leaned my back against the frame, feeling like we were treading on conversations that deserved vulnerability which would be hard to achieve with my body draped over hers. Instead, I opted to pull her against my side.

Voice as raw as my mind, I said, "Tell me I'm not the only one that pictured you all these years. Tell me you imagined it was my hand you were riding when those jackoffs made you come like that."

"Nobody made me come like that," she countered, voice still soft. Of course, she'd look out for my feelings, even when I was painting the painful picture of our wasted years.

"Way to let me down easy," I breathed. "Stroking my ego, El?"

Her brows winged up, and she repeated, "Nobody made me come like that."

I studied her for a beat, some purely male piece of me basking in her words before I muttered, "Idiots."

The snort my comment earned was entirely unladylike. I loved it. Loved that she didn't have to be the polished version of herself that she offered the rest of the world when it was just the two of us.

"You're not wrong."

"Thought I was going to hell."

"What?" she breathed back, brows pinching.

"For wanting you like this. For picturing *you* when they were on their knees for me. For wishing it were your hands on me all these years." She stiffened against me, and I rotated so I could have a clearer view of her face, which had pinched in something between anger and frustration.

"I don't want you thinking about them when you're sitting here with *me*."

The urge to smile tugged at my mouth. "*Jealous*, El?"

"That they know what your cum tastes like? Or that I imagined your hands on my skin as you bottomed out in me a million times before I felt it? *Yeah*. I'm fucking jealous. Jealous that bitch got your twenties when I would've killed for them. And I hate that feeling. Why are you *smiling*?" she demanded, and I just tugged her tighter against my side.

"I like you jealous," I admitted. "It's kinda cute."

"Not an emotion I'm acquainted with or one I intend to

feel again, so you better fuck it out of me before I change my mind about this whole damn thing."

I reached up to snag her wrists as she shoved against me, like she'd pry herself free. Looping them between my fingers, I held her in place, the hand around her shoulders sliding up to grip her neck, pulling her forehead to mine before claiming her mouth. She nipped at my lip with more force than usual, and I chuckled against her lips.

"Me either, Pix. But goddamn, if seeing Pierce panting after you didn't shred me to pieces."

"Pierce?!" she questioned, smirking like I was an absolute idiot.

"Six-foot-two, blonde, winner of the competition," I listed off.

A muscle in her cheek twitched as she supplied, "Gayer than Maxamillion?"

I blinked down at her as she grinned back at me, looking way too smug for my liking.

"Are you telling me I thought about ripping him apart the entire week in Vegas and he wasn't even after you?"

"So violent," she said with mock disapproval.

"You lied to me?!"

"Excuse me?" she barked, laughing in a way that brought her sanity into question as a hand settled on her chest. I was too irritated to buy the innocent act, especially as she countered, "I never lied to you."

"We had it out in the elevator about his *ulterior motives*."

"Oh, no you don't, Allen. I never said he was interested in me or that *I* was interested in *him*. I said he was a solid prospect and was about to tell you I got his number *for Max*, but you went all pissed-off neanderthal on me."

"Thought you were being naïve. He was so damn

touchy feely. Fuck, El, I spent the entire week hating him for putting his hands on you so freely."

She giggled then, equal parts mischief and smug victory. "And you did *all of that* to yourself, big guy. Could've spent one evening with us and put all that angst to bed."

"Well, fuck me," I groaned, leaning back into the mattress as she laughed skyward.

"Again? Christ, you're relentless."

"Har-har."

"What do they say about making assumptions, Professor?"

Shaking my head, I bent down and nipped at her neck. "Took two years off my life and you were setting *Max* up."

"Yep."

"I feel like a dumbass."

"That's a warranted emotion."

"You're evil," I teased, tickling her side and grinning as she squeaked and tried to squirm away.

Still giggling, she nipped back, "Remind me how evil I am when I'm swallowing your cock later."

Elora

NEVER IN MY life had I been banged into a sex aversion, but the decadent ache between my legs was a promise for absolute devastation if we didn't figure out how to keep our hands to ourselves this week.

Thanksgiving was freakishly quiet. As a matter of fact, I didn't think I'd ever seen a family gathering so small. Was this what normal families felt like during the holidays? No chaotic chatter or a dozen voices vying to hold the conversation at the same time? No competing for the last roll or theatrical game of charades after dinner? It was... disconcerting, to say the least. I was missing the chaos of a full house, while simultaneously soaking up the calmer, quiet tempo of an intimate group. Noel prepped half the dinner herself, and James popped over to Broderick's around ten am to put the tiny turkey in the oven. The guys sat down to watch football, Axel joining in around noon. We had a video chat with Broderick's parents, Rob and Marley, before dropping food off to his grandfather. Our cousins, Jake and Charlie, and Charlie's kids, showed up not long after. We'd all laughed and played cards while the games rolled across the television, eaten and served up pie and ice cream in an oddly comforting routine. Is this what it would feel like if Brod and I decided this was our new normal? The two of us entertaining the family, making the kids giggle with traces of pumpkin on happy cheeks?

I'd always loved watching Brod with kids around the island, but somehow, seeing him with little Sterling hit so much harder now. Harder because, *God*, I wanted that. At the base of all of this yearning and pining sat a deeply rooted need to have the entire picture. I just wasn't sure what that looked like.

"Wait, wait, show me again!" Sterling demanded, bouncing on the balls of his feet as Broderick laughed. At seven years old, there was absolutely nothing Charlie's youngest loved as much as sleight of hand magic tricks. My multi-talented lover had been entertaining both kids for the better half of dessert.

Our not-so-little Junebug turned eleven this fall and was attempting to appear indifferent as she peered over the rim of her novel, watching with enough focus that I assumed she was trying to catch the science behind the magic.

"Pay attention, now," Broderick said, holding up a too-shiny quarter. I wondered if he got it fresh from the bank for just this purpose. He held it up to the left, and bright Rhodes' blues followed the motion. The kids both shared Charlie's warm olive complexion but got their late mama's dark jet-black hair. "Don't lose track," Broderick encouraged, shifting the coin from one hand to the other. That tiny dimple popped up in Sterling's cheek as he followed the motion. Meanwhile, June's eyes narrowed, like she could focus her way past the illusion as Broderick moved it again. "If you blink, you're bound to miss it," he added and with a flick of his wrist, the coin vanished.

"*How do you do that!?*" Sterling demanded, both his volume and enthusiasm at their max.

"It's just a trick," June said dismissively, lifting her chin and dropping her eyes to her book all in one movement. I smirked as Broderick did the same thing, but he kept his eyes on the still mesmerized Sterling.

"I'll teach you some day, but you have to follow the magician's code."

"The magician's code?" Sterling demanded, grabbing Broderick's hand and peeling it open, only to scowl at his empty palm.

"Everyone knows the magician's code," Broderick said sagely. Sterling's silver eyes snapped to me, looking for confirmation.

"It's true," I said, nodding. "Everyone knows the magician's code."

"What is it?" he asked eagerly, peeling open Broderick's button up sleeve as he searched for the quarter. Grinning, Broderick held up one finger with a flourish.

"One—you can tell no one how you did it unless they've sworn the oath. Two—" a second digit joined the first. "You can never perform the trick without practicing it until you've mastered it." Another finger went up. "Third, you have to escape the Monster of Mayhem!"

Before Sterling could ask about said monster, Broderick's eyes went wide, his hands snapped up like T-Rex claws, and he growled, lunging for Sterling, who yelped and bolted away. I realized I was grinning like an idiot when I caught June's smile directed at her pages. Eleven going on thirty, evidently. Something cold nudged my elbow, and I turned to find a beaming Noel offering me a glass of red.

"Something about a good man who's good with kids," she said, shaking her head adoringly as she handed over the wine. "Just makes my ovaries explode, you know?"

"He'll be a wonderful dad someday, won't he?"

"One of the best. James loving on those two was the end for me, I swear."

"They've both always had a soft spot for Charlie's kids," I supplied, feigning indifference with no more finesse than Junebug as I attempted not to watch every move of their theatrical game.

"You guys talking about kids?"

I nearly choked on my wine before my brows winged up. "Excuse me?"

"You were just here *helping prep* this morning?" she said dryly, laying the skepticism on thick. If by 'prep' she meant fucking each other's brains out so our lust wouldn't infect the whole gathering, then yes, we were *prepping*.

"Yeah," I said, voice tighter than it could be if it needed to convince anyone.

"Prep *what?*" She laughed. "Slicing canned cranberry sauce?"

"That stuff is shit. We made ours fresh," I bit back, smirking.

"Sure," she said, arching a brow, but then beaming as a tiny voice bellowed for Jameson.

"Unca James!!! *Help!*" Sterling squealed as he bolted around the long dining table, still covered in dessert and abandoned plates and drinks.

Jameson's head snapped up from his conversation with Charlie, and he threw Noel a wink before taking a nearly identical dinosaur stance to Broderick's and bellowing a, "*Raaawr!*"

"Don't wait too long, El. Good men only come around once or twice in a lifetime."

Blinking, I turned to my friend who knew that reality more than any woman ever should. For the first time, the truth tiptoed down the length of my tongue before I beat it back. "Yeah, I just gotta find one."

The lie tasted sour. Because we both knew the man tickling the dickens out of my cousin's ridiculously cute kid was the best of the best.

It was as Broderick's elated brown eyes found mine that my stomach twisted. Leaving on Monday was going to be the most acute kind of torture.

TWENTY-TWO

BRODERICK

I glanced at my watch before movement at the end of the street caught my attention, and then I didn't bother to bite back my smile. Waiting in the misty alleyway between houses while pretending to take out my trash probably wasn't the smartest deterrent for nosy neighbors, but the street was quiet, the houses dark and the world soft with winter snow. Like a happy little penguin, El waddled around the corner, wrapped in one too many layers to convince anybody she'd grown up here. The snow had given the entire town that soft, almost unnaturally quiet kind of tranquility and the crunch of her feet was the only sound between us. She looked uneasy on the icy street, like she'd forgotten how to keep her feet on the slick surface.

Leaning into my gate, I pushed it open, making room for her to dart past me and through my dark yard before we zipped inside.

Rounding on her, I couldn't help but mirror her smile, her cheeks rosy with cold as she beamed up at me. "Hey, stranger."

"Hey, baby," I breathed, still in a bit of disbelief that

this was finally our reality, closing the distance and weaving our fingers together. The kiss we shared was gentle, leisurely, free of that desperate lust that ran us haggard. Her scent filled my lungs as I tasted her lips, and the sweet lingering hint of mint. Like she'd brushed her teeth before heading this way. "Sneak out okay?"

"Yeah, I don't think anybody noticed." A full body shiver wracked down her frame when she peeled off her winter coat, and I chuckled as she blew out a frozen breath. Skintight leggings and an oversized...

"Is that *my* Mistyvale University hoodie?"

"Maybe. I didn't let James see it, if that's what you're thinking."

That did something disconcerting to my chest. Thirty-five-year-olds could have heart attacks, couldn't they? Needing to redirect, I just shook my head and said, "Can't say I'm surprised they wanted you to stay with them." Jameson and Noel had *passionately* insisted El stay at the big house with them. When their parents, Milo and Juniper, retired to Florida, leaving the boat to James, the reigning Captain Rhodes moved into the family's main house. With the two of them keeping the family property and business running, Jameson's old place became a vacation rental that turned a pretty profit. This time of year was dead for tourists, though, so she could've stayed there if they'd been a little less insistent.

"Good luck arguing with either of them, though. Am I right?"

"That would be impossible."

"At least I know all the sneaky creaky floorboards," she said with a mischievous grin. I narrowed my eyes, remembering teenage life in that old oceanside house.

"You climbed out the window, didn't you?"

"And didn't hit a single creaky board on the way," she quipped back without missing a beat.

"Some things don't change. I know he'd never say it, but I think James is missing having everyone around."

"Me too," she said, her eyes going pensive. "He seems okay, though?"

"Yeah. He's got Noel. Charlie and I meet up with him at the gym, and Axel's around quite a bit."

She nodded pensively. "Good. So, what's the big plan, professor?"

I smiled when she looked around, leering around the corner, like she'd get a better peek at the living room. They'd barely left when I shot her a text inviting her over tonight once the love birds were in bed. She'd responded within a heartbeat, and I'd gotten to work setting up.

She froze as she observed the living room. I'd piled every pillow and blanket I had on the sectional and enormous accompanying ottoman, in front of one of those television Christmas fireplace screensavers with the crackling sound effects. I'd neatly laid out snacks for the movie–all the classics displayed on a tv tray I usually used to eat when I was on my own. Hot cocoa was steaming away beside the deck of cards I'd set to the right of the licorice. I had two additional board games set out on the end of the footrest; in case she wasn't in the mood for cards tonight. I had to admit the fat flakes of snow drifting through the darkness past my window added to the cozy, inviting effect of the space.

"You made me a magic snow-night-in date?"

"Yes, ma'am."

"You got me Rolos," she said, something tight in her voice making me nervous.

"Do you not like those anymore? I grabbed Milk Duds

and Red Vines too." My shoulders relaxed the instant she turned to look at me, revealing the sweetest smile and glassy eyes before she threw her arms around me, nearly knocking me back a step.

Chuckling, I said, "Hey, Pix. Did I do good, then?"

"You're perfect." She stepped farther back than strictly necessary, and I wondered if she was fighting to keep space between us. I certainly had to battle to not just wrap her up and kiss her breathless the instant she was within reach.

"Nobody's perfect, but I try."

"So. What am I kicking your ass in tonight?"

"Excuse me?"

"The cards? What game did you pick for me to destroy you in?"

That made me laugh, unable to even feign indifference. "Poker, Rummy, Slapjack, pick your poison and I'll raise that bet, baby."

She lifted a hand to her heart as she said, "Slapjack!? Heck, I don't remember the last time I played Slapjack."

"High school, maybe?"

"Maybe!" She slowly backed into the space in a cocky little saunter that made not smiling impossible. "Sure about this, Professor? Pretty sure it gets a little intense, if I remember correctly."

Christ, she was cute when she tried to talk shit. "I once survived a five-hour debate on the existence of time. Now *that* is intense."

El rolled her eyes as she kicked off her shoes and climbed up onto the layers of blankets and pillows over the makeshift living room bed. "Oh, spare me the intellectual superiority complex. We're talking elementary school games, not quantum mechanics."

"Fine. But don't underestimate me because I use my brain for a living. I've got lightning-fast reflexes."

"*Please*, the last time I saw you move like lightning was in high school."

"Hey now," I said in mock offense. Hell, she seemed to enjoy watching me move in Vegas. "I'll have you know I beat both your brothers in the town dodgeball competition last year."

Laughing, she plopped down between two pillows. "Welp, for your sake, I hope that Salmon Fest championship holds up."

I sat down on the opposite side of the TV tray, gently nudging her mug and coaster across to her as I snagged the card deck to shuffle and deal. Elora did this adorable, full body wiggle as she looked down at her cocoa, complete with whipped cream and marshmallows. She wrapped her entire mouth around the tip of the whipped cream pyramid before sucking in a mouthful and giggling as she covered her messy lips. How could something so ridiculous and so adorable also get me hard? The two sensations should not walk hand in hand, but with El, it seemed like I was in a perpetual state of raging desire.

"With mini *marshmallows* and everything?!"

"Go big or go home," I supplied with a shrug.

"Amen. Now, if you were a *true* hot cocoa connoisseur, there *would* be sprinkles."

Smirking, I plucked a tiny shaker of peppermint sprinkles from the pile of candy and handed it to her. I chuckled when she narrowed her eyes.

"Oh, you *are* good."

"Don't forget it," I jabbed back as she popped the lid and gave a few generous shakes over her cup, speckling all that fluffy white in tiny red crystals, like a terrifying glitter explosion. As if I hadn't noticed her love for diabetes in a cup. Sliding slick cards between my fingers, I shuffled the deck and dealt, card for card, between our two piles. A long, dramatic slurp interrupted the subtle slap of them hitting the table and I looked up right as she lowered her mug with a deeply satisfied expression on her face.

"Aren't you going to drink some?"

"Yeah, in a sec. I sampled my bodyweight in it as I got the ratio right. Actually called my mom to make sure I had the recipe down."

"I knew I recognized that flavor. God, she was always the keeper of the good cocoa."

"The baton has been passed."

"Don't get too cocky. Hers is better."

I brought my hands to my chest, tossing my head back dramatically. "You wound me, Rhodes."

"You'll live," she said with a giggle as I set the last card in place. A vaguely warm, very damp finger poked my nose, and I jerked back, narrowing my eyes on a satisfied feline smirk. Wiping the melty whipped cream off my face, I popped my finger into my mouth, shaking my head as she stifled a laugh.

"Easy, Pix. Don't start a fight you can't win."

"For your ego's sake, I'll let you keep believing that."

"You're incorrigible."

"*Why, thank you.*" She took a long sip from her mug, giving me another satisfied full body wiggle and looking all too pleased with herself as I shook my head. With a dull clunk, she set her drink down and snatched up her stack of cards, turning to face me head on and clearing the couch of all things fuzzy. "You're going down, Allen."

"Maybe later. Play me first."

"Ha-hah, *so funny*," she said with an eye roll before an

equally dramatic deadpan. "Now, play." We both started setting cards down in rapid succession, but that didn't stop her from adding, "If I remember the rules correctly, the loser buys the winner's dinner?"

"Is that so?" I pushed back as our cards *tap, tap, tapped* onto the growing stack between us. "Thought we were just playing for bragging rights."

The smirk that lifted her cheeks was nothing shy of maniacal. "Consider it an added incentive to win."

I jerked my eyes back to the growing deck as we continued to *tap, tap, tap* cards into place. "You trying to distract me, Pix? Cause it won't work."

"I'm insulted, Brod. Just stating the rules of the game, but if you're feeling nervous...?" the end of her sentence trailed up and off, but I refused to look up at what was an inevitable Cheshire smile.

"Please," I scoffed, shaking my head as I watched our cards hit the middle pile. *Ace, eight, six.* "Steady as a rock, baby."

"We'll see about that," she said slyly as I set mine down. After watching to make sure it wasn't a jack, she leaned back, casually setting aside her half of the deck and stripping my hoodie off her body in the next motion. The extended lines of her abdomen were on full display as she tossed it across the back of the couch like a lazy basketball shot, smiling coyly as I let my eyes scrape over her frame. I palmed my jaw, admiring all that skin and the way the red bra boosted her tits up in the most inviting fucking way. She wasn't just gorgeous, she was confident in her body, and that was a deadly combination.

"Like I said. Steady as a rock." But I couldn't help but wet my lips, wishing my tongue could run over those sexy lines of muscle instead. Slide up the center of her generous cleavage. *Tap, tap, tap.*

"Hard as one too, by the looks of it."

I held onto my next card, locking eyes with her as my smile grew. There was no need to confirm her claim. My dick was at full attention. Painfully so. It took very little effort for her to get it to stand up these days. "Keep running that mouth, and I'm going to give it something hard to *do*."

"If that's your idea of a threat, you've got some work cut out for you."

"You say threat. I say promise."

"Big words, big man."

Chuckling, I shook my head, subtly tossing my card on the pile but holding her stare. "Nice try, baby," I muttered as I set my palm over the jack. Her eyes flared as she lunged forward and then yelped, clapping her hands together in a loud smack and throwing her head back.

"Dammit!"

"Do you generally win your games by getting naked?" I asked, adding the cards to my stack.

Flippantly, she tucked her bangs behind her ear and said, "It's a new strategy."

"Not a very good one."

"That tent in your trousers begs to differ." *Tap, tap, tap.* She lost her battle with a nervous little giggle when I narrowed my eyes on her, tonguing at a molar to keep from bursting out laughing. She paused after my turn to sip on her cocoa, and I did the same. Only, her hand swatted out with cat-like efficiency, pushing the cup up and dipping my face in whip cream.

Yep. Should've seen that coming. Fighting a smirk at the elated laugh that burst from her lips at the sight of my whipped cream beard, I slowly set aside my drink, snatching hers and adding it to the tray before pushing it back to a safe distance.

My eyes locked on hers for a beat before she yelped and tried to flee. Too little too late, because I already had her wrist gripped in my fingers, locking her in place as my other hand snaked around her waist. She reared back, trying to keep her face away from mine as I dove forward, pinning her to the couch, scrambling to secure her wrists above her head and transferring them into one hand before burying my mess of a face between her breasts. She shrieked with laughter, and I smiled as I popped up, shifting my weight over her body, making sure she could feel that erection she kept pointing out.

"You know, when I've thought about covering you with whipped cream, it was in a much more dignified manner."

Her frantic giggles came to a breathy end as she grinned up at me, full breasts heaving against my chest. "*Is there* a way to be dignified while covered in whipped cream?"

"Laying naked on my bed so I can decorate those tiny nipples before sucking them off sounded nice to me."

"I agree. Much more sophisticated than you motorboating my boobs," she said firmly. My brows rose, smirk hooking wide as her gray-blues went round and she barked, "Don't you *dare!*"

Her attempt to squirm away just got me harder, and I ground my hips into hers to hold her steady, still pinning those delicate wrists in one hand as I bent down and did exactly that, coming up with a full face of whipped cream and my woman cackling so hard tears formed in her eyes.

"You know, I thought you on your knees for me would be the only time I enjoyed seeing your mascara run, Pix," I said as I leaned onto my elbow, releasing her wrists. "This might be better."

El couldn't compose herself long enough to articulate a comeback. Every time her laughter tapered off, she'd make this hilarious little humming sound before erupting back into giggles. One delicate hand found its way to my face, and she smudged away the sugary topping, popping a finger between her lips as hysterical machine gun bursts of laughter escaped.

I shook my head, snatched her hand and slowly slid a finger in my mouth, sucking it clean and reveling in her mouth hanging open and eyes sliding closed, before ruining the illusion of the moment by releasing her hand and lapping straight up the valley between her breasts instead.

Elora

OUR WHIPPED CREAM war resulted in an impromptu shower, and me wearing Broderick's oversized hoodie and my lace undies with nothing else, while we cuddled up back on his gray sectional to watch *Inception*. By the time the movie ended, we were both teetering on a sugar coma and completely exhausted. Broderick finished brushing his teeth and ducked into his room before I'd wrapped up my skincare, so I wasn't shocked to find him already gloriously shirtless and in bed when I came out of the ensuite. He had one knee propped up to brace a book where he could keep it at eye level, but his eyes strayed to mine as I closed the distance.

"Gosh, it doesn't matter how many times I watch it, it's just one of those films that leaves you questioning everything you think you know, isn't it?"

"Kinda *the point*, Pix."

"It's like a dream inside a dream inside a... well, you know. And fuck, that ending gets me every time."

"Maybe we're living inside someone else's dream *right now*," he teased, waving a conspiracy hand around, his book falling to rest on his thigh.

"Maybe! *You don't know*," I insisted as I flopped onto the mattress beside him. "I hate open ended plots. Unless there's a sequel to tell me how it concludes, I can't deal with it. Because then the questions just torture me *forever*."

Patting the pillow beside him, Broderick skipped my dramatics with a subdued smirk and said, "Come on, baby. Under the sheets."

"You probably love open ended plots."

"I do," he confirmed simply.

"Endless room for theorizing."

"I do enjoy theories. Come on, come get under the blankets with me, and then I won't make you move until morning."

"Ugh," I whimpered. "My *abs* hurt. You laughed me new abs and now they hurt."

He chuckled before admitting, "Actually, my face is sore, now that you mention it. Are smile-ups a thing? Because my cheeks feel all bruised."

"Serves you right."

"You started it."

"Didn't expect it to escalate that quickly," I pointed out, smirking as I begrudgingly rolled onto my hands and knees and crawled up to him. It was impossible to miss the way his pupils flared as he tracked the motion, but my attention locked on the bed when I threw the comforter back. He had two hot pads neatly laid out under the comforter on my side of the mattress, little red lights illuminated on the controllers. Blinking, I glanced to his side of the room, and when I didn't spot any cords, jerked my gaze back to his. "What's this?"

He shrugged a nonchalant shoulder as though the gesture warranted no explanation. "You don't sleep if you're cold. It's going to snow tonight, and these windows are terrible."

"You... you pre-heated the bed for me?"

That made him chuckle, his hand finding my hip as I scooted under the blanket beside him. "Seventy-two degrees or higher for a happy Elora pastry." I nestled in right next to him, practically purring when the heat from the pads hit my skin. Damn, that was cozy. My eyelids instantly became just a little heavier. "You sure you can get away with sleeping here, Pix?"

It was officially hard to keep my eyes open. "I usually work from the coffee shop in the mornings," I said with a yawn, stretching before nestling into his side as he scooted down to cradle me against him. "I figure as long as I pop in with my laptop long enough for the baristas to remember me coming by, then nobody will be any wiser."

"Okay. I'll wake you up with me."

"Mmmkay." My eyes sealed shut, head lolling against his chest, muscles melting between the snuggles and warm bed. Voice barely audible, I mumbled, "Whatcha' reading?"

"Brandon Sanderson."

"*Dragons?*" Even my ears thought I sounded drunk. Could you get drunk on *happy?*

"Sometimes," he chuckled. "Goodnight, Pix."

"Tell me about the dragons tomorrow?"

"Okay, baby." The heat of his palm settled against my cheek, pulling a contented little hum from my chest as he pushed the hair away. "Sleep well."

TWENTY-THREE
BRODERICK

"I don't know. Maybe I just gotta swear off women," Axel groused as we packed our nasty gym clothes into duffle bags. After a whopping six months, he and his most recent flame fizzled out, and he was less than pleased at the prospect of getting back in the game.

"Famous last words," I declared, smirking over at Jameson, who scowled because it was true.

"Maybe stop dating women half your age," he suggested, stuffing his hoodie deeper into the black space and sliding the zipper closed.

"Christ, dude, they're not half my age. I'm not a pedo."

"Just saying–did you meet this last one in homeroom?"

"What can I say? Apple doesn't fall far from the tree. Worked out just fine for you and Rhyett."

"First, the apple thing is for kids, not brothers. Second, fucking watch it," Jameson growled. But Axel's jab earned a round of laughs from Charlie and Jake.

"Don't give him a complex," I muttered, slinging my bag over my shoulder and palming the basketball from where it sat on the wood bench. "Took a great deal of effort to make Noel stick." There's honorable and then there's insufferable. Jameson was so bent out of shape about the eight-year difference he almost threw away the best thing that ever happened to him. Last thing I wanted was these bozos making him second guess that, so I opted to redirect their focus. Turning on Jake, I asked, "What about you–any prospects on the horizon?"

"Gotta be looking to have prospects. Haven't bothered to look since...I dunno, Sterling was born?"

All of us halted, collectively turning to pin him under incredulous eyes. At five-foot-eleven, Jake was the smallest of the group. While he possessed those signature Rhodes eyes, their youngest cousin had light brown hair, olive skin, and a baby face. It was Axel to vocalize the collective thought.

"I mean, I knew it had been a minute. But...you haven't dated in *seven* years?"

Fidgeting under our focus, he shrugged. "I mean, a couple of hookups."

"You're not even thirty," I pointed out.

"And the dating scene blows. Women are fucking crazy."

All of us weighed his words before turning for the door as Jameson muttered, "The good ones are out there. Might have to go off island to find one we're not related to, though."

I snorted, shaking my head. "In your case, that's true. You Rhodes pop up like rabbits."

"How about you, teach?" Charlie asked as we walked through the open free weight space. "Haven't heard you talk about Sarah in a few weeks. You doing alright?"

Smiling as I realized I hadn't so much as thought about my ex since Vegas, I smiled and said, "Never better," and pushed open the door to the daycare so we could spring Sterling and June out of baby jail. With the woman behind that 'never better' in mind, I suggested, "Anybody else need a cup of coffee?"

ONE THING I'd always loved about El was her capacity to dive so deeply into her focus that a war could start while she was working, and she wouldn't even know. She never even bothered to look up as the seven of us came into the Grizzly Grind, Rhyett's coffee shop on the harbor, and made our way to the counter to order. Kara, the sweet little blonde behind the counter, beamed down at Sterling and June as they bounced on their toes, blushing a little when she looked up at Jake and Charlie. She held her shit together, though, which I always thought was admirable.

"Hey, guys! What can I get for you?"

We rattled off our orders one at a time, but it wasn't until I stepped up to the counter and into El's periphery that her head snapped up, her smile stretching wide before she waved enthusiastically at the other four. "Long time no see," she quipped. "A whole twelve hours, and you're all back together. Why am I not shocked?"

"Thought we'd burn off those mashed potatoes of yours," I said, leaning an elbow onto the bar to prop myself up.

She canted her head before asking, "Basketball morning?"

"Yeah, took a steam after," Axel added. Nobody else seemed to notice her eyes flick to me.

"You in here working on a holiday weekend, El?" Charlie said, grinning. "Leave the no personal life up to first responders, cuz."

"No rest for the wicked," she chirped, standing and stretching out her back before squatting down to talk to the kids. The guys were chattering about Paxton's game yesterday, but I was stuck, mesmerized by Elora.

Our orders came out at the same time, and I lifted my to-go cup in salute. "Good bumping into you," I said as the guys finished taking turns giving her big bear hugs.

"As always," she said back, fighting that smile teasing the corners of her lips. "What else is on the agenda today?"

"Eh, we're all taking off, heading home," Jameson said with a hand on her shoulder.

"Grabbing groceries to make Grandma's curry tonight, then try to be in bed by eight," I said, hoping I achieved some sense of nonchalance.

"Nice, nice," she said, patting her brothers on the back as she walked our huddle to the door. The guys all filed onto the street, but as I walked past her, she said, "Can I bump into you again later?"

"In a town this small?" I smirked in her direction as I stepped onto the sidewalk. "Inevitable, don't you think?" Fuck me. Her smile took my breath away.

"Inevitable."

Elora

FIVE DAYS WEREN'T ENOUGH. I'd been well aware that it wouldn't be when I'd booked my flights, but it didn't make it any easier to wake up in Broderick's arms Monday morning, knowing our stolen days were over. From movie nights to his family's century old South African curry recipe that brought tears to my eyes and made me sweat a waterfall, to a Sunday brunch whipped up on that magnificent island, with his arms around my waist, it was the cruelest blink at bliss.

Then it was over.

We couldn't even share a proper goodbye, because the town was too damn small to get away with it. So, I begrudgingly allowed Jameson to drive me to the airport and brushed off his concerns about my panicked resting bitch face as he set my suitcase on the scale. He'd wrapped me up in a great bear hug before holding me at arm's length.

"You're welcome home any time, El. You know that, right?"

"Yeah," I said, nodding and trying to ignore the stinging at the bridge of my nose. *Home.* Home was six feet of long, lean muscle and rich brown skin, a laugh that carved a grin on my face, and a breathtaking smile that lit my core on fire. "Yeah, I do. Thanks, James."

He stooped, like he could compensate for being six-foot-four. "You sure you're okay?"

"Yeah," I said, mustering a smile and a nod. "I get to see Pax when I'm in Chicago in a couple of weeks. That'll be nice."

"Yeah," he said, but the pinch in between his brow said I hadn't convinced him. Hug him for me."

"Will do."

"Fly safe, El."

MARA

Awe, poor bébé is homesick?

> ELORA
> God, I never knew how people could miss a place until now.

IT WASN'T SO MUCH the *place* as the man living within it, but with Hadlee on this thread, I decided I should probably keep my mouth shut. Three people in the know was likely three too many.

> ALICE
> I miss everyone so much it makes me nauseous. Captain Hartless is on a terror.

GREYSON HART WAS a ruthless mid-thirties media mogul, and Alice had bestowed a handful of less than flattering nicknames over the last two years working for him, including 'Hartless' or when he was being spectacularly dickish, 'Captain Hartless', 'The Fire-breathing Dragon', and my personal favorite; 'Mr. Ass Face'.

> MAX
> And now you're all so scattered it's costing me a small fortune to bounce around to see everyone.

MARA

Hold on, let me call an ambulance for Mr. Whines A Lot.

MAX

What? It was easy when all fourteen of them were on one rock.

MARA

Poor little rich boy has family all over the country to stay with.

MAX

Little salty there, Mara?

MARA

Nate is teething. There is no sleep to be had. I need a vacation. And a fifth of tequila.

ALICE

You know where you can find a state-of-the-art spa resort?

ELORA

Hmmm. IDK, maybe Emerald Bay?

ALICE

PLEASE come visit me. The Harts own one uptown and I can get us in at forty percent cost.

ELORA

Like hosting the twins aren't enough people in one apartment.

ALICE

The dragon has depleted my dopamine so sufficiently, I gotta chase any hit I can get. Starting with your cute asses on my couch watching a LOTR movie marathon with sea salt and caramel chocolate ice cream and mashed potatoes.

MARA

Po-Tay-Toes.

MAX

Weird combination. I'll allow it.

HADLEE

You're all obnoxious. Do you realize there are four hundred and sixty-eight notifications on this text thread?

MAX

How nice of you to grace us with your presence, Hads.

HADLEE

I've been boon-docking!

MAX

Why?

MARA

Apocalypse preparedness training?

ELORA

Hads is a minimalist.

HADLEE

Experiences over things is my MO.

MAX

Welcome back to the land of the living.

HADLEE

Thanks. First stop is a bathtub.

Elly, why so homesick?

MAX

Yeah, Elly. Why so homesick?

GOD, I missed Broderick. Had been missing him even more since leaving Mistyvale nearly two weeks ago. He was like a phantom limb, an omnipresent ache for a piece of me that was never there when I went reaching for it. Yeah, we talked every night and texted all day—hell; we spent the evenings watching the same movies or playing the same music. But it wasn't the same thing as waking up in his arms on those stolen days back home. He was meeting me here on Saturday night, and we'd go watch Pax play Sunday together, shielded by the family box and thousands of fans.

I never thought I wouldn't want to take another speaking gig, but fuck, having to say goodbye to him again was even worse than Las Vegas. By my fourth year on the speaking circuit, I'd learned to make my presence dependent on my comfort—flat water instead of sparkling, and the right coffee and snacks in a private dressing room, or hotel room on site, where I could run through my breathing exercises, visualization, and rehearsal before stepping out on stage or in front of a boardroom.

When I first started, I would've labeled them weird asks or a prima donna attitude, but I was good at what I did, and deserved the space, tools and reinforcement to deliver the information at my full power. It was only there that I could serve my clients in the way they deserved, anyway.

Men were never second guessed when they had specific requests, and yet women always were. That's what we needed to change.

This company was woman owned, and—low and behold—didn't bat an eye at my signature 'weird asks'. As a matter of fact, they'd been prepared for it, and even had a welcome basket with my favorite juice and cute little mini muffins when I got there. I'd happily given them an extra half hour of Q&A time before we dismissed the meeting. Their hospitality played into my nonchalance when I saw the flowers and a card sitting on my bedside table when I got back from the presentation.

It was only when I noticed they were daisies, rather than some kind of ostentatious roses or a mix, that I hesitated. The Leaning Tower of Pizza postcard finally sent my heart sprinting.

I FLIPPED over the postcard to see his hastily written note, a smile on my face just seeing my name in his handwriting.

> Dear Elora,
> I watched the most beautiful woman present on stage today. She took my breath away.
> Congratulations on another legendary speech,
> Pix.
> Answer the door.
> Brod

HEART IN MY THROAT, I flipped it back and forth, like more of an explanation would somehow appear, but then two solid knocks sounded on the door. I laughed when a familiar voice called, "Room service!"

Shaking my head, I bolted for the door, throwing it

open and nearly sobbing as I hurled my arms around his neck. Broderick staggered back a step as he caught me, wrapping me up tightly in those corded arms and chuckling as he buried his face in my hair.

"Hey baby," he husked. "You were brilliant today."

"What are you doing here!?" I squeaked.

"Couldn't miss my girl on stage in the Windy City."

"You weren't supposed to be here until Saturday!"

"Got big plans, Pix?" He chuckled, squeezing me tighter before unspooling our limbs.

"Porn and a pint of ice cream."

"What?!" He barked, eyes shooting wide as his brows flew up to his hairline. God, it was fun to make him squirm. "You were going to sit and watch porn with ice cream?"

"Sir, I am a *lady*. I don't watch porn." I leveled him with a glare as his eyes narrowed on me.

"No," he said, smirking. "But you read it."

"Guilty," I chirped. "Some good inspiration in there."

"Oh, I've heard."

"Have you now?"

"Evidently Rhyett has reaped the benefits."

Wrinkling my nose, I stuck out my tongue, making a gagging sound. "Ew, raging lady boner instantly vanquished."

He stifled a laugh, mock scolding over every inch of his face as he said, "He's got a baby. Do we need to have the talk, El?"

"Vaguely knowing my brothers screw like bunnies and *thinking* about it are two very different things." I latched onto his arm, yanking him inside my room and kicking the door closed in the same motion. "Now. Back to the subject at hand. How are you here!? Don't you have classes?"

"Even professors get sick, Pix." He mock-coughed into his fist twice.

A manic laugh burst from my throat, my hand slapping over my mouth as I watched that gorgeous smile of his grow. "Are you *sick*, professor?"

That grin hit blinding proportions and I couldn't help but mirror it. "I'm elated to say it's terminal."

My heart did thrilled little pancake flops, at the idea of this thing between us being a lifelong sentence. Did he mean that? It took all my focus to quip back, "Is it contagious? Should I be worried about you infecting my team?"

"Nah baby," he said, snaking a hand around my waist and pulling me into him, a now familiar warmth saturating my senses. "This fever is just for you and me."

"Cheeeeeesy line, sir."

"But did it work?" he asked with a chuckle, voice now low with promise that rippled goosebumps down my arms.

"Maybe," I breathed back, wrapping my arms around his neck as he lowered his mouth to mine.

FUMBLING the back of my earring into place, my eyes flicked up to Broderick, now freshly showered, as he came back into the room. He had a knack for planning our evenings, and I wasn't even a little mad about it. Frankly, it was nice to not be the only person capable of making a decision for once. We were going to eat at the Leaning Tower of Pizza and then to watch a movie. Regardless, I'd opted for a cute fitted long sleeve black dress, and furry boots beneath my winter coat.

One broad hand came up to rub over his mouth as his

eyes scraped over me. "I ever tell you that you're painfully gorgeous?"

"Not nearly enough," I teased, eyes dropping to my feet as he stepped in closer.

"I intend to remedy that immediately." He set those warm palms on either side of my hips, giving me a little squeeze as he leaned down to nip at the lobe I'd just stuck an earring in. His breath over my ear sent an anticipatory chill down my spine. "Regretting this whole going out thing."

"We don't have to," I whispered back, bringing my palm up to settle against his cheek as I nuzzled against him.

"As tempting as that is, my girl deserves to be properly courted."

"Courted?" I giggled. "Tell me, will you present Milo with one pig or two?"

Broderick groaned, leaning into my cheek. "Oh, man."

"What?" I asked, turning in his arms to bring our foreheads together. "I've been so anxious about telling your brothers that I didn't even think about needing to talk to Milo."

My dad, much like Jameson, was a big teddy bear under a six-foot-four exterior. But there's something about a sun-weathered Captain, subject only to the sea, that makes people cower. Maybe it was the towering frame, or that men go missing in the storms every year, but knowing him for who he was, I couldn't wrap my head around them all being intimidated by him.

I straightened Broderick's sleek blue tie before running my palms down the slick heather gray vest and giving him a pat. "Of all the men that could proposition his daughter, you're the only one I could see him being thrilled with."

"I don't think you understand how men operate, baby."

"Don't get me wrong, he's a dad at his core, which essentially means that nobody will ever be good enough for his kids, but...as far as prospects go, I'm more than confident in mine."

Expression melting into something like affection, he brought those warm palms to cradle either side of my face, pressing a light kiss to my forehead as he murmured, "Thanks, Pix. I hope to earn his blessing in this. Which means we can't hide forever."

Anxiety stirred in my chest, because as long as this was our little secret, I could revel in the emotions of it, in the bliss of it. But the moment I shared him with my family, the moment we became an 'us,' this would be... real. And we would be subject to their scrutiny. I loved my family. Truly, I did. But thirteen other very loud opinions were thirteen too many.

"I know," was all I breathed back.

"Any intention of breaking our silence soon?"

"Maybe."

"The longer we wait, the worse it will be if somebody finds out by accident, baby."

"And the faster we tell them, the faster this stops being our personal escape, because it will be everybody's god damn business," I blurted back. Knowing curved the lines of his mouth, the warm brown skin around his eyes crinkling.

"Like keeping me your dirty little secret?"

"Nothing little about you."

"First up—damn straight and don't you forget it. Second—then we gotta have a plan, baby. It's only a matter of time before one of us slips up."

"Excuse me, *sir*, I am a *vault*," I said with mock insult, miming locking up my lips and tossing away the key. The no nonsense deadpan he gave me said he didn't believe me as far as he could throw me.

"And Max? Alice? Mara? How long will they keep this close to the vest?"

Groaning, I buried myself in the crook of his neck, soaking in his scent, wishing I could just hide myself in this lovely little bubble of ours. "I know. Okay. So... soon, okay?"

He scowled down at his watch, tapping the face with a perplexed furrow to his brow. I narrowed my eyes at him.

"What are you doing?"

"Looking for soon between eleven and noon."

"Oh boy," I muttered, disentangling and grabbing his hand. Leading him to the door, I rolled my eyes as the man continued.

"I could check my calendar. There might be a month I'm not aware of. Or a national holiday I missed?"

"Very funny." The hotel door clicked shut behind us, the lock buzzing into place as we walked away, Broderick trailing in my wake.

"Secret day of the week?"

"You're *hilarious*."

Chuckling to himself, he followed me down the hallway to the fire escape stairs. We were greeted by crisp air—seriously, I could almost see my breath in there—and the creak of ungreased hinges. It was the moment the heavy metal door clanged shut behind us that Broderick pulled me back against him and spun us, caging me in against the icy wall of the secluded stairwell, planting a knee between my legs to pin me in place. My breath halted as he towered over me, a forearm propped above my head in a way that saturated all of my senses. Those dark eyes held a seriousness in contrast to the smile playing on his luscious lips.

"I'll play your games, El, because I meant what I said. You're the ultimate prize life could ever give me." He brushed my hair away from my face, eyes tracking where my throat bobbed before he slid just his thumb down the line of my jaw. The pad of his finger grazed over my bottom lip before gently pressing it down. I fought back the need to suck his finger into my mouth like some kind of feral animal in heat. As his eyes found their way back to mine, I rolled that lip between my teeth. "But this is questionable territory we're treading in. And a man is *nothing* without his integrity, so I'm asking you again; when can I honor mine? Your brothers. Your dad. Mama Juniper. They all deserve to hear this from us."

I could feel the rapid-fire tap of my heartbeat hammering in my throat as his now-flat palm brushed down my cheek, my jaw, bracketing my neck as his thumb hovered over the pulse point. Breath coming in tight little inhales under his intoxicating proximity, I nodded. Who the fuck knew that integrity could be so damn sexy?

"You'll make a plan?" he pressed, those brown eyes narrowing slightly.

Still nodding, like that was all my brain remembered how to do, I breathed, "I'll make a plan."

"Good girl." He dropped a reassuring kiss to my lips as my core went molten, rendering me barely capable of kissing him back. Somehow, he breathed life back into me before pulling back with a sweet smile in place. "Let's go eat."

Without further ado, the man returned the air to my lungs when he whooshed away from me, leading me down the concrete stairs with echoing steps without another word.

"GOD, I forgot how damn good this place is."

"You didn't oversell it," Broderick said, grinning as he wiped his hands on a napkin. He was adorably out of place in the greasy little pizza joint—wearing his classy button-up shirt and vest—and yet somehow so GQ he pulled it off.

"The wax pizza tower is lame, albeit practical."

"Totally lame. But it would be ethically appalling to remake the tower on a regular basis."

"Obviously." Rolling my eyes, I finally slid my plate away in surrender. "Suddenly, I'm not so mad about that movie tonight."

"I think I'd get a side ache if we adjourned any sooner."

I smiled, glancing across the bustling restaurant and reveling in the chaos surrounding our circle of ease. There was something spectacularly comfortable about dating someone I knew on such an intimate level—a friend who knew all about my ugliness and celebrated the beauty anyway—compared to the prolonged unease around dating strangers. We didn't have to fight to impress each other. Didn't have to pretend a romp in the sheets after eating our body weight in cheese sounded like an enjoyable experience.

Broderick had seen me at my worst—hell, he'd ridden in like a dark knight in shining armor to salvage my prom night when I was stood up—and at my peaks. There wasn't a part of me he didn't already know. Which meant enjoying time together was just that. Enjoyable. Effortless.

At least, it was until my eyes snagged on graying blonde hair and a familiar face across the restaurant. "No fucking way," I muttered, my mouth hanging open as my feet fell to the floor from where I'd perched them on the foot of Broderick's chair.

"What?" he mumbled, glancing over his shoulder in the direction I'd been gaping in a most unladylike manner.

"Don't look," I hissed. "Mrs. Anderson is here."

TWENTY-FOUR
BRODERICK

"Like...lives-next-door-to-Jameson, Mrs. Anderson?"

"Yes. Taught us all seventh-grade science. Five-foot-four, blonde hair, blue eyes. Takes her steaks pink in the middle. How many Mrs. Andersons do you know?"

I choked on a laugh before glancing over my shoulder. This was *not* subtle. We were staring like a couple of lunatics. Sure enough, retired Mistyvale Middle science teacher, and Jameson's next-door neighbor, Mrs. Anderson, was standing at the hostess stand waiting to be served. Shaking my head, I muttered, "What are the damn odds? Man, it's a small fucking world. A country between us, and we end up in the same pizza parlor?"

"What the fuck is she doing here? Chicago isn't exactly vacation central, especially this time of year."

"I thought Alex landed in Wisconsin." Her kids were years ahead of me in school. Her youngest son, Alex, was three years older than El's oldest sister, Jeanne, and the reason she'd originally gone out with her now ex-husband, Lincoln–good man, just shitty circumstances.

"Me too."

"And why is she out alone?" I straightened, more than a bit irritated. "Who lets their seventy-year-old mother walk Chicago streets alone?" As if on cue, Alex and his wife came in behind her, a baby carrier tucked into the crook of his elbow. "*Oh, look*, Alex."

"Fuck me, because one person wasn't enough?"

I chuckled, ducking down but watching as the four of them reunited in the entryway. "What are the odds they don't see us if we stay put?"

"Not great. What do we do?" she asked, a bit panicked. I didn't know how to articulate it, but her nerves irritated me. I got to hold El for four days and didn't want to spend a moment of it ticked-off, so I did my best to shake it off, opting for humor.

"Smile and wave?" I breathed back, mimicking her dramatic stage whisper.

"Christ, are you that penguin in *Madagascar*?"

"Why *were* there penguins in *Madagascar*?" I asked, smirking, and not remotely bothered by the current predicament. This was inevitable. Albeit, how we got away with her week back on the island only to bump into someone in *Chicago*, I'd never understand. "El, we're friends. Is it so odd to be seen out together?"

"Dressed up for a date night in a city *four-thousand* miles away, just the two of us? Yeah. I think it's weird. I think it's the end of our charade if she catches us." Her subtlety had reduced notably as she leaned over the table, gesticulating between us. Which I found hilarious, poorly hiding that fact behind my fist as I propped my elbow on the table.

Shrugging, I pressed, "So what, El?"

"What do you mean, *so what*?"

"What if I *want* to be seen with you? We just talked about telling the family. Might as well get it over with."

She blinked, looking a little dumbfounded, before the words tumbled out. "Right. *Us* tell them not Mrs. Anderson and her bingo-playing biddies down at the pool hall. We won't even have time to talk it out before it gets back to Jameson, and then all hell will break loose."

Something about her urgency to get the hell out of dodge didn't settle well. Frustration planted in my bones as she extended a hand across the table. I winced when I looked over my shoulder and saw the hostess marching towards the front stand to greet them.

Sensing my unwillingness to budge, El added, "We don't even have answers to the million and one questions any Rhodes or Mistyvale busybody will hurl in our direction. Don't you think that's important? Don't you think we should be prepared to explain to Rhyett and Jameson what our plan is, so they don't beat you half to death?"

Okay. She had a point there. With a sigh, I snatched her extended hand and stood, pulling my wallet out of my back pocket with the opposite hand, fishing out a fifty, and tucking it under the short rose in a little vase on the table.

I followed El between patrons for the back hallway, shaking my head as she glanced over her shoulder to make sure we weren't busted. Boisterous Italian music came from the speakers, which I found ironic given the very American pallet of the menu. We wound our way to the back, and with one last glance over my shoulder to scan for the Andersons, El leaned into the kitchen door.

Her grin turned maniacal before she led me through the space, head held high as if she belonged here—as if that would ward off suspicion. Much to my dismay, it did. We somehow scooted between counters and servers bellowing, "Corner!" Without causing alarm, or having rotten tomatoes lobbed our way by pissed-off chefs.

When she pushed outside into the filthy, frozen back alley, a heavy breath rushed from her lungs and she shuffled sideways to collapse into the cold brick, like we'd just had a near-scrape with death instead of a seamless escape from a near-sighting with an elderly neighbor.

"You look like you just escaped a bear, not a seventy-year-old woman," I noted, aiming for lightheartedness and evidently missing the mark. At least, judging by the sarcastic glare she shot my direction. I reached forward to snag her dainty fingers in my hands, stepping into her space as I asked, "What are you so freaked out about? We're going to tell everybody anyway—would it be the end of the world if we were discovered at a kick ass pizzeria?"

"I'm not ready."

"To explain yourself to our middle school teacher? I think she knew we were endgame back then," I chuckled. Despite the focus furrow between her brows, the whites of her eyes grew, and I shook my head. "El, you gotta talk to me here. You're freaking me out."

"I'm not ready to explain myself to...anyone."

"Baby, I'm trying to be understanding, but I'd be lying if I said I was okay with that. Are you *embarrassed* to be with me or something?"

Pain lanced across her expression, oddly stilling the ache in my chest. "God, Brod, *no*."

"Okay. Because I know we joked about it, but I don't actually *want* to be your dirty little secret." Judging by the way her jaw popped open, I'd done a shit job of hiding the edge of hurt lingering in my tone. We wasted a decade pining for each other, but deciding to make El mine was the best thing I'd done in my life. If she said 'go', I'd scream it from the damn rooftops. Consequences be damned.

"You're not. I just... my family is complicated. And huge. And overwhelming."

"I *did* crash in that house more nights than not for about twenty summers." Some nights, it felt like half the high school landed at the Rhodes' on Friday nights. But the summers turned that old house into a clown car of teenage angst and rank smelling football gear. The entire varsity team would pile in under the guise of pizza pockets and electrolytes, but I always suspected I wasn't the only kid that needed a hug from Juniper Rhodes.

El was right about one thing though—even when it was just the family, it was still a lot to handle. "That piece, at least, I understand."

"And this sounds ridiculously petty, even in my head, but is it so wrong that I just want you all to myself for a little while longer? I've shared you our entire lives, Broderick. Just... for now... I want to be selfish. Please."

Well, that was unexpectedly endearing. I grabbed the back of her neck and pulled her to me. I'd never get sick of kissing this woman. Of feeling the subtle give of her body against mine, or the moment her lips surrendered, and she melted into my hungry demands. This remarkable woman —who'd walked the globe twice over, who had CEOs eating out of her delicate palm—was asking to keep me for herself. As deeply as I wanted to come clean, to claim her publicly, as I tasted her lips and my hands traveled over her warmth in a frigid city, some part of me decided just to do what it took to keep her happy. Despite the gnawing in my gut that said this was going to bite us in the ass, I nodded and peeled away from her just as a gentle snow floated down between us.

"Okay."

"Okay," she said, tone slightly more chipper, although not entirely certain.

"We're not in Mistyvale anymore, Todo. We better get out of the dark alley before trouble finds us," I said, glancing around to ensure we were still alone and relieved to find the space empty. Her giggle dissipated the unease a bit.

"True." She leaned up to tickle bunny kisses across my nose and then led me off into the glowing snow globe of a winter night in Chicago. I followed her through wonderland, wanting to believe everything she said. Wanting to believe she wanted to prolong this oasis of ours. But a part of me felt like the reality was I'd yet to fully earn her trust. And who could blame her? For a decade, I wavered like a fucking pussy as we both hung onto the hook. It would take a lot more than a few weeks and a surprise trip to earn her faith in me. I just had to be okay with doing whatever it took to do it.

Elora

THE SHARP SMACK of Broderick's palm against my ass trapped my breath in a bubble in my chest the following morning. My surprise turned into a coy smile when I found him smirking down at said ass, looking all-too satisfied. Sweat glistened over his beautiful biceps, leaving damp spots on his cutoff t-shirt.

"Couldn't have the gym bros confused about who you're going home with," he said cheekily, amused eyes flicking up to mine.

"They just recognize me from the vlog, but don't know why." When his smile turned into a deadpan, I laughed and glanced around the crowded space. Most assisted machines were taken, the free weight section we'd happily made camp in no less congested. Lo-and-behold, a few guys with headphones on looked between us before turning to their machines.

"You were saying?" he said, closing the distance to trail warm fingers over the skin between my tank and leggings.

"That you have excellent taste in women. Take the compliment?" Clearing my throat, I offered a quick smile before rising on my toes to press a quick kiss to his lips. Setting my hands on his chest, I said, "Besides, you look awfully tempting curling those dumbbells."

"I've got nothing on you with your ass in the air cranking out deadlifts." My cheeks flushed, and I glanced around outside our little bubble. The best part of most gyms was that everyone lived in the cocoon of their own headphones. His fingers gently pinched my chin, tilting my face up to his so he could press a firm kiss to my lips before saying, "Alright, coach, what's next?"

Grinning, I supplied, "Squats."

"Trying to kill me, Pix?"

"You seem to appreciate the results just fine."

"Yeah, yeah, let's get this over with."

"For a football coach, you sure whine a lot in the gym."

"For a business coach, you sure lift like you're preparing for war."

"Your point?" Laughing, I disentangled, nodding towards the weight wrack. "Will you spot me?"

"Not like you need it."

"No," I agreed, not dropping his gaze as I backed over towards the towering barbell wracks. "But I like your hands on me."

He groaned as if I'd inflicted a physical pain, head

rolling back as he followed me, and I couldn't even wipe the grin off my face when I turned to load plates onto the bar. There was a euphoria that seemed to emanate between us during the simplest of activities, a sensation that I'd yet to experience. Weights loaded, I stepped under the bar and positioned myself, but it was Broderick's careful evaluation that I watched in the mirror. The only description for the look in his eyes was...protective. And I loved it.

"Good girl, keep your form," he instructed, tugging my ponytail playfully before pulling it over the bar so I didn't place the weight on it. With one nod of approval, I began my set, smiling as each rep got harder, my breath coming hotter, legs shaking by the fifth. I was about to roll the weight back onto the hook when he shook his head. "You're not done. Keep going, baby."

"Fuck," I breathed, but lowered again, something like pride swelling in my chest as he grinned and nodded. His eyes stayed on me–those broad palms upturned and ready to step in if I maxed out–while mine watched him in the full wall mirror across from us. The chaos of the gym was nothing but a blur, I'm sure partially because of the adrenaline-endorphin combo in my roaring bloodstream, but my zeroed in focus was all on him.

"That's my girl, you got one more," he said when I extended, giving my ass another light slap.

"Gonna...kill me," I gritted out, but shifted on my feet, mentally preparing for the fight of it. Through the scream in my quads, I squatted down, the smooth metal purr of the weight sliding down the track permeating my fog as I watched him step forward, his hands under the bar, but not touching until I'd extended. There if I needed him, but not doubting my ability to do it my damn self. Fuck, I loved the man. I rotated the bar back onto the hook with a heavy clunk. My breath exited in a relieved little whoosh as I straightened on shaking legs, grinning at him as he raised his big hand for a high-five. When my palm met his, he laced his fingers into mine, pulling me against him with his other hand as he brought our foreheads together, dropping that hand to my waist.

"I ever tell you how proud I am to call you mine?"

I grinned through ragged breaths, shaking my head.

"Mmm, we'll have to remedy that," he said, the promise in his tone sending a shiver down my spine before he claimed my mouth with a kiss that set fire tearing through my bloodstream. "A man has never been prouder, Pix."

As we stepped apart, I watched that glorious smile, and wondered if a woman had ever been prouder of *her* man than I was to call him mine. More than a decade worth of internal Elora's preened, and I decided that wasn't possible.

CONTENTEDLY NAKED, I lounged on the bed that evening, fingers absently curling in my hair as the other hand traced the long lines of Broderick's bare chest. I'd never thought story time would be erotic, but Broderick's low timbre tracing words more prose than pulpit certainly did it. Sure, it didn't help that the room smelled like sweat and sex, or that sensation was just returning to my fingertips. We'd squeezed in a quickie back in the room between the gym and my meetings, but there was nothing like getting to take my time with this man. Luxuriating in the feel of his skin on mine, his breath hot against my neck as our bodies did the talking.

With the chapter finished, he slid the bookmark into place, set the book aside and rolled over to smile at me, although I immediately missed the feel of his head resting on my belly.

"You look awfully sleepy for a woman with a date in forty minutes."

"You look awfully tempting for a man with plans in the city," I countered, running my nails over the pronounced vein in his forearm where he'd brought his hand to my bare waist.

"Insatiable creature."

"Guilty as charged." The gentle caress of his fingers over my body made my eyes flutter closed. Melting into his touch, I said, "You feel too good."

"Don't fall asleep, baby. I only have three nights with you, and we can sleep when we're dead. Gotta take advantage of a city where nobody knows our names." He bobbed his head, a sheepish grin curving his full lips as he evaluated. "Well, where only three people know our names."

My chuckle turned into a pained groan when he pulled his fingers from my skin. "Mm-mm," I protested, shaking my head. Shimmying down the bed, I relished in each inch of warm, naked Broderick against my body. I scooted until I could bury myself in his chest. His laugh rumbled through my ribs as he wrapped those long arms around my body, nuzzling his face against the top of my head. I wiggled my nose when the fine smattering of his chest hair tickled it and then turned my face to cuddle tighter against him. It shouldn't be legal for a man to feel so good. "I could stay here forever, and it wouldn't be enough time."

Goosebumps pebbled my skin when he began to gently scratch up and down my back. "I know, baby. But I gotta enjoy showing you off while I can. And I think you're going to like it."

"Why do you have to be so sweet when you're a pain in my ass?"

He chuckled darkly before giving me a little squeeze. "Come on."

"Mmmm," I croaked.

"Pants."

"Overrated."

"Dress, then? Something I can flip up over that ass the moment we're alone again tonight?"

I peeled one intrigued eye open, soaking up the warmth of his smirk as he leaned up on his forearm. "Why, Mr. Allen, are you insinuating a public romp?"

"It's on the bucket list," he said, his nonchalance betrayed by the way he was watching me for a reaction. "The idea of bending you over in some bathroom or pinning you up against the wall and making you come with my hand over your mouth so you can't scream... Fuck, I'd never forget it."

Smirking, I teased, "Mr. Ethics risking public indecency? I never thought the day would come."

"There are a lot of things I want to do with you that wouldn't occur otherwise."

"Like?" I whispered, my curiosity getting the better of me.

"Like... the white picket fence, golden retriever, matching jogging suit thing."

Throat thick, I wet my lips. Broderick Allen wanted to build the American dream with me? "Two-point-five kids?"

"I'd prefer rounding up to a solid three."

Nerves had me battling my smile, my previously brash display of my birthday suit suddenly immensely vulnerable. The picture of three little Brodericks running through the sunlight-filled living room of my dream house played through my vision. Squeals of laughter reverberating off a vaulted ceiling as their daddy and I sipped on tea and watched the fog roll in over the coast. Fighting the twitch in my cheeks, I asked, "You want a family?"

"Someday, yeah. Don't you?"

"I don't know," I answered, a bit too honestly. He didn't retract, still stroking steady lines across my back. "I mean, yes. *Maybe*. If the timing was right. Not a big one, but a couple of kids sounds nice. I just... With my career taking me everywhere, and hitting my thirties, I kinda figured my chance at that Norman Rockwell painting vanished."

"If anyone can paint their future, it's you, Pix."

Something about his certainty brought my fingers to his face, gently following the broad planes of his cheeks. His eyes slid shut as I rounded the line of his brow. I wanted to commit every inch—every breath with him—to memory. "Maybe not."

"I know it's old fashioned, but I always thought if I had a son, I'd name him after my dad."

I smiled at that, before catching the hope swelling in my chest and rolling my bottom lip between my teeth. "I always thought the same thing about mine."

"Robert Milo Allen has a nice ring to it."

And just like that, every scrap of composure exited my body. Hell, maybe my soul went with it, some kind of existential elation rolling through me. "Yeah," I breathed. "It really does."

His eyes narrowed on my face, like he could see the way my heart and mind were racing. Racing with what ifs and how's? "Hey, we figure all this out one day at a time, baby. You don't have to plan our whole life out right now."

Nodding, I asked, "You can see us building a life together?"

"Baby girl, there's not a woman alive I've ever seen that playing out with... *except* for you. You make it easy to see that complete picture. The late-night feedings. The diapers and potty training and picking the right schools. With anybody else, college tours would stress me out. But if I was doing it with you..." That smile that owned every inch of my heart grew. "That's the dream, right there."

TWENTY-FIVE
ELORA

The rich scent of garlic and veggie sauce loaded with meat mixed in the air with the soft sounds of Louis Armstrong singing "La Vie En Rose" like a magical transportation device that erased the Chicago skyline in favor of my memories of Europe. Our instructor, a boisterous middle aged white man with a generous belly and not quite enough neck, walked around grinning–first at the stations and then at his eager students. He insisted we call him Gio, although a handful of us playfully insisted on calling him 'Chef.' A subtle bubbling sound drew Broderick's attention, and he leaned over to stir the sauce, inhaling deeply.

"God, I'm salivating," he breathed happily.

"It's not my fault this time."

"For once," he muttered, bringing the wood spoon, which was loaded with Bolognese sauce, up to his nose. I snickered, using the back of my wrist to wipe stray strands of hair away from my eyes. He hadn't been spectacularly confident, but there had been something disproportionately sexy about watching him chop all the veggies during prep. Broderick had this way of looking suave, even while he compulsively re-checked our instructions, nervously watching Gio in his rotation around the room, like we'd retroactively fail school if he missed a step. It was disconcertingly endearing.

"Is *per*fect!" Gio exclaimed excitedly across the room as he peered over the shoulder of a rather anxious looking pair of Korean women that had to be sisters judging by their matching looks and laughter. His accent was as thick as the scent of simmering veggies and herbs.

"How's it coming, Pix?" Broderick questioned as he slid back to my side, pinching more semolina and dusting the wood board generously as I portioned out a fresh ball of dough. A stray plume drifted toward my apron, and I giggled as he muttered a curse under his breath.

"Easy, Professor, you're getting flour everywhere."

"Beg your pardon–I am *clearly* masterful at flour distribution." Even as he said it, he lost a battle with a laugh. Honestly, I was more than a little surprised when he announced our plan for the evening. Broderick generally stuck to activities he had practiced in, not a big fan of trying something new and failing in front of an audience. Which meant this stretch outside of his comfort zone was solely for me.

"*My Renaissance man,*" I said, feigning a swoon as I leaned back into his chest. He moved around my body, one dusted hand landing on my waist on top of the red apron, lips finding my neck on the opposite side.

"My *muse*," he whispered huskily, his voice coasting over my skin as sweetly as his possessive hold on my hip. He swiped up the remaining dough, and wrapped it in the plastic film, like Gio had shown us. Evidently, keeping the dough from drying out was more than a little crucial. Leave it to me to shoot straight for the fun part and Broderick to look after the details.

"Thanks," I muttered, feeling a little silly for forgetting.

"Of course. Nice work on the Tagliatelle." He wrapped me back up, resting his chin on my shoulder as I worked the dough with the rolling pin. We stayed like that for a beat, Broderick guiding me through a subtle little sway with a hand on my belly and his hips against my ass as Etta James' *A Sunday Kind of Love* took over on the understated speakers. A happy little hummingbird fluttered in my chest where my pesky heart had long since liquified. Wordlessly, he brought a hand around to hold the edge of our rolled dough when it came time to wrap the sheet around the rolling pin. Together, we mimicked the soft little rock with the pin that Gio had shown the class, and I tried not to break skin as I chewed on my lip nervously. It's not that I was a poor cook, but something as intricate as authentic Italian pasta was well outside *my* wheelhouse as well.

"Okay, so now we flip it, right?" I leaned toward him, smiling as the heat of his breath ghosted over my lips.

"Right," he affirmed. I gingerly unrolled the dough, smiling when Broderick lifted his hands out of my way and dusted the board with flour again when I peeled our sheet from the wood surface. I laid it back down, bringing the rolling pin back to continue the motions we'd learned. Before I knew it, Gio was peering over my opposite shoulder, his cheeks rosy enough they belonged on *The Night Before Christmas* illustration of St. Nick.

"Get your hands on it," he encouraged in that thick Italian lilt. "Not too thin, not too thick. You gotta *feel* it."

Broderick subtly nipped at my earlobe, and when Gio spun toward our neighbor he muttered, "Dying to feel *something*," but obediently brought his hands down to test the dough with me, ensuring all the edges were even.

"It doesn't have to be a perfect circle. Is alright if some are small and some are bigger," Gio encouraged as he walked down the aisle between stations in his white apron and light blue button-up shirt with his hands braced behind his back.

"That's not what she said," I mused, and Broderick choked on a laugh, resting his forehead on my shoulder to keep from losing it. "Glad you enjoy my ridiculous humor."

"Some things never change."

"Thank God for that." Despite the shake of laughter through his chest, we completed the pasta rolling process together in a wordless dance of movement, interspersed with my nervous giggles. Simultaneously canting our heads, we both stared down at the big blonde blob, and I wondered if he was also wondering if we could do anything else or if we'd completed the step.

From the corner of his mouth, Broderick hissed, "I think we did it?"

Laughing, I agreed. "I think we did."

It was right about then that Gio boomed over the chatter and vocals to remind us of that ultimate test. "Molto bene! You should be about done and remember to hold it up." He peeled his own example off the front station and held it to the light, opposite hand wiggling behind it and casting shadows through the sheet of dough. "See my hand through it?"

Broderick carefully did the same thing, an adorable trace of pride in his tone as he said, "Not too bad for a couple of amateurs, huh?"

"Speak for yourself, Professor," I said, shrugging. "I think we can give Gio's Nona a run for her money."

His eyes flicked to mine, equal parts nerves and humor as he muttered, "I usually think your confidence is ungodly sexy, but let's not get ourselves beaten with a cannolo."

"Gio left the gun behind?" I said, grinning ear-to-ear that he'd just made a freaking *Godfather* reference in our Italian class.

"Exactly," he said, smirking. "Besides, I wanted to see you blow it." Logic said that he was referencing Gio's other test to see if the dough was ready to be cut—evidently dough at the proper thickness waved like a flag when blown upon. It seemed like a comically unsanitary, albeit effective, way to test it in my humble opinion—but I couldn't help my smile as I shook my head in mock disapproval.

"Relentless man," I chastised as he laughed. God, that sound made my insides go molten. I could listen to Broderick Allen laugh for the rest of my life. The thought brought me up short after our earlier conversations. Yes, I didn't have to have all the answers right now, and should probably just try to be present, but that didn't keep my mind from wandering down years' worth of questions. Things like where the hell would we live? When I traveled, would he come? Would he keep teaching? Because those two thoughts were not conducive to each other.

All the worries in the world couldn't eclipse the way my body melted as he wrapped around me, his chin returning to my shoulder as he folded our dough. He felt like home to me. Felt like everything I'd always known he was in my life without the hope of him choosing me over them. But there he was, sliding the knife over the wood surface and slicing our Tagliatelle with anxiously precise strokes. He gave it a few gentle tosses before setting the serving aside to rest. I turned in his arms, looking up and smiling as his eyes met mine.

"Thank you," I whispered softly. When he quirked his head, I shook mine before looking pointedly around the room. "For this. I enjoy having firsts with you."

That knockout smile burst across his face like the early rays of sunrise. "To many more firsts," he said, reaching for the wine glasses and handing me mine.

Nodding, I clinked our glasses together in cheers and agreed, "To many more."

Broderick

"WHAT ARE the odds we walk away with a win?" El hissed Sunday afternoon, her fingers digging into my thighs like that might keep her anchored to the plush seats Pax saved us in the team's friends and family box.

El had unavoidable business to attend to on Friday, and even a few calls on Saturday, but we'd taken advantage of every second of time in between meetings and after dark. Memorizing her body would be the highlight of my lifetime at this rate. The sweet little whimpers she made, the cranky edge to her voice if she needed to eat. Made even more hilarious because her assistant, Chris, could hear it too, and we both knew we had t-minus seven minutes to get protein into the woman before an explosion or meltdown. Which brought me to the next thing I loved—the respect and adoration her team showed her, the way they catered to her drive and dedication, anticipating needs both in and out of the virtual boardroom. It wasn't just Chris, but her social media girls, the blogger who said very little on the video meetings but smiled to herself every so often at something they said, the PR team that sat in on strategy calls—they all loved her.

But there was nothing quite like the way she smiled as I settled over her naked body and read my current novel aloud for her to enjoy. She was always tracing feather light fingers over the veins in my arms. Weird kink, but I loved it. It was like she was working just as ardently to memorize me as I was her. Beyond the best fucking sex of my life, we'd *talked* this weekend. Finally, *really* talked. Future, past, it all came out between us.

The game had been riveting, and my girl was bouncing at the edge of her seat, eyes trained on the field, those pearly teeth digging into her lower lip as Pax and the o-line took their places after the Wolves called a timeout. They were down by a field goal with less than sixty seconds on the clock.

"I don't know, baby, but I've seen them pull off wilder comebacks."

"Pax has something up his sleeve, right? God, he's always got an ace tucked away."

I chuckled, watching her lip lose color as she worried it with a canine. Reaching up, I pushed her lip free with my thumb, turning her in my direction for a quick kiss before she wiggled with anxiety. I chuckled as those brows winged up, like she wasn't sure what to do to dispel the energy of a nail biter match. The stadium went eerily still in home field anticipation. The echoing hush of one hundred thousand people holding their breath was a surreal kind of high. We dragged our eyes back to the field as other people in the box stood, hands braced over their mouths.

"Come on, Wolves," she muttered under her breath, anxiously tapping her clenched fist against her lips. "Let's go, Pax."

The entire stadium sucked in a breath when they hiked the ball. The defense was gunning for our man though, and bellows of frustration filled the stadium when the line broke, and Pax bolted sidelong, before throwing the ball away.

"God dammit," the man behind us muttered. He'd been thrilled to learn we were here to support 'that Rhodes prodigy'.

"He saved his skin, he'll make it up," the woman to his right said as the ref announced the penalty, and the team made the walk with sagging shoulders.

"With forty seconds on the clock?" the man snipped back skeptically.

"Give him a break. This is *Paxton Rhodes* we're talking about—he's got forty seconds, two time outs, and his best receiver out there, and we just need a field goal to go into overtime. The game ain't over," another woman muttered. Did I take pride in our little Mistyvale hero inspiring that level of faith? Yeah. The kid was like a little brother to me. But it was nothing compared to the beam and glow of the woman beside me as she preened.

"There's our boy," I said, nodding to the mega screen and giving El a little squeeze. She hopped up, tugging me with her and looping my arm around her shoulders as Paxton's face—which was *so* like his brothers—popped up on the screen, partially concealed behind his face guard. He looked entirely unfazed by the setback as he barked directions to his guys. That didn't stop Elora from winding her arms around me like I might keep her anchored through the anxiety.

The entire stadium lost their minds when they pulled off a killer trick play before the opposing coach called a timeout.

"Motherfucker," El barked. "They're just fucking with their momentum, the fucking fuckers."

The woman singing Paxton's praises hacked out a gulp of cola, hand flying to cover her mouth as she battled between laughter and choking. But I was grinning like an imbecile. If I hadn't already known that I loved this woman, watching her swear like a sailor with a freakish grasp for my favorite sport would've done it.

"That sums it up," the man behind us with the handlebar mustache said.

"I'm starving, let's grab a snack in case we end up in OT."

"Remind me to sell off my left kidney to thank Pax for these seats when we get home," I said as I followed her toward the in-suite smorgasbord where Mustache's wife was walking away with a couple of sodas. Snacks were a luxury in a match this tight, and there's absolutely no way we could survive the lines in the main stadium and make it back in the two minutes they cut away to sell cars and more soft drinks. But then my stomach did this little sinking thing because I'd said *we*. When *we* get home. There was no 'we' when that happened. It would be me, back in my townhouse on my own while El started her book tour. Nope. Didn't like that even a little bit. Now wasn't the time to mope, though.

"I already gave him my right one, so we're all good," she tossed over her shoulder playfully. But my eyes fell to the way those dark pants hugged her curves. El was wearing a purple jersey with her brother's number on it, their last name emblazoned between her shoulders. She tied the jersey above black jeans that sat over her belly button, tan skin playing peekaboo between them. Black boots that doubled as a weapon really topped off the look, and I couldn't wait to peel it all off her and bite that perky ass she'd been teasing me with for the last three hours. She was unbearably appealing in her purple Wolves beanie and matching scarf. Yeah, it looked like the apparel shop threw up on us, but her dedication was adorable. When we reached the buffet, I jerked my gaze up to her face as she asked, "So, Professor, what's your go-to snack these days? Smoked pork loin? Barbeque shredded beef? In more of a drink your calories kind of mood?" she asked, motioning to the wet bar.

I nodded to the pretty blonde attendant who blushed when she smiled before turning my attention to El. The attendant shuffled away, ducking out of the room like she had been all afternoon when supplies needed replenishing. "Tough choice, but I'm leaning toward chips and queso—something crunchy to dispel some of this anxiety as Pax works his magic."

"Can't beat the classics." Her smile twisted sideways as she added, "I'm less concerned with Paxton's magic and more with what's going through that head of yours."

"What makes you think my mind is occupied with anything but football?" I asked with a shrug. "I mean, I was definitely admiring your ass on the walk over here."

Her eyes flicked sidelong, ensuring the attendant hadn't come back, her voice low as she said, "Still thinking about what you did to it last night?"

"Thinking about all the things I'd *like* to do to it," I countered.

She gave a little groan that made my balls tighten. It was the same sound she made when she needed me. "Fuck, you make it hard to focus on anything else."

"Pot, meet kettle."

"Glad the feeling is mutual." Eyes sparking, she reached up and rubbed her thumb between my brows, like she could dispel the ache there. "But... this little furrow, for starters," she supplied, answering my initial question. El lifted onto her tiptoes to press a peck to my lips. "And because every time I've caught you looking at me, you seem like you're solving a very complicated puzzle."

"Ahh, that. Well, *nosy*, if you must know, I've been pondering whether you're more of a wine or whiskey girl these days."

The little tick in her jaw said she knew I was full of shit, but the amusement in her eyes knew she wouldn't get anywhere if she pressed. Relief sluiced through me when she shrugged and said, "I'm a woman of many tastes." Before I could respond, the announcer came over the loudspeaker, and her eyes went wide. *Saved by the bell.* "Oooh, shit. It's game time, Professor."

"Go. Sit and watch. I'll pour drinks."

"You sure?" she asked, but she peered around my shoulder like she could somehow see the field.

Chuckling, I jerked my head back toward our seats and said, "Yeah, Pix. Go keep an eye on your brother."

She blew out a stressed little breath that made me smile. "Yeah, *okay*. Thanks, babe."

It was a physical fight not to scoop her into my arms at the sound of the pet name, but I resisted. Fuck, I'd waited for what felt like a lifetime to be more than just 'Brod' in her world. She hustled down to our seats, and I grinned as I watched her, the anxiety of the game seeming to return to that beautiful little body as the announcers came on the speaker, words about as clear as the teacher in *Charlie Brown*. We'd talk about our plans, but today wasn't the day. Today, I was just going to enjoy being with her. By the time I made it down to our seats, everyone was shifting nervously, El included. She rocked on her seat as she accepted the plate of assorted snacks.

"Here we go. Fuck, I might puke."

"No puking," I said at the same time as our friend with the mustache. We all shifted in our seats as the team took their places. Then they were moving—Pax faked left and juked right. His guys held the line, and he bided his time. My stomach sank as I saw the break in the line, but Pax saw it too, quick on his feet as he shifted, eyes still downfield as opponents closed in. One was tackled with a brutal clap, but the other had a clear shot as Paxton wound up and let the ball fly like he shot the pass from a canon a beat before both players went flying out of bounds with an audible crack that had everyone wincing. Everyone *except* for Elora.

Her hand flew to her mouth, but when I glanced her way, her eyes were down the field, not at her brother on the sideline. Downfield, as that rocket flew sixty, seventy, *eighty* impossible, gorgeous yards, directly into the open hands of a sprinting receiver as he crossed into the end zone.

The stadium *erupted*. But it was Elora, her arms around my neck and mouth pressed to mine, that consumed my mind. A dull cloud of cotton swallowed the outside world as everything in my body pulled into her. I tugged her little frame into mine, mind buzzing as I soaked in the feel of her. There weren't words adequate enough for the sensation of getting to touch her like this in public and I decided right then to do whatever it took to keep her forever.

The frenetic roar of the stadium needled through the Elora-haze, mind replaying the last sixty seconds. She was incredible–such a badass little winner. Even through her own nerves, she'd kept her eyes on the goal, on what her brother had just put his body on the line to accomplish. Hell, her enthusiastic collision with my mouth was her priority before she peeled away to find that number thirteen on the field. Like she just trusted that he was okay.

Much to my relief, the cameras all trained on Pax as his team mobbed around him.

"That kid may have just set an in-game record," Mustache roared over the crowd behind us. But my eyes were no longer tracking Pax after the guys dumped a cooler of electric blue liquid over his head as he shared a congratulatory hug with their coach. No, they were locked on the smaller screen off to the side of the main one. The one with a red heart and 'Kiss Cam' written across the top, replaying Elora jumping into the air with her arms up in victory before slamming her mouth against mine.

"Well, shit."

ELORA WAS WATCHING me with a permanent furrow in her brow as I paced the length of the room, my phone pressed to my ear. She had Max scouring the internet for the footage, and blessedly coming up empty thus far. But that didn't stop her from chewing a hole in her lip as she fast-forwarded through the replay on her computer. It seemed like the coverage had been properly trained on the celebratory chaos on the field.

It was only a matter of time, though, once they realized who had been in that private box. The golden boy's big sister might not get coverage, but Elora Rhodes, the internet sensation, certainly would.

The obnoxious ringing finally gave way to that telltale click, and a gruff, "Hey, man. Good to see your name. How's it going?"

"Uh, good, good. Everything's good."

His low chuckle filled the line a beat before he said, "Why do you sound like you're convincing yourself of that?"

"Nah, all good here. How are you guys?" I desperately attempted a redirection. Elora buried her face in her hands with a groan that sent me smiling.

"Great! Noel just wrapped up work down at the office and is heading home."

So, we had a minute. Hopefully, it would be enough. "Nice, say hi for me." Right as I was going to ask if he had time to chat, he beat me to it.

"I've been meaning to call, man. You got a sec?"

Running my hand over my face, I blew out a breath as I said, "Yeah! What's up?"

"I need your help."

"We burying a body, or something less eventful?"

"Fuck, dude, we don't discuss felonies on the phone," he laughed. A real one. Those were far and few between with Jameson, and my interest piqued despite the anxiety telling me to rip off the metaphorical bandage.

"You're right—my bad."

"But I really could use your help. No felonies—or misdemeanors, for that matter."

"Shoot."

"I'm going to propose to Noel."

My head snapped up from where my gaze had settled on the plain gray carpet. "I'm sorry. Am I having a stroke?"

His laughter emanated enough that Elora clambered over the mattress to stand beside me, pressing her ear to the opposite side of the phone. Smirking, I flipped my cell into my palm and hit the speaker button.

"I mean it. She's it for me. Known for quite a while now. I'm thinking I'll do it during Christmas in Florida.

We'll have the whole family together, in her hometown. I figure do some Florida Christmas shit—I dunno what that is—and ask her to be my forever."

"Damn," I muttered, as my stomach constricted. If anybody deserved a happy forever, it was Jameson and Noel. "Congratulations, bro. That's... huge."

"I know."

"How you feeling?"

"Really, really damn good. I've had the ring for months, just waiting for the perfect idea. And I think this is it. Is that good enough?"

"It's great, James. Surrounded by your big ass family *and* hers? She'll love that." When I found Elora's eyes, they were glossy, her hands crossed over her heart and face so sappy I could have laughed. It would've ruined the moment, though, so I held it together.

"So, I need your help planning."

"Of course."

"And you're coming."

"To the wedding? No kidding."

"To the Christmas proposal, smartass."

That earned a chuckle, but my eyes slipped up to El, who was grinning like the Cheshire Cat. *I just got invited to Christmas.* "My parents will be on that cruise with Max's folks."

"Perfect."

"No ideas on where you want to do this?"

"I was thinking about the house. Maybe hide it on the tree or something? She likes romantic shit like you read about—oh shit, she's home. Gotta run. Love you, man."

Before I could respond, the line died, and I was left staring down steel-blue eyes a beat before Elora *balked* like a chicken.

"Get your smartass over here," I snarled as I chucked my phone onto the pillows, lunging for her as she shrieked and fled. One tickle fight and a quickie later, we were cuddled up under the sheets when I called Rhyett but got his voicemail instead. It seemed the odds were not particularly favorable outside of the game today.

TWENTY-SIX

ELORA

While gloriously victorious, that last hit had done a number on poor Pax, and he'd spent his evening laid up or rotating between an ice bath and sauna to ramp up his rebound before playoffs. Only his title as world's best little brother allowed him to humor me with dinner last night.

Having decided we would tell the family together in Florida, I watched as Broderick's anxiety ratcheted up by the hour, even as he steered clear of coming over to see Paxton when I did. Something about not being able to lie to him if he wasn't around. Luckily for us, Paxton had been spluttering on a mouthful of electrolytes and then toweling off under unending congratulations when that damn kiss cam focused on us.

Max had combed through all the footage from the game, and set up some fancy keyword search trigger thing in case our names popped up anywhere new online. I didn't know how it worked; I just knew he swore it would.

It was stupid on my part, obviously, for us to have been affectionate at all in such a public setting. But fuck me sideways, if I could keep my hands off Broderick for more than a heartbeat. Let alone with adrenaline pumping and victory screaming through my veins.

That Hail Mary had been *incredible*. And incredible things deserved to be celebrated with my incredible man.

And he *was* my man, I'd decided, even as his anxiety drove him from bed Sunday night.

"Come on," I mumbled, wiping the sleep from my eyes and dragging him out of the room. "Get your fine ass in swim trunks. We're going to the pool."

"It's five in the morning, are you insane?"

"It's *five in the morning*," I countered saucily, holding his gaze as I peeled my shirt off, satisfied as his eyes roved over me. "Get with it, professor."

Which led us here, relaxing in the rumbling bubbles of the hot tub before breakfast. Broderick's corded arms were spread out to either side of him, braced on the slick gray concrete, his head lolled back as he soaked in the massage of high-powered jets. My legs were straddling his, my arms resting on his shoulders.

"So, after Christmas, what's next?" He asked. I wasn't sure if he was scrambling to keep himself thinking of anything but the looming conversation, or if he was actually trying to make plans.

"Going to visit Alice in Emerald Bay. Batch record the next two months of episodes for *TrailblazeHer*. The book tour starts the middle of January, so it'll be nice to hang tight with the girls for a few weeks. Slow down after months on the road."

"Nice. Trade one beach for another."

"Whenever humanly possible, that is my goal."

"How are the twins?"

"In SoCal heaven. Kaia already picked up a gig at a

local coffee shop, but Leighton is holding out for something more long term."

"Figures," he chuckled, but it was halfhearted at best. Needing to get his mind off of things, I glanced around to ensure we were alone, and then slowly drug my body over his groin, smiling coyly when his dick twitched against my entrance through the flimsy layers of fabric. "Fuuuuck," he said as his hands flew to bracket my bare waist. It shouldn't have been possible for something as simple as his palms against my bare skin to feel so decadent, but he'd yet to touch me without my body lighting up like a Christmas tree. From simple caresses to lavish licks, the man activated more synapses in my brain than any one person should have a right to.

This cobalt blue swimsuit did absolute wonders for my figure, the top freakishly supportive and high-waisted bottoms beautifully forgiving for days of bloat. Today though—I was feeling myself today. The color emboldened the blue in my eyes, and the last lingering hint of tan in my skin. And this incredible man was running his gorgeous, vascular hands over me, his eyes suddenly focused and locked on mine. Dark with flared pupils, like a predator about to enjoy every ounce of its prey. God, I wanted to be Broderick Allen's prey for the rest of my life. His to break apart and piece back together again.

I rocked against him, humming when the friction of his rapidly swelling dick hit my clit.

"You feel *incredible*, Pix." A truncated chuckle rumbled in his ribs, and I canted my head.

"What's so funny?"

"Nothing, baby, just thinking."

"I'm mostly naked grinding on your dick, it's not great

timing for that kind of thinking without sharing with the class, sir."

He dug his strong fingers into my hips, pulling me forward over the long, hard ridge of his impressive cock. "Just thinking that when I dropped out of the grant competition, I never thought I'd end up here, with you humping me in a hot tub a month later."

My mouth popped open right as realization sparked in his eyes. "Wait, what do you mean—?"

His lips came down on mine, one hand slipping beneath the scrappy fabric of my top and finding my nipple, giving it a hot, hard twist that sent heat spilling through my body. But not even expertly wielded lust would clear my mind of what he'd just said.

I peeled our lips apart, and then clamped my hand over his mouth to keep him from distracting me with the promise of body trembling, mind numbing, IQ eliminating ecstasy. "You can't kiss your way out of that one. Answer me, Brod. What in the fuck did you just say?"

"That I never thought I'd get this lucky." he supplied quickly, giving me something like the man equivalent to puppy eyes.

"Yes, I got that, you're very cute, but stop being evasive. Did you... did you drop out of the grant competition?"

"Look, uh, it didn't work out the way I meant it to," he mumbled against my hand until I removed it. "But yeah, I figured you'd kick that big lug's ass. I wasn't going to say anything because I didn't want to make it worse. Wait, why do you look so horrified?"

"Brod," I breathed, shaking my head as my stomach churned. "Baby, I dropped out too. I had the same train of thought."

His brows winged up and I couldn't tell if he was ticked

or amused. "You're telling me we handed the funding to Pierce because we *both* bowed out?"

"Yeah, my agent called Chris, and he called Mara and me. We got picked up by a reality television network. The school is going to be fully funded once we can land on a location."

"Baby, what?! That's incredible—"

I shook my head, cutting off his enthusiasm. "*You* deserved that funding. You worked so hard to get there and put your best foot forward. I was so damn proud of you. Of the business plan. Of how it would impact the island. *Why?* Why would you do that?"

"El, isn't it obvious?" Those big brown eyes softened, flicking between my own. When I just stared back, he rasped, "Baby girl, I'm in love with you."

My jaw fell open, eyes flying wide as emotion welled up in me. I'd yearned to hear those words from his lips for my entire adult life. Plus a few years, if I was honest. I could barely breathe as I said, "*What?*"

"I'm in love with you," he repeated without flare, as if it were as natural a statement as the sky being blue. My heart soared as his forehead came to rest against mine. His thumb brushed over my cheekbone as he chuckled, adding, "And I'm an idiot for waiting so long to tell you."

When his soft lips came down this time, they were gentle, yet urgent as his hands guided my body over his, rocking my hips. He didn't wait for me to say it back, didn't leave the declaration hovering in the air. Instead, he stole away my breath and sent heat flaring through my core. Perhaps I'd known—had certainly hoped—before he said it. Seen it in the way he tailored our time together, in the decade of collected post cards, and thoughtful little details like hot pads in our bed so I wouldn't freeze in Mistyvale. It was glaring within his determination to talk me into telling my family. And now...he walked away from the grant of his dreams because he believed it would give me a leg up, for pity's sake.

The bridge of my nose stung, but all thoughts vanished as he gripped my hipbone, dragging me forward as he ground my clit against him, lust teetering through my system as decadent kisses made my head spin. My hands found his hard cock beneath the thin fabric of his trunks, and he bit into my lip, gently dragging it between his teeth. As my fingers slipped below the elastic waistband, needing to feel him against my skin, but hindered by the angle, Broderick chuckled.

"You a closet voyeur too, El?"

I glanced around, ensuring we were still alone. "There would have to be people, wouldn't there?"

"I believe the prospect of them is plenty."

Grinding over him, I lowered my lips to hover over his. "I'll make a rebel out of you, yet, Professor Allen."

"Perhaps," he said with a chuckle, but it was the heavy metallic creak and clang of the door that had him sliding me off his lap and tucking me against his side. "But apparently not today."

I burst out laughing as the space filled with the echo of excited children. "A sex scandal probably wouldn't look great to the network," I allotted under my breath.

"I'm just about ready to get outta here. How about you?"

"*So* beyond ready."

"Come on, Pix." He rose from the bench as the kids all whooped and started canon balling into the pool in a rapid sequence of splashes. A mother with exhaustion shadowing her eyes—clutching two hotel branded cups of coffee to her chest like they were a lifeline—slumped into a blue plastic pool chair. Normally, my sympathy would have been off the charts after years watching my mother wrangle all of us kids, but my mind was still trapped in our conversation. When I turned to Broderick as he climbed from the hot tub, I couldn't help but admire every inch of his body as the water sluiced down it.

"Hey, Brod?"

"Yeah?" he said, glancing over his shoulder, biceps flexing as he rotated toward me, and the warm water sloshed against my belly.

"I love you, too."

The smile that carved his features would live in my memory for the rest of our lives. But it was his words that sent my heart hammering. "I know, baby."

TWENTY-SEVEN
BRODERICK

After what was decidedly the best Monday morning to ever exist, we ate breakfast together, and El hopped online for her meetings while I lounged like a bump on a log with a book in my lap. I couldn't help but watch her as she led her full staff meeting like the pro she was, as they evaluated their final location choices for the show. It seemed like they'd come down to Los Angeles or Seattle, which would at least keep her on the west coast.

"Commute time is about the same," Chris pointed out. His voice had become familiar to me over the last few days, as he was her most vocal contributor to most group conversations. "But air quality is better in the Pacific Northwest."

"If you don't factor in endless fog and rain," Mara contradicted, shaking her head. "LA puts us within two hours of Emerald Bay with Alice and the twins."

"Valid point," El said, weighing her words and reactions carefully, refusing to give too much away.

"You could plant yourself between the two and have an hour in either direction."

"An hour commute to work *every* morning?" Chris challenged. "That's fourteen hours a week in the beginning. That's a part-time job."

"Okay, so she stays in the city, and drives the two hours to Alice. It was just an idea."

"An idea that needed to be vetoed for the sustainability of her mental health." Chris' protest made me chuckle, mostly because he sounded like Max with his need to look out for her. He wasn't wrong. But I couldn't help but wonder how this would play out for *us*. Was she going to live there year around? If she was following a traditional school schedule, it was at least nine or ten months of it. And those were the same months I'd be bound to Mistyvale. Suddenly, the idea of her pursuing this school made me anxious. But god, she needed it. Needed to build that dream. For her and her future students. A sinking sensation in my gut matched the dread pinching my brows as I attempted to force my eyes back to the book in my lap. The words seemed to blur into some other dimension, because all my brain could understand was that I couldn't derail all of that. The rational option was staring me in the face; I would be the one to uproot my life and follow her. But that meant leaving my family. My parents and surviving grandparents. Jameson and Noel as they started their family. As he was the closest thing I had to a brother left on the island, that one hurt the most.

El was happy to wander from place to place never growing roots as she rode wherever the wind took her, where I was like a coastal redwood, every ounce of my being settled in the mountains of Mistyvale Island.

But, for El... I could start over. So what, if I'd dedicated six years to Mistyvale University? I could start that run for tenure over. Even though my chest felt heavier just thinking about throwing that away.

My phone lit up with an incoming call, and I sat up, a bit relieved when I saw my dad's name on the screen. As quietly as possible, I slunk from the room before answering.

"Hey, Dad."

"Brod!" No matter how long or short our absence, the thing I loved most about my father was that he possessed the enthusiasm of a Labrador Retriever at a Fourth of July barbecue when he answered the phone. As far from the stereotypical, solemn lawyer as you could get outside the courtroom. "How's my son?"

So much to unpack there. Opting for the simplified version, I said, "I'm great. How's the trip?"

"Your mother says I've caught a tan," he supplied with a chuckle I couldn't help but echo. Of the two of them, dad's South African bloodline made the concept laughable next to Mom's light skin. And the joke was one she never seemed to tire of.

"So, the island hopping is going well, then?"

"I've gained ten pounds," he said with significance.

"Congratulations, you can be black Santa again this year."

"Always my greatest honor," he said, tone entirely jovial. Mistyvale had come a long way as far as diversity went in the last few decades, but logically speaking, Filipino Santa would have made a lot more sense. Regardless, Dad had played the role for five years running, and loved every moment. Every hug. Every affirmation spoken over kids that might just need to hear they were good and shown that they were loveable. "How is everything back home?"

I weighed the question and decided it wasn't a lie to skirt my current whereabouts. "Home? Home is good."

"Mmm," he said, tone astutely suspicious. Good luck lying to a lawyer. "And my *son*? How is my son?"

"Your son is good."

"Should I ask *where* is my son? Would that be more accurate?"

Dammit. "Uh, I'm in Chicago at the moment. Fly out tomorrow morning."

"Now, with all due respect, you *lead* the conversation with something like that. Why the hell are you in Chicago?"

"I got to watch Paxton throw a game-winning Hail Mary pass yesterday."

"Ahh, the *Wolves* won again. Pax is about to get himself another Super Bowl ring, isn't he?"

"Pending the playoffs, it's entirely possible."

"Good. Very good news for a talented kid. But you didn't answer my question."

I palmed my face, dragging it down across my mouth as I groaned, and he laughed at the sound.

"You used the same deflection techniques as a teenager. I asked *why* you're in Chicago, not what you've been doing." I glanced back at the room door, thinking that those were details he certainly didn't need. "Is there a new woman in the picture?"

"Now, why do you sound so hopeful?" I pushed back when his voice was just a tad too cheery for my liking.

"Seriously?" he husked back. "Sarah was a real piece of work, Brod. Tried to warn ya', but you weren't open to advice."

"Yeah, I remember."

"And then you moved her in with you, and it became poor form to remind you."

"Mom wasn't exactly subtle," I contradicted lightly.

"She wasn't particularly fond of her," he allowed as mom's voice snarked in the background.

"That snake was a real cunt."

Dad choked on a laugh as I covered my mouth, eyeing two mid-forties women as they passed me by.

"*Marley Allen,*" Dad scolded as I re-composed myself. She wasn't... wrong?

"What?" she croaked indignantly.

"Nice small-town mayors don't talk like that, mother," I interjected, my sentence likely swallowed by the two of them squabbling.

"Bitch brought another person into my baby boy's bedroom, and I'm not allowed to call it like it is?"

"I'm not saying that, but can we at least pretend to have some decorum in public?"

"Guys?" I chuckled, shaking my head as I paced down the hall on bare feet, the soft threads of carpet brushing against my skin. They didn't seem to hear me.

"Decorum belongs in town hall and inside the courtroom, Robert. Not sitting in a bikini sipping margaritas in the Dominican Republic."

"My love, our son had his heart stomped on, I don't think he needs you poking your nose in—"

"*Guys,*" I attempted again.

"Like *you* weren't inserting yourself in his love life not thirty seconds ago?" she protested, and I heard the faint click of ice in a glass.

"Mom has a point," I said, laughing as her triumphant voice cut through the background.

"*Hah!*"

"That's different," my dad protested.

"Oh really? Tell me, Robert, how that's different from his mother butting in?"

"Mine was a sneaking suspicion about his future."

"So, speculating about future women is acceptable, but criticizing past women is not?"

"*Guys.*"

"It was the language used."

"Was it inaccurate, your honor?"

Snickering, I said, "Alright, it's been *great* chatting with you."

"Wait, baby! Hold on," Mom protested. I shook my head but stayed on the line. My mother was nothing if not predictable. "Why *are* you in Chicago? Your father has my interest piqued."

Sucking down a long breath that released in a sigh, I glanced up at the sleek, chrome, wall-mounted sconce and admitted, "I came to see Elora speak for a local business." When silence beyond the crash of waves was all that crossed the line, I cleared my throat. "Guys? You there?"

My father's resonant laugh filled the line as my mother said, "Dammit, Brod."

"What?" I barked. *"You like El."*

"*Love* her. Winner. Totally not a cunt-a-saurus. But you just lost me twenty bucks."

"*What?*" I startled, choking on my saliva.

"When she moved out of state and Sarah moved in, I thought you wrote the whole thing off. Last summer, your dad swore up, down, and sideways you were 'looking after Miss McShane,'" the air quotes in her voice were irrefutable, "in order to make a move on Elly. I told him the ship had sailed, but he insisted you two would finally get together this year."

"Woah, woah, woah, who said anything about getting together?"

"Because grown men regularly fly four-thousand miles away to see a *platonic* friend? I don't think so," Dad supplied, voice high like he was still laughing to himself.

"I fly to see Rhyett all the time," I argued.

"And is that what this is, son?" Dad pressed. "Flying to see a *friend*?"

Throat thick, I admitted, "Not this time."

A smacking sound amputated dad's victorious laugh, followed by *harder* laughter.

"Mom, did you just five-star Dad?"

"That's neither here nor there—"

"Right on the ass," Dad protested through his rumbling humor, but my mother carried on like he hadn't said a word.

"I'm happy for you, baby."

"Well, don't run off getting too excited. We're just...*feeling this out*, seeing where it can go." *Understatement of the year award goes to...* "I haven't gotten to talk to the guys about it yet."

"Don't wait too long on that front, son. Jameson especially won't take well to you hiding this from him. Rhy... he'll get on board as soon as he processes it."

"Very astute," I said flatly, heart heavy, knowing I'd already let it go on too long. "We're going to tell them together at Christmas."

"Sounds like a plan," Dad said sagely.

"As much as I want the whole scoop, sweetie, we've got to run. We were just in port for a quick stop and hunted down some internet with our food to give you a buzz. We have to head back toward the ship."

"Yeah, okay. I'll fill you guys in when you're back."

"Sounds good, sweetie. Give Elly our love."

"Will do. Love you guys."

"Love you too," they said in unison, smiles dripping from their tones. Albeit Dad's was a little more obvious. The line clicked off, and I was still shaking my head when I came back into the room, feet stuttering to a halt when I spotted El bracing her head in her hands.

She rubbed tight little circles into her temples and didn't look up as I closed the gap. Cautiously, I crouched beside her chair and asked, "What's up, baby girl?"

She took a very long, unhurried breath before softly telling the tabletop, "Decision fatigue, I think. I'm just... very overwhelmed."

"With the show?"

"With... life. I think? Too many choices needing to be made and time is of the essence."

"Well, I do evaluate human nature for a living. Maybe I can help."

"*You're* one of the decisions," she mumbled into her palms, voice cracking as my stomach dropped.

"Okay. Well. *Especially* then, I'd like to be a sounding board."

"Start having babies in my mid-thirties, or skip that phase and adopt? Skip it all together? Honestly, I'm growing tired of the travel life. Hell, I'm just... too old to sleep on shitty hotel beds ninety percent of the time. I miss my apartment. The cracks in the bricks. The creak of the wood on those first steps in the entryway." She huffed out a tired sounding breath. "Now, the network really loves the idea of basing in New York but will accommodate the West Coast. I just have to decide where I want to plant roots for the foreseeable future. And I have to have some kind of family nearby. Alice would at least be close to LA. But I need to decide quickly, because they need to get the ball rolling on all the legal shit."

"Ahh. That's where I factor in?"

"Obviously," she groaned, her defined shoulders curling in. "You're everything I've ever wanted for *me*. But... this show is more than I even dreamed of for *the vision*."

"And you're worried about the distance?" She nodded into her hands, and I settled my fingers around her wrist, gently guiding one away from her face. "Look at me, Pix." Slowly, eyes downcast, she lifted her face before tentatively meeting my gaze. "For once in my life, my decision is perfectly clear, and I need you to hear me. Are you listening?" When she finally nodded, I said, "I come to you."

"*What?*" she squeaked, eyes going wide. Wider, when I shrugged my shoulders. "Your life *is* Mistyvale."

"*My life* is sitting in this chair, stressing over losing me or her dreams. That's not a choice I'm willing to compromise. I've been thinking about this a lot the last few days, and the answer is easy." My palm settled against her back. "I'll move where you move. I have an exceptional track record at Mistyvale U. I'll put in my notice, finish out the academic year in the spring, and find a new placement in whatever city you decide to build our life in."

"Brod, that's too much. Your family, your job, your gym, your team. The vision for the youth center. You'd be losing too much."

"No, baby. Continuing life without you now that I know what it feels like to wake with you in my arms and call you mine... *that's* losing too much."

ELORA

. . .

HAND-IN-HAND, we walked down the icy streets of Chicago on our way back from the restaurant down the block. Broderick's declarations had scrambled my brain like eggs, and after one too many minutes of me resting in his arms without speech, he pulled me to my feet and declared it was time to eat. He wasn't wrong. I'd been so focused on my meetings, on planning and researching, that I'd skipped right past lunch time into early-bird *dinner*. Luckily for me, my man didn't mind a lunch-dinner combo, and said nothing about how quickly I inhaled a plate full of food before asking the server for seconds.

"Better?" he finally asked as we passed by a rather ruckus bar, despite it being an early Monday evening.

"Mm-hmm," I assured, even though I wasn't feeling remotely better about his proposition. Broderick and his family weren't Rhodes family intertwined, but he was close with his parents, and even closer with his surviving grandfather. He coached the high school football team with Jameson and volunteered around town when he wasn't occupied by filling the minds of the next generation. Taking him from all of that... it planted this white-hot kind of pain in my chest. Guilt, I realized. But he seemed so sure. So damn certain that I was worth hocking everything he knew aside.

"You bullshitting me, Rhodes?"

"Mm-hmm," I repeated, shooting an apologetic glance his way and earning a laugh.

"Cut it out, baby. I overthink enough for both of us. Don't do that. And definitely don't tell me you're okay if you're not."

"It's just...a lot. There are solutions for this. I know there are. I just...haven't found them yet."

"You know one constant I've learned in all my reading, El?"

I shook my head before deciding the crack in the concrete was particularly fascinating as we stepped over it.

"In all my books. Philosophy. Plays. History. Literature. Fantasy and romance and historical fiction. The one constant is this; love isn't a fixed resource, El. It's not going anywhere. It never dissipated when you left town, or when I hid behind Sarah—"

"The bimbo," I cut in, shooting him a pointed glance. God, how I'd loathed that woman.

"Yes, that. When I hid behind the bimbo," he chuckled. "And it won't diminish now, no matter how tricky it is for us to get situated. I've loved you for nearly as long as I can remember."

"Same."

"So, trust me, when I tell you I'm prepared to do whatever it takes to stay beside you now that I have you."

The bridge of my nose burning, hands shaking, I nodded before tugging him to a stop and stealing a kiss as the air nipped at my icy skin. When, at last, it seemed the oxygen returned to my lungs, I turned to continue our walk, but Broderick held steady, jerking his chin up. I followed his gaze to a tan sign that read *The Happy Potter*.

"Wanna throw some clay?" he asked, a chipper little hop between his words.

"I think I'm good," I said, shaking my head.

"Come on El. Let me teach *you* something for once. To many firsts, right?"

"I *suck* at arts and crafts," I protested, but didn't resist when he stepped past me and led me over to the front door.

"This is a terrible idea. My junior high turtle looked like a Picasso painting gone very, very wrong."

"Oh, *I remember*," he said cheekily, and I peeled my hand from his to smack him on the ass. "But I'm actually decent."

"Not helping. So, *you* can sculpt some custom vase to sell at auction and I can make deformed Dumbo, the fucked-up turtle?"

The snow swallowed his laugh, but he didn't slow down before opening the metal door with a clang and motioning me inside. Shaking my head, I followed him into the warmly lit space.

"Hey, dudes," the *very* white, very scrawny twenty-something with teenage acne and questionable dreads said as we stepped into the warm studio. Every raging stereotype of a stoner was embodied in this one grinning human, with his half-hooded, bloodshot eyes, surrounded by hippy decorations, wearing a Rastafarian beanie, and setting a matching hacky sack on the counter. As though we'd interrupted his game in our attempt to patronize the establishment.

"Hey," Broderick said back, squeezing my fingers when I didn't immediately follow him in or greet him back. Frankly, I wasn't sure which offense earned the pinch, but mustered the energy to both follow him and speak words.

"Hi there," I chirped in a too-sunny voice. Broderick's ensuing smirk and not-remotely-subtle side eye had me laughing to myself as he forged on ahead, as if I wasn't a begrudging captive. A begrudging captive now staring at that perfect bubble butt as he walked in. I left the men folk to talk, turning to study the plates and bowls, and little jewelry dishes that were glossed and awaiting pickup on metal shelving to the side of the room. When Broderick materialized beside me, he held up two steaming mugs of tea.

"Happy tea," he said, grinning. "Bobby promised it's just Kava, not weed, despite his chosen aesthetic. Also, evidently it aids in relieving anxiety and insomnia, both of which I feel would be beneficial today."

Shaking my head, I snagged a cup from him before eyeing the potter's wheel Bobby was motioning us over to with the same level of distrust I'd allot to a coiled snake.

"I might prefer weed for this," I muttered. "Tell Bobby to stop bogarting the good stuff."

His grin was fantastically contagious as he shook his head. "I ever tell you that you're dramatic, baby?"

"Probably not often enough," I laughed, looking to my steaming mug before taking a sip and grimacing at the bizarre taste.

"Ahh, man, that'd be the valerian," Bobby said sagely as he eyed my displeasure. "Works miracles but tastes like gym socks."

"Got a lot of experience ingesting gym socks, Bobby?" I asked, laughing when Broderick knocked his shoulder into mine.

"More than I'd like," he admitted in his dopy little voice, grinning up at me under sleepy eyes. "Got bullied a lot as a kid."

"Oh good, *I'm* the asshole," I said, more to myself than them, but both of the guys laughed.

"Nah, it's a fair assessment," he said, bobbing his head as he set a crate of clinking supplies beside the wheel. "Stuff tastes nasty but does the trick. Hella chill, and you should sleep like a baby."

"It's not even six o'clock," I pointed out.

"Didn't say your timing was fabulous. I'd plan an early

nap." I was still laughing when he said, "Alright Mr. and Mrs. Allen. You two are set. Enjoy."

"Thanks, Bobby," Broderick said, not bothering to correct his assumption. *Mrs. Allen*. That did something crazy inside my chest. Judging by the satisfaction in his smile, Broderick liked it too. I could have sworn he winked at the little hippy dude before he sauntered off like there was no rush in the world. A beat later, Tom Petty started over the speakers, and I turned and grinned at him. He shrugged and said, "Cool kid. Now, come here, baby."

Eyes narrowed, I shook my head. "I'm sipping my dirty sock tea." I did. And it was just as terrible the second time. Broderick was still shaking his head as he stepped forward and gently pried the mug from my grip, set it up on the bar top, and returned to snatch my hands in his.

There was a row of beige aprons hanging from pegs on the wall, like we'd stumbled into a grown-up Montessori school. Mara's kids went to one, and I could swear the canvas smocks were identical, just on a larger scale. We slipped out of our coats and Broderick set his tie and button-up shirt aside, leaving him in his undershirt, looking way too hot to sit at a pottery wheel.

He hooked an apron around my neck, smirking as I begrudgingly tied it while he got his own. After going through the motions of washing hands, and bopping to the music, he led me back to the stool and had me sit before dragging a second one behind the first. Wordlessly, he returned to the wall, swiping his tie off the hook before closing the distance. Nerves skittered through my chest as I eyed the silky fabric warily.

"Whatcha' doing with that, Professor? I don't think we can implement it in this adventure, although I have alternates in mind."

"You'd be surprised," he said, tone dripping with too much satisfaction as he straddled the apple box behind me, scooting in tight so his front was flush with my back. Of course he'd just leave my bait hanging on the hook. He pressed a kiss to my cheek and whispered, "Follow my lead for once, baby." I nodded stiffly, and then he said, "Close your eyes."

With butterflies going manic in my center, I burst out laughing as he brought the tie around my face. "Is there a piñata I don't know about? Or am I pinning a tail on a donkey?"

Evidently ignoring my nerve riddled questions, he asked, "Ready to get your hands dirty, baby?"

"Born ready to get dirty, but I can't say blindfolds were part of the plan." Even as I said it, I felt him tug it snug over my eyes. The sudden sensory deprivation sent my heart sprinting.

"Just adding a little mystery to the experience."

"Because stumbling around blind with clay covered hands is everyone's idea of excitement?"

"Because if we eliminate the possibility of perfection, you won't be so hard on yourself."

Well. That was...an interesting theory. "Of all the hobbies you could have taken up in the last decade, this was the last one I would have expected."

"Don't knock it till you try it."

"Not knocking. Just...surprised," I admitted as his breath went hot against my neck, long arms looping around me.

"Just, relax. Trust your hands—*and me*—and let your instincts take over. It's not like the clay is going to bite... *hopefully*."

I snickered, my limbs a little shaky as I leaned back into

his chest, anchoring myself in the heat of him. I'd give it to Broderick, for a man who thrived on routine, he did spontaneous surprises rather well.

"So, if I end up with Dumbo, the misshapen blob, I blame the blindfold?"

"Precisely."

I turned my face to the side, where his lips brushed over mine, listening as he moved around my body. Something whirred to life—I assume he'd woken up our wheel—and then wet kneading sounds told me he was prepping the clay. Every so often, his stubble grazed over my cheek, or his lips brushed over the shell of my ear, sending goosebumps down my arms.

"Ready?" he breathed softly as *Listen To Her Heart* took over on the speakers and I gave a little shrug.

With mock bravado, and absolutely no expectations to speak of, I quipped, "Tell the clay to prepare to be dominated."

Sliding his hands around the back of mine, Broderick ran what felt like his thumb across my knuckles. "That's the spirit, baby. Let's see what kind of masterpiece we can create... or destroy," he said with a chuckle.

"A disaster-piece is more like it," I muttered, but still followed his lead as he brought my hands forward. My nose wrinkled when he led my palms around the wet ball of clay, the slick blob melding where we softly braced around it as it spun against my hand. "That's fucking weird," I said, but followed his lead as Broderick's fingers gently guided mine into the cool, silky mass as it yielded beneath the pressure. A chill wracked down my spine as goosebumps pricked across my skin.

"Who knew all I had to do was blindfold you, and you'd be rendered silent?" he whispered, nipping at my earlobe.

"Throw in some ice cubes and candles, and you have inspiration for later."

"Noted," he chuckled. "Do you always just say what you're thinking?"

"It's been my rule of thumb for quite some time now, and I find it serves me well. You certainly seem responsive."

"Baby, you could ask me for just about anything, and I'd break my back to comply."

"Please don't," I quipped. "I quite like you exactly as you are, spine and all."

"Yeah?"

"Yeah."

"The feeling is mutual. *Here*, relax your hand."

Breath quicker than the situation warranted, I did. Silencing my mind, I followed his lead, allowing Broderick to guide my hands, my thumbs, each finger against the smooth surface as a subtle, wet squelch and rush of material told me we were making larger changes.

"Good girl, just like that."

I barked an obnoxious laugh before regaining control of my faculties. "This is not a scenario where I ever expected hearing those words from your lips."

"Do I not praise you enough in the bedroom, baby?"

"Is there such a thing?"

His breath coasted over my shoulder in a rushed exhale, I assumed in humor, but trusting my ears in the absence of my eyes was daunting. "Apparently not. Because you're perfect, El. My new life goal will be to make sure you know it."

"Nobody's perfect," I argued.

"Perfect for me, baby. Perfect for me."

The earthy scent of clay-in-motion filled my nose, and I smiled as I asked, "New life goal, huh?"

"Yep."

"Not world peace?"

"Nope."

"Solve world hunger?"

"My future wife will solve that," he teased, thighs giving my hips a little squeeze.

My laughter punctuated the rhythmic sound of our hands across the wheel as he continued to act as puppeteer, the blob submitting to our joined hands.

"Future wife, huh?"

"She's pretty brilliant."

"Should I be worried?"

"Everyone should. This is Elora Rhodes' world. We're all just living in it."

That was the sentence that sent me cackling, and Broderick yanking my hands off the wheel until I wasn't shaking with amusement. "You'll do well to remember that," I teased, leaning my face toward him and smiling when he brushed his lips across the tip of my nose before bringing them to my ear.

"I've waited since I was sixteen to live in your world, Pix. I'm not going to forget now that you're here with me. I meant what I said. If you asked me to steal the moon, I'd find a way to scale the stars to do it."

"There you go, spitting prose again."

"Did it work?"

"My mouth says *no* but the state of my panties has a different tale to tell."

His chuckle caressed my neck as he said, "One stolen moon, coming up."

"How very *Despicable Me* of you."

"Always did want a villain era."

"Good. Now let's finish fondling this pile of mush so I can take you home and show you just what you do to me."

"Hell, woman—"

"*My mouth?*" I cut in teasingly.

"Is both my favorite feature and greatest source of anxiety."

"Didn't your dad say that once about your mother?"

Broderick was quiet for a long moment, just the squish of clay and whir of the machine accompanying the rotating playlist as he molded our project. The clay almost seemed to come to life beneath my fingers, shifting and growing, bending and curling.

After a while, he said, "You know. I think he did." He pecked my cheek before adding, "But taking you home sounds so much better than sitting here. Let's wrap this up."

At some point, he placed a cold, slender rod into my fingers—I assumed it was some sort of metal based on the feel—and gave me instructions to be very gentle. But broad hands and steady fingers guided every motion.

He said little, just guiding my hands as I nervously broke out in spontaneous giggles. I was well aware I likely looked ridiculous and could feel the splatters of wet against my forearms but found that I didn't particularly care who else existed in the world... so long as Broderick Allen did.

TO MY SURPRISE, the blob was actually impressively bowl like, with elegant curves like flower petals.

"To many more firsts," he breathed against my ear before pressing a sweet kiss to my cheek. "Thanks for trusting me."

Something so simple, but as I washed the residue from

my skin, I realized outside of my siblings, there weren't many people I actually trusted enough to relinquish control to. Broderick handled shipping information with Bobby, and then wrapped me against him when we ventured back into the cold.

It wasn't until I'd stripped the jacket back in our room that I realized just how much fun it had been to relax in his arms and let him lead. Which, naturally, meant the universe would conspire to bring me back to reality.

Laying across the bed, he'd just cracked open our book when his phone rang, and he scowled over at it before jerking upright.

"Give me a sec, baby. This could be important."

I nodded sleepily, the consequences of the dirty sock water evidently in full effect as I drifted out of consciousness. The door quietly closed, and I peeled my eyes open to see Broderick with a focus furrow carved deeply enough between his brows the fog cleared from my head.

"Babe?" I asked as unease brought my feet to the floor. He palmed his mouth, opening it twice only to close it before tugging at the back of his neck.

Broderick's mouth was still parted, his eyes wild in what appeared to be disbelief, when I rushed over to him. My heart ratcheted up, convinced somebody must have died. Looking more than a little stunned, Broderick brought those rich brown eyes to mine and said, "I uh... I just got offered tenure."

TWENTY-EIGHT
ELORA

Fear collapsed under a wave of relief, and I threw my arms around his neck. Evidently in some kind of shock, Broderick staggered a step before returning my embrace, wrapping those muscular arms around my back and tugging me close as he inhaled deeply into my hair.

"Babe, that's incredible! *You're* incredible," I breathed, cupping the back of his head as we rocked in tight little motions together. Pulling back to look up at him, I grinned, and said, "Congratulations, Brod. That's amazing." He nodded yes, but the pinch in his brows adamantly disagreed with the motion. Quirking my head, I asked, "Why don't you seem excited about that?"

"When they didn't grant it in August, I—I didn't think I got it. All that work. All the reviews. I…"

"You're processing?" He nodded when I said it, but with the way his lip rolled between his teeth, conflict shadowing his eyes, it felt like more than that. "Brod, you gotta say something. You look like you saw a ghost."

It wasn't an exaggeration. Haunted eyes fell to mine, that furrow never leaving his brow. "Baby girl," he rasped, lowering his forehead to mine before brushing our lips together ever so gently. "My entire career has been building up to this point. I was about to give up—did, I guess. I guess they wanted to present it formally before the break and told me they hope I'm feeling better." He shook his head as if to clear it. "The idea of starting over somewhere fresh didn't bother me at all, because I didn't think I'd get it. But..."

When his voice drifted off, icy, liquefied lead shot straight into my spinal column and down my legs, cementing my feet in place as my lips popped open in understanding. "You can't leave Mistyvale."

THE WEIGHT of our additional complication settled in the air between us on the ride to the airport, and through security. He kept his hand in mine, but it didn't seem like either of us could formulate a sentence, much less a solution. Hell, I'd forgotten all my people skills beyond basic grunts of acknowledgement, and I'd never been more grateful for being on the TSA pre-checklist than I was when I eyed the enormous line at airport security.

We both buzzed on through, that line between his brows evidently a permanent fixture on that beautiful face. Even serious, he was unfairly gorgeous. I never stood a damn chance. But why did it have to come down to our relationship or our careers? All my life, I was told that women could have it all. The job, the family, the love story worth immortalizing on countless dead trees, so it might lend hope to a young woman just beginning her journey.

Lies. All of it.

In the end, one of us would sacrifice the last decade of work to be with the other. Or...

My stomach churned, nausea threatening the deeply unsatisfying burrito I'd forced down once we'd found our gate. Broderick was still doing his best impression of a mime, shoulders curled where he slumped into the uncomfortable airport chair, his eyes trained on the runway beyond great panes of glass. The gray of winter cast soft light across his rich complexion, brightening the eyes I loved so much, even as they were weighed down with choices that were entirely unfair.

He wrapped one arm under the other like a pensive elbow shelf, the other braced atop it so he could cover his mouth.

I'd seen him retreat inside his head countless times over the years, but this was the first time I thought his silence might actually kill me.

"Say something," I whispered after what felt like a lifetime of letting him stew, my gentle voice evidently yanking him back into the stiff seat. He turned to look at me, the weak smile on his cheeks miles away from reaching his eyes.

"I love you," he said with such conviction it beguiled the ache in his voice.

"I love you, too." My whispered echo seemed inadequate, but I needed to say it. Some part of me collapsed in on itself like a rotting pumpkin because I had a horrid feeling I wouldn't get to say it enough. "We don't have to solve everything right now, do we?" A nondescript turn of his head, and flexed muscle in his jaw, were his only responses. Rocking my weight forward onto the balls of my feet, I began nervously bouncing my leg before collapsing back into my seat in defeat. "I just want to pretend this is real. Just... until we leave Florida. Pretend we can both be happy."

"Baby, this *is* real," he rasped. "You're the only part of my life I am certain of."

"Then... why isn't this easier? I thought a good relationship would actually make sense." The speakers crackled to life as airline attendants called names and gave instructions for the flight before ours.

"The relationship, and the extenuating circumstances, are two very different things. Or so our predicament suggests."

"You're using your professor voice," I pointed out. He made a noise I thought was supposed to be a laugh but sounded too forced and pained to be one. His eyes fell to his lap as he stretched his arm around my shoulders—the contact lending some semblance of ease where panic had shredded my sanity—and I nestled closer under the safety of his wing.

"I'm sorry. I'm—I guess I'm not used to having someone else to think about when my brain is trying to process. Explaining my emotions has never been my strong suit. I can handle logic, but this... not so much." The confession felt raw, given the absolute pandemonium around us. Chicago's O'Hare was certainly the last place I would have selected to have a heart-to-heart, with its bustling concourse and overflowing waiting areas as more and more flights were delayed because of inclement winter weather. Not sure how to respond, I glanced at the ticking screen, relieved that at least our flight to Tampa would still arrive on time.

"Can you try?" I finally asked, turning to weave my legs over his, irritated by the placement of the immovable arm rest. He finally dropped his hand away from his mouth, as though he'd been holding all the words inside.

"I don't know the answers yet, El. I want to say it's easy. Want to tell you it doesn't change anything."

"But it does," I supplied, my throat aching as I swallowed down the unintentional injury the words inflicted.

"I just worked so damn hard for that professional validation. The security of it." He shook his head, jaw feathering again. I wanted to smooth out the lines on his forehead, only that thought made me realize I needed to relax the muscles in mine. They ached like I'd been pinching pennies between my brows. Finally, he turned to meet my eyes, an echo of my trepidation reflected at me there. "This feels like some kind of cosmic joke. Start over after twelve years of school and nearly six years of teaching, or wedge myself into a long-distance relationship with the woman of my dreams? If there is a god, it certainly has a sense of humor."

WE TOUCHED down on the Tampa tarmac with a jolt, and Broderick wordlessly squeezed the back of my neck in reassurance. Florida was known for very few things more than their bipolar weather, which meant the descent had been bumpy, at best. At least it was an accurate depiction of my mental health today.

On the tail end of a long inhale, he managed a one-word question with more hope in his voice than in his eyes. "Beach?"

"They say that answers are often found on the sea." Hell, even I heard how forced my voice was.

"Is that a yes?" he asked, the first hint at his sincere smile tugging at the corner of his lips.

"That's a yes." I smiled back at him, hoping for a stroke of genius to strike one of us like lightning. "But coffee first?"

He rose from the aisle seat and unlatched the luggage compartment to retrieve our bags. Hope stirred in my chest as he seemed to thaw out a bit. "At least some things are dependable."

"Like my love of sunshine and caffeine?" I asked, sliding out into the aisle beside him.

"Yes, like those," he said, gently setting my bag down and sliding the handle up to pass over to me. "And also, how much I love you."

Broderick

"PEOPLE CAN SAY what they want, but there's nothing quite like a Florida beach."

"No, there's not," I agreed, sidling up next to El, where she halted in the shallows, surveying the impressive stretch of white sand packed full of people. Music blasting, seagulls cawing, people laughing, and not a single flake of snow or wrap of garland to be seen. It was loud and overwhelming, but the sun was as warm on my skin as the sand was on the soles of my feet. I had to hand it to the sunshine state; seeing people with heritage from every corner of the world all in one space was certainly refreshing.

The ride had been...*uncomfortably* silent.

I didn't have a suitable answer for us, so I understood why El had spooled herself inside her head, but that didn't ease the way her withdrawal had me panicking. She was wearing a bright blue two-piece that made those steel-blues pop. Using some kind of witchcraft I didn't understand, she'd piled her feet of hair into a solitary clip, stray pieces blowing in that hint of breeze the gulf was known for.

The bare, tan strip of skin between her top and expertly tied wrap was just begging me to run my fingers over it. But it felt...wrong. *Stiff.* Like her formally straight spine, and shoulders pulled back were preparing her for battle, not affection. Like her eyes were on the crowd to avoid me, instead of absorbing the commotion.

"So, this is it," she whispered. "Our last stolen moment of alone time."

"I mean, for a bit," I amended. Clinging to hope that one of us would craft a solution we could both live with.

"For a bit," she agreed, but the sugared smile on her face didn't bring any life to her eyes. *Vlog face.* My gut sank.

"Yeah," I said, not bothering to hide the fact that the reality of it sucked. Well. Here goes nothing. My Hail Mary pass. "The sooner we rip off the bandage, the sooner I can hold you in public again. So, when should we tell them? Ease into it one at a time, or tackle the entire group together?"

"Um..." She turned down the beach, where laughing kids were flying kites and splashing in the shallow turquoise water. Innocent. Beautifully oblivious to the man trying not to puke as he walked a tightrope. "Listen, Brod."

Fuck. Me. My stomach sunk like a rock off the pier. "Please don't say what you're about to say." I shook my head, the familiar vice of panic constricting around my body. "Please don't 'listen, Brod' me—"

"I don't think we should tell them," she blurted over the end of my sentence before pressing her palms to her mouth, then smooshing them over her cheeks like she could rub away the emotions in her skull. She brought her hands together in front of her lips as if in prayer, and I watched them as I tempered my voice.

"Don't ask me to keep lying to them, baby. Please don't make me do that. I want to parade you around the city—want everyone to know you're mine. I've been working up to telling your brothers how much I love you since I was seventeen."

"It's not fair to get their hopes up when the odds of this working in the long run are as grim as they are."

I straightened my spine, cocking my head as my heart... *stopped*. Not that she could see it, as she expertly avoided looking at me.

Composing myself, I said, "Christ, baby, you make it sound like one of us got a diagnosis, not offered job security."

"I know," she said under her breath, taking slow steps through the shrinking fingers of the waves. I watched the water rush up again, erasing the print of her footfalls with a horrible sinking sensation in my stomach. "But in terms of a functional relationship, being long-distance for nine months a year is about as optimal as a cancer in the body."

"What are you saying?" I asked, snatching her wrist and tugging her to a halt. The warm waves collided with our feet. Birds yelled as they dove to scavenge prizes from the crowd, and my pulse attempted to slam directly through my skin as my life tried to slip through my fingers as fluidly as the sand between our toes. Suddenly, the blaring sun and chattering voices were too much, pressing against my skin, even as her glossy eyes came to mine.

"I'm saying that I love you. And that *because* I love you, I cannot rob you of *eighteen years* of effort. You already gave up the grant trying to give me a leg up." Those brimming tears crept silently from the corners of her eyes. It should've been a crime to make Elora Rhodes cry, I decided. Just watching that dam break sent a hot rod through my chest. I couldn't help but reach up to wipe them off her cheeks. To my relief, she leaned into my hand as she worried her bottom lip, eyes locking on mine. "I'm also too smart to turn down an endorsement like a television network. This is it, Brod. This is that big break moment. I will not beat the resources and exposure they can throw at this school. Not by a long shot. Not even Paxton could get us in front of this many eyes as often as they will."

"I would never ask you to give that up," I assured her, cursing my voice for coming out so weakly. My hands found her waist on autopilot and I finally inhaled when she didn't resist me pulling our bodies together. "You gotta slow down, Pix. We gotta *talk* before you just throw out the best thing to happen in my life... unless there's another reason you don't want to be together?"

"God, no," she sighed, brows winging up as her hands came to wipe at her face again. "The logistics are just—"

"Then *hold up*. Because I'm not willing to let you go—"

"And *I* can't ask you to give up tenure, Brod. That's not a minor accomplishment."

"Fuck." I freed one hand from where it rested on her back to rub over my jaw.

"*Heads up!*" A distinctly male voice broke our moment, jerking both of our attention to the side as a football made a beeline for Elora. I spun her behind me, stretching the opposite hand out to catch the ball.

"Jesus," she barked, hands in front of her face as I clamped my fingers into the laces.

"Damn!" I now realized 'the voice' belonged to a grinning young man with a willowy frame and skin a shade darker than Dad's. *When the hell did I become the old guy?* "*Nice catch*, man!" A couple of buddies jauntily sidled up beside him as I tossed it back, earning a, "Thanks!" and a happy wave from the lot of them.

"Have a good one," I called back.

"*Learn how to aim*," El muttered petulantly. Her irritation reminded me of the way Dad was always soothing my mother's temper, and I narrowed my eyes.

"You and Marley aren't allowed to be friends."

She grinned, shaking her head and taking a steadying breath as she tipped her face up to the sun, just breathing it in for a minute.

"So, we have some evaluation ahead of us. Some pro and con lists."

A little giggle broke free from her lips before she said, "You can say that again. We're in... a pickle."

"*Okay*, this is more than a pickle," I allotted, earning a watery little laugh.

"But we tackle this together. I didn't wait my whole damn life for this just to lose you in the end."

"Me either," she admitted. "But I don't have answers for Rhy and James right now."

"Then we take a few days. We analyze. *We talk*. We decide together what the hell the best next move is." I brought my hands up to hold either side of her face. "Right?"

She sucked down a breath before giving me a nod. The tone in her voice said she was still convincing herself as much as me. "Right."

TWENTY-NINE
ELORA

"There, all better, huh?" I cooed as Quinny's dimples popped into existence. "Just needed a change, and some cuddles, and all is well. Huh, baby girl?"

"Aoooom."

"*Aooom*," I echoed back, my cheeks aching with how much this girl made me smile. "Aooom," I repeated, mostly because it made her giggle, but partially because if I allowed my brain to go silent, it rapidly sunk into spiraling panic. Panic over Broderick. Panic over the show. Over what I actually wanted amongst all the unknowns. If I eliminated all the factors out of my control, where did I want to settle? Did I want to keep traveling? Speaking? Doing book tours? Or did I want to plant roots somewhere, and if I did plant them, *where?*

Oh god. Opting for a safer topic, I squeaked, "*Aooom.*"

"*Momomom*," she babbled back, bending in half to pull her little toes toward her mouth.

"Yes, I know. But mom mom is getting some time with dada."

"Dog."

"*Da-da,*" I emphasized each syllable.

"Dog," she repeated, before popping a big toe into her mouth.

"Ew," I said, wrinkling my nose and trying to free her chubby little digit. "We don't suck on toes, Quinny." I pursed my lips, narrowing my eyes at the little sunspot, now sporting a clean diaper and the cutest glittering red tutu dress that showed off priceless *Michelin Man* worthy rolls on her arms and legs. I needed to squeeze her forever and ever and smother her in so many kisses it was ridiculous. The palm tree wrapped in Christmas lights on her chest was even cute, although I wasn't entirely convinced spending Christmas somewhere warm wasn't sacrilege.

Noel was surprising Jameson with not one—but *two* puppies for Christmas, each of them dubbed after the main character in his favorite movie, *A Knight's Tale*. Quinny, Brex, Max and I had gone on a stealth mission to retrieve them, and our little cherub had been babbling about dogs all night, much to our chagrin. Honestly, I just needed the time away from Broderick and my brothers, and the drive to clear my head while Max and Brex chattered at each other.

"That's alright. Uncle's not that bright, and I bet I could convince him you were talking about Royal."

Royal. I love all animals, really, I do. But Brex's golden retriever had a weird affinity for the rabbits on our parents' property. So much so that she nearly got Rhyett killed a few years back when the house caught fire and she wouldn't abandon a baby bunny under the deck. My beautiful big brother refused to abandon *her*, the big lug. Come to think of it, the man probably saved Royal because she was secretly his spirit animal or something.

But she was cute and sweet and Quinny's biggest fan, despite the fists full of fur regularly liberated from her shiny coat. "Should we go find Uncle Max? *Should we?*" I cooed again. What was it about babies that just liquified my brain cells?

"Mah."

"Ma*x*," I mimicked back, emphasizing the *x*.

"Mah."

A phantom pressure settled between my shoulder blades, but I just cleared my throat before saying, "Yes, *Max*. Come on, Quinny." When I scooped her into my arms and turned on my heel, I came face to face with the one man I'd never gotten over. It turns out, I could officially, *undoubtedly,* say that getting *under* him certainly wouldn't have helped the cause, despite the suggestion being thrown my way for a decade.

Because now that I had...when I straightened and met that molten gaze where he leaned against the doorframe, every inch of my being lit up with expectation. His laugh, his touch, his scent, the image of him ranging over me—all hard lines beneath warm, rich skin—before he knocked my breath clean out of my lungs with that magnificent dick. *Seriously*. Other dicks could only aspire to his level of greatness.

"Hey," I managed awkwardly. Fuck, I *hated* that it was awkward. But it was. *God*, it was. The house was packed, in true Rhodes form, and we'd barely seen each other in the last three days. Yes, we shared the kitchen for cookie baking, but with the guys all shelling nuts, stringing popcorn, and talking shop, and the girls all focused on layering the entire island in flour, we hadn't gotten to say more than a few words.

Jeanne was back gallivanting the planet—*only God knew where*—and Alice was locked down helping Captain Hartless with something she didn't feel like discussing.

She'd had *two* migraines in as many weeks, and Rhyett, Hads and I were seriously discussing an intervention if things didn't look up soon. But ten of us, plus Brex and Quinn, Noel and her sweet family, and Max and Broderick made for a chaotic three-thousand square feet.

Much to my simultaneous disappointment and relief, Broderick had been pressured into staying with Rhyett, Brex, Jameson, and Noel, while the other eight of us invaded our parent's house like a swarm of candycane laden locusts.

"Hey," he husked. I couldn't help but wonder if I wasn't the only one using the crowd as a shield. Using the chaos to keep myself busy and try to think through our options. Regardless, every inch of my body was screaming to close the distance, to go to him and let our bodies talk in a way words couldn't. Because, fuck, I loved him. But continuing on as we were—fighting to connect for a few days at a time or stuck on phone calls for *weeks* at a time—wasn't an option.

A timid smile curled one side of his mouth as he eyed Quinny, who gave a stilted baby wave and a, *"Ba-oop."*

"Hey, baby girl, you sure are beautiful," he said softly, but I didn't miss the fact that his eyes were on me as he said it. "Your auntie sure looks good with a baby on her hip, too."

"Thank you," I mouthed back, not trusting my voice. My throat was too tight, tongue too leaden with all the unsaid things. Some horribly condemnable, selfish part of me wanted him to pick me. To pick *us* and walk away from that going-nowhere fishing town. The rest of me...was unspeakably proud of the love of my life for setting his eyes on a goal and becoming one of the best along the way. His hands flexed at his sides, and he took a stiff step forward before swallowing hard and stuffing his hands in his pockets. Those gorgeous eyes found his feet as he rocked on them.

A heartbeat later, Rhy popped into the doorframe, tapping on the molding to announce his presence. Broderick must've heard him walking down the hallway. He gave Broderick's arm a playful smack, grinning like a kid that just spilled their bucket of Halloween candy over the carpet to inventory.

"Hey, guys! It's time. Come on," Rhyett said excitedly. Quinny reached out chubby grabby hands for her daddy, who scooped her up without hesitation. The two of them led the way, leaving Broderick and me to follow their matching blonde noggins.

"Do you think he'll change his plans once he meets the puppies?" I asked out of the side of my mouth, needing to fill the silence, to cut through the tension between us. Jameson's plan was to propose to Noel tonight when the entire family—both ours *and* hers—gathered for Christmas dinner. At this rate, my parents needed to build a big ass barn to accommodate our growing tribe. To my relief, Broderick chuckled, the sound punching through the invisible wall between us and letting the light through.

"My money is on ice skating tonight."

"No way," I argued halfheartedly. He was probably right, but it was more fun to play. To pretend, even if just for a moment, that everything was normal between us. "Too cheesy."

"Bet you five bucks."

"Deal," I quipped back, relieved he was humoring me. My mistake was turning to look at him. *Fuck me*, I missed his lips. The warmth in those eyes, and the smile lines framing them. Three days, and I was breaking apart at the seams, just praying I hid it well.

"Think she'll say yes?"

I leveled him with a side-eye, only to find his smirk full of mischief. I missed him. *God*, I missed him. Playing with him, laughing with him. "William and Thatcher would be strange gifts from a woman who wouldn't," I pointed out, grinning back at him.

"True. God, I know Noel's got energy, but *two* puppies??"

"Best of luck to them both."

Chuckling, he said, "Really though, I couldn't be happier for them."

Nodding, I glanced to where Rhy and Quinny had vanished at the end of the hallway before saying, "No matter what happens, I need you to know I couldn't be happier for *you*."

"WHAT THE HELL IS THIS?" Broderick asked later that night as he glared at the five-dollar bill in my outstretched hand.

"You bet me he'd propose on the ice rink."

Laughing, he pulled Thatcher—who had been laying on his back chewing on Broderick's shoelaces—into his lap. I might've been crazy, but between the two brother retrievers, Thatcher had the lighter ears. I sat down beside him to steal some puppy snuggles, but not before tucking the cash into his button-up pocket.

"My 'never getting married', 'forever alone', 'unlovable' big brother proposed to the love of his life on a plastic ice rink tonight."

Broderick scoffed, his humor palpable as he made a big claw, shaking his hand before coming down over Thatcher's snout and grinning as the puppy gave his best, most ferocious play growls back before releasing him again. "He did it well."

"There were tears."

"For him and for me," he admitted playfully. I looked back out at the bizarre, orchestrated magic of twinkle lights and enormous gingerbread house beside the striped red and white walls of the rink in question. The image didn't compute with the sheen of humidity on my bare legs and sweat dripping down the low of my back. Jameson and Noel were still skating in circles over the waxed surface. Nat King Cole played over the loudspeakers, and the scent of peppermint cocoa competed with the savory spices of the Cuban restaurant across the circular park. It was like a Florida themed snow globe, complete with lights wrapped over palm trees, making an undeniable phallic shape.

"Nothing says Christmas spirit like twinkle penises."

Eyes closed in something like amused resignation, he just shook his head. "Your mouth," he muttered, clawing Thatcher again. This time, his floppy little ears fanned out like tiny gold wings, eyes comically wide as he nommed on his fingers.

The familiar joke somehow warmed my chest and tightened my airway at the same time. I wanted this to be our normal. Wanted everything to fall into place.

"Think of anything?" I asked, scanning the caramel corn line and finding Pax, Finn, Hads, the twins, and Max. My eyes had just found my parents, Rhyett, Brex and Quinn, across the way on the merry-go-round together when he spoke up.

"I *think* you're the most beautiful piece of the sunshine state tonight." A gust of warm, salty air kicked up, blowing the glittering fake snow over our way. But the pressure of his focus brought my eyes to his. He smiled softly, leaning forward to pluck a 'snowflake' off my lashes. "I'm thinking that I'm the luckiest man alive because you let me call you 'mine'. And there is no happy ending to my story if you're not at the center."

Eyes stinging, I held his gaze, until a laugh burst up my throat when he barked, "*Hey*," and jerked his hand away from tiny razor puppy teeth. "Little piranha. Just had to ruin the moment?"

"Brod?"

"Yeah?" he asked as Thatcher squealed and backed away from the hand now encircling his mouth. Broderick let him go, but narrowed his eyes when the puppy shot him a disbelieving stare. Evidently, both quick to forgive, the standoff ended as abruptly as it started when disproportionate puppy paws clumsily bound over Broderick's legs, landing on his lap.

"You wanna get out of here?"

Still working to wrangle the fluffy piranha, his eyes snapped to mine. "Fuck, yes."

While Broderick returned Thatcher to his new daddy, I walked the perimeter of the market, admiring sweet families as they shared cotton candy the size of my head, or pulled apart cinnamon buns, or climbed up on the merry-go-round. Who knew that admiration and envy could walk hand-in-hand? I wanted that. But where on earth did kids fit amongst book tours and filming schedules?

My phone buzzed, and I fully expected Hads or Noel to be tracking me down, which is why it was so damn strange to see *Lionel calling* across the screen. What in the hell was my agent doing calling on Christmas?

Determined to find out, I swiped the button and said, "Lionel? Merry Christmas! Everything okay?"

"Merry Christmas is right," he said, sounding a little bit out of breath and *a lot a bit* excited. "Are you sitting down? You'll want to be sitting down."

"The last time someone said that, Chris was telling me we'd been acquired by the network."

"Well. The little shit stole my line. But you're going to thank me for crashing your Christmas."

BRODERICK

THE BROAD FAN of our headlights spanned over the Main House. Funny, having grown up in what was dubbed 'the main house' back in Mistyvale, like a center point where kids and cousins and aunts and uncles all congregated, only to see the home base shift five-thousand miles away. This one was modernized. A nostalgic white farmhouse surrounded in Florida green.

Our music abruptly amputated when the engine turned off, and we sat in ponderous silence for a long beat, just staring through the dark at the house only illuminated via Christmas tree through the oversized living room windows, and fat bulbs that left the wood patio in a golden glow.

"So," I finally said, breaking the pregnant silence.

"*So*," she echoed back.

"Time to make decisions?" I asked, but even my voice gave away my desperation. She nodded and my shoulders slumped. I reached down between the seat and the door, and longed for the days of a pulley lever instead of a button that slowly leaned the seat away from the wheel. "This feels ridiculous."

She side eyed me, smirking as the seat buzzed, easing back so I could turn to face her. "If it means anything, it also looks ridiculous."

"Can you imagine this thing in an emergency?" I growled.

"Certainly not going to bust out of a garrote with any kind of efficiency."

I barked a laugh, shaking my head. She really did just say whatever she was thinking, didn't she? The best part was, I loved her all the more for it. "Do you regularly escalate to being *murdered*?"

"Sorry," she laughed, not looking sorry at all. "I've been binging true crime shows this week."

"Nothing says *cozy Christmas bedtime story* like serial killers."

"Exactly." She unbuckled her belt and turned to sit crisscross in her seat, back pressed against the window. With a timid little shrug, she added, "Kept my mind off of you when I couldn't sleep."

"You mean you didn't just stew in self-loathing for the last seventy-two hours?"

"I would've come out of my skin."

I chuckled, but looked out the window when movement caught my eye. Royal happily trotted across the yard with a rabbit in her wake. Shaking my head at the strangest animal alliance I'd witnessed in person, I found El studying me, half her face in shadow.

"I'm not giving you up," I stated matter-of-factly.

Her eyes fell to her lap. "I'm moving to New York City."

An out-of-body kind of buzzing erased our surroundings as her words burrowed into my stomach. My mouth failed. So did my lungs. *Say something*, some coherent corner of my mind snarled.

"My agent called tonight, and the network took my hesitation as a need to sweeten the deal because they knew we had multiple offers. They can swing a larger budget—not just for me, but for scholarships, equipment, everything—if we re-use a building that they purchased for another project that didn't make it past the pilot. Already renovated. Historical, so it has the character I wanted. We'll just need to outfit it." She paused, looking at me like she was fighting the waves, and I was the only person with a lifeboat. New York. *Manhattan*. Hell, I'd never even been in Manhattan. Finn lived there, and with Pax in Chicago, at least they put her within visiting range of family. But... I'd never imagined myself in a *city*, let alone one as savage as New York. When the best response I could muster was my mouth opening and closing twice, she cleared her throat.

"They need me to fly in tonight and sign off."

"*Tonight?*" I demanded, doing a crap job at curbing the panic in my voice. "El, it's Christmas. You think the family isn't going to flip their collective lid?"

Throat bobbing, El shook her head. "There's some monster blizzard headed for the city, and they anticipate grounding flights the next few days. I either fly in tonight before it hits, or the storm doesn't clear out until the end of the week. Network wants a commitment or a refusal, and I can't blame them. I've strung this along for weeks already."

Voice rough, throat tight, I asked, "You can't just... sign electronically?"

El sucked down a breath, like she was bracing for backlash. "I want to see it in person before we finalize things. Mara already booked our flights. Pax is going with me."

"And you just... decided all of this on your own?" The implied 'without me' was betrayed by the break in my voice. My mind was running a million miles a minute, the familiar holdover overwhelm creeping in.

"I'm sorry. I... Pax, Mara, and Max all already signed off. They're waiting on me. And this is the kind of opportunity that can create generational wealth, not only for me, but for the women whose lives we'll impact. The media attention will bolster my book sales. It's, overall, just..." Pained eyes—more than a little wild—looked frantically between mine before she clambered over the middle console to straddle my lap. Her hands found my neck, my jaw. Mine automatically settled on her waist. I turned to press a kiss to her palm as she pled her case. "Brod, this is so much more than I ever prayed for. Please understand. *Please.* I can't throw away ten years of effort. Mara and I have talked about this forever."

"I know," I breathed against her palm, soaking up her warmth. The feeling of her settled on top of me.

"And it's important to me that you take your time making your next choice. I've been working toward this goal for no more time than you have yours. I won't ask you to throw that away without doing your due diligence and thinking it through."

"I know, baby. I love you, Pix," I said, pulling her closer, smiling as she rocked her hips over my groin, "and I'm *so* fucking proud of you."

Her lips came down on mine, hard and desperate, cutting off my questions, my protests, the million and one things that I needed to say. Because as urgently as we needed to talk, we needed each other. El immediately went for the buttons of my shirt, popping the first three apart until she could slide under it, a breathy, contented hum purring in her chest when she found my chest bare.

"Perks of southern heat," I muttered as my hands went for her naked thighs beneath the scrap of a dress she'd taunted me with all day. Each touch, each pull of her lips and scrape of fingers became laced with both need and the kind of care I would never articulate in all my years.

I *loved* her. This fierce, independent, relentless, brash woman. I poured that reality into each stroke up her thigh and over her hip, each clash of teeth and graze of our lips.

"*Bed?*" she panted, and I nodded against her, reaching to unlatch the door, and kicking it open in the next beat. She yelped when I scooped her up and out of the SUV with me, landing on my feet and kissing her all the way across the yard to the unlocked back door.

"Gonna make a habit of carrying me around?" she teased.

"Until we go gray, baby." Maybe if I just kept saying it, she'd get the picture. There was no quit once we started this. She might want me to take time, but I'd already made my choices. Her. I chose her. The moment I touched her in Vegas, I'd made my choice. The universe was just testing it.

Yeah, there'd be a transition period before I could respectfully leave home, but she could ask a million times and the answer would stay the same. For now though, I just needed to hold onto her. Honor her choices. Let her process. Or at least that's what I gathered from her books.

We bumped into a corner or two, but I got to the room she was staying in before settling her on her feet. She turned, pushing the unlatched door open, only to stop so abruptly I walked into her back.

"Now, what the fuck?" she muttered, canting her head. I craned around the doorframe to spot *Royal*, happily sleeping with *three* fucking rabbits curled up against her warmth. "In the goddamned house?"

Panting, dick straining against my zipper, I looked around, snatched her wrist, and yanked her inside the hall bathroom.

"Close enough?" I muttered.

"God, yes," she breathed back, shutting the door behind us.

"Come here," I demanded, hands settling around her hips to pull her in front of the vanity. "I want to see you, baby."

She nodded incoherently as I bent her over the counter, her hands flying out to brace herself. "I've been dying to flip this skirt over your hips all day," I said as I did just that, giving her shapely ass a light smack, and loving the way it halted her breath.

"*Good*," she gasped. "I've been dying to touch you."

I spied the wet spot on that silky excuse for underwear and smiled at her in the mirror. "Wet for me already, baby?"

She arched a brow, eyes dropping to my blatant erection in the mirror before countering, "Hard for *me* already, babe?"

Grinning, I yanked apart my belt buckle, followed by the button and zipper of my slacks. "All you gotta do is smile at me, and I'll be ready, El." I shook my head as I freed my aching cock. "Touch me like that—*tell me you want me*—you can bet I'm dying to make you scream, baby."

"Then do it," she challenged, pulling out that bravado that undid me entirely. With no further delay, I slid aside her red thong, running the crown of my dick up her wet slit. Her eyes slid closed where I watched her in the mirror, mouth falling open as I repeated the motion, giving her clit a hard tap before lining up and thrusting home, her body somehow fighting me and welcoming me all at once. That hot, wet channel gripped me without mercy. Her lungs filled in one hard breath as mine faltered. As though I'd granted her the air in my lungs in one abrupt motion. "Fuck, baby, you're so tight." Eyes flying wide, she locked her gaze on me in the mirror.

"I love you," I said, watching the emotions shift over her face like a rapid-fire strobe.

"I love *you*," she repeated. There was no lead up this time. No foreplay or teasing. I went straight for the devastation I needed from her, needing to see her come undone around my cock, body melting under my hands.

Palms roamed. My thrusts quickened, and she cried out my name like a prayer in the air between us.

"You're *mine*, Elora Rhodes. At the end of this life, that's all that fucking matters to me. *Do you hear me?*" I growled, pistoning into her, my pace growing punishing. This was a claiming. A declaration of intent. She couldn't just run off making all the decisions for us alone. She was *my* girl. My *world*. And I'd find a way to prove it to her. There was the dull thud of what I assumed was Royal jumping off the bed. But the world was fuzzy beyond my need for her. Beyond the warm slide of my palm over her hip and slap of skin against skin. The wet sound of her body pulling me in.

"Yes!" she cried out, and I clamped a hand over that pretty mouth just in case, the other tightening my hold on her waist as my hips snapped forward.

Buried deep, bottomed out at the end of her, I held steady, our eyes locked. "Then stop making decisions for both of us. Give me a chance to figure this out. Because the only future worth living in is one where I have time to worship every inch of you. Understand?" She nodded against my palm. "Good girl. Now fucking come for me, baby."

Her walls fluttered around my cock when I returned to that punishing pace, release barreling for us both. But right as we tumbled over that edge together, the door flew open, the room filling with hall light.

A frantic, feminine yelp proceeded a screeched, "Oh my god! *Oh my god*! I'm so sorry!" The door slammed shut, but not before I caught a flash of red hair and wide brown eyes. I'd barely pulled out, El's dress pouring back over her hips as she lunged for the door. Yanking my pants up, I rushed to follow. But El was hauling Noel back inside and kicking the door closed while she pinned her up against the wall with a hand over her mouth.

"*Noel*," she said with a disconcerting level of calm. "You can't say *anything*."

THIRTY

ELORA

"*Wahdoomeeahca*," Noel rapid fire mumbled into my palm before her eyes went cartoon character angry and she *licked* me. I yanked away from the impressive assault of saliva, wrinkling my nose.

"Breathe," I instructed, as she opened her mouth, her eyes flying wide. There was nothing subtle about Noel—she was big, bright, animated, and currently, her passion was directed at me.

"What-the-fuck-do-you-mean-I-can't-say-anything?" she trilled so quickly it took a hot fucking second for my brain to catch up. I blinked as it buffered, but evidently not fast enough, because she immediately popped a hip, hand hitting it as she glared Broderick's direction. "You know Jameson and I don't do lies. I'm *not* lying to him. Don't ask me to do that—you're both better than that."

"We're going to tell them," I said, hands raised defensively as her brown eyes narrowed.

"When?" she demanded, eyes flicking from him to me.

"Soon," Broderick promised, voice low and soothing, even to my frenzied brain.

"When is soon?" She barked back with a bit too much enthusiasm. All three of us nervously eyed the door, and she flinched like she was also remembering how hard she slammed it.

"Is everybody out there?" I redirected the line of questioning.

"Yes! We came back to go carol for the neighbors, and Rhyett and Pax broke out champagne, and then everybody is gonna watch *A Knight's Tale,* and cuddle the puppies and *what do you mean by soon?*"

"How do you do that?" Broderick muttered as I just blinked back at her. "Do you take micro inhales or something?"

"Stop changing the fucking subject and tell me what the hell is going on or I'm really going to show off my lung capacity."

"We're going to tell them," I repeated, glancing over my shoulder to Broderick. "But we're navigating the logistics and want to be prepared with well thought out answers on how we'll make this work before we tell the guys."

Broderick stepped in closer, settling his hand at the low of my back in silent reassurance. "I'm sure all three of us can agree going out there before we're ready to answer all their questions is as good as stepping in front of a firing squad."

"Can you understand why we don't want the family to know yet?" I added pleadingly.

"Maybe. Maybe *a bit.*" She immediately seemed to think better of her statement. "But then you shouldn't be boinking in the bathroom at Christmas fucking dinner."

"*Boinking?*" I barked right as Broderick busted out laughing.

"I mean, dinner was over hours ago, and we thought you all were at the festival for a while yet."

A little furrow pinched in her brows, brown eyes flicking between us, and then down to where his fingers had slid across my back to hug my hip, pulling me into his side. "How long?"

"I'm going to New York tonight—"

"*Tonight!?*" she yipped. I just continued; tone dulcet as if soothing a panicked animal.

"And then Broderick and I will talk and make some decisions. We'll present this to them together once we have a strategy."

"*No.* Not how long before you two *tell them*. How long have you been doing *this?*" She pointed an accusatory finger between us before crossing her arms over her chest and rocking back on a foot.

Not sure how to summarize an eternity of pining, I opted for the simple truth. "Just since the conference last month."

"Sweet baby cheeses! I *knew* something was going on!" she squeaked before her hands flew up to cover her mouth. When she threw her fists down to her sides, I got the distinct impression of a ginger *Tinker Bell* throwing a tantrum. This time in a stage whisper, she said, "At pie night! I *knew*! I knew you were there for him."

I scratched at the back of my head, brows winging up as I slowly smiled over my shoulder at him. But Noel's mouth had popped open, and she danced in place.

"You weren't *writing* at the *coffee shop* at *six* in the goddamn *morning*, were you?" I shook my head, grimacing at her volume as she barked, "This whole time?!"

"*Shhh,*" Broderick and I both hissed together, stepping

toward her, although what either of us would do to shut her up was beyond me.

"No, no. No *shushing* me. You don't get to shush me when you've been lying to your brothers—your best friends," she added, leveling Broderick with a glare.

"I know. I know, and I'm sorry. We want to tell them ourselves; we just want them to know we've put a lot of thought into this whole thing. That neither of us is taking this lightly."

She blinked before saying, "Why on earth would either of them think that? You two are obviously made for each other."

"Jameson certainly won't see it that way," Broderick spoke up, his anxiety dripping from the words.

"He might surprise you, you don't know," she argued. "But either way, don't you think he has a right to react however he's going to react?"

"Yes," we answered together.

"Just let me solve the *where I'm living* part, so Broderick can weigh his options." I reached out, grabbing both her shoulders, and holding my ground when she turned her face toward the door, as if she could peer through it back to her fiancé, clearly uneasy with the whole concept. "It was important to me that Broderick didn't lose his friendship with the guys if things didn't work out between us. I only wanted them to know once they wouldn't feel like they had to protect me."

"And now?" she asked, voice softer, gaze still on that steady rotation.

"Now we're..."

"Figuring things out," Broderick summarized. "I was just offered tenure back in Mistyvale. El's possibly moving to Manhattan. There are a lot of factors at play."

"Factors Rhyett and Jameson will expect answers for," I emphasized. She sucked down a hard breath, blowing it out with just as much gusto before giving us one curt nod and turning for the door.

"Twenty-four hours, El. I want an update tomorrow, because I'm not keeping this from James. We don't *lie*. We don't keep secrets. I won't tell him tonight, but if he puts it together somehow—if he asks me—"

"You won't lie for us," I surmised. She shook her head, eyes somehow heavier for it. "That's totally fair. I'm not asking you to lie for me. I'm just asking for more time."

"You both deserve each other. Seriously. One—" she held up a finger, "I called it. Two—" her voice lowered when that second digit went up. "Our family deserves the truth. Let them make their own beds, and deal with it then."

"We will. I promise, we will."

"James and Rhyett have been my ride-or-dies since we were kids," Broderick added. "I swear, we'll tell them everything."

Noel sucked in a pained sounding breath before giving us a blunt nod and turning for the door.

Only... when she opened it, Jameson and Rhyett were both standing outside like a couple of predators about to pounce. Noel startled back a step, her hand flying to her chest. Broderick automatically positioned himself between my body and their looming frames. A muscle in Jameson's jaw flexed as Rhyett leaned forward to brace a forearm on the doorframe, lips rolled between his teeth. It was Rhyett to break the loaded silence.

"Uh... You got something to share with the class, teach?"

Broderick

"TELL US WHAT?" Jameson demanded through a stiff jaw. And here it was. The reason I hadn't wanted to keep this to myself in the first place. If a man could light another on fire with his eyes, Jameson would have turned me into a kabob on the spot.

"Don't be mad," El said from where she wrapped her hands around my bicep. 'Don't be mad' was basically the male equivalent of 'calm down'. Light a match and pour some kerosene because shit's about to go up in flames. I didn't miss how quickly Noel skirted out of the space to stand behind Jameson's back, her allegiance in this firmly established.

"Tell us *what*?" Jameson repeated.

"Look, you guys were never supposed to find out like this," I hedged, not sure where to look. At Jameson, whose face looked dauntingly like it had before he beat Noel's ex within an inch of his life. Or at Rhyett, who looked…rocked. "We planned to sit you down and talk to you tonight, so we could do it with the whole family."

"Alright, so let's talk," Rhyett instructed.

To my chagrin, Axel's bulky form appeared behind his brothers, leaning against the wall with his arms crossed, looking particularly displeased. "I'd kinda like to hear this conversation myself," he added.

Oh good, because the two of them weren't enough.

"What the fuck did Noel just stumble in on?" Jameson demanded. "It takes a lot to rile my girl up like that."

"We'll explain everything," I reassured, pointing back toward the main living area. "Can we go sit down?"

"Hey, guys! What are we—" Maverick's lanky frame appeared beside Axel, peering around Rhyett's shoulder but hesitating as he read the space. "Uh. *Who died?*"

The guys' stern gazes all landed firmly on me.

Swallowing, I repeated, "Let's go talk. Might as well head to the living room."

"I think this is as good a spot as any," James countered, grinding his teeth as he leaned back into the wall. Like he wanted us caged in. Noel turned into his side, looking torn as her eyes darted between all of ours. Deciding it was Jameson's gaze I needed to meet, I lifted my chin and held it, reaching down to grab El's hand. Was he pissed? Yeah. But the part that sent my gut churning was the pain there. Honesty had always been our number one.

"El and I are seeing each other," I announced softly.

"*When?*" Jameson demanded, not dropping his gaze.

I felt El shift uneasily behind me but held his stare. "We kicked things off at the conference."

"Last month?" Rhyett asked, his even voice drawing my attention. Where Axel and Jameson's anger rolled off them in waves, only his pinched brow gave away his frustration. I nodded.

"Oh shit," Mav said before skirting away from the impending storm. Smart kid.

"This whole time?" Jameson growled, looking past me to his sister. "He's why you came back. For Thanksgiving. You didn't want to leave."

"Yeah," El said softly. "Long distance isn't easy."

"No shit," Jameson said, pushing off the wall and beginning to pace in the tight space. I couldn't help but think of a prowling lion before they struck. "So, you've been lying to me for what—*six weeks?*"

"Look, man—"

El cut me off, stepping out from behind my arm, where I'd tucked her behind me. "I asked him to keep it quiet. If things weren't going to be serious, I didn't see a point in riling up the family or putting him in the position to be ostracized by our siblings if things didn't work out. I didn't want him losing that home away from home."

Rhyett quirked his head, a fierce scowl carving his features as he glared down at her. "What the fuck, El?"

"His friendship with you meant too much," she added, shaking her head and straightening her spine.

"So fucking *lying* was the solution?" Jameson asked in blatant disbelief, glaring back at her.

"We never *lied*," she argued.

"Bullshit," Jameson muttered, running a palm over his hair.

"A lie of omission is still a lie," Rhyett countered coolly. Jesus, hadn't she told me that once?

"So, *what happened*? You just jumped at your first chance to get her alone? It is *Vegas*. Could've just sprung for a hooker. But you took advantage of a woman we've all watched pine for you for *years*." Axel's rapidly hurled accusations earned the first visceral reaction in my body— heart ratcheting up, hair on end, muscles bristling, vision zeroing in on his pissed-off face. It was the glassiness of his eyes and pink in his ears that told me he'd had one too fucking many. The feral smirk curling one side of his mouth said he wasn't just drunk, but looking for a fight, and knew he'd hit his mark.

"Listen up, kid. I love you, so I'm going to tell you this once," I said, my voice low as I squeezed her arm where I held onto her beside me. "Watch how you speak about *my* future wife, or I won't hesitate to knock that smile off your face—trashed or not." My snarled words had the desired effect. El straightened against me, her fingers tightening on mine. Noel's head snapped to me so fast she popped her neck. Jameson stopped his feral prowl as Axel straightened off the wall, anger and confusion muddling their faces.

Rhyett's brows winged so far up they nearly merged with his hairline. "Uh, I'm gonna need you to say that again."

"El! We gotta get going," Paxton came sauntering around the corner, his pace slowing as he surveyed the testosterone filled space. "Sooomebody gonna tell me what's going on?"

"Brod's been—"

Before Axel could say something especially stupid, Jameson clamped his hand over that angry smirk, yanking him against his chest and growling, "Ax, shut the fuck up and go walk it off," before shoving him down the hallway. Axel glared over his shoulder, but complied, muttering epithets as he vanished into a bedroom.

"That's *enough*." Milo's resonant timbre brought everyone's attention to him as he stepped out of his bedroom. "For Christ's sake, I raised you boys better than all of this."

Rhyett started, "Hey dad, we're just—"

"Go sit down," he barked, pointing toward the living room. Milo was just a grayer, older compilation of his boys. Like he really had whittled a layer off his metaphorical block for each of them. But his voice was just an aged version of Jameson's. "All of you. Now." As El and I inhaled in unison, making to follow Rhyett and James as they led the march to what would be an inevitably uncomfortable conversation, Milo's hand came down on my shoulder. "I think we both could use a drink for this, don't you?"

With tempers quieted and seats taken, everyone

gathered in a tense silence in the living room. Axel was still absent, but I couldn't say I was mad about it. He'd always been an angry drunk. He'd feel like shit tomorrow. Come around with his tail between his legs. Always did.

"Mr. Allen," Milo started, leaning back in his armchair to cross an ankle over a knee, resting his glass on his leg as he rotated it. Thirty-five years old, and I felt like a teenager all over again. "I believe you were trying to share something with the family before my boys started behaving like Neanderthals."

I cleared my throat and gave El's hand a little squeeze. "Elora and I had planned to talk to you all during the holiday but didn't quite get the chance. We started dating while at the conference in Las Vegas."

"It wasn't planned, but it wasn't... unexpected, either," El added. "I've had feelings for Brod for years."

"I don't understand. This feels like it came out of nowhere," Rhyett argued, while Jameson remained silent, his eyes on his hands where they hung between his knees.

"*Oh please,*" a chorus of feminine voices echoed from the kitchen where Brex, Noel, Juniper, the twins, and Quinn were *all* staring at us.

"Even I knew that," Brex said, rolling her eyes. I couldn't help but smile.

"Look, I love you both, but are you really that dense?" Noel's eyes were pleading, but Jameson didn't bother to look up and meet them. "I picked up on the sparks between these two idiots my first week on the island."

"Hey," El protested, but I was smirking.

"Don't *hey* me, Miss, straighten my hair and skirt when he enters a building," Noel quipped back, pouring herself a generous glass of wine. Rhodes gatherings were always chaos, but this one was...insane. Dogs were barking in the yard. Juniper was watching me with pain in her eyes as she came to sit with Milo. Pax was nervously glancing between El and his watch, where he still leaned against the arch of the hallway. Mav perched on the back of the couch with headphones on, although I suspected they were silent. Every pair of eyes was rotating to us and then whoever was talking. And I found it very, very hard to breathe.

"Look, I hate to do this," Pax cut in. "But El and I booked the last flight into Manhattan tonight, and odds of anybody getting off the ground tomorrow are slim to none."

"You're *leaving!?*" Rhyett asked, whipping his head to El.

"I didn't exactly have family intervention on the calendar tonight," she explained.

"What about Christmas?" Jameson bit back. Fuck, it wasn't just the sag of his shoulders, but the gravel in his voice that said he was hurting. This whole dumpster fire could have been avoided with a phone call. "Did you have *Christmas* on the calendar, sis?"

"I will not argue with you guys about this. I'm sorry to bail early, but this is a once in a lifetime opportunity, and I will not miss it for the sake of one holiday movie night."

"What time's your flight, baby?" I asked before anyone else could protest.

Pax grimaced as he checked his watch for the millionth time. "We've got just over an hour and a half until boarding."

"Fuck," El muttered, planting a kiss on my cheek. "I'm so sorry. Do I stay?"

I shook my head as her pleading eyes caught mine. "No, I got this. Nobody flies on Christmas—you should get through security fine."

Nodding, tears springing to life in her eyes, she said, "We'll talk?"

"We'll talk," I reassured, threading my fingers through her hair, and pulling her lips to mine in a desperate plea that this wasn't goodbye. When we came up for air, she made a beeline for Pax, who already had their bags by the door. Everyone else was staring at me.

I assumed this was what it felt like to be a fish inside a tank and leaned back onto the couch. As the door slammed behind them, Rhyett cleared his throat.

"This... this isn't like a casual hookup kind of thing."

"It is not," I confirmed.

Jameson didn't look up as he asked, "When?"

"In Las—"

"No. When did you catch feelings for our sister?"

Well, fuck it. I ran my tongue over my teeth, sucked down a breath, and began. "I thought it was just some kid crush I'd grow out of. I was... I think, *seventeen*, when I knew she would be something special. Eighteen, when I knew I was in love with her. But she was...too young." I shook my head, raising my eyes from where they'd settled on my hands, unsure of whom to look at. Landing on Milo, I added, "And you trusted me to protect her."

"Jesus Christ," Jameson growled, barely audible as he palmed his face.

"Why didn't you say anything?" Rhyett asked, his voice soft but heavy.

"So, I *wasn't* crazy," Leighton said, more to herself than any of us. A dozen siblings, a dozen unique voices—and a dozen hearts I needed to mend, when all I wanted to do was run out that door after her. But I'd told her I had this. So, I'd handle it. It was long overdue, anyway.

"No, you weren't crazy," I said, shaking my head. "I've

loved El since before I understood what it was to love a woman."

"Answer my question. *Please*, Brod," Rhyett asked again, as Brex came to settle into his lap and stroke her fingers over his jaw. For the first time, I was aware even Finn had wandered into the room, silently observing as he picked up Quinn. And just like that, I remembered exactly why she'd put this off. I wasn't just chasing Elora for the rest of my life. I was committing to all of them, too.

With a defeated shrug, I said, "The pact, man."

"The *what?*" he asked, quirking his head.

"The fucking pact!" I snapped, rising to my feet. "*Fuck* the pact, guys. I love you. I really do. But the love of my life just left for *New York City*, with a blizzard rolling in, and I should be with her. We should make these decisions together. Should have told her I'd follow her *anywhere* under the sun. That so long as I draw breath, my heart is with her." I palmed my jaw, blinking back the burning at the bridge of my nose. "*That's* what I was working up the courage to tell her. That I'd leave home, turn down tenure, find a job at a school in Manhattan. Follow her to the end of the fucking earth and back." I brushed an angry hand over my short hair. "But we got swept up in each other again, and then Noel walked in—"

"*Sorry*," she grimaced before chugging her wine, but I couldn't stop now that the words were all coming out.

"And now I'm facing down the Mistyvale *Brady Bunch* when all I want to do is tell her I love her. That I'd do anything for her and I'm *so damn proud* of how hard she's worked. That I love you both, but if a stupid high school pact is more important than our friendship, I choose her. If that means I'm no longer welcome here, I understand. I'll respect that. But I. Choose. *Her.*"

Teeth audibly grinding, Jameson glared at me before standing abruptly, crossing the room in a few aggressively long strides, throwing open the front door and slamming it behind him.

"I got him," Kaia said softly, hustling to grab sandals and follow him outside. With that outburst fizzling away, I collapsed back onto my spot on the sofa as Noel pursued her in a rush, shutting the door at a much more acceptable volume than her future husband.

"I gotta be honest, B. I don't even remember the pact," Rhyett said, shaking his head. "I'm just...bummed you didn't think you could come to me. All this time?" When I just nodded back at his question, he said, "Brod, you're the best man I know. El is a lot. A lot of strength. A lot of opinions. A lot of control. If you love her after seeing all of *that* for the last thirty plus years..."

"Agreed," Finn piped up as he humored a grinning, babbling Quinn, who was shaking his fist around by the thumb. "If our sister has to land somebody, I'm glad it's you."

Well, that brought an unexpected wave of warmth to my chest. I turned my attention to their parents, where Juniper had perched on the arm of Milo's chair, her hand working the ends of his salt and pepper hair.

"I'm so sorry I didn't come to you first. I owed you both that. And that was a misstep that I don't expect to be forgiven."

"*Broderick Allen*," Juniper scolded—her tone almost... insulted?—as a truck engine roared to life out front.

"Son, I say this with all the love in the world, but you're an idiot," Milo said, shaking his head. Leighton, Brex and Finn burst out laughing while I tried to numb the hit to my ego. "Do you think a father could watch a man defend his daughter's honor, have her back when she went rogue, and then boldly declare his intentions in the face of a house full of pissed-off, fully grown men who brawl *for fun*... and not be grateful for him?" When I raised my eyes, he smiled in that fatherly way of his. The same one he used when we messed up as kids. Kind, but firm. "You've always been a son to me, Broderick. If you want to make it legal by marrying the most bullheaded of our daughters...I couldn't think of a better fit."

I would *not* cry in front of *Milo Rhodes*. The lump in my throat begged to differ, but I reached for the whiskey glass closest to me on the table and knocked it back, just in case.

"That's uh...a hell of an endorsement, sir."

"You're a hell of a man, Mr. Allen."

The front door banged open, and Jameson took two long strides before huffing a harsh breath. "Let's go."

"What?" I asked before he leveled me with a glare.

"Come on. Get in the truck."

"If you're going to bury me in a swamp, the one at the back of the lot will do."

Jameson dead panned, the sigh sagging his shoulders speaking to years of exhaustion. "Get in the fucking truck, Brod."

"*Now, James*," Milo started, but Jameson rolled his eyes, pointing an aggressive arm out the door.

"I'm not gonna kill him," he scoffed, rolling his eyes before looking at me with expectation on his face. "We're gonna go catch his fucking girl."

THIRTY-ONE
BRODERICK

Jameson took the last turn into the airport like his hair was on fire, rubber squealing across the rain-slicked asphalt. Never had an 'oh shit' handle been squeezed as tightly as mine while he mobbed through the city in a classic Florida rainstorm.

"Maybe the weather delayed it," he said hopefully.

"They're supposed to be boarding right now," I pointed out as my stomach turned in one last somersault.

"Still not picking up?" Noel asked from her precarious spot sitting between us. I just shook my head. I'd called Elora half a dozen times since we tore out of the driveway, but she hadn't answered once.

"We'll catch her," James said, frustration still seeping off him as he tapped Paxton's face on the touch screen again.

"I still don't understand why you're helping me," I admitted.

"Because I love you, asshole."

"You seem mad," Noel pointed out.

"I *am* mad."

Grimacing, I said, "I couldn't help but fall for her, man."

"I'm not mad you *fell for Elora*," he ground out as we caught air over a speed bump.

"You're not?"

"No, dumbass. I'm mad you fucking hid it. That you didn't do what would make you happy for *seventeen* goddamn-fucking years and *I'm* to blame."

"I don't blame you," I countered.

"We made that cocksucker of a *pact* when I couldn't escape Mindy because Hads kept bringing her around the house. It is my fault. You've always been too damn good for me."

"*Bro*," I protested, but he was shaking his head.

"Talk later. Unbuckle and get ready to roll," he instructed as he blew by the five mile per hour sign.

"Maybe don't tear into the terminal like we're pulling a heist," I suggested, but the comment just earned a wry smile and an arched brow.

"Where's the fun in that?" And with that, he pulled into the departure line, finally slowing to accommodate the barrage of speed bumps. He'd barely eased to a roll when I hurled the passenger door open and was out and running a beat later.

"Good luck!" He barked after me. Boarding pass loaded on my phone and ID in hand, I slowed to an acceptable speed-walk when a security guard scowled at me. Waving apologetically, I hustled through pre-check and into the mostly empty concourse before sprinting toward the departure gate. I'd flown in and out of the Tampa airport enough times in the last two years that the layout was familiar.

Which is why my heart dropped through the floor

when I finally spotted them closing a gate at the end of the eternal, shining hallway.

"Wait!" I barked. "Hold the door! Please!" Jesus, I'd already worked up a sweat, heart pounding as I prayed to any god that was listening. I called out the gate number, but nobody seemed to care about the psycho yelling for help in a dead sprint through the empty airport. *"Hold the gate!"* This time the attendant with long brown hair in a high ponytail snapped her head up at me, eyes wide before recognition sent her whirling. By the time I reached her, I was out of breath, humidity sticking my shirt to my skin.

"Hi...ma'am, hold the plane...*Did you?*" I bent over, bracing myself on my knees as I sucked down air, vaguely aware I sounded like a pathetically winded *Yoda*.

"Sir, are you okay?" she asked, bending over to check my breathing. I gave her a thumbs up.

"The plane?" I panted. "Get on—I need to get on the plane."

"Sir, I'm so sorry, but the gate is closed."

"Gate is closed. *No.* Christmas. Blizzard. Need to—" I sucked down a lungful of air, forcing myself to stand upright as I palmed at my eyes. "I need to get on the plane. I have a ticket. Ran from the parking lot. Big ass airport. Need on. No more flights. New York."

For each disjointed word, the empathy in her eyes seemed to deepen, and she glanced over her shoulder toward the window, where the male attendant—who looked a disconcerting amount like a short-haired Max—was on the phone, eyeing me warily.

"I'm so sorry, Sir, but once the gate is closed, we cannot open it."

"Sure, you can. Door has a handle." I set my hands on my hips. Maybe I needed a little less weightlifting and a little more cardio. *Does my heart always try to expel through my temples like that? This is what a stroke feels like. Airports have doctors, right?*

She shook her head, blue eyes glossy above a freckled nose. "It's not that simple. Federal security protocol prohibits us from—"

"*No,*" I said, the little air I gathered crushed from my lungs as I collapsed onto her stand. She set an awkward hand on my shoulder. "Broke thirty laws to get here. Sprinted from the lot."

"I see that." She shook her head empathetically. "I really am sorry."

Elora

"SIS, I've got this. Do what you gotta do."

"*Are you sure?*" How Pax understood my blubbering through the waterfall of tears and hiccups I would never understand. But my not-so-little brother smiled as the airline attendants gave the last call for our flight, stooping from that nearly six-foot-four vantage point to meet my eyes.

"I'm sure. I know *you*. I know the *plan*, and what you need. You and Brod come first." His dimple popping into existence was oddly comforting, as was the just-hard-enough-to-smart sock to my shoulder. He flicked my chin up with his index finger, booped me on the nose, and ordered, "Go get 'em, Sparkplug."

Despite the shuddering sobs I couldn't seem to get under control, I laughed. It was watery, at best, but the twenty-nine years of brotherly nostalgia punched through the mess of emotions that took me captive the moment we hit the freeway. "Okay. *God*, thank you, Pax." I threw my arms around him, and he scooped me up, tucking me against his chest before settling me back on my feet.

"Hurry, El. He's probably getting eaten alive in that house right now."

I took a shuddering breath. "I know. *God, I don't know what I was thinking.*"

"You were thinking about kicking ass and changing lives, not about what your heart actually needed. Now you need to run and save him."

"I'm running. Right now."

"Good. *Go*," he said with a little salute as he backed onto the ramp to the plane. "Love you, El."

"Love you, little brother."

He smirked, and then turned on his heel as the male attendant glared at his watch, a little pinch in his brows. "We've got one more," he said to the woman coming over to check his list. I gave them a little wave; aware my chin was trembling again as the last six weeks all caught up with me at once.

I only made it as far as the bathroom before the tears started fresh. Ducking inside, I rushed for an open stall, heaved my duffle off my shoulder, and fucking lost it.

Collapsing up against the cold tile wall, my rain jacket screeched the entire way to where my descent stopped, squatting on the dirty bathroom floor as fat tears tore loud, ugly sobs from my chest. The pathetic noises competed with the obnoxious, endlessly looping elevator music they insisted on playing in surround sound. This wasn't the 'I just said goodbye to my boyfriend' kind of cry. This was the catastrophic, life ending fuck up kind of sob.

Burying my aching face in my hands, I thought about Broderick. That damn smile that shattered me entirely.

How mouthwatering he looked stretched out poolside, with all that gorgeous skin on display. The stories he told me about his family history while we made his Grandma's curry. Over a decade's worth of postcards. Wildflowers. Where the hell did the man find a single long-stem rose in Las Vegas, for pity's sake? His warm hands guiding my fingers through slick clay to forge something beautiful together. The delicious burn of his stubble on my thighs.

Broderick was effortless. Not the relationship—the logistics of two very different lives attempting to blend. But...actually being with the man? *That* was effortless. His laughter brought life to my lungs. A why to my existence.

That's what I realized as we drove to the damn airport. That this network deal could very well leave me farther apart from the one person I'd ever loved like this. Success without Broderick would be a hollow life sentence that left me aching with a million 'what if's'. And God, if we couldn't survive this and I had to watch him move on? That would kill me. The idea alone made me want to crawl deep into the earth to rot with my shattered heart.

And he would move on. A man like Broderick Allen wouldn't stay single for long. Not when someone experienced how sweet, how thoughtful, how absolutely incredible he was.

He had to come first. *We* had to come first. And here, I'd left him to fend for himself with the sharks. Like that wasn't a psychological bloodbath waiting to happen. I never should have abandoned him to face my brothers alone. Stakes be damned.

Hell, I never should have left, period. Because it was Christmas. *Our first Christmas.* And instead of spending it in his arms in ugly sweaters, I'd spent it sobbing my heart out and telling Pax everything. From my junior prom, to last summer, to how he'd shown me what it felt like to be loved.

Paxton—bless him—told me to get the hell out of here.

Which is what I needed to do. Now. *Right now*. Before they made him feel so guilty that I lost the best thing to ever happen to me.

I shook my head to clear the hysteria. Tear tsunami finally slowing, I wiped at my face and shakily found my feet. Blowing my nose, I decided it was actually disgustingly impressive how much snot could come out of one face after an hour of crying.

Some kind of commotion broke out beyond the bathroom as I washed my hands and splashed my face, hoping nothing too terrible had happened. I was still scowling when I rounded the corner. I was just heading for the main hallway when said commotion broke into distinguished words and a timbre that I would know anywhere.

"Broderick?" My voice cracked, so soft I could barely hear it. But I tentatively wheeled my suitcase back toward the gate, unwilling to hope. But there he was, leaning his elbows on the counter, hands braced against his mouth as if in prayer—*pleading*, I realized.

"Ma'am, I know you're just following policy, but you don't understand."

"I'm so sorry, sir. I can look for another flight."

"Listen, Kimmy—can I call you Kimmy?" She nodded, and he continued, "I don't need another flight. I need *that* flight. The love of my life is on that plane, and I need to go with her." My chest warmed as I closed the gap, heart quickening, tears brimming all over again. *He'd come after me.* "She's moving to the city, and I didn't tell her I'd drop everything. Didn't tell her that home is where *she* is. That maybe starting over means I can finally figure out who the hell I am without people expecting things from me. Or that I would teach anywhere if it meant I get to wake up with her every morning and make her coffee, just how she likes it." A silent sob shuddered through my ribs, hand flying to cover my mouth as if it could contain it. He was shaking his head, reaching forward to plead his case, and my heart was breaking and mending all at once. "She's the most frustrating, beautiful, courageous, impossibly stubborn woman you will ever meet," he said with a stilted little laugh, as though he was suffocating his own emotion. But I could hear it. So could the stewardess, her chin wobbling as she looked back at him. "I love her. Kimmy—I have loved Elora Rhodes since I was seventeen—and I could lose her tonight, if you don't just open that door and let me go after her. And I can't lose her." He shook his head vehemently. "Not again. It would kill me."

"Sir, I..." The helpless looking employee shook her head. I crept ever closer, tears streaming all over again as my pulse hammered against my skin.

"I know. I know about the policies and you're just doing your job, but I can't lose her, Kimmy. Please. She's my world. My everything. I don't care where we do it, I just want to live a life where I get to raise a tiny Elora that looks like me and see her little face light up every Christmas morning." Eyes burning, I rocked on my feet, hands both covering my mouth now, as I tried to keep my shit together. He meant it. Every damn word. Even with a view of those tight shoulders, I could hear it in his voice. "This woman is my better half in every sense of the word. And I need to ask her to live and die together as my wife."

"Say it again," my voice cracked as I said it, but he whirled, eyes wild as they locked on me in utter disbelief.

Frantically, he studied my features before he seemed to jerk out of a spell. Lunging forward, Broderick wrapped his arm around my waist, scooping me to him as his lips came down on mine. Hungry fingers threaded through my hair, his hand finding its way up to my jaw so he could pepper my face in desperate kisses that sent me laughing through my tears.

"Fuck, baby, I love you so damn much." His thumbs absently wiped away the tears on my slick cheeks. I was vaguely aware I likely looked like I'd tried to make out with a beehive, but he didn't seem to care.

He was here.

He was here and proclaiming his love for me for the world to hear. When Broderick finally pulled back to look at me, his eyes were glossy and his smile tentative, I just nodded.

Yes, I wanted all of that. Felt all of that. Straight to my marrow. Our bodies melted into each other as he cradled my face, our foreheads coming to rest together.

"I love you too." Breathing in the love of my life, I repeated, "Say it again."

EPILOGUE
ELORA

May

"Yes, Chris, I ate, thanks for checking though," I laughed, shaking my head as I wheeled my carry on across the sleek Terrazzo floor. The chatter of countless voices competed for my focus beyond Chris in my ear, my eyes straying out those great walls of glass to the beautiful, spring morning beyond.

"Okay. Everything is good here, and my flight out is in five hours."

"Chris."

"I've checked and re-checked, and everything is done."

"Chris?" I tried again, with a sharper tone. Evidently, it wasn't enough to pull his attention away from his spinning top of a brain.

"Security system is enabled. Movers are ready. The last of our books don't get in until we're all back in the city. Also, I double confirmed vendors for Saturday, and nobody has the audacity to forget or be late."

"Christopher?"

"I confirmed with Max, and the last of the security system went in this morning."

"*Christopher!*" At last, the line went silent, my mind vaguely aware of the click of my heels and purr of countless rolling rubber wheels against the hard floor. "Everything is accounted for. You may now clock off, my friend. Pour a margarita. Get a massage. Or a good lay. I don't care which, just breathe while you do it."

"Everything is accounted for," he echoed back, and I laughed at the breathless panic in his voice.

'Chaos' would be an understatement for the last six months of espresso-fueled madness. It turns out that having a breakdown after abandoning the love of your life to an inquisition of feral piranha siblings and spontaneously deciding it was a good day to learn how to delegate... was a lot harder than it sounded.

But I'd done it. Or... begun to, at least.

With Chris already in the city, and Pax, Max, and Mara all on board, my brother headed to Manhattan in December to approve the building, and I'd simply...*let go*. Free fell off the cliff of anal retention into the flight labeled 'trust your team'. The biggest problem was getting the disgusting mix of fluids to stop leaking from various orifices of my face. Snot. Tears. Probably some stray saliva. It was the ugliest ugly cry of my life, made more humiliating by the fact that it took place in an airport.

Reuniting with Broderick in the waiting area had thrown me for a fucking loop, and the water works began all over again until I'd soaked through his shirt.

It turns out, all the success in the world wouldn't mean shit if I didn't have him to share it with. Evidently, he agreed, because while he held me to his chest, sitting on the filthy floor of the Tampa airport, Broderick Allen asked me to be his wife. Post haste. My enthusiastic acceptance and our rather inappropriate public—but not actually very public—lip lock had earned a congratulatory round of applause from the limited remaining staffers.

And so, my real life finally began.

With Paxton and Mara on location, we'd unanimously forged ahead with the new building, and signed our first network deal after Lionel's meticulous review and approval.

In the months since, we'd grown, trained and honed the team. Broderick gracefully declined tenure and submitted his notice that after the academic year, he would be moving on to new adventures.

As if tackling our big, hairy, audacious vision wasn't enough, the team had also helped me plan the perfect intimate wedding back home, where I could finally marry the love of my fucking life. After all, we'd waited seventeen years to be together. It was time for the wait to end.

With the school year and filming both starting in August, what better time to tie the knot than right after the academic year ended, but just before the fishing season started?

"Okay," Chris breathed, somehow more flustered sounding than I was.

"Hey, I have dibs on the frantic, panicked bride role today."

"You get that for one day only." He cleared his throat, the smile obvious when he asked, "You gonna tell him the big news before the wedding?"

"That's a hard yes, my man." Finally taking a deep breath of rather stale smelling air, I checked and double checked the gate number before slinking into the stiff seat. "Lord knows I can't be within proximity of that man before

I blurt out anything significant these days. Mama Marley also seems to have just as innate a sense for detecting malarky as her husband." Broderick's parents had been just as—if not more—supportive of our relationship as mine had been. Once the initial shock wore off, our families celebrated over video chats in the weirdest long-distance family barbeque in history. It was kinda cute, though, despite feeling absurd propping multiple phones on the dining room table.

Robert in particular had hugged me so tightly the first time I made it back to Mistyvale that I thought I might suffocate. When he released me, his eyes had been glossy with something like pride. According to him, I was just like his mama, and she would've loved me like her own. Before I knew it, both Broderick and I were teary-eyed right along with him.

"Kept enough secrets for one life, boss?"

"You can say that again."

"But I won't."

"Thanks for that. So. I'll see you tomorrow, right? You're not bailing on me?"

"I wouldn't dream of it."

"Thanks Chris."

"You got it, boss."

"No, but like. *Thank you*, Chris. I couldn't have done all this without you."

"I know. Maybe let's not do a book tour next time, though?"

"Once was enough," I said, laughing. A rather elderly looking couple made their way into the seats beside me, their complexions freakishly close to Broderick and mine, only they were both a little ashen with the honor that is age. God, what I would give to grow old together. He lent her a hand as she took her seat, obviously both tired from the effort of travel, but it was the way he brought his forehead to hers that did me in. "I want that," I muttered, evidently aloud.

"What?" Chris asked quickly.

"The old and gray, but still in love thing."

Chuckling, he said, "Babe, if you and Broderick aren't that, all hope is lost in this world."

"Thanks, Chris," I said, pulling my eyes away from the lovebirds so I didn't turn into that crazy stalker lady. Reaching to pull my laptop out of my bag, I said, "Travel safe."

"You too, boss."

Line disconnected, I drank my half-caf latte—*what a joke*—and finished the last of my work for the week, firing off a few emails before they called our flight, and passengers began to file on board. How very different these flights traveling to each other had felt as the big day crept ever closer. Because after this weekend, there would be no more long-distance visits. No more reuniting in echoing airport atriums or stealing away for too-short weekend escapes.

As I wheeled my way down the ramp and onto the plane, I couldn't help but smile because in less than ninety hours, all of my high school notebooks would at last be vindicated when I actually became *Mrs. Allen*.

Bags stowed, nestled in my first-class seat with headphones in my ears, I paused my audiobook when the speaker came on, because the *pilot* was standing at the front of the plane with the radio in hand. What was left of his hair was silver, his face clean shaven, and both his smile and eyes were kind as he looked down the length of the bustling plane. I wasn't the only person to notice—the man across from me sitting up a little straighter with concern lining very blond brows.

"Good morning, passengers and crew for flight A-S-three-oh-five. I know this is unusual—normally my lovely attendants give you the safety brief, so don't mind my ugly mug stealing your attention." Curiosity bit through me, intensifying as I realized it was emotion welling in those pale blue eyes, not concern. "But today we have some extra special guests aboard—you're all fantastic, don't you worry—but my wife, Cheryl, and our sons, Marcus, Jim, and Vinny are all here with me to celebrate my last flight across these skies. I gotta tell you, folks, I thought I was ready, but you're never really ready to walk away from something that's been a part of you for over thirty-five years."

He wet his lips, throat bobbing. I glanced back to where his wife and grown sons were all looking a little verklempt themselves and raised a hand to rub at the knot forming in my chest. His voice over the speaker pulled me back to the front of the plane as he went on, "But through all the flights, through all the cities and situations and complications, all that ever truly mattered to me were those four people sitting in the back of the plane today. Show of hands–who all has kids?" Most of the passengers raised their hands, as mine fell to flutter over my still flat low belly. "There is nothing—nothing this life offers—more important or more fleeting than the years with your children. Cherish them. *Don't blink!* You blink, and you miss it." He snapped his fingers, a bit of sadness shadowing his sweet smile back at his boys. "The diapers. The sleepless nights. The exhaustion, and worry, and *exhaustion*, decision fatigue, praying that you don't mess them up too badly, the sports games, the... *exhaustion*," he repeated, smiling softly. "It's all so fleeting, in the scheme of things. I was blessed with a career that I loved. The freedom of open skies beneath my wings. But...when it comes down to it, all I've ever been doing is what all of you are fighting for. At the heart of things. We're all just... finding a way back home."

BRODERICK

IF NOSTALGIA HAD A SMELL, it was parchment, leather, freshly sharpened pencils, and burnt teacher's lounge coffee. For the final time, I looked up at the lecture hall full of students. Not just my usual attendees, either—nope, I spotted faces that graduated years ago, others who were just a few years ahead, all piled into seats in the lecture hall that had been a second home to me for the last six years.

There was a kind of electric anticipation in the air today. Maybe I was imagining it, but I didn't think so. The thing about teaching in a town as small as Mistyvale is that you actually get to know your students whether you mean to or not. Which means...they get to know you, too.

These were my kids. But they were also my friends. Because they knew I'd finally proposed to the girl of my dreams. Knew she would be here tomorrow to get ready for our laid back Mistyvale beach wedding. Which meant that nostalgia-anticipation cocktail in my stomach was echoed through the too-crowded space.

"As we wrap up the spring semester, I just want to thank every single one of you for being incredible students. Incredible scholars. For challenging thought for thought's sake." Stuffing my hands in my pockets, I leaned against the desk nobody ever actually used, and scanned over the room, meeting as many smiles as I could as a pang struck my chest. I'd never walk here before the sun was warm with a coffee in hand again. Never sit in the silence of an empty Mistyvale lecture hall waiting for students to stir to life in the cocoon of this campus. Drawing in a deep breath, I added, "Whether your grades will be posted this weekend, or were already handed down a semester—*or years*—ago," nervous laughter graced the space and I smiled. Like I would be disappointed they snuck in to see me off, or something. "If I leave anything behind for you, may it be a love of learning. In the words of Socrates, the only true wisdom is in..." I bowed my head, gesturing with a hand for them to finish and smiling as they did.

"Knowing you know nothing."

"Very good. So, carry on—dare to know nothing, seek *everything*—"

"But, Professor Allen," a familiar, teasing voice sent goosebumps down my spine, eyes closing as amusement lifted my cheeks. Laughter rippled through the rows as I turned, scanning for the face that had become my anchor point. "We can't forget Descartes." I found her then, tucked in a particularly crowded huddle toward the top of the hall. That glorious, wicked mouth was painted a bold pink, stretched in a feline smirk. El's arms were crossed over a curve-hugging dress where she leaned back in her chair, chin lifted in a theatrical defiance. "Cogito, ergo sum."

"Ahh, Miss Rhodes," I said formally, eliciting a ripple of laughter. "Always keeping me on my toes."

"I think, therefore I am. Isn't that right, Professor? I know I'm a little out of practice, so I might be misinterpreting René's work," she said casually, as if he was an acquaintance rather than a historical figurehead. "But I believe he spoke to the very essence of knowledge and existence."

I smiled up at my almost-wife, I shook my head as her feline smile grew. If we had ever been anything to each other prior, it had been beneath the umbrella of *challengers*. I didn't much expect that to change. Prayed she would never stop. Truthfully, I lived for it. That push and pull of her. That push and pull *to* her. Which is what had me clasping my hands behind my back as I made a steady saunter to her side of the hall. "Perhaps wisdom has very little to do with certainty, and...everything to do with challenging our own perspectives," I said, unclasping my hands as I began to ascend the stairs.

"And... being courageous enough to chase new beginnings?" She rose from her chair, shaking her head as she descended toward me until we met, face-to-face, in the middle.

"To new beginnings," I said, and then I wrapped her up and kissed her breathless to the ruckus applause and obnoxious wolf whistles of my students, like we'd been performing a play, and this was our ovation. Even in the chaos, her lips on mine sent heat down my spine, body eager at her proximity.

Peeling apart, she rested her forehead against mine, her voice low this time. Just for me. "To new beginnings. Perhaps we'll start by changing my last name, and in about seven months, begin again with Robert Milo Allen."

Thank you for reading!

WHAT COMES NEXT?

If you're not on my reader's list, make sure to join and be the first to know about pre-orders for Alice & Greyson's story, *Salvaged Hearts,* the first book in the next Rhodes universe series, *The Hearts Of Emerald Bay.* Join the list here!

Love the Rhodes? Applications for the street team are open! Apply here!

AFTERWORD

Dear reader,

In addition to most stubborn, El and Broderick hold the title for my most swoony, most inevitable couple. I didn't have their romance planned, but from the moment she sent Rhyett that picture in *South Of The Skyway* (and in every interaction after), I knew they were just dying for a chance to tell me their story.

Never in my life have I backspaced over *so. Many. Words.* But these two wanted it their way, not my way.

Fun story; I had a 3rd act breakup outlined for this duo, and Broderick just pursed his lips, shook his head, and gave me the silent treatment for a whole damn week.

"Nope. Not doing that," was all he'd say until I threw my hands up, drank an entire pot of coffee and let him take over. In retrospect, I would've saved a whole lot of words (and frustration) if I'd just let it flow the way they wanted it to. So you can thank him for that.

Theodora Taylor says that she's a 'vessel' for her stories, and my God, was this a confirmation of that.

Thank you for reading their story, and I hope you fell in love with this quirky pair as deeply as I did.

Big hugs,
   Sydne

ACKNOWLEDGMENTS

My readers, my midnight 'oh my god' DMers, my 'when is the next one'?! Grayshell Babes posters and raving reviewers, **you guys are my why**. *The light on dark days, and the reason I keep swinging when I want to quit. Love you all so much.*

MY HUBBY, thank you for showing me that strong men lead with kind hands and gentle affirmations. For showing me they're quick to forgive and quicker to ask forgiveness. For showering me in more belief and praise than any girl dares to dream of. Thanks for being empowered by my ambition rather than intimidated by it. You're the real deal, Mr. Barnett.

HEATHER, my darling, thank you for being the backbone of this chaos party. Thanks for throwing spaghetti with me at literally all hours of the night. I wouldn't want to try this without you.

JESSICA, thank you for the endless encouragement, *especially* in hard times. Thanks for all the love you pour into our writing partnership, and the characters we craft together.

HALAIA, My muse! Thank you for all the initial El and Brod brainstorms, for breathing life into El and sweet love into our gentle but protective Brod. We finally made it to the finish line.

SAM, you are the coolest editor to ever wield a pen like a blade. Thank you for your patience, your input, your invaluable feedback, and endlessly humoring my memos. Thank you for talking me down from the edge of panic more often than not. *Fucking legend.*

P.S. I am *Batman*.

SHANNON, thank you for our gorgeous covers for this beautiful baddie—they're my favorite yet.

To all of my amazing indie author friends. This would be an impossibly treacherous, very lonely road without you. Love you all dearly.

ABOUT THE AUTHOR

Sydne Barnett is a lover of spunky, badass heroines, and heroes that embrace their wild. She's an avid reader, never turns down a good cup of coffee, loves hiking with her hubby, and lives for finding their next adventure.

If she's not writing, you can probably find her behind her camera, swimming, or curled up with a homemade pastry, watching Friends, HIMYM, or Gilmore Girls.

Raised in the Treasure Valley, Idaho, Sydne has a love for one-light towns, and winding backroads, but refusing to ignore her soul's call for adventure, she hit the road with her family, and now they call the world their home.

Let's connect!

Reader's Group: https://www.facebook.com/groups/grayshellbabes

Tiktok: https://www.tiktok.com/@barnettbooktalk

Instagram: https://www.instagram.com/barnettbooktalk/

Newsletter: https://shorturl.at/acJSZ

Patreon: https://www.patreon.com/GrayshellUnhinged

ALSO BY SYDNE BARNETT

Nomadic Rhodes

<u>South of The Skyway (book 1)</u>

Brewing Temptation (book 2)

The Hearts of Emerald Bay
(Rhodes universe continued, billionaire edition)

Salvaged Hearts (Coming fall, 2024, now available for pre-order)

Romantic High Fantasy as S.J. Barnett

Commanding Flame And Shield (Grayshell Rising, book one)

Commanding Earth And Shadow (Grayshell Rising, book two)